SH

PRINCE

Demon Hunter Book Two

Tim Niederriter

COPYRIGHT PAGE

Shadow Prince

http://timniederriter.com/

https://dwellerofthedeep.wordpress.com/

Published by Mental Cellar Publications

You can get a free Demon Hunter story and regular insights from the author by signing up using this link.

https://BookHip.com/KQDXQJ

ACKNOWLEDGEMENTS

Thanks to all those who assisted with the process behind this novel.

Specifically, I'd like to thank my proofreader, Barrie. Special thanks to Reinhardt for his work formatting the book.

And of course, a fair bit of appreciation to the podcasters and authors I chat with regularly (And not so regularly) as I worked on the book. Some support can be as simple as a good conversation.

Finally, my brother, Joe, needs a mention because I might have given up without his enthusiasm for this story and world it's set in.

Thank you all.

Tim Niederriter, September 2020

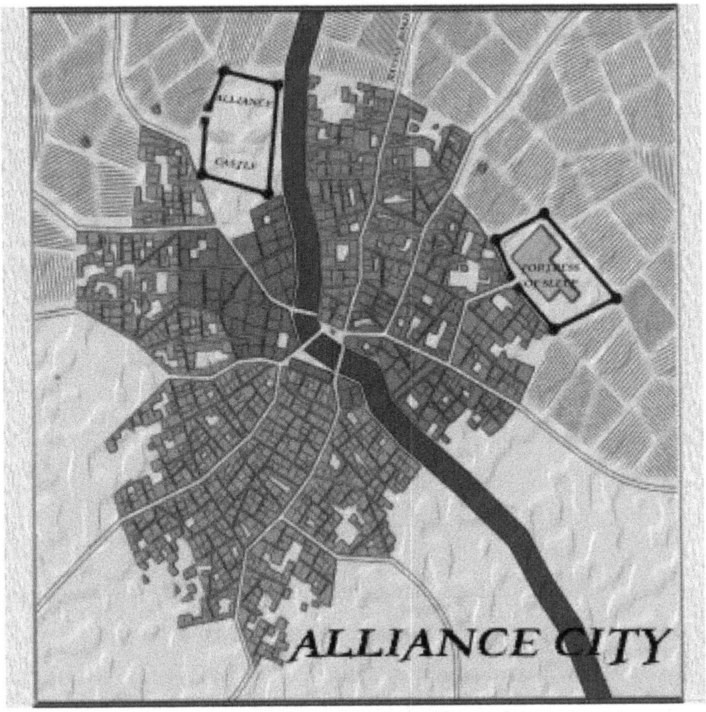

"No matter their order, poets of Tancuon seek truth. Each of us demonstrates our skill in different ways, but the chasm is almost universal. Studiously divide each line in twain, and you won't soon forget the difference between the mortal and eternal, between humanity and Mercy, herself."

-Nahron Yenger, The Art of Poetry. 2590, Imperial Jadiketzian Reckoning.

"What a cut divides The chasm's sister sides?
Curious, our baited Minds must be sated
When high families Rot under soft ease
Awaiting respect They'd hold out their necks
And speak of kindness, Love, death, remind us
Of Mother Mercy, who by just decree
Offers our remains To worms 'neath the plains.
Highborn but low-lived Ever death's divide."

-From "Termita" by Catricha Maltos, 2631, Imperial Jadiketzian Reckoning

CHAPTER 1

CATRICHA

Torches lit the path to the palace south of Alliance City. Colorful dresses and the faces of young nobility from every family of note danced beneath arched rooftops. It was the night of Prince Saviron's final ball of the summer, and Catricha Maltos lacked any desire to dance.

The palatial manse of House Halth resounded with music and the steps of moving feet. Catricha gazed upon the dance floor from the balcony that overlooked the ballroom. Beside her, the famed cynic poet, Porfiria Amburen, shook her head in a cascade of black tresses.

"Pathetic, aren't they, Cat?"

Catricha leaned with both hands against the railing of cool metal. She trusted the balcony with her weight as much as she relied on Porfiria maintaining her public image, and her friend never let her down. As a trained mage, Porfiria was here to protect the entire party. Their friendship made Catricha grateful for the older woman's presence for entirely different reasons.

She turned to Porfiria, a smirk turning the corners of her mouth.

"You know what I think of them," Catricha said. "Funny. The more they dress up, the more gruesome they look."

Porfiria laughed, stifling the sound with one pale hand covered in a black lace glove patterned with thorns.

"I take it *he* irritates you more than ever, now that you two are wed?" She gestured with her eyes toward the center of the dance floor where Prince Saviron's best friend and steward, Adias Halth, danced closely with some girl from a lower family.

Adias wore a pale gray doublet and maroon jacket. His hands glittered with the twin rings of his family status and a collection of lesser jewelry. His intense eyes, some called them smoldering though Catricha scoffed at such words, locked on the face of the golden-haired girl twisting before him.

As Catricha and Porfiria watched from above, Adias' hand touched the girl's waist, then moved along her navel. He led her from the dance floor, moving toward the chambers he nominally shared with Catricha.

"Of all the men I could be forced to marry," muttered Catricha, face growing hot with embarrassment. "I had to be joined to him for life." Her nose wrinkled, remembering the corrupt stench of Adias' lust from a previous dalliance she'd interrupted.

Porfiria's gaze traced Adias and his paramour's path across the ballroom. Catricha's friend lacked any way to soften the impact of the scene playing out below them. For that, Catricha didn't blame Porfiria. *A woman must carry some burdens alone.*

"I suppose I ought to interfere." Catricha feigned a yawn, covering her mouth with her palm. "After all, it'd be vastly improper to simply let him run amok so soon after our wedding."

"Perhaps," said Porfiria. "Will you let me accompany you?"

"If you would," said Catricha, grateful to accept the offer.

Porfiria smiled slightly. "Of course, my dear. I'll help when I can."

The two of them left the balcony and descended the spiraling tower staircase to the dance floor. Many young nobles of lower status capered in the middle of the room. The guests included members of every household, with only those families dwelling on the furthest periphery of the city's northern territory having no members in attendance.

Catricha and Porfiria marched as swiftly as their long-skirted summer gowns would allow them while remaining decent. They followed Adias and his latest object of affection through the palace.

The girl's laughter echoed along an opalescent hallway. Catricha took the lead, hitching up her skirt to allow her faster movement, now that they were out of sight of others. She didn't want to be seen as desperate to catch her husband in his adultery. Still, that would make an annulment possible, potentially. The glow of torchlight cast Catricha's shadow ahead of her as if the dark thoughts outpaced her body.

Catricha and Porfiria followed the echoes of the blond girl's laughter. Yet, their path took them not toward the estate's lordly bed-chambers, but to a balcony overlooking the River Duenn where the waters flowed north toward Alliance.

The last winds of summer blew with an evening chill, rustling curtains in the doorways, and carrying autumnal cold into the halls of the estate. Catricha shivered. Her shoulders and arms were exposed by her low-cut gown, leaving her little protection against the gathering night.

The west wind carried the unmistakable stink of unseen blood from the woodlands surrounding the Halth's family holdings. Catricha wrinkled her nose, only able to imagine one smell worse. She did not relish her time living in Adias' house in the future.

Catricha's marriage to the young lord of House Halth couldn't keep her prisoner indefinitely. *Thank Mother Mercy.* She could have their union annulled, as symbolized by the gift of a dagger to him as a final step. Until then, the estate was her home as much as his.

Annulment, Catricha thought, *will be difficult, given his close ties to Prince Saviron.* Even the obvious infidelity Adias pursued at every opportunity, and his refusal to touch Catricha, might not be enough to win her freedom. Seemingly, she was the only woman in the city her husband did not lust after, though she'd hardly prefer the alternative.

She and Porfiria entered a hallway where Catricha estimated the last gale of the girl's laughter had originated. A single torch burned low in the wall bracket, leaving most of the corridor in shadow. Drawn curtains concealed the balcony where the hall ended. Heavy breathing came erratically from behind the dark, satin drapes.

Catricha glanced at Porfiria. "Damn him to the pits of the world," she said softly.

Porfiria touched her shoulder with a gentle hand. "I'm here. Remain aloof. You knew what he was after."

Catricha closed her eyes and took a deep breath, then released the air from her lungs, expelling some of her anger. She marched to the curtain, then gripped the dark cloth in calm fingers. She pulled back the shroud that hid her husband's indecency, walking alongside the moving curtain to avoid any contact with the amorous pair.

But Adias was alone. He lay on his back, his body convulsing violently. Blood ran from a deep crimson wound in his chest and from the edges of his eyelids where he squeezed them shut.

The sight of her husband's ruined body in the dim torchlight made Catricha's eyes widen in shock. She gasped for breath as the spreading pool of gore from beneath Adias touched her sleek, black dancing shoe.

"What—What happened?" she managed to say, tears streaming unbidden from her eyes.

Porfiria reached Catricha's side, then recoiled as she saw Adias. A single glowing moat of magic, a mystical essence called a sprite, floated from Porfiria's hand and then circled Adias' bloody chest.

"That wound is mortal," she said in a hushed voice. "His heart is gone."

Adias coughed, spraying droplets of blood down his red-stained front, coloring the once-gray doublet a darker shade than his jacket.

Catricha swayed on her feet, dizziness threatening her from the sight of so much blood. "The girl," she managed to say through stammering lips. "What happened to the girl?"

Adias shook his head, unable to speak. He shuddered once more, then his convulsions stilled. Catricha's heartbeat echoed in her ears. For once, Adias didn't get the last word.

Catricha stared at the limp form of her long-time tormentor and recent husband. *He's dead. What should we do? What should I do?* She failed to put her thoughts into speech, shaking in silent horror.

Screams rang out behind them in the estate, echoing to where Catricha and Porfiria stood by the bloody balcony. Porfiria glanced the way they had come, brow furrowing.

"They're talking about the prince," she said.

Catricha turned toward her friend with frost clawing at her heart as her gaze left Adias' fallen form. "Tell me what they're saying, please." Tears ran unbidden down her cheeks.

Porfiria's eyes widened, looking at Catricha, large and dark. "The Prince has been attacked! Prince Saviron..."

New ice formed a hand around Catricha's heart. *Adias and Prince Saviron, both murdered in a single hour.* She blinked back her tears, then leaned against Porfiria.

"That can't be..." Catricha murmured. "Porfiria, do you know what this could mean?"

Her friend touched her hand. "Please, Cat, we don't know enough—"

"We need to do something." Catricha brushed off Porfiria's touch. She took off running through the house toward the ballroom. Her legs pumped, skirts hitched up and flying about. Porfiria's sprite-quickened stride caught up with her, and together they returned to the ballroom at speed.

Catricha stumbled to a stop before a moment of frozen horror on full display to all the noble scions. Everyone stared at the place where Prince Saviron Davaltz lay behind the high table. His sword servant and bodyguards surrounded him.

The eyes of the gaunt chief bodyguard, Layne Kasol, moved around the room, frantic, wild. His hand rested on the hilt of a short sword. Catricha's eyes narrowed. None of the guards held naked steel, only sheathed weapons.

Only the prince's sword servant carried a bare blade.

Terrell Varder, dark of complexion and eye, held the prince's bane sword in both hands. The infused weapon's pale glow gave his face a tinge like old parchment. Terrell had been the sword servant of Saviron's father as well, and now both father and son lay slain. Varder spoke no words but glared this way and that, steely eyes searching for an enemy. Despite his quest, no threat presented itself in the frozen scene.

"No..." Catricha said, masking her disbelief under her breath. "No."

Porfiria sent sprites flying from her hands with a sound like the chime of bells and flickers of streaming light. Her sprites circled the open space left by the staring nobles on the dance floor, outlining the scene of the fallen prince of Alliance.

Catricha stared at the broken form of Prince Saviron. His once tall, lean figure now lay torn and shredded on the floor by the high table.

His cloak, always dark and lined with purple, was now stained with blood. The crimson pool around him spread from multiple wounds in his chest and side.

Who could have attacked him here? And how?

The scene before Catricha overflowed with fear, running red like the blood on the floor.

"Where were you?" Terrell Varder shouted at Porfiria, "What's happened when you took your magic wards down?"

"My essences still line this room," said Porfiria. "I only left momentarily with Lady Maltos."

"And where were you?" bellowed Varder.

"We were following my husband," said Catricha, her own voice sounding distant. Her hands, though they shook with the chill in the room, felt numb. "My husband is dead."

Varder's eyes widened, shot with bloody streaks, and the bane sword trembled in his grip. "What did you do?"

Catricha gritted her teeth and stepped forward. "We only followed him and his latest lover," she said. "He was dying, and she was gone before we caught up."

"No. Impossible..." said another nobleman as he broke from the crowd, and advanced toward the bodyguards.

Catricha recognized the man by his hulking frame and graceful movements, as Vual Kuldettan, heir of the most powerful family in the city. Even House Maltos was second to their influence. Vual always carried his own sword, and its sheath glimmered at his side.

Vual had been friends with Adias and Prince Saviron for as long as the three had been alive. He stared, trembling, large hands clenched together. "I don't believe what you're saying. Adias cannot be dead. You must be mistaken."

"I'm sure as this room reeks of murder." Catricha clasped her hands together before her heart. "Mercy rest him and his promiscuity." She hung her head, hair swinging to cover her face, hiding the fact that she was crying.

Vual took a step in her direction. "How dare you! My friends lie murdered, and you continue your games?"

Varder lowered the bane sword, then motioned to Vual. "Please, my lord. Choose calm." His eyes flashed, and he turned to Catricha. "We saw no attacker. Did you?"

"We saw no one," Catricha managed, wiping her eyes with the back of her hand.

A high-pitched laugh rang through the room, followed by the sound of parchment ripping and falling apart as if someone had touched a mummified corpse and the remains collapsed in on themselves.

Varder spun, looking in every direction. The prince's sword glowed, illuminating a shadow creeping across the wall, the outline of a man but gaseous, outlined by light rather than vanquished by it.

The shadow fell across the high table, then bent down over the prince's body, reaching for the quill pen the prince kept with him. The quill danced off the floor, and a shadowy hand dipped the point into the prince's blood.

The shadow flew to the wall. Everyone stood, transfixed, their eyes staring at the words that formed in the wake of the pen. The stone behind the high table bore a message in blood.

Catricha read the words in a whisper. "Whosoever shall hold the throne of Alliance shall suffer the fate of those arrogant enough to call themselves royal over others."

Porfiria stepped forward, hands thrusting forward to direct her essences toward the shadowy form. Before her sprites could catch the shape, it faded into nothing. Darkness scattered like motes of smoke. The prince's bloody quill chimed against the floor, the tiny sound echoing in stunned silence.

Catricha put her hands on her knees and sank to the floor.

Vual stared at the words written on the wall, teeth gritted.

Terrel Varder lowered the bane sword, and the blade's light dimmed. His eyes furrowed, tears dripping from them. "The Prince," he said, "and his steward, Lord Halth are dead."

Catricha shook her head, unable to bear the finality of the proclamation.

Porfiria knelt beside her, brushing the hair from Catricha's forehead. "Come," her friend whispered. "We have to tell them where we found Adias."

"Lord Halth is on the balcony," said Catricha, raising her voice. "Please, someone go find him there."

The sound of footsteps drew close. She looked up, hair falling away from her eyes like parting curtains. The handsome, almost delicate jawline and even Palavian features of Sion Arver, the sword servant of House Halth, appeared before her as he bent to speak to her close.

"My lady, I will go find your husband and do what I can for him."

"Your lord is dead," Catricha murmured. "Do what you must, and see for yourself."

Sion's lips trembled, and his facade of calm crumbled as tears began to flow. He worked to straighten himself, but remained uneven, then stalked past Catricha and Porfiria, followed by a pair of house guards. Catricha choked back the curse forming in her mind. She chose not to utter the profane words, for once. For a brief moment, she kept her hatred to herself.

He deserved this, she thought. *Damn him, but none of us deserve what will happen if we can't replace the prince.*

Porfiria put her arms around Catricha, keeping her eyes averted from where the prince's ruined form lay below the message on the wall. "Breathe, Cat. Just breathe."

Catricha's world spun. Despite the scene before her, she fixated on the image of Adias' bloody eyes and gaping chest wound. She steadied herself on Porfiria, her breathing ragged. *How could this evil happen at such a frivolous party?*

"Mercy." Catricha gasped out a harsher curse. "To the pits with decorum. Worse is coming."

Porfiria brought her face close to Catricha's. "Jadiketz falls." She spoke the curse in a soft tone. "But, I hope you're wrong, Cat."

Catricha pressed her forehead to Porfiria's. "I'd hope so too. Except I'm not."

They leaned on each other for stability. Saviron lay motionless except for the spreading pool of blood. *What can hold the four families of Alliance together without a ruler?*

Creeping dread stopped to rest in Catricha's chilled heart, fueled by the fear of what would happen next.

CHAPTER 2

CATRICHA

Rain was sprinkling when the funeral procession arrived at the complex of tombs in the center of Alliance. Catricha climbed from the carriage alongside her father, just within the gates of the necropolis. Her mother followed, along with Catricha's younger siblings. The six of them stood before the grand mausoleums of the princes and the four families, Alliance's rulers for the past thousand years.

All the noble houses buried their dead in the necropolis.

The massive central tomb of the city's princes dominated everything else, a majestic structure, the dome of an ancient temple to a forgotten religion. The building's foundations went deep into the earth. The dome aboveground loomed six-hundred hand-spans high, dwarfing every other construction near the river.

In lighter times, Catricha might have remarked on the first prince's odd arrogance in choosing a conquered foe's temple as his final resting place. A few snide lines began to form in her mind, and she worked to dismiss them. *Not today.*

Catricha frowned as she considered the curse of mortality would one day bring her to this very place in a casket.

The morbid thoughts and the silence of the procession as they wound their way toward the Halth mausoleum gave Catricha the urge to shiver. She gripped her red shawl, where it hung over her shoulders.

Black covered Catricha's frame from head to toe, but she'd deliberately chosen the scarlet hair-covering. Her parents allowed the splash of color, but no one else wore anything other than black or dark gray clothes in the procession, leading the four families.

Each family, Maltos, Paroth, Kuldettan, and Graef, held a significant power base in the city. Their ancestors, along with those of the prince's line, had conquered and renamed Alliance. Five families, after many generations, now dwindled down to four. The princely family had been their figurehead, uniting the rival houses behind one leader.

That ancient line of Davaltz now lay at its end, and the threat to the city's unity grew daily. House Maltos was ever at odds with Graef and Kuldettan. House Paroth, meanwhile, remained aloof from political contests, but their members were few in number these days.

Many nobles from all across the Lands of Mercy had gone east to fight when Catricha was young. Lord Paroth and Kuldettan both returned to the tombs of Alliance directly. Their bodies rested in the family mausoleums.

Years later, when her widowed mother retired, Nansoela Paroth took over leadership of the family. Nansoela walked at the head of her retainers and junior family members, parallel to the Maltos family. Golden hair shimmered at the edges of her black shawl, framing her elegant features. She didn't look in Catricha's direction and maintained a prim and stoic silence. Such manners befitted her well, as the foremost canon poet in the city.

Behind the first two families marched the representatives of Houses Graef and Kuldettan. Both of the trailing households carried powerful magic in their veins. House Kuldettan, in particular, was descended from the immortal called Deckard Hadrian and his first bride.

Rumor had it the immortal man flew north, toward the city, and Catricha dreaded his arrival if he joined with his descendants in their enmity against House Maltos.

The funeral column moved under umbrellas borne by black-clad gentle servants. The edges dripped, heavy with rainwater. Even the younger children, including Catricha's siblings, looked grim under the downpour.

Catricha and her father climbed the steps to the mausoleum belonging to House Halth. Lord Enrin Maltos remained no stranger to loss. Though her father survived the devastation his generation suffered, many of those lost had been his friends, including Lord Paroth. So many gone left a scar in the city's society.

Gone. Like Adias, Catricha thought. *Damn him to the pits of the world.*

Despite her hatred of her husband, Catricha felt an instinctual pang of wrong for an instant, damning him.

He might have lived. If it wasn't for his lust.

"Welcome," said the parson officiating the ceremony. "The casket may be placed within."

"Thank you," said Catricha's father. "And thank Mother Mercy."

"Mercy be praised," said the parson in a hoarse voice.

Pallbearers carried Adias's remains sealed in a heavily-engraved coffin into the tomb. The wounds he suffered must have killed him in seconds, but the way he stared at her, left Catricha wondering if his death could be some kind of justice. In the weeks since his death, mere days farther from their wedding, she accepted one fact. Adias earned her hatred.

The other family representatives followed them inside. Catricha would shed no tears for House Halth, she wondered if the one who brought up the place of honor at the rear of the train of mourners felt the same.

Kizoni Duhikzo, the prince's widow, came from the Rosado Desert, many leagues south of Fulster and Alliance. She'd dwelt in Alliance for two years with her long-betrothed husband but always fit with the rest of the nobility better than Catricha ever had.

Kizoni walked with Terrel Varder and the prince's bodyguard, Layne Kasol, as they approached the tomb. The group climbed the steps slowly, reverencing every movement. Beside them, walked Sion Arver, the sword servant of House Halth, and the last member of the family's retainers not dismissed by Catricha after Adias's death.

"Don't say anything," whispered Enrin to Catricha. "He might have treated you well or poorly, but he doesn't need your brand of bile today."

Sion always treated Catricha well, despite his friendship with Adias. She almost liked the young knight. Catricha turned her gaze from the other parties climbing the steps. She approached the casket. In the tomb, with light filtering through the panes of translucent crystal on the far wall from the entrance, Catricha silently read the inscription on Adias's casket.

Here lies interred Lord Adias Halth the third, last of his family name, last of his household. His marriage to Catricha Maltos was his last public act.

If only that were true, thought Catricha as she read on.

The inscription continued, *Adias was a well-loved lord of noble contrasts, but his love for all women and men transcends his life to join Mercy's House on high.*

Catricha hid a grimace in her red veil, wondering who scribed the fawning inscription. The words seemed ironic now, given how he perished unfaithfully chasing some woman for what lay between her legs.

Enrin bowed his head. The rest of the gathered nobility did the same as Kizoni and Sion entered. The sword servant was not noble but descended from a knightly household. Though he remained ever loyal to his master, he had an air of superiority towards Adias, despite their friendship. That disdain endeared him to Catricha.

He was of the knightly Order of Dreams. His knightly household, guarded far more knowledge of magic than most of the nobility except for House Kuldettan.

Too bad, Catricha thought, *a knight has no status compared to one of us.*

Sion's features set in a grim expression of resolve. His mouth became a thin line, and his eyes remained downcast.

Ashamed, Catricha reiterated her previous thought. *Someone like him should have been higher born.*

She stifled her emotions and turned to face the casket as Sion approached her side.

"He is at rest," said the presiding parson. "Let the ceremony begin."

Kizoni and Sion stood opposite each other on either side of the casket. The parson and assembly began the ritual that would seal the final chapter of Adias's life. Mother Mercy promised an afterlife by her side for those who repented their evil. Catricha wondered if he'd had time to repent, or even consider it.

"We all transgress," the parson said. "We all know the way of mercy."

"We all know the way," said the gathered people.

"Let him who knew of any acts of evil this man committed, step forward now," said the parson.

Traditionally, the friends and family of the dead declined to step forward at this moment.

Catricha retreated one pace from the casket, taking her stand at last.

Enrin glanced at her, unconcealed frustration pulsing in the vein of his neck. His jaw clenched. Catricha feared a similar expression must also be growing on her mother's face.

"What would you say of your husband?" asked the parson, turning toward Catricha.

"I would say," said Catricha, "that he and I were never husband and wife."

She waited for a moment, letting the words sink in and watching the rage in her father's eyes. Enrin's anger was matched by the expression of pure fury building in the twisted features of Vual Kuldettan on the other side of the casket from Catricha.

"If I could call him my husband," said Catricha. "I would."

"How dare you?" said Vual under his breath. "Here lies the son of a noble house, the last son of the stewards of Alliance, and you speak ill of him?"

He seethed beside Kizoni, stepping away from the casket. His hands shook, and the sword he wore on his belt, in defiance of noble tradition, told Catricha she may have transgressed too far for safety.

"If you have something to say to me," said Catricha, "say it later, Vual, because I carried a greater burden for Adias than any other. I carried his disgust."

Vual trembled, lurching sideways to maneuver around Kizoni. The prince's widow turned, eyes narrowing and lips forming words that went unheeded as Vual marched past on his way around the casket.

Sion Arver blocked his way before Vual reached Catricha. Both men carried swords, because Sion still bore the sword of House Halth.

"Whatever you would say, Vual, say it from there," said Sion.

"Stand aside," Vual growled.

"Parson," said Catricha. "Please continue."

"No." Vual's hand remained on the hilt of his sword, restless. "You'll answer for your crime, Catricha Maltos."

"What crime?" asked Catricha. "Marrying at the will of my family rather than my own?"

"Catricha!" her father said, putting a palm out to her. "Be silent."

"Let her speak," said a soft voice from beside the coffin. "Lord Maltos, let your daughter speak."

Catricha looked for the source of the words and found Kizoni, her hands clasped together and shaking. The prince's dowager regent had spoken. Kizoni gazed at Catricha and Enrin with shining eyes, clearly on the verge of tears.

"But Lady Davaltz..." said Catricha's father. "I—"

"—Please," said Kizoni. "We all need truth better than comfort today. We need truth."

Quiet followed the widow's words. The steady drum of raindrops on the mausoleum roof became the only sound in the wake of Kizoni's statement.

Catricha turned to the parson. The skinny priest cleared his throat with a cough, eyes moving nervously to Vual's sword hand. Vual removed his heavy fist from the hilt and then bowed his head.

"Speak, Lady Maltos," said the priest.

Catricha folded her hands despite the heat rushing to her cheeks. She half-closed her eyes.

"I married Adias Halth at my parents' request," she said. "Yet, he made me less than a wife. I will speak no more ill of him today, but I offer this dagger..." She lifted up a sheathed blade in both hands. "...that belonged to my forebears, as a sign of our union's end." Catricha gulped, feeling tears bead in her eyes. In spite of herself, she couldn't tell if her physical response came from fear or relief.

Certainly, though, grief did not enter into her feelings.

She remembered Adias as a young boy, already chasing after girls, even at thirteen years old. His eyes lingered on her often, but always carried scorn when they did. More than seven years gone by since then, she'd not once dreamed of a moment when she'd be free of his presence, least once she married him.

Her friends, her family, and every man who met her gaze with more than derision, all these people outlasted the last Lord Halth.

His life is over, and his line ended. I live on.

Catricha bowed to the priest. "Thank you, Parson Stohan. I've said my words."

The priest's eyes were wet with tears. Expressions warred on his face, mingling sorrow and forceful dignity. "The Church of Mercy will consider your request, my lady," he said.

She kept her head bowed but noticed Vual staring at her, eyes wide. She rarely spoke anything but jests in a crowd. Vual turned his back on her without another word. His shoulders rippled with muscle under his black jacket, but Catricha could not tell if fury or grief impelled the motion.

She waited through the rest of the service, then left with her family in the rain. The entire party marched in traditional silence through the tombs. No mortal voice broke the peace of the tombs until the birds started calling.

Crows perched on the ornate stone arch of the gate to the city streets hopped and fluttered in the slackening rain. No amount of storm could keep those blackbirds from congregating, as if ordained by Mother Mercy herself to preside over funerals.

Catricha pulled her crimson shawl tighter as she walked under the birds. The low sound of thunder rumbled somewhere in the distance, though Catricha missed any flicker of lightning.

She composed a few lines in her mind, adding up syllables three at a time.

No more words No more light,

March silent Into night,

Quiet world's Shadowed plight.

Catricha frowned as she climbed the carriage step, escaping the drizzle. The verse she'd just conceived felt too pretty for this scene.

CHAPTER 3

MELISSA

The wooded ravine northeast of Alliance stirred with hints of movement. From the road beside the slope, Melissa Dorian paused to survey the forest below. Wagons from the caravan bumped past on their way west, but her friend, Elaine, stopped beside Melissa.

"This place has a grim reputation," said Melissa. "Best stay on guard."

"There are demons down there," Elaine said. "Demons and their spawn, all mixing and breeding..." She shuddered. "I'm glad you signed on to guard the caravan, but please be careful if anything comes at us."

"I know," said Melissa. "I've walked this road before."

"This time, perhaps you won't leave empty-handed." Elaine looked at Melissa's face, her shorter frame more noticeable when they stood side by side. Her dark hair shimmered around her head. "With a little luck, we'll find your parents in Alliance."

"Right," said Melissa. "I'm not sure if I'm excited or afraid. Am I ready?"

Elaine nodded. "I wonder if I'll feel the same way, the next time I have a chance to meet him."

"Hadrian may not even realize you're his daughter," said Melissa in a soft voice. "I'm not sure how he'd react either."

"I hope, and I hope, but I don't know for sure about anything." Elaine patted Melissa on the shoulder, then kept walking.

Melissa gripped the handle of her spear, noting another rustle among the trees in the ravine. Mostly the ravine's foliage took the form of scraggly pines or the kind of gnarled oaks common in the lands north of the Rosado Desert. The haunted governance of well country lay east of Alliance. Still, the demonic presence in the ravine offered the same threat.

No doubt world wells as dangerous as any in the eastern valleys lay hidden under those branches. Demons sometimes climbed from the pit of the world and emerged to wreak havoc on mortals. Only the most powerful mages could defeat such beasts.

"See anything down there?" asked Elaine, her glance following Melissa's gaze.

Melissa motioned at the tree she'd seen shake with her spear. "Maybe there?"

Elaine squinted into the shadows of the trees below them. "I can't see much."

"There was movement," said Melissa.

"It could be anything."

"I understand." Melissa lowered the point of her spear. "I doubt even strong demon spawn would risk an attack on a large convoy. And our caravan has only gotten larger, the further north we've gone."

One of the carriages nearby slowed to a stop, horses stamping the ground on the side of the road. Perhaps twenty men on horseback and a few smaller carts followed the carriage. A man in a worn black riding jacket turned his horse toward Melissa and Elaine.

Melissa frowned, not recognizing the young rider. He doffed a dark messenger's cap to them.

"You ladies are keeping an eye on the ravine. The guards should show you some gratitude."

The man looked no older than twenty-five, his hair short and dark, and his eyes intense, hazel, and roving.

Melissa shouldered her spear. "I am one of the guards."

The man smiled. "Forgiveness, please. I concluded you were too well-dressed for that, but I see I was in error." He coughed into his fist. "Manners. Excuse me. I am Heron Olfrus, lord of my household, I suppose.

Having come all this way from the Chos Valley's edge, I couldn't help but notice the odd music about both of you."

Melissa looked at her trousers and tunic. Their quality didn't seem obvious to her after so long on the road.

"Our essence songs?" asked Elaine. "You can hear them?"

"I'm excessively curious," Heron said. "Why do you two, out of everyone in this caravan, sound different?"

"We're mages." Melissa stepped back from the edge of the ravine and approached the Olfrus family carriage.

"Careful around my horses," said Heron. "I happen to be new as lord of the family, and it's my responsibility to keep every man, woman, and animal safe."

"You care a great deal for your people." Elaine smiled at Heron. "I wish more lords felt the same."

"As do I," said Heron. "I take it the two of you are on your way to Alliance?"

"City of poets," said Melissa. "Why not see it for ourselves?"

"Something about your tone makes me think that's not why you're on this road," said Heron. "But never mind. Have either of you need of employment once the caravan reaches the city?"

Melissa took a step back from the carriage. She studied Heron's face. He might be young, at most a few years older than Melissa. A young lord traveling with his whole household must have a strong reason for going west.

"Why are you going to Alliance?" she asked.

"I'd prefer not to explain that myself. Here." Heron smiled slightly, then waved to another rider on the far side of the carriage. "Meet my sister."

The woman rode around the carriage to join Heron, Melissa, and Elaine beside the ravine. She wore a gray jacket and dark trousers, and her eyes lit up with excited alertness as she drew closer.

"My name is Niba. I'm in charge of finding mages to assist the household."

"Why do you need mages?" asked Elaine.

"To be honest, we're looking for more than mages. We need experienced warriors capable of wielding essences in battle."

"Your brother can hear our songs," said Melissa. "Can you?"

"Better than he can." Niba smirked. "I've been trained in that, but I can't do magic, just sense it."

Melissa glanced at Elaine. Her friend nodded. "We both could use employment once we reach the city," she said.

"Perhaps we can make an arrangement," said Niba. "Your soul songs are extremely vivid, and I note something especially affecting in yours, Melissa."

"How did you know my name?" Melissa frowned.

"Forgive me. I've been listening carefully during our journey," said Niba. "I want my brother and our family safe once we reach Alliance."

"Why wouldn't you be safe in Alliance?" asked Melissa.

"You didn't hear?" Niba sighed. "The city's last prince was murdered near the end of summer."

Melissa frowned. "Royals kill each other. Nobles do the same for power, and I suspect a commoner like me would be in little danger. What about you?"

"We are nobility," said Heron. "House Olfrus was native to the Chos Valley even before the conquest by Jadik."

"So says our family lore, anyway," said Niba. "My brother is trying to say we have aspirations beyond mere nobility."

"Aspirations aside," said Melissa, "As nobles, you may need bodyguards, but ordinary warriors will likely be enough, in Alliance."

Elaine silently touched Melissa's sleeve, making her pause.

Melissa raised an eyebrow. "Elaine," she said. "Do you think we should take this job?"

"I see the value in it," said Elaine. "After all, I still haven't mastered my sacra form, and without one, I'll never be a full wizard. I could use funds to continue training."

"You say that as though Melissa has mastered a sacra form," said Niba.

"I have," said Melissa. "Just over the summer."

"Phenomenal," said Niba. "I'll happily hire both of you if you'll agree to protect my family."

"I've been tutored far longer than Melissa," said Elaine. "But my apprenticeship ended over the summer, the same as Melissa's."

"It sounds as though you both have potential to explore," said Niba. "Heron, what say you?"

"I say, sign them on for fifty silver a week each," said Heron. "We'll need all the help we can get once we reach the city."

"Fifty silver?" said Melissa, eyebrows rising. "You pay well."

"Don't make me regret it." Heron laughed. "I trust your powers are worth the price."

"The city is just hours away," said Niba. "We couldn't have met you at a more opportune time."

"Alliance is near," said Heron. "But sister, don't forget. First, we must take a detour. Let us move."

* * *

Alliance's towers rose before them as Heron, the young lord of House Olfrus, led his carriage and his family northward. They just passed the ravine and were already circling across the where the river emptied onto the plain. They crossed the river on a wide stone bridge.

Melissa and Elaine rode in one of the Olfrus wagons on their way a stronghold on a hill overlooking the ravine.

"The House of Graef is one of the great family's of Alliance," said Niba. "They could become an ally for us, and we'll need support if we are to become the princely family."

Melissa squinted over the driver's board at the fortified house on the hill overlooking the ravine. "What sort of nobility are they?"

"Hunters," said Niba. "They mind the demons that emerge from the wells in the ravine."

"Demon hunters?" Elaine frowned, tapping her lip with a finger. "That sounds familiar."

"Familiar, how?" asked Niba.

Melissa shook her head. "I don't believe we've explained what happened before we left the south lands," she said. "We fought in Soucot when a fleet from Kanor attacked late in the summer."

"Kanor must be a terrible opponent," said Niba. "I received letters from a noble friend before we left the valley. There is still strife in the river land."

Elaine nodded, her eyelids drooping. "I'm sad to say I expected as much."

"But the demon hunter we met in Soucot wasn't native to the south," said Melissa. “I've heard he's been flying north."

“Flying?” Niba's eyes widened, and she reached over her horse's reins. She grasped Melissa's arm. "You two met Deckard Hadrian?"

"We were in the governor's service in Lowenrane," said Melissa. "We worked with him there."

"Fascinating," said Niba. She cleared her throat. With a cough. "I've heard Hadrian is one of the most beautiful men to walk the world, is that so?"

"I'd say..." Melissa started.

"He's handsome," said Elaine. "But not exactly the type for everyone, or indeed anyone."

"What does that mean?" asked Niba.

"We weren't on the best of terms with him when we parted," said Melissa. "One of us better than the other, but neither of us expects him to be helpful in the future."

"I wouldn't go that far," said Elaine. "After all, you fought alongside him in the battle."

Niba looked from Elaine to Melissa, mouth half-open. “You more than met him, then?”

"We both did," said Melissa. “But we earned more pain than glory."

"I see." Niba hung her head. "Forgive me for asking."

"It's not your fault," said Melissa.

"Melissa," said Elaine. "We lost too many people in the fighting."

Melissa's eyes would have welled with tears had she not pushed the memories to the back of her mind. Pains stirred in her heart as she considered the battle claiming the lives of her friends and fellow mages.

"The governor's people trained me as a mage," said Melissa. "I owe them much beyond my grief. I simply couldn't stay after that."

"You're like my brother. Very open," said Niba. "Has anyone ever told you?"

"Never," said Melissa. "I suppose I'm changing."

“So you traveled north again," said Niba. "You've come a long way to escape your memory."

"If you'd been there," said Elaine. "You'd understand. We both lost friends. But those who fell in battle were not the only cost we paid."

"I'll ask no more about the battle," said Niba softly. I think I understand. Still..." Her tone brightened. "What kind of magic do you wield?"

"I'm still fairly new to the arts," said Melissa. "I barely mastered my sacra form by the time of the battle."

"A sacra form is a powerful tool," said Elaine. "Soon perhaps, I'll be able to afford a scroll to study to become a full wizard."

Melissa nodded. The demon of her sacra form, Fanhedon, always resided at the back of her mind. Fanhedon hummed a soft song only the two of them could hear.

Niba rode ahead, waving for the wagons to follow her. The caravan went through the open gates of House Graef.

CHAPTER 4

MELISSA

In the great hall of House Graef, a noblewoman danced among others, red hair flying about her.

Melissa sat beside Elaine at one of the lesser tables as Heron and Niba discussed an arrangement with the head of the Graef family. Meanwhile, the daughters of the house continued to move on the dance floor as the conversation diminished. The minstrels played louder.

The dinner meal was cleared away, and guests began to join the dance. Though the family was supposedly poor by the standards of Alliance, Melissa saw more than one lavish gown and fancy doublet.

"How do you stand it?" she asked, leaning toward Elaine. "I could never wear a dress like that."

"I'm sure you could," said Elaine. "You have the shape for it."

Melissa shook her head, turning away to hide her reddening face. "I certainly do not."

"Say what you will," said Elaine. "I'd wager your footwork would be as agile as anyone else here."

"I'm fast," said Melissa. Swift on my feet, but I wouldn't necessarily call myself nimble."

"Again." Elaine smiled. "Say what you will."

Melissa shrugged and turned toward the high table, testing her ears to listen to what Lord Graef was saying to Heron.

Lord Graef was a skinny, aging man, his hair as red as his daughters' where it had yet to go gray. His beard was thick and white.

"You see," said Heron. "If we were to form an alliance, as it were, the cities power could fall into our hands when we take what we can from the other houses. I'm offering a substantial change of fortunes should we win."

"A pity," said Lord Graef. "I've no son to marry your sister."

"I heard as much in my travels," said Heron. "However, I've yet to take a wife."

"In this household," said Lord Graef, "the women are free as men to choose. I wouldn't have a daughter of mine marry anyone unless she agreed with me on the decision."

"Perhaps one of them will," said Heron. "But let's not get ahead of ourselves."

Lord Graef gave a heavy belch, the sound surprising, given his skinny frame. "Excuse me," he said. "My manners are not what they once were when I lived in the city."

"Neither are mine," said Heron. "I rarely entered Empire, or any other cities in the Chos Valley, when I dwelt there."

"I have heard of your family, Heron Olfrus." Lord Graef nodded to Niba. "You see, you're almost as famous among demon hunters as we are, and your people spread further east."

"Unfortunately, we're on hard times," said Heron. "I have little to share with anyone. But if we were to join forces, your funding and my craft, honesty, and guile may be enough to win the throne."

"Now, now," said Lord Graef. "Don't be so forward."

"Pardon him," said Niba. "My brother is eager to reach the city and stabilize matters."

"Of course," said Lord Graef. "I wish the city to return to order as well. I'm not yet sure if you're strong enough to be worth an arrangement of the kind we're discussing."

"The reputation of House Olfrus goes before us," said Heron, "Yet, you insist that we prove ourselves?"

"Of course," said Lord Graef. "I see no reason why you shouldn't show me what you can offer firsthand."

"We will have a hunt, then," said Heron. "What say you to that?"

"In the ravine, you mean?" said Lord Graef. "Don't be foolish, boy. The place is far too dangerous for anyone without magic at their command to hunt."

"I've heard your eldest daughter rides the ravine often," said Heron. "Or is that just a tall tale?"

"Bethanelle hunts in the ravine, true," said Lord Graef. "Still, don't put your life on the line just yet. I've something else in mind for you to show your worth."

"Go ahead," said Heron. "What did you have in mind?"

"Hunting is not a skill I need right now," said Lord Graef. He frowned in Melissa's direction. "But I sense some eyes on us. Perhaps we should discuss the rest of this in private."

"Of course," said Heron. "Sister, please tell Lady Dorian not to listen in further."

Niba rose from the high table and approached the lesser table where Elaine and Melissa sat. Melissa flushed, thinking how obvious she must've been staring and inclining her head to listen in on their conversation.

"Forgiveness," said Elaine. "We did not mean to overhear so much."

"It's no sin," said Niba. "But we must be proper."

"True," said Elaine. "Forgive the impoliteness, and please tell Lord Graef the same."

"It might mean more coming from your friend, Lady Dorian," said Niba. "No need to bow your head and beg pardon for something you were not the greatest part in, Elaine."

Melissa's face grew hot. No doubt, she flushed a bright red. "I will request Lord Graef's forgiveness. I know well how nobility excludes the weak of blood."

"Now, don't get so personal," said Niba. "I've heard the name Dorian in these parts. Everyone has." She shrugged and then motioned for Melissa to stand. "Come with me, and we'll sort things out."

The two of them returned to the high table, Melissa trailing Niba by a few paces. She bowed to Lord Graef as they approached him. *I can act as required, so long as I'm employed to do so.* "Forgive me. I did not mean to offend by listening in."

"Clearly not," said Lord Graef. "You mages are more curious than formal, in general." He smiled slightly. "I take it you were listening to protect your master's interests. That is loyalty I admire. Your attendance to such details has me considering you more a bodyguard than a hired mage."

"I'm not a bodyguard or sword servant," said Melissa. "I've been a caravan guard, though."

"A caravan guard?" Lord Graef snorted, his eyebrows elevating. "Is that not a bit tedious for someone of your talents?"

"Before I learned magic this past summer, guarding merchants was my only skill."

"Since summer? How much magic do you know?" said Lord Graef. His eyebrows bent together. "I'm curious, mage."

Melissa folded her hands. "I studied with the rest of the Governor's Hand in Soucot."

"So..." Lord Graef frowned. "The tales are true."

Melissa inhaled deeply, tasting the lingering smells of the feast. "Lord Graef, I know not what you mean."

"It is unfortunate," he said. "I was told to expect one with your family name approaching from the south. The Dorian mercantile company has holdings in Alliance, and I take it you're of the same blood."

"Indeed," said Melissa. "I've not seen my parents in some years."

"As much as I'm curious about your history, we must dismiss matters for now." said Lord Graef. "I can say the Dorian leadership is not here in Alliance. After you leave the city, I will tell you where you can find them. Not before."

Melissa frowned. "Why not?"

"That also, I cannot tell you before you leave Alliance. Please, don't listen in further. Lord and Lady Olfrus and I should finish this discussion in privacy."

"As you wish," said Melissa through gritted teeth. "Elaine and I will wait."

"Do so," said Lord Graef. "And your listening in is forgiven."

Melissa rankled at his insistence on keeping secrets. Perhaps he was right, and her parents were not in Alliance. If so, she should simply leave now, but her contract with Heron was too immediately valuable. *To the pit with them all*, she thought. Her family's holdings in Alliance could wait.

"What little we know," said Lord Graef, "can certainly hurt us."

Melissa turned, hiding her grimace of annoyance. She walked stiffly to Elaine's place at the lower table. "They want us to wait. Night is gathering fast."

"We can practice outside, yet," said Elaine. "Are you prepared for a lesson?"

"If your fit to teach," said Melissa. "But it is growing late. Perhaps we should simply spar."

"A good idea," said Elaine. "The situation here doesn't suit at the moment."

Melissa nodded. "Lady Tanlos."

"Now, don't call me that." Elaine sighed. "I only wish to escape my parents," she said. "If we're lucky, maybe we can avoid Calferis for another few weeks."

"The family demon." Melissa gave a low whistle. "How long will he search for you?"

"Who knows?" said Elaine. "But, regardless, we should stay out of sight while sparring. Nothing flashy for now."

Calferis, despite being a demon, took the form of a flock of blackbirds. However strange, he could be stealthy, especially with darkness in the sky. If he was trying to retrieve Elaine, caution remained sensible.

Melissa and Elaine rose from the table. The two of them went out into the household's walled yard.

* * *

The sound of essences clashing faded into the night.

Elaine turned to Melissa. "I was afraid you were going to tell them about me."

The two of them sat side-by-side on the steps, breathing heavily, after the exertion of sparring as the night grew darker.

Melissa touched Elaine's shoulder. "Never."

"Thank you. I didn't know I needed a friend like you until I had one."

"Neither of us has many friends right now."

"You think that." Elaine shook her head, a rueful smile on her face. "I know it. Far too many, both men and women, wanted to be my friends when I lived in Geteren. I've not written to any of them since I went south."

"Your father," said Melissa. "I mean, Lord Tanlos must have an idea where we are."

"I'm sure his Calferis is still on our trail." Elaine sighed. "My only doubt is that he won't be strong enough after the battle to fly north alone."

"Demons are immortal," said Melissa. "You don't need to worry about him."

"I'll still worry, regardless," said Elaine. "I grew up around him, after all."

"Of course you do," said Melissa. "That's you. Do you think Lady Nasibron could be looking for us too?"

"My teacher never would..."

"But your mother?" asked Melissa.

"She's the same woman." Elaine folded her arms and heaved another sigh. "Until we find your family, there's no way I want to face her."

"I get it. If you want to go back to Geteren, I'll understand. Though, I'm grateful you're here."

The door behind them creaked open. A single set of footsteps approached from the great hall, soft and careful, like those of a hunter. Yet, these feet were no-doubt clad in something softer than even a ranger's shoes.

"You two?" said a girl's voice. "You shouldn't have been sent out."

Melissa turned and looked up into the eyes of the red-haired girl who'd been dancing after dinner.

"Who are you?" asked the daughter of Lord Graef. "My name is Bethanelle."

"We're wizards." said Elaine. "The Olfrus family hired us on the road just today."

"Heron seems to have a magnetism to him," said Bethanelle, tapping her chin. "I'm not sure what my father is waiting for, he hasn't even asked my opinion of the man yet."

"Perhaps your father is being protective," said Elaine.

"Or he doesn't want anyone to know his thoughts," said Melissa. "He's secretive."

"Quite so," said the young lady. "Ever since my mother passed, he has not let anyone close except for my little sister."

"So you're the oldest child?" And Melissa.

"Yes, I am the heir of the house."

"Bethanelle, you said? That's quite a name." Elaine climbed to her feet. "It sounds familiar."

"Mother took it from a canon poem," said Bethanelle. "One of the epics rumored authored by Zidon."

"Zidon, the immortal?" said Melissa. "I've read about him."

"He was one of the warriors who rode north with Jadik," said Bethanelle. "So, he fought alongside the founder of the Empire, and lived for many years as Jadik's right hand."

"And wrote poetry apparently?" said Melissa.

"Are you not familiar? Alliance is called the city of poets." Bethanelle smiled. "I'm surprised a wizard wouldn't know."

"I've not been a wizard long." Melissa gazed into the courtyard's gloom. "There's still a lot I don't know, even about the mortal world."

"Alliance, city of poets and knights," said Elaine, "Known both for the arts of battle and writing."

"I never paid enough attention to verse," said Melissa. "I'm more apt in reading histories and guides, which is why I know Zidon's name. Wasn't he given the city after the conquest?"

"So legend says," said Bethanelle. "But he was more a monk than a prince. Perhaps that's why he gave up his rule to the line of Davaltz."

"He didn't stay to rule the city?" Melissa's eyebrows rose. "I guess I need better histories to study."

Bethanelle laughed. "If you want to go to a library in the city, I can take you there. We can find books on far more than history. My father will approve. He thinks I should spend more time in the city, rather than the ravine."

"What do you do in the ravine?" asked Elaine, wrinkling her nose.

"I hunt," said Bethanelle. "My house guards and I keep the well demons and their spawn from getting out of control."

"That sounds dangerous," said Melissa.

"It is, but my family has tools to slay demon spawn."

“I hope the city appreciates that, Bethanelle,” said Elaine.

"I overheard a conversation from the guards, which reminded me. The prince's funeral is tomorrow night. Perhaps a better day to go to the library will come soon after. I nearly forgot the funeral," said Bethanelle. "I must be one of the few noblewomen in the city who did not know Prince Saviron well."

"They say he was murdered," said Melissa. "That's the rumor on the road."

"Indeed." Bethanelle bowed her head. “The prince was killed at his party over the summer while he sat alone at the high table. Somehow, no one saw his attacker until it was over."

"His attacker?" asked Melissa.

"A shadow," said Bethanelle. "Whatever the attacker was, he must've been magical in nature. That's probably why Heron wants mages to join his mission. Whoever seeks the thrones must deal with shadows. The killer threatened the next prince and any who would hold the throne."

Melissa's eyes narrowed. "I dared hope to have a quiet position. After all, I have my own reasons to be in Alliance."

"What are those reasons?" asked Bethanelle.

"My own," said Melissa. “Some secrets must be kept close.”

"Very well," said Bethanelle. "I couldn't help but notice your name is Dorian, and there is a merchant company by that name in the city, the largest traders on the river Duenn, in fact."

“That's true.” Melissa shrugged. “I could have relatives everywhere, perhaps?”

Elaine glanced at Melissa, then smiled. “It's possible.”

"I'm going to Prince Saviron's funeral tomorrow night," said Bethanelle. "It would be impossible for me not to represent my household there. Still, I may attend another event while I'm in the city." She brandished a letter.

"What is that message?” asked Elaine.

"Nansoela Paroth is having one of her parties the very night the prince's funeral," said Bethanelle. "I suppose when you're the most renowned poet in a city of poets, you have real nerve."

"Lady Paroth," said Melissa, "doesn't seem broken up about the prince's death. So much so, she's invited fellow nobles to a party on the night of his funeral."

"Could it be she means to celebrate the prince's life, rather than his passing?" Elaine clasped her hands and turned to Bethanelle.

"Prince Saviron loved poetry, from what I understand," said Bethanelle. "But, I do have one other question for you, my ladies, before you retire."

"Speak, then," said Melissa. "We'll see if we have answers."

"I overheard my father speak of Lord Hadrian earlier when discussing things with Lord Olfrus. It seems the immortal flies this direction. I'd heard he lived near the town of Fulster, some miles south of Alliance, but he hasn't been there since I was an infant."

"Who can say?" Elaine unfolded her hands and set them on her knees. "Lord Hadrian is a mystery to us, no matter how many times we speak with him."

Melissa nodded. "Elaine tells the truth. I'm afraid if we encounter him, he may not be pleased to see either of us."

"Then perhaps you should stay far from him," said Bethanelle. "The immortal is legendary. The last of only two remaining in the world."

"What is an immortal?" said Melissa. "Who dies?"

"I don't know." Bethanelle gave a nervous laugh.

"A mortal, who's been prolonged?" said Melissa with a smirk.

"Please don't laugh," said Elaine.

"It seems apt." Melissa shrugged. "Apologies, Elaine."

"You'll pardon the joke, I hope, Elaine. Now, I'll have our servants show you to your quarters," said Bethanelle. "They won't be anything luxurious fancy, as Lord Olfrus has quite the number of other retainers. He and his sister are the only ones receiving private chambers tonight. Still, we'll find ways to provision you better than on the road."

"Thank you," Elaine said with a nod.

Melissa got to her feet, turned, and faced Bethanelle. "Thanks indeed."

Bethanelle waved two young women, both dressed in the solemn clothes of gentle servants. Their long black skirts flattened against their legs in a stiff westward wind. "See the guests to their lodgings," said Bethanelle. "Please inform me when they're ready in the morning."

Melissa arched an eyebrow. "You're keeping eyes on us?"

"Mages are quite dangerous," said Bethanelle. "I should know, as I have a bit of talent myself."

"I don't like it, but I understand," Melissa said.

Bethanelle folded her hands. "I meant to ask if both of you would honor me by accompanying me to Nansoela's party tomorrow evening? I only wanted to ensure you did not find yourselves otherwise occupied first."

Melissa shrugged. "Fine by me. Elaine?"

"I'd like to go meet a famous poet," said Elaine. "We can act as bodyguards if nothing else."

"Practice and train," said Melissa. "But we'll see if Heron needs us elsewhere."

Bethanelle smiled. "Of course. You must serve him first."

As long as he pays, Melissa thought. She and Elaine went to their lodgings in an empty stall in the stables. Bethanelle was right. It was more comfortable than the road.

CHAPTER 5

VUAL

The essences within the training room produced a haunting tune. Resonances in the mingled songs of sprites and banes told Vual his foes were preparing to attack. They stood around him, a circle of five major servants, each trained in hedge magic. Every man bristled with additional battle-ready essences. Despite himself, Vual's eye twitched with nervous tension.

Mortality felt closer since his best friends' deaths. Both Adias and Saviron had failed to survive a summer party. Vual faced five highly-trained warrior mages. The fact this was a sparring match did not diminish one clear truth. These servants intended to beat him to the point of death if he couldn't defeat them.

Vual flexed his hands, sensing essences in his fingertips. The banes flowing through his heart made their song known in a deep, discordant ripple, the kind of song that menaced Vual when he heard it from another mage. The men around him hesitated.

Sprites extended from his body, forming a kind of halo of glowing particles around him. His banes began to build in volume. Their combined songs, rough and crunching, enveloped him.

The five warriors broke their hesitation and surged toward him.

Each of them formed their essences into a magical attack. One used a blade made of sprites, another hurled elongated essence whips at Vual, trying to grab his arms. The others were less immediate threats, weaving a single slower spell together.

Vual possessed superior skills to each of them. Yet, without the power of a fully-controlled sacra form, he remained careful. His opponents could still best him. He took as deep a breath as he could while avoiding each foes' attacks.

Calm notes echoed in Vual's heart song, as in the eye of a whirling storm.

He jumped to one side, avoiding flailing essence whips that cracked against the floor. A blade from the second warrior slashed past him, tearing through the air with a wail. The other three mages came from his opposite side as a group, sprites and banes combined to hurl burning magic. The net of heated essence cut off Vual's movement on one side and scorched at his extended fingertips.

He leapt over the net, boosting his jump with sprites matching the muscles in his legs. He landed behind the three men carrying the net and dropped them, each with blows from his fist. The three fell, writhing in pain. Vual pivoted to face the two remaining assailants. The one with the essence sword advanced, slicing in a rhythmic pattern with his blade.

Vual retreated bit by bit as he drew an essence sword of his own between them. He parried his foe's sword once, twice, three times, and then grabbed the man by the wrist. He spun and tugged the swordsman off-balance. Vual smashed the man into the oncoming whip-wielder. The two men went down, and their magic evaporated, sprites returning to their unconscious bodies.

He grinned, then looked down at his hand, smarting with pain where he'd thought he avoided the blade altogether. His fingers weren't burnt from the net's heat, but a trickle of blood ran along his palm, it's source a small cut near his wrist.

Not fast enough.

"Stop," said a man's voice.

Vual turned to see Uncle Terek standing beside Vual's mother, who waited with her usual stern demeanor.

Filavaye Kuldettan nodded to her brother. "Explain to my son his error."

Terek stepped forward, motioning for the servant mages sparring with Vual to stand down as they recovered. "Well done, for the most part, nephew," he said. "You suffered a cut." He motioned to Vual's hand.

"I noticed," said Vual. "It hurts a little."

"As it should," said Terek. "After all, a single cut from the right weapon could kill you."

"Are you trying to chastise me?" asked Vual. "Or are you aiming to congratulate?"

"A little of both." Terek smiled. "You've come far. I expect you'll have your sacra form mastered soon."

Vual shrugged. "That doesn't matter anymore."

It's too late, he thought.

"Why doesn't mastering the most salient feature of a full wizard matter now?" said Terek. "You've worked for it your whole life, boy."

"True. I've struggled to become a wizard my entire life," said Vual. "I may be young, but I've done much to reach my place. Now, a different challenge rests uneasy on my mind. Isn't that right, mother?" He turned to Filavaye.

Filavaye nodded. Terek turned toward her, eyebrows raising with an unasked question.

"Correct, my son," she said. "The city is in chaos. Vual should be our representative to ascend the throne to replace Prince Saviron."

"It won't be easy to attain the princely seat." Vual frowned. "Even for our family. We carry an immortal's blood in our veins. Guessing by the rumors of his recent travels, I wonder why he flies for Alliance."

Filavaye frowned, her teeth bared in a grimace. "Deckard Hadrian is not our enemy, son. He's an honored ancestor, and I expect he will be the least of our worries once we engage in the succession conflict. Everyone must be prepared to do their part."

"If I fail to lead our way, would you have Ruar try for the throne? Even with his other dalliances?"

"Your younger brother is not fit for the throne," said Filavaye. "He is less able as a mage and less powerful as a warrior."

"I only fear that if I go forth to claim the throne, someone else will attempt to pull our power from under our feet."

"Who in the city can best you, my son?" Filavaye gave a derisive snort and shake of her head. "Are you really doubtful, Vual?"

"I have my worries," he said, slowly diminishing the blade he'd formed of his essences until it disappeared completely. "Saviron and Adias, my friends both, should be the ones to hold power to choose a successor, but they're gone." Vual gritted his teeth, hands shaking as he lowered them to his sides. "The dowager regent holds the seat for now."

Ever since they'd been young, Vual, Saviron, and Adias had been inseparable. The three were once the strongest allies of their cohort in the city, and best friends to each other.

"Saviron left no instruction as to who would succeed him beyond his steward, Lord Halth," said Filavaye. "As a friend to them both, you are the clearest to succeed. Ruar didn't know them the way you did. Even the dowager regent will see that."

"I knew them a way no one else did," said Vual. "Nobody else, not even that wench from House Maltos who married Adias. And forget the princess from Ettayeed, who married Prince Saviron."

Filavaye folded her perfectly manicured fingers. "Don't speak that way with anyone else," she said. "You must show respect to both those widows, my son. After all, our family has appearances to keep up."

"I'll call Catricha Maltos whatever I damn well please," growled Vual. "Mother. I lost both my best friends in one night. I will not tolerate that half-noble woman acting as though she is mourning. We all know how she felt about Adias and how he rejected her. Their marriage was of convenience, but I can scarcely imagine why they were promised to each other for so long."

"The former Lord Halth and his father wanted the two families to become one," said Filavaye. "Adias' line was dwindling, but things failed completely because of the two of them. The old Lord Halth would be turning in his grave if he saw how they treated their marriage."

"Filavaye," said Terek. "Perhaps not now."

Filavaye waved her brother away. "Vual must listen." She turned to him and his glare. "Your friends were far from perfect."

Vual bowed his head, trying to hide his seething anger. "Don't speak ill of them."

"Don't command me in my house," said Filavaye. "After all, you're not Lord Kuldettan yet."

"By your design," said Vual, "I will never be Lord Kuldettan, but I may yet become Prince of Alliance."

"Fairly spoken, my son," said Filavaye. "If you are chosen as prince, you will no longer be an official family member. You will start your own household, and I expect you will not spend the time deriding those you can use as stepping-stones and bearers of children when the time comes."

"I never hated Maltos the way Adias did," said Vual. "And I never chased women like him, either."

"Vual," said Filavaye, "you must reach acceptance. I don't dare hope that will happen immediately, but you must understand that lesson, just as you must master your sacra form. You must learn to forgive insults. Mere words must become as nothing to you."

"Impossible," said Vual. He reached inward, brushing against his angry banes as their song began to build within his heart.

Terek backed away, his hands folded. Filavaye glanced at her brother. "Don't be a coward, brother. Straighten your back."

Vual's uncle bowed to Filavaye, then straightened himself like a sturdy tree.

"Good," said Filavaye. "be an example to my son and the entire family."

"Thank you, sister," said Terek. "Filavaye, please, don't be so harsh on the boy. Vual has trained hard, even since Lord Halth's funeral. It is my opinion he doesn't need further pressure at the moment."

"I can bear the weight." Vual turned to Terek. "Thank you, uncle."

"Of course." Terek did not smile but gave a nod of satisfaction, the sort Vual recalled from his younger days.

Filavaye drummed her fingers on her elbows. "See that you do, my son."

Mother married late and lost her husband in the wars with the Kism. Vual was the eldest of her three children. He held the position of immediate successor to the family seat while Ruar trained equally as a poet, mage, and warrior, and remained more an artist than anything else. He certainly fell far from the heroic leader Vual trained to become. Their younger sister, Palladia, remained Filavaye's favorite. Only twelve summers old, she was the source of mother's rare joy.

Vual met Filavaye's gaze. "I will do what I can, mother. I will achieve the goal you've set for me, and I will do it my way. I will become the Prince of Alliance if that's what you want. I will even replace my dead friends if that is what you demand. I will do whatever it takes to topple the other houses if you desire it, mother."

Filavaye raised an eyebrow, face serene except for a small twitch of her lips. Vual suspected he may have touched a nerve. Filavaye might be the most controlling head of any of the four houses, but she was also human. No doubt, she considered her goals as higher than Vual's. He'd spent his whole life learning how to handle a taskmaster far stricter than his uncle.

"Mother," said Vual, "May I leave for the moment?"

"You may go," said Filavaye. "Don't tell anyone I'm considering you as successor to the prince."

"Of course not," said Vual.

Not yet, he added mentally.

He strolled through the halls of the Kuldettan mansion, making his way toward his chambers.

He encountered Ruar. His brother sat on a stool in an alcove under a window, sketching on a piece of parchment with a pen.

"What are you doing, Ruar?" Vual asked.

His younger brother looked up from the page and frowned at Vual. "It's not much, just an attempt to record the gallant poetry I've been composing."

"Gallant?" said Vual. "I wasn't aware you cared so much about the respect of the knights."

"I want to leave something behind," said Ruar. "I need to make a name for myself apart from being in this family. You'll always overshadow me here, brother."

"True," said Vual. "Though, you could train harder in magic and war. Your skills in both fields could use work."

"Why compete?" said Ruar, "when I can go my own path?"

"That's some wisdom," said Vual, "That I didn't need to hear. Brother, you might be a better warrior than me if you put your mind to it. But you're divided."

"I'm not divided," said Ruar, "Not any more than you. I just happen to focus my temper on being productive."

"What does that mean?" Vual clenched his fist and stalked a few paces into the nook where Ruar sat. Vual leaned over him, his bulky frame eclipsing the light from the lamps shining behind them. His arm cast a shadow in the sunlight from the alcove window.

Ruar shrugged. “Please, move out of the light, brother.”

Vual grunted, then stepped aside. “Forgiveness. I haven't been as calm as I should be lately.”

Ruar nodded but said nothing.

Vual turned and marched away, forcing himself one step at a time to leave his brother in the nook and continue to his chambers.

CHAPTER 6

DECKARD

There was wine on his breath when he left the tavern early in the morning. He took to the air, his robe billowing in the gale as the feather sprites within took all the weight from the iron garment.

Deckard Hadrian, immortal demon hunter, flew north. He'd taken his time to mourn those lost in the battle of Soucot. Hunting in the river lands eased the pain. The demons he'd encountered suffered his anger worse than ever during the intervening weeks. Deckard only ceased his wandering prosecutions when his closest holding in the north called to him.

Fulster was a little town, overlooked by the glass-walled fortress known as Hadrian's Keep. The place remained close to his heart, even though he rarely spent time there of late. The keepers of the village paid him homage, fed him, and kept him in good spirits when he stayed there. When Deckard thought spirits, he thought of alcohol.

"Good wine is hard to find," Deckard said as he glided over the land, carried by storm winds toward the north.

He was still a thousand leagues from Fulster when he spotted shapes on the horizon, too large to be birds, but not large enough to block his view of the ring peaking through the clouds above the world.

Whatever the shapes were, they flew toward him with purpose. Deckard only hoped if the flying shadows belonged to demons, they'd waited for their proper place in the order of those who wanted revenge against him.

Despite his early-morning drinking, Deckard's gaze was steady. He could fight a few demons in the air, and there were only three of them. Perhaps more could be hidden in the clouds. There were always possibilities.

He flexed his fingers, tested the readiness of his sprites and banes while the potential foes were over a mile away. They did not change course. Deckard prepared himself to clash in the air. The sword at his belt, taken from the governor's armory in Soucot after the battle near the end of summer, was no ordinary blade.

When he left, he'd requested a demon-fighting sword to inflict intense pain on the banes that dwelt within every monstrous heart. So far, three rogue beings had tasted the blade's edge in his travels.

The presence of the same essences comprised humans and demons when combined had interested many philosophers across the land over the centuries. Mortal scholars possessed little knowledge of essences and the types of creatures they combined to create.

"Let's see..." Deckard murmured, extending the tip of a bane dart from each finger. The low hum of his battle essences mingled with the usual sound of glorious trumpets that accompanied his feather sprites. Deckard didn't like the idea of flying across the land and deafening everyone for miles. Fortunately, most mortals couldn't hear such songs, no matter the distance.

He squinted ahead, unable to make out precisely what demons approached. He could catch breezes and bend them to his will, but his senses remained those of an ordinary man.

The silhouettes indeed appeared demonic, with the two on the flanks far larger than any human or bird. The one in the center appeared as a glimmering shape. It was awkward to distinguish the central figure from the slender sunbeams emerging from the clouds. With half a mile between them, Deckard caught a snatch of song belonging to a particular being he knew all too well.

Ilrona, he thought. *Mother Mercy shouldn't have sent you to confront me. I'm not in the mood.*

He closed the distance quickly, releasing his readied bane darts, so they retreated into his fingers.

Gliding toward the demons, he noted the other two must also be servants of Mother Mercy. He didn't know their names but recognized the long serpentine bodies and feathered wings common among their breed of demon. Deckard fixed his attention on Ilrona.

Her humanoid form was divided between light and shadow. The songs of each side rang out entirely differently from the other. On one side, darkness took a feminine shape, while on the other half, pure light composed a brilliant mirror image of the void. Though she lacked wings, Ilrona flew with ease.

Her voiced greeted him with an echoing call. The two feathery serpent demons parted from Ilrona and winged their way around Deckard. The lady of light and darkness slowed her pace as she drew near to Deckard. He quieted the wind a little, leaving just enough of an updraft to keep him aloft.

Ilrona was Mother Mercy's handmaiden and messenger. No doubt she'd come to talk.

The dark side of Ilrona's face rippled for a second. "Deckard Hadrian." Her voice warbled in the air. "Descend to the earth, so we may speak."

"Surely, whatever matter you have for me can wait until I arrive at my destination," said Deckard.

He felt the wine bottle in his robe, despite all its weight being borne by his essences. He didn't like the idea of Ilrona noticing him drinking. Since Soucot, he hadn't been clear with Mother Mercy about how he handled the losses suffered. He'd not known many, but some of the mortals lost hit him hard enough he drank to forget. *Niu. Kelt.* The faces of the fallen members of the governor's mage hand burned in his mind.

"They cannot, Hadrian," Ilrona said. "You are headed to Fulster, no?"

"I'm aimed in that direction," said Deckard. "Do you need me to change course?"

"No," said Ilrona. "I only wish to give you Mother Mercy's latest message."

"Then fly with me," said Deckard, "if your snakes can keep up."

"They can," said Ilrona. "I chose the fastest of their sort."

"What do you call their kind?" asked Deckard.

"Air serpents will suffice for now. They are friends of an ancient rival. Anovot the Silencer once commanded these two."

"And now they serve Mother Mercy?" said Deckard. "Consider me skeptical."

"I trust them well enough." Ilrona glided to Deckard's side, then pivoted effortlessly in the air. She grinned with the bright side of her mouth. Her shadow side never betrayed such emotion. "Deckard, I want you to serve our master as well as I do."

"Perhaps you'd serve better if you were more cautious of your allies," said Deckard.

"You'd do well to heed the same advice." Ilrona's smile vanished. "I heard you let several individuals of questionable repute escape after the fighting in Soucot."

"Obviously, a demon doesn't understand the value of life," said Deckard. "Those ones could be useful in the future."

"Yet they could pose a danger in the present," said Ilrona. "That demon hunter from the east...What was his name?"

"Leave it," said Deckard. "He's not here now, and we're not going to find him anytime soon unless we fly a few thousand miles in the opposite direction."

"An astute point, demon hunter." Ilrona turned her gaze to face the northern horizon as she propelled forward. The air serpents followed them at a distance.

Deckard had to push the winds from behind him harder to keep up with Ilrona. She was faster than him and moved without apparent effort. Her powers remained a mystery even to Deckard. The source of her abilities could be from either side of her nature. He didn't know which one allowed such defiance of natural forces.

"Mother Mercy has a message for me?" he said.

"She does."

"What is her will this time?" asked Deckard.

"One with a dual purpose," said Ilrona. "The Prince of Alliance lies dead."

"I heard," said Deckard. "I was friends with his father before the last war."

"The battles with the Kism had regrettable consequences," said Ilrona. "Too many mortals fell from Mercy's lands to be called a victory."

Deckard grunted in agreement. "What kind of mission do you bear?"

"The prince's steward was slain as well. Alliance lies in chaos between the four families. Others would claim the throne as well."

"Is that an issue?"

"Normally, it would be no trouble," said Ilrona. "Mother Mercy and the mortals themselves believe there is more to these murders than simply a move by one of the noble families. The nature of both deaths is more than suspicious to Mother Mercy. Something is loose in Alliance."

"Something worse than a rogue demon?" said Deckard. "Or do you already have suspects?"

"Alliance has not seen a promortal demon for many generations," said Ilrona. "But their time may soon be upon us again. They are worth an investigation."

"The promortals?" said Deckard. "Do you really think they would return to Alliance?"

"Many things have changed since you flew south," said Ilrona. "A particular stirring has begun in the essences of the world, both below and on high. Matters could mean we must attend the great pinnacles."

Deckard grimaced. "Pinnacles. To the pit with them. Surely you don't intend to approach one of those awful things."

"Not yet," said Ilrona. "They are far too dangerous to investigate on mere suspicion, even for you."

Deckard breathed a sigh. "Who is the steward of Alliance right now?"

"At the moment? The dowager regent, Kizoni Duhikzo, reigns. But given time, she'll need a strong enforcer."

"I'm sensing your implication for my role."

"Hadrian."

Deckard shook his head, long hair streaming in the breeze. He felt the weight of the wine once again. "I don't know if I'm ready to engage in such a position. I've only recently detached from Soucot."

"The southern river land is not like Alliance," said Ilrona. "Alliance is by the heart of the old empire."

"I know. For that reason, perhaps Cyrus would be better to take the reins." He scowled, already guessing what Ilrona intended to say next.

"Don't deny you lack trust for your fellow immortal," said Ilrona. "And don't deny you're curious, what's become of your family in Alliance."

"Just because they are descended from my children," said Deckard, "doesn't mean they're family."

"Are you feeling contradictory today?" Ilrona's bright side beamed a sardonic smile. "Or have you been so angry since the battle of Soucot?"

"I'm a particularly bad mood since then," said Deckard. "I'd say that's obvious."

"Deckard Hadrian," said Ilrona. "You are one of only two immortals left in the lands of mercy. Whether it is your mission in the world or not, it falls to you to sway other humans. Cyrus Bode has his own mission from Mother Mercy, and it occupies his attention completely."

Deckard nearly bit his tongue. "What is he doing that's so important now?"

"You will learn in time," said Ilrona. "For now, Mother Mercy wishes you to go to Alliance and oversee the turn of power."

"Fine," said Deckard. "I was on my way to Fulster already."

"For this mission, you will need to take up residence in the city itself," said Ilrona. "Find who killed the previous prince if you can. More importantly, protect those potential heirs to the throne. The killer threatened them all when he slew Prince Saviron."

"So there's a monster stalking the nobles of Alliance," said Deckard. "I suppose protecting the Kuldettan's should be on my mind. But it's not."

"Your role in existence is to protect humans," said Ilrona. "Didn't you tell me that, once?"

Deckard put a thumb to the corner of his mouth, accidentally wafting the stench of alcohol from his breath to his nose. "I scarcely remember what I said to you last time we spoke."

"Luckily, I have an itemized list of foolish words you've spoken that I can return to you from times past," said Ilrona. "Right now, you may be grieving, but there are still humans who need your help. Fly to Alliance, find the destroyer of Prince Saviron, and bring him to justice. The killer may indeed be a demon. Reportedly he took the form of a shadow."

"A shadow? Now I see why you brought me this message," said Deckard. "I heard rumors that Prince Saviron did not die by mortal hands, but I dismissed them. Alliance is as safe a city as any in the land, and has been for a century."

"The city of poets is no longer as safe as it should be."

"Your air serpents," said Deckard. "I don't trust them enough to continue. Before I ask this question, please have them drop back further."

"They can't hear us as we are now," said Ilrona. "I assure you of that."

"Fine. I'll just ask. What could Mother Mercy want me to do that only I can in a city where but a single demon is likely running amok?"

"Besting rogue demons is your specialty," said Ilrona. "Is it not?"

"I asked my question first," said Deckard. "But it's true my skills are ideal for such a hunt."

"Mother Mercy values the outcome of this situation," said Ilrona. "As do I."

"The succession of one of the most important city-states in the land of mercy, is, of course, a concern for all," said Deckard. "At the moment, I don't think I'm quite suited to the task. Still, if Mother Mercy commands—"

"You understand well what you must do."

Deckard bowed his head to Ilrona and put his fists together. "Consider it done."

"Of course," said Ilrona with a smirk. "I always do when I give you a task." She slowed her pace, falling behind little by little.

Deckard glanced over his shoulder as Ilrona, and the air serpents rejoined each other. The three demons flew toward the sky, disappearing into the clouds, undoubtedly bound for the city above.

The ring around the world held the maladrite city on high, where the house of Mother Mercy stood. Within those walls, no one could tell how many beings dwelt, or what powers hid. The same might be said about many structures on the ring but of Mercy's house most of all.

"To the pit," Deckard muttered. He brought up the wind and hurled himself north. He fished out the wine bottle and took a drink as he flew.

CHAPTER 7

DECKARD

The bottle was empty before Deckard arrived on the balcony overlooking the River Duenn. He touched the floor beside the railing, deep within Alliance's walls. The house was a grand building almost three centuries old, so not much younger than Deckard. Arched windows and smooth walls showed fine stone-craft in every line.

The house belonged to the famous Porfiria Amburen. Deckard had not conversed with her in some time, not having been in Alliance to call upon the cynic poet. Her last letter had reached him years ago and far away, relayed by a messenger from Deckard's retainers at the time.

The letter, the words within it, and even the messenger appeared faded in Deckard's memory. Fine words they had been, when first written.

Deckard crept quietly inside, his robe making no sound. He'd removed enough weight to allow silent movement even for a garment made of metal. He approached the door leading into the master bedroom. Though more than ten years had passed, Deckard suspected he would find the place with but one occupant.

He stepped into Porfiria's chamber, observed the high writing desk along one wall. The desk's slanted surface remained polished, lacking any sign of wear. Beside that pulpit, stood a short and rough-looking stool, which barely came to Deckard's waist. Ink stained a small table in front of the stool.

Deckard guessed which place Porfiria wrote at more often. He marched through the room, his footfalls light as air.

His essence-song doused, even a trained mage like Porfiria wouldn't notice his presence from elsewhere in the house. The bed lay empty before him, sheets neatly arranged as if never used.

"It's you," said a woman behind Deckard. "I heard rumors you were flying north."

He turned, arched an eyebrow, and smiled slightly. "Lady Amburen. You were expecting me?"

"The smell of wine led me here." Porfiria waved a hand before her face, lips curving slightly. "I only suspected you would come when you heard of Prince Saviron's death." She shook her head, making black tresses bounce. "I didn't realize you would be the source of the odor. The rumors say you stopped drinking."

"They were right. For a time," said Deckard. "I don't believe the smell is that bad."

"It's not bad," said Porfiria. "Not at all."

Deckard grinned. "Now, we understand each other." He took a step toward her, taking in her finely-lined features. More than ten years had passed since he'd last seen her, yet she maintained a sultry air. Her full lips parted slightly as he took another step forward.

"Lord Hadrian, what brings you to my abode, of all places in Alliance?"

Deckard paused in his approach. "I understand you saw the murders the night of the attack."

"I did," said Porfiria, face falling.

"Is there anything you can share about the events?"

"Of course, my lord."

"Don't 'my lord' me," said Deckard. "We've been on first-name terms for too long, Porfiria."

"Of course. Forgive me," she said. The years left her more polite than in her youth. "You might also want to call upon my friend and fellow poet, Catricha Maltos."

"I don't know her," said Deckard. "I know you."

"We were together the night of the killing. I went with her because her husband was the steward of the city. He was...unfaithful. Not a good man at all."

"Is that the case?" said Deckard. "Perhaps that provides a hint of the killer's motive."

"Motive?" said Porfiria. "Of the women in the city, Catricha and I were the least likely to have anything kind to say about Lord Halth."

"Adias Halth," said Deckard. "He died the same night as the prince, and they were born on the same day. Did you know that history?"

"I did not," said Porfiria. She blushed slightly. "Though perhaps I ought to have. I was nearly a woman by the time they were born."

"Indeed," said Deckard. "Though I can't say exactly why I recall that little fact. I never met either of them since they were children."

"Now, the family of Halth can only be found in their tomb," said Porfiria. "Prince Saviron is to be buried tomorrow night."

"Tomorrow?" said Deckard.

Now I see why Ilrona wished me to hurry here.

"I think it's right to share," said Porfiria. "The city moved on, but while we mourned for thirty-three days, it is now autumn, and the month is nearing its pinnacle day."

Every month in the eleven-month calendar of Tancuon had thirty-three days. *Four weeks late*, Deckard thought, *and a pinnacle day too slow.*

Deckard nodded. "He's been gone for almost a whole month. It is unusual to leave him above for so long."

"Indeed. Perhaps the city needed more time to mourn the passing of a Dire-Lord, the last who might ever rule us," said Porfiria. "I fear he is not your reason for coming to the city, though his killer might be."

"Did you see what happened the night of his murder?"

"That night," Porfiria said, "I witnessed an essence fly free from the prince and join with his killer's shadow. That's all the killer appeared to be, a moving shadow."

Deckard tapped his chin with one long finger. "Whoever killed the Prince, collected one of his essences?"

"Yes. My Lord, have you flown far to reach us today, the day before the prince's funeral? Where were you this past month?"

"I can travel quickly," said Deckard. "But I didn't intend to visit any city so soon."

"You preferred to stay away." The way Porfiria spoke left no question in her voice.

"I was honest," said Deckard. "I don't lie lightly."

"Some say you do." Porfiria smirked. "Or is that a different kind of lying?"

"Perhaps you can find out," said Deckard. "Or should I say we can."

"I don't find this the best time, Lord Hadrian. Given your inebriation, perhaps your mind isn't on what should hold your focus."

"My dear," said Deckard, smiling. "Porfiria, you wound me."

"I know the stories," said Porfiria, "you never come back. Once you've shared a bed with a woman."

"I only share a bed once?" said Deckard. "That's not so, or there'd be no Kuldettan family."

"The Kuldettans." Porfiria's dark brows furrowed. "Do they know you're here?"

"Not yet," said Deckard. "But until I find permanent lodgings in the city, I noticed the master bedroom sits empty. The lord of the house would stay here, but I take it that position remains vacant."

"True," said Porfiria. "What need have I for a Lord to serve or be served by?"

"No children," said Deckard. "That suits you well."

"What kind of father do you make, Deckard Hadrian?"

"A bad one, I'm afraid," said Deckard.

"Ah. Speaking of, you should visit Filavaye Kuldettan and her family. They will expect to hear from you."

"I will be back, Porfiria. Please, have the servants prepare guest quarters where I may keep a locked door."

"Will you even need a bed, Deckard?"

"Just because I don't require sleep," said Deckard. "Doesn't mean I can't enjoy a fine mattress and blanket."

"You haven't slept in years then," said Porfiria.

"No," said Deckard. "I took rest more recently than that."

"Rest?"

"Yes," said Deckard. "For the moment, that doesn't really bear thinking about, does it?"

"Perhaps it does."

Deckard nodded. "I'll take that to mean you accept me as a guest."

"You may," said Porfiria. "But, my lord, your hands will remain to yourself."

"Unless asked for," said Deckard.

"Unless requested." Porfiria closed her eyes, and Deckard glimpsed a flush in her cheeks. "Deckard, you don't get refused much, do you?"

He said nothing as he turned from Porfiria and paced across the room. He walked onto the balcony and then stepped onto the ledge overlooking the river. Porfiria followed him outside, silently searching for words.

"Deckard, please answer my question," she said.

The river flowed north through Alliance, moving toward the seas of the northeast, far away. Deckard gazed over the dark water, noting it seemed deeper than the last time he'd been in the city. *Deeper and darker*, Deckard thought, *just like the mystery before me to unravel.*

He took to the air before Porfiria could say another word.

* * *

The Council of Alliance met that afternoon, at the same place the nobility assembled for the prince's ceremony to begin the funeral. The ceremony began at sunset that evening and would end at the next sunset. Most of the nobility only attended the beginning and the end, leaving the priests, knights, and ordinary people to manage the rest.

Deckard Hadrian stood befzore the council in the princely palace. He waited at the head of Saviron's coffin, silently watching the assembled priests, nobility, retainers, and servants approach the great hall of the palace. The domed ceiling overhead glimmered with orange sunlight.

The peak of the dome was indeed a solid crystal. It's many facets gleamed with the brilliant light of the late sun. The rain of the past day had fled, leaving clear skies ahead of Deckard's arrival.

Beside him, the beauty of the dowager regent remained hidden behind a veil of mourning and a conservative black gown. Kizoni Duhikzo kept her grief silent except for the occasional sniff to fight concealed tears. Only Deckard stood close enough to notice such a detail.

The households gathered before them, and Deckard spotted a hint of what remained of his bloodline in the city.

Filavaye Kuldettan and her son Vual walked at the head of the procession, looking as serious and grim as anyone in the mortal world. She was slender, though she carried more weight around the middle and bust than the last time he'd seen her. The strains of motherhood, though distinct, truly became Filavaye. She'd had only one child when Deckard had last been in Alliance. Vual had been a small boy at that time.

The present Vual towered over his mother and their retainers, almost as large as Deckard himself. His arms were thickly muscled and hands rough with calluses from swordplay. His eyes still held the predatory glint as when he'd been a six-year-old.

Deckard noted the full scabbard Vual carried at his side. Most nobility preferred to leave their tool of challenge to a sword servant for honor-keeping. Vual must be a ready duelist as well as the mage his family required of him.

At just more than twenty years old, Vual appeared ready for any kind of fight a human with less than a hundred years of training could imagine.

"Lord Hadrian," said the priest nearest the coffin, "Will you lead the ceremony?"

"Once I have addressed the nobility," said Deckard.

Beside him, the dowager regent nodded.

"Very well, Lord Hadrian."

Deckard bowed to her. "Lady Regent."

"Deckard Hadrian." Filavaye drew near the coffin. "Honored ancestor, thank you for arriving in our time of need."

"Too late for some." Deckard recalled Porfiria's words from just earlier that morning. He met Filavaye's eyes. "As the day wanes to night, take care. The killer could strike again, and tonight would be the perfect time to inflict more terror and chaos on the city."

"What do you care of the city?" said Filavaye, wrinkling her nose. "No doubt, you would return more frequently if you gave any damn care about anyone here."

"Charming as ever," said Deckard. He turned to Filavaye's son. "Vual, leave your sword with the palace guards until the end of the ceremony. A weapon has no place at a funeral."

Vual snorted. "Even an honored ancestor can't make me relinquish my blade at the moment. You said yourself the danger is real."

"Then keep it," Deckard said. "It is my hunch a sword will be of little use this evening."

Filavaye shook her head. "No ordinary blade could touch a shadow, but that is one of yours."

"You have one of my relic weapons?" said Deckard. "I see."

"Deckard," said another voice from nearby.

He turned to see the shape of a shadow creeping to the hall, moving over the people's heads. He blinked in the dimming light, and the shadow evaporated like a silent cloud.

"You," he said to the nobility, raising his voice. "You are all doubtless vying for a chance to win the throne." He shook his head. "I say, as protector of Alliance, where I stand now, I will not simply give the throne to the most powerful or best-liked. The regent will decide. I am here to advise her, but she must make the choice."

"Truth," said Kizoni in a soft voice. Then, even softer, "thank you, Lord Hadrian."

"Is that all?" Filavaye said under her breath.

Deckard ignored his descendant's snide tone. "From today on, until a new prince is chosen, I will protect your city. Thus, reach out to me if you see any danger that I may prevent." He turned to the priest near the coffin. "You may begin, parson."

CHAPTER 8

CATRICHA

Catricha stood at the foot of the Hill of Forges, which lay at the center of guild workshops and smithies on the northwestern edge of Alliance. The area just outside the demonstone city walls formed a district wholly dedicated to the arts of metal-craft.

When Catricha had been small, her mother had taken her to the hill to show where she had grown up. Hyla of the Forge had joined House Maltos eagerly. Without her renown in the sacred order of the Forge Maidens, she never would have the opportunity. Catricha's mother was of common birth and darker skin, her heritage coming from the southwest of Tancuon.

Though her bloodline made Hyla's children stand out more than the rest of the city's nobility, it was not as great a trouble as her lack of a powerful bloodline. Catricha inherited father's status, mother's skin and stature, and along with these material aspects, the mind to use them. Not a day passed when she wasn't grateful for her unusual parentage.

She marched up the hill alone, looking for the Market of Words. The cool breeze caressed her face and tugged at the cloth of her silk trousers. She knew from experience the market boomed daily with finely wrought scripts and poetry. Raised text, engraved on metallic plates, made for the most prestigious way to distribute poetry in all Tancuon.

The lines she composed were copied, sculpted, and dressed using magic, metalwork, and paint. The resulting pieces appealed to the commoners and merchants who could afford them as well as noble patrons. Thanks to the Forge Maiden's abilities to duplicate such artifacts with relative ease, such art became widespread throughout the homes of both commoners and nobles. Much of that artistic proliferation could be attributed directly to Catricha's mother.

Hyla had brought the Forge Maidens into the fold of the city by marrying Enrin Maltos. After that, she'd put the resources and renown of the Maltos family into her passion. Gold and silver flowed into their coffers and elevated them to stand as the most powerful house in the city. None could say Lord Maltos had married poorly after that.

Marriage, Catricha thought. Her parents' union still lasted strong after over two decades, while Catricha's wedlock had survived less than a week. Where Adias died, Catricha could go on living. As a widow, she would be forced to absorb scorn from the city's people. She'd experienced plenty before, but the fear and suspicion of being the wife to discover her dying husband left her in a socially uncomfortable position.

My dying husband...

The night of Prince Saviron's death still horrified Catricha to recall. In a city of whispers, she was doubtless suspected by some as the culprit in both cases. Every member of the nobility could say honestly, Catricha despised Adias. His inevitable faithlessness only compounded her troubles. Despite his status and position as the prince's best friend and steward, Adias never learned how to act nobly.

His responsibilities never bothered him. Now he was gone except for his reputation, hanging like a grave shroud over her head. Despite herself, Catricha almost felt sorry for him.

She let her feet carry her up the hill. She reached the turn onto the street of the Market of Words. There, poets, both those in canon and not, dealt their wares on the hillside. Her latest plate would be available for the first time today. She called the poem *Termita.*

Termita, because seemingly by small insects native to the distant southern land of Aushuek, her world had been devoured from the inside.

Adias may not have been a good husband, but the attention he brought her had been useful. Her responsibility to keep them out of trouble had gained her the good graces of some other families. After his passing, she only perceived fear and disgust from most of the other members she knew. She still didn't dare consider approaching any of those she'd been close with, apart from Porfiria.

Catricha made her way into the Market of Words. The street roared with the chatter of commerce. The far off din of metal craft rose steadily from the hill below, adding to the noise. The city never got louder than when the forges were hard at work. The hubbub and trade of metal goods provided enough clatter to disrupt any possible silence.

She marched through the streets to the market stall where she and her friends sold their poetry, both in books and plates.

The apron-clad young forge maiden Catricha employed stood behind the table at the front. To her surprise, Catricha saw not one but two more faces she recognized there. The maiden bowed to Catricha and greeted her as she drew near. Catricha smiled, then nodded back. She turned to the two women standing before the table. She had no greater respect for anyone than for Porfiria Amburen.

Her friend stood near the table, and at Catricha's metaphorical side. Porfiria remained steadfast, even after the death of Adias. The other woman perusing the table was also a fellow poet, but Catricha knew her less intimately.

Nansoela Paroth, the foremost of the recent canon poets and youngest master within the city, looked at the plates for sale. The word *Termita* was printed in the metal at the top, followed by the rest of the poem in smaller words below. "The engravings are beautiful," she said.

Porfiria nodded, glancing at the forge maiden behind the table.

"Thank you for saying so, my lady," said the maiden.

Porfiria raised her eyebrows at Nansoela. "I suspect you may want to move along soon. After all, this is outrage poetry, not the canon form that uses the rules you employ. Your reputation could be blemished by associating with the weavers of such verses, no matter how skillful."

Nansoela laughed. Her high-pitched voice pierced the air clearly, even over the clang and clatter of the metal trade. "A fair idea. I would be afraid of losing face in this situation if my work wasn't already beyond reproach. I find the way the young Lady Maltos scripts far more exciting than any of my peers, I'm afraid."

Porfiria smiled. "I'm glad you see things that way. I doubt many canon poets feel the same."

"Most people, even most poets, are not as educated as you and I," said Nansoela.

Porfiria waved Catricha closer. Catricha felt a smile grow as she looked at her friend. "Apologies for running late."

"Nonsense," said Porfiria, "it is still not yet noon."

Nansoela glanced at the timepiece on the second-story arch of a building across the street. "It may not hurt my reputation to be here, but I suspect I should move my feet. I have a reading to perform on the other side of town at the sun's height."

"Farewell, Nansoela," said Porfiria.

"May your lines stay sure," said Catricha.

"Both of you consider yourselves invited to my party this evening." Nansoela smiled. "Just don't act beyond reason if you take up my invitation. Please accept the small gift I've sent to your house, Lady Maltos." She bowed to Catricha and Porfiria separately, then turned and swept her way out of the market.

"I don't see how she can get to the other side of town in time for the reading," said Catricha. "Though, I'm sure she has her ways."

"We all do," said Porfiria.

"True," said Catricha, thinking of the network of carriages and different drivers she used to hurry through the streets when late for an event.

Porfiria motioned to the plates on the table. "I know you composed much of the poem before it happened, but how do you think the verses read now?" She smiled at the metal plates and leather-bound books on the tables.

"It's poetry I love," said Catricha, "but unfortunately, poetry is not my greatest concern right now. All that said, I think the beauty of the metalwork on *Termita* exceeds my expectations."

Porfiria arched a brow. "I don't see how poetry should be anything but your foremost concern now, my friend. Cat, you don't know who attacked the prince that fatal night. No one does."

"The two of us know more than most," said Catricha. "Still, I see your point. I truly do. Though, I know only a few details better than the other attendees as regards Prince Saviron. Among those details is one I see as most important. I know I am innocent."

"Most people probably don't believe you killed Adias," Porfiria said softly.

"Of course they do," said Catricha.

Despite herself, she wanted to cry again. She thought of Adias, on the floor, eyes bleeding and heart rent asunder. She knew she shouldn't feel sorry for him. Infidelity defined his life. However, she felt as though their fates had been intertwined even more than before in those final moments.

"I suspect," said Porfiria, tapping her chin, "you are not as concerned with Adias, as you are with Prince Saviron."

"Now why would you say that?"

"I would say that because you are never going to be charged for Adias' fall. Everything else said I'm here as a witness. I'm not the only one who knows you're innocent of both ends."

"Thank you," said Catricha. "But, Porfiria, I doubt my reputation will survive another blow should the matter ever go to a judge."

"We can always hope the matter never goes so far. That night won't live in peoples' minds forever."

"I don't want to merely hope."

"Perhaps we should talk somewhere else?"

"No. This place is fine. We do business here. If we can't talk about what happened right here, we can't discuss things anywhere. What we do in darkness is inevitably scrutinized by daylight."

"Very well," said Porfiria. "If we talk in public, do you want us to be overheard?"

"I'm hopeful, perhaps, in that regard."

"Cat," said Porfiria, "Hope may even be too much to ask if things don't go in your favor. If the princedom's succession is taken by an insensitive or hostile household, your chances at poetic fame will disappear. A chance at marrying again will be lost next. Consider the danger watchful eyes and illusive whispers place on your family's claim to the throne of the city."

"I know, Porfiria," said Catricha, "Still, I have to attempt to prove my innocence."

"It is possible everyone outside your family suspects you," said Porfiria, "Except me."

"I know. That is why I need to convince more people of the truth."

"Indeed, that would be of use," said Porfiria. "But how?"

"I won't guess," said Catricha. "I want to find what truly happened that night."

Porfiria folded her bare arms. "That remains the great mystery of the present. Where would we start?

"I would start where I can. I would think to start with finding the girl who took Adias from the party. She led all three of us, Adias, you, and me away just before the prince was attacked."

"I suspect she could provide us more clues, yes."

"Porfiria," said Catricha with a frown. "Are you suggesting you plan to help me?"

"You've caught on." Porfiria gave a small smile. "You're my most promising project as a poet. I don't consider you a student, I consider you a friend."

"I'm glad. I feel the same toward you."

Porfiria glanced over Catricha's shoulder. "Look, here comes another potential customer."

Through the crowd of moneyed poetry patrons, advanced a figure in a dark cloak, making his way toward them, behind a tall young woman with wavy hair. The woman carried a short spear and moved with the elegant grace of a warrior. Porfiria once discouraged Catricha from practicing combat. The woman's stride provided evidence no one ever suggested she train less with her weapon.

The man behind her moved almost as gracefully as the woman. He looked to be slightly older than the spear woman. Though his face was youthful, his bearing spoke of someone used to being obeyed. He was no noble Catricha recognized, but he must be of some importance somewhere, if not in Alliance.

"Greetings," said the woman with the spear. "What are you dealing here?"

"We offer our poetry. These are plates engraved with my latest work," said Catricha.

The woman stepped one side, allowing the man behind her to face Kat and Porfiria fully. He approached the table and poetry. He looked down at one plate. "*Termita?* Does this involve those awful burrowing insects?"

"As a metaphor does," said Catricha. "Even the greatest poets only seek their power in the individual, but in outrage poetry, as I practice, we attempt to subvert expectations."

The man nodded, then flashed a smile. "My name is Heron Olfrus. I am new to the city, and this..." He motioned the woman. "...is my bodyguard and a wizard in my employ, Melissa Dorian."

"Melissa?" said Porfiria. "I've heard that name recently."

"I doubt that. My name is hardly common," said Melissa with a small frown. "Though there are people in the city from my family. We are not nobility."

"Dorian," said Porfiria. Then she snapped her fingers. "You are a member of the merchant family, correct?"

Melissa shrugged. "I was, at one point. I'd heard my parents may still dwell in Alliance."

Heron picked up a plate with *Termita* written upon it. He turned the poem over in his hands, examining the small text and the printed seal at the end of the metal-wrought lines.

"What form of metal is this worked in?" he asked.

"We have versions of the poem engraved in both bronze and gold," said Porfiria.

Heron peered at the plate in his hands. "In gold? That is rare, especially in outrage poetry."

"It is," said Porfiria. "But *Termita* is a rare work. I suspect soon, outrage poetry of such quality will be regarded at least as well as any canon currently taught or circulated."

Catricha's face grew hot. "Porfiria, please don't burden me with such weighty praise."

"I speak my opinion," said Porfiria. "Of course, the gold carries more than its weight in value. Because gold is among the most incorruptible of materials when it comes to a demon's touch. Every created entity, even those seen on high, may appreciate such work. Even the smallest..."

"Even the smallest," said Catricha, starting to smile despite her embarrassment at the compliments. "even the smallest will be glorified."

"Is that from your poem?" said Melissa.

Catricha nodded, face hotter than ever.

Heron hefted the plate of gold he held. "It is," he said. "And it belongs to a great line, I see."

Catricha smiled, cheeks burning. "Thank you for saying so, Lord Olfrus."

"Like your friend, Lady Maltos, I say what I will." Heron smiled brightly.

"I take it, you're new to the city?" said Catricha.

"We are," said Heron. "I have come from the east, my ancestral home lies near the Chos Valley, but my family has moved to Alliance."

"If I may ask, say, for what reason did you come here?" Porfiria said.

"I am here to claim the title of prince," said Heron.

"You seek to become prince?" said Porfiria. "Truly?"

"Truly, I have come to ensure the city's stability. And I will see to it that the laws of succession are upheld as I lead one of the more powerful families now present in the city. I suspect the selection will go well for my side, depending on who acts as judge and steward during the process."

Catricha frowned. "I would not be so sure," she said. "You must know each of the four families are powerful, especially mine."

"Of course," said Heron, "but the challenge makes an attempt all the more worthy."

Catricha nodded. "Do you wish to buy that?" She motioned to the plate.

"I do," said Heron. "Even in a family conflict, I can appreciate skillful lines of poetry."

He opened a coin purse.

Melissa watched both directions to make sure no thief attempted to run by and snatch the purse. Heron paid for the plate. He tucked the poem under one arm bowed to Porfiria and then to Catricha.

"Thank you. I'm pleased to have met you both, my ladies. May I ask your names?"

"Catricha Maltos," she said.

"Porfiria Amburen," said Porfiria.

"Good to meet you both," said Heron. "I'm sure we'll be seeing more of each other in the future."

CHAPTER 9

CATRICHA

The funeral procession wound through Alliance, bearing Prince Saviron to his final resting place in the tombs. Catricha and her family marched dutifully with the other nobles. Her mind lingered on the dress she received from Nansoela. The gown came earlier that day, bundled up in a cloth that hid its shape. *Good,* Catricha thought. Her parents wouldn't wish her to wear that out tonight if they saw it.

The funeral was scheduled at dusk, and the sky was clear. Catricha watched the priests from near the front of the procession, waiting, among other families, as they spoke their words and said their prayers. They beseeched Mother Mercy for her gifts of repose and afterlife. No one, not even the immortals, spoke of Mother Mercy in anything but respectful terms, Catricha thought. Some figures were impossible to mock, even for an outrage poet.

She glanced through the crowd, noting only one noble among them carrying a sword, Vual Kuldettan. She wondered if that was going to continue even if the prince's killer was caught. *No reason to think he wouldn't because he's done it ever since he grew up.*

Nansoela Paroth wore the same style of conservative black gown she had worn to Adias's funeral. Everyone here was fully garbed in ritual vestments beyond where the nobility stood, except for one man.

Deckard Hadrian stood, raven hair blowing in the wind, and watched from within the fortress of his iron robe. His eyes darted back and forth, bright and glimmering. *Could he be searching for the killer?*

Catricha doubted the immortals would consider it possible the attacker of the Prince and Adias would be so close to the funeral as to be ready to attack again. She must be among the suspects. Hadrian must consider the nobility, especially Catricha, among the potential assassins.

Never mind the fact that Catricha had never studied magic, and her power of words was nowhere near cutting enough to rent out a man's heart and steal his eyes. Especially, she thought, when she was not present at the killing. Of course, they might suspect her of keeping secret magic.

Magic she didn't have could become troublesome if it made her more suspicious to other nobles.

Porfiria and her small household stopped one side, she waited with her head bowed. Her servants knelt. They were but servants, as Porfiria had no husband or family or children. Her friend had never taken a hiatus from the poetry scene and thus was unlikely to have ever had a secret child, unlike some others.

They spoke their pieces, and the authorities and priests laid down their prayers until the daylight began to fail. Stars glimmered on the horizon, growing larger and brighter as the sun sank away.

Catricha glanced at the rest of her family. Her younger siblings and their light-skinned cousins looked both bored and solemn until the songs began from the tombs.

The choral music rang out as singers marched forth from the side streets at the end of the ceremony proved enchanting. Catricha rarely targeted that kind of music in her works of satire. The songs prevalent in the temples left her wordless to confront such beauty. Sweet refrains, guided souls toward the ring where Mother Mercy sat, enthroned on high, so the dead might rest at her side for eternity.

The funeral ended gradually as the crowds began to disperse. Noble families mounted their horses or carriages and turned toward their manor houses. Countless people of lower status streamed through the streets around their swifter lords and ladies.

Deckard Hadrian took to the air as if part of the breeze itself, floating like a dark bronze leaf in the autumn wind. He drifted skyward and then finally vanished above the city streets, disappearing behind the smoke billowing from chimneys into the gloom.

Catricha wondered if the immortal would have any more words for the nobility before a successor was chosen. Despite being the progenitor of House Kuldettan, he appeared not to be their friend, judging by how irritated Filavaye seemed with him the day before the funeral.

Perhaps Catricha could learn more at the party that night.

The new Lord Olfrus, freshly announced in Alliance, would be at the ball tonight, Catricha suspected. He might send representatives and not attend himself. After all, the nobility were meeting for their council, and Olfrus himself would have to be there.

More importantly, every poet of note could attend Nansoela's party. The guest list doubtless included many known and unknown line-smiths. Catricha meant to speak with one of the less famous ones tonight. He'd been avoiding her for too long.

* * *

Catricha looked at the dress in her chambers within the family manor. The gown was white. That fact alone would be enough to instill her in the memory of any who saw her tonight. The funeral was too close for anyone to wear such a dress.

Neither of the shadow's victims had possessed much sense of decorum—especially not Adias, who'd frequently flaunted his lack of care for rules and etiquette. Consequences for him were always light.

Catricha might be an outrage poet but could still suffer backlash. Consequences of a widow wearing white could be harsh in the public eye. That only began to describe the ridiculousness of wearing such a bizarre gown tonight.

The hem and shoulders were patterned after human teeth as if her mantle consisted of gleaming incisors. The small jewels hanging from the waist appeared similarly patterned, carved to fit the shape of tiny teeth.

Nonetheless, Catricha began to dress. Nansoela had sent the gown, and that made her opportunity clear. *Who cares about the feelings of dead men?*

She adjusted the skirt before fastening the back of the dress. Despite a high slit on one side, the skirt itself was otherwise long enough to cause her no additional trouble. No more time remained for second-guessing her career path. How could one outrage the city more than appearing in such a bright, morbid gown just days after the funeral for a husband and just hours after the prince's interment?

"Are you done in there?" asked Porfiria, waiting outside the door.

"Almost," said Catricha. "Is the carriage ready?"

"They're waiting downstairs," said Porfiria. "I'm surprised you sent for the House Halth carriage. Why not use the one kept here?"

"The House Halth owe their service only to me for the moment," said Catricha. "I'm the one paying them, and I don't want to subject my parent's servants to this indignity."

"Yet, you're at peace with putting other servants through the same?"

"The consequences for them will be light because they have little say in the matter," said Catricha. "Everyone knows the common folk work for the coin of the realm. I only ask with money in hand."

"Indeed," said Porfiria. "And money opens doors as well as minds."

"Open minds are what we need," said Catricha fastening the ties on the back of her dress. The white gown revealed too much. Despite her will to excite tempers in the crowds of nobles at Nansoela's party, Catricha had her doubts. Her face grew hot as she considered what some might say. She took a deep breath, steeling her resolve.

"I'm ready." She set her jaw, looked in the mirror, and then nodded to her reflection. "As ready as I can be."

She marched to the door as Porfiria opened it.

"That is quite a dress," said Porfiria.

Heat returned to Catricha's face. "Nansoela has an unusual idea of what's appropriate for a canon poet."

"What's appropriate probably never even entered into it," said Porfiria. "Judging by what she sent, she may be using the dress to play a game with you."

"If one evening gown is enough to destroy what remains of my reputation, I don't deserve any fame." Catricha smiled slightly. "I'm already a widow seeking a divorce from her dead husband. I suspect that will never go over with those who love him."

"Adias is gone," said Porfiria. "I hope you can be your own woman, Cat."

"For the first time," said Catricha with a rueful frown. "I'd barely come of age when they betrothed us."

Porfiria nodded. "I don't understand why they moved things so quickly. and yet assumed two people who'd grown up as enemies would be able to preserve the partnership they forged through relations."

"They thought they could do anything," said Catricha. "After all, I am loyal to my family."

"Too loyal if you ask me," said Porfiria softly. "But, never mind that."

"Shall we go?" asked Catricha, glad for Porfiria dropping the subject of family.

"If you wish," said Porfiria. But put on some kind of shawl or over-cloak. We don't want to show you off too early."

"Is it really that revealing?" asked Catricha, her face heating up even further.

"The dress leaves little to the imagination on the top," said Porfiria. "And on the slitted side as well."

"I was afraid of that," said Catricha. "But as Jadik invaded the north with nothing except faith in Mother Mercy on his side, I shall go to this party no matter how little I'm prepared to deal with what others will say."

"You shouldn't compare yourself to the founder of the empire," said Porfiria. "I'd wager you have more courage than he ever required."

"Now who's speaking outrage," said Catricha with a smirk.

"Only one who has much practice at it," said Porfiria. "Now, don't let me steal your essence, either."

"Oh," said Catricha. "I'll have a line or two of payback ready for you soon enough." She barked a laugh, then composed herself again. There would be no room for such harsh expression at Paroth Manor.

The two of them descended the staircase. Catricha used a brooch to fasten her cloak about her shoulders, hiding the tooth dress.

Catricha and Porfiria proceeded to the courtyard. They walked out of the massive doors to where the carriage waited.

Beside the carriage, stood Sion Arver, wearing the sword of House Halth in a scabbard as his side. Catricha gratefully touched the brooch that allowed her cloak to conceal her gown for the moment.

"Sir Arver," said Catricha. "I didn't realize you were going to escort us tonight."

"I thought it proper," said Sion. "After all, you are still my lady."

"Only as long as I remain a member of House Halth," said Catricha. "Those days may be numbered, my loyal friend."

"Friend?" said Sion with a smile. "I suppose that title fits."

"Shall we go?" said Porfiria. Sion bowed his head, then motioned toward the carriage doors. "This way, my ladies."

* * *

The carriage arrived at the party as night closed in like a choker of deep blue steel around the city.

“My ladies.” Sion turned to face them as Catricha reached for the carriage door. "Will you allow me to accompany you into the party as well?"

"I see no reason why not, Sword Servant Arver," said Catricha.

"What happened to *friend*?" asked Porfiria.

"In public, we must keep up appearances," said Catricha. "It would be wrong of me to suggest my departed husband's sword servant is indeed close enough to be called by such a word."

"Sion," said Porfiria. "Sir Arver, please, lead the way."

Sion opened the door. "Which of you cares to take my arm?"

"Why not both of us?" said Catricha.

"Splendid.” Porfiria smiled slightly.

The three of them dismounted and then linked arms with Sion in the middle. They proceeded up the steps to the glowing halls of House Paroth.

Catricha separated from Porfiria and Sion after they made it inside. She went to the cloakroom to remove her outer garment.

She was reaching for her brooch to remove the pin when she heard footsteps behind her.

"So," said a voice, "you're here too?"

She looked over her shoulder, one hand still holding the brooch at her chest. The large shadow behind her left no doubt. Even here, Vual Kuldettan wore his family's relic dueling sword.

"Vual," said Catricha. "Why wear a sword to a party?"

"I take my sword where I choose," said the heir of House Kuldettan. A snarl peeled his lips back. "I have a sense of decorum but also a sense of honor."

"A pity." Catricha sniffed. "You'd be far more attractive if you carried less sense of violence about you at all times. After all, what woman wants to be associated with a warrior? In this city, of all places, where many parents, fathers, and mothers both, died at war far away."

"Save the stage play for your sycophants," said Vual. "It's not your place to shame those who fight for the lands of mercy, no matter how far they travel to meet the foe."

"Your opinion is noted," said Catricha. "In a book destined for the back of a shelf. The city's people probably don't want to open that volume again."

Vual's brows darkened. "Don't insult me—"

"Lady Maltos," said a voice from behind Vual. The heir of Kuldettan twitched in annoyance.

"Sion," said Catricha. "Wait a moment. I'm about change."

"Not with the Lord Kuldettan in there," said Sion, "Surely?"

"Of course not," said Catricha. "I merely meant that once he has removed his cloak. I'll be ready to do the same and join you all outside in the hall." She figured Vual would be further incensed by the sight of her toothy dress.

"You first," said Vual. "After all your insults, I doubt you can do worse tonight."

"Unlike some other nights," said Catricha with a smirk. "I've seen you stare at me in the past."

"Unlike Adias." Vual wrinkled his nose, cheeks reddening. "Now, perhaps we can remove our cloaks together?"

"Your cloak," said Catricha. "Best be the only garment your remove in my presence."

"Likewise," said Vual. He reached for the amulet that held his cloak in place. He removed the pin, then snapped the mechanism into place. His mantle fell back revealed a doublet and jacket beneath as bleak and forbidding as ever. Both garments were mostly black, but with traces of gray and patterns like spiderwebs creeping at the corners, made her sure Vual intended a grim appearance.

She put her hand to the brooch, reluctant to show him with only Sion present. His temper might overwhelm his sense.

"Go," said Vual. "I've removed my cloak." He folded the garment on the bed. "Now, you do the same."

Catricha's mouth felt dry. "Very well." She swallowed and removed the brooch.

The cloak fell around her shoulders and settled onto the rack behind her. Vual stepped forward, his face turning red, and his fists clenching.

"You..." He said. "Is this how you honor a prince at his death?"

"This is how I honor my husband's murder," said Catricha, smiling. She could show him as much disdain as necessary. *No, he can't be any angrier with me than he is already.*

Sion stepped further into the room. "You both disrobing in front of each other hardly seems proper."

"Don't worry about proper, Sir Arver," said Vual. "This prostitute has never known what is proper."

Catricha shrugged, then tossed back one arm in an exaggerated faint. "To be an outrage poet and a woman is to be called a prostitute," she said. "But to be a man and a noble is to be wicked to the core."

"Wicked, am I?" said Vual. "Perhaps you will understand how to taste steel when I introduce you to it."

"You will be introducing me to nothing," said Catricha. "Sir Arver, please escort me into the party."

Sion bowed his head, but his eyes remained open. His face was flushed. Surely, he'd not expected what he saw covering Catricha's frame."

"As you wish, my lady."

"Have you no pride, Sir Arver?" Vual snorted. "You still call this whore your lady?"

"Do not speak any further insults," said Sion calmly. "You're more uncouth than Lady Maltos when it comes to foul language."

"Please," said Catricha. "Forgive my departure," she smiled at Vual, putting in extra curl to her lip. "I have a party with more talented folk to enjoy."

"Go," said Vual. "Before I drive you from this house."

"What would our host to say to that?" asked Catricha in a sweet tone. "Don't presume you know how Lady Paroth will react if you start attacking her guests, especially fellow poets."

"Get out," said Vual.

She smiled at Sion. “Really, Sir Arver? Am I not more foul-mouthed than him at times?”

Sion shook his head, a flush bright on his cheeks and no words on his tongue.

Catricha obliged Vual’s request. She marched into the front hall of the house, where the lanterns glowed on every surface, making the room bright as day. Together, Catricha and Sion met the party with a provocative dress and a knight’s scabbard between them.

CHAPTER 10

DECKARD

"I have questions, Enrin," said Deckard, alighting on the balcony outside Lord Maltos' master bedroom.

Enrin Maltos turned from the mirror in his chamber, dark eyes narrowing. "You're earlier than I expected, Lord Hadrian. Grown tired of your lover, and your ever-numerous descendants quickly have you?"

He had aged in the time since Deckard last saw him. That intense gaze that once made noble girls swoon now resided in a face softened and cracked by the years. Enrin's features nearly made Deckard envious. After three hundred years of the same face, he was weary of his reflection and the attention his looks attracted.

"My other lines of inquiry are more vital than catching up with my descendants." Deckard shook his head. "Besides, I've always found you interesting, if not agreeable."

"You'll have your answers, Hadrian," said the graying Lord Maltos with a shrug. "Just let me finish with this—" He gestured to his collar and the twin black sashes, each tied around a separate silver ring, one on either side of his chin. "My funeral attire is less than convenient without a gentle servant's help."

"I hope you remain as cooperative as you suggest," said Deckard. "I recall you've been less than forthcoming with me in the past."

"Speak plainly, Hadrian. I long ago tired of funerals."

Deckard clenched a fist. "As have I."

Enrin set to work on the ties of one sash, offering no reply to Deckard's words.

"Your eldest daughter has my attention, Enrin," said Deckard.

"You've never met her, have you?" Lord Maltos scowled, a vein bulging in his temple. "Catricha is recently widowed, and you'd dare—of course you dare–to insinuate some kind of relationship between you. I know you, Hadrian, but this is a new low."

"And I know you, Enrin, as I've known your forebears. Besides, this is no romantic matter. I speak of Prince Saviron's murder."

Enrin's lips quivered, his face turning a dark red color. "My family is called the shield of Alliance. That you'd dare accuse my daughter of conspiring to kill Prince Saviron is unthinkable. Even you will not escape such slander, no matter how many rumors Filavaye spreads."

"I dare," said Deckard, "because the prince lies dead, and his steward is slain."

"In the name of Mother Mercy, Hadrian," said Enrin. "You ought to have learned enough wisdom not to accuse my daughter of anything before even meeting her. She was at that final party, but neither she nor her friend, Porfiria, who I'm sure you've already spoken to, can be tied to the killings. Virtually all the noble youth who were of age attended those parties, so why don't you go accuse Vual Kuldettan or someone else with more to gain than lose?"

"Doesn't that make it more mysterious?" asked Deckard. "I'm not accusing anyone yet."

Enrin sighed through his teeth as he struggled with the ring for the sash. "What answer do you want from me?"

"I need to know about the prince's parties," said Deckard. "You've already given me a hint."

"You're better off asking one of the young ones," said Enrin. "I've not attended anything like that since my wedding."

"I recall you frequented similar parties often when you were younger," said Deckard. "Even beyond what a gentleman should."

"I'll ignore your implication," said Enrin. "I was young once. As were you, I imagine, centuries ago."

"Indeed," said Deckard softly.

He pictured the flower country in the southwest where he'd grown up. Fields of bright grass waved on a day no living mortal could still recall.

"Which ones would you recommend I speak with among the next generation?" Deckard asked.

"Catricha never much liked those parties," said Enrin. "That's probably because few among her peers liked her once she began darting them with her lines."

"Then who?" asked Deckard. "Perhaps her friends?"

"Catricha doesn't have many friends among the nobility these days," said Lord Maltos. "I fear she is growing isolated."

"I know little of your city's young generation," said Deckard. "I suspect there will be fewer parties with the prince and his steward lying in their tombs."

"Now, there is a grim thought." Enrin abandoned his fight to untie his sashes. "There is but one party tonight. It is hosted by Nansoela Paroth at her family's house. She is one of the finest canon poets in the city but has grown to be a spinster as she nears thirty. Perhaps she also enjoys her parties too much."

"Nansoela," said Deckard. "I've heard her name in other places from time to time."

"Who among us has not?" asked Enrin. "Catricha sees her as something of a rival, I think. Still, Nansoela has nothing to do with my daughter's form of poetry, besides practicing the foil to her style."

"Perhaps that's where I will find my answers tonight." He turned to the balcony. "See to your sashes, Lord Maltos."

"Get gone, I say." Enrin returned to fiddling with the rings around his collar. "I hope you won't need me again, Hadrian."

Deckard said nothing as he took to the air.

* * *

Deckard soared over the city, then descended toward the House of Paroth. He spotted the lights of the house, gleaming up over the street, outshining almost all the other lights of the city. Deckard circled once, then dropped on the rooftop, he landed softly, his feather sprites keeping his weight from making an impact.

He slipped across the rooftop, the dome and arches easily negotiated by leaps and bounds of his light feet. He came to a stop beside one window and peered into the room before him.

The party was well-attended, despite the grim nature of the day. The prince's funeral evidently had not discouraged many guests from attending. Deckard spotted a cluster of three women moving outside the ballroom. Two of them were all-too-familiar. "Melissa Dorian," he said under his breath. "And Elaine Tanlos."

He frowned. And slipped back from the window so no one would see him.

"What are they doing here?" He asked himself. Then he considered the woman he'd seen beside them. He did not recognize her, but her red hair suggested she belonged to the Graef family or its relatives.

"Have they become bodyguards again so fast?" Deckard muttered. He regretted taking so long wandering. The dead were beyond help. Those before him still lived.

His job tonight was to find the identity of the prince's murderer. Deckard waited silently for the three women to pass, then slipped into the vacant passage outside the ballroom. No one saw Deckard as he crept onto the gallery overlooking the dance floor.

CATRICHA

"Announcing Catricha Dire-Maltos and Sir Sion Arver," called the gentle servant standing by the entryway to the Paroth's grand ballroom.

Faint musical chimes from glowing sprite-lamps, joined the sound of a piano, creating an ethereal tune on the dance floor. Catricha paced forward deliberately, arm-in-arm with Sion. She mustered all her poise and coolness of expression to draw the attention of the other guests.

Most of the dancing nobility dressed in more somber tones. Catricha's snow-white gown stood out, tooth-patterns and all.

She did her best to appear aloof as her fellow nobles and poets stared.

Nothing could have been further from the rush of energy filling her. Vual was here, and there was no way the heir of Kuldettan had come without his brother.

She looked for Ruar Kuldettan. Not many others knew him in these circles yet, but he was a talented poet. His slow growth in status came from pursuing the challenging path of gallant poetry. Of the disciplines of poetry seen as viable in Alliance, gallants were perhaps the most out of place. To be a gallant poet, a writer needed deeds to their name beyond verses and lines. Somehow, Ruar had taken it into his head that such acts would present themselves in time, and such heroics were not necessarily dangerous.

When she first met him, Ruar had been just fifteen years old, and she only seventeen.

The two of them were fast friends. They steadily grew closer over two years before they first kissed.

Unfortunately, Catricha's parents had made their plans with the steward's family before she could tell them of a potential liaison with Ruar. Marrying between Kuldettan and Maltos seemed impossible then, and remained so to the present. Having missed him at the funeral and not seen him since before the night of the final party, Catricha had begun to miss Ruar, even if he was doomed to remain just a friend.

"My lady?" said Sion. "May I..."

"You may relieve yourself," said Catricha. "Is that your question?"

Sion smiled. "How did you know?"

"I'm practiced in determining when someone is carrying waste," said Catricha.

Sion bowed, then left her side, releasing her arm, and marched toward the lavatory. Even his motion when heeding the call of nature looked knightly, Catricha thought. The cut of his trousers and jacket certainly did not do him any disservice, especially not from behind.

Catricha made her way through the party, avoiding the dance floor for the moment, as she looked for Ruar.

Nansoela, head haloed by yellow hair, caught Catricha's eye, from a distance and then grinned. They changed course to meet each other.

The Lady of House Paroth hid her earlier glee as she made her way slowly forward to converge with Catricha's path. Catricha followed the edge of the crowd, still unable to find Ruar.

Nansoela met her. About halfway through the room, near where a cluster of noblemen stood whispering. Catricha stopped walking and gave a small curtsy to Nansoela. "Lady Paroth. A good evening you've set, and you make a fine hostess."

"Polite," said Nansoela. "But I'm sure others here are wondering what you're really thinking, wearing that dress tonight."

"I wear this dress because you supplied it for me," Catricha said, leaning in to speak quietly to Nansoela.

"Of course," said Nansoela. "It suits you, Lady Maltos."

"You knew it would make a stir," said Catricha. "So did I."

The men talking behind them moved off, taking their whispers and stolen glances with them. They shot the occasional bemused expression at Catricha and Nansoela.

Men.

Catricha smiled slightly, pleased that at least those fools-in-fine-clothing noticed her, even if their feelings were ambiguous. She turned to Nansoela and said, "I am pleased to wear it."

"Are you now?" Nansoela shook her head. "I fear it may cause you trouble."

"If it causes me trouble, recall, I made the choice to put it on. You only sent me a dress."

"That is true," said Nansoela. "I've been reading your poetry, you know. *Termita* is a fantastic work, but when shall we expect to see the next part?"

"I didn't intend to write another part," said Catricha. "I've been somewhat slower than I'd like, writing long-form in the month since my husband's death."

"You make for a stunning widow," said Nansoela. "But a widow nonetheless."

"Have you seen Ruar Kuldettan?"

"Ruar?" asked Nansoela. "Do you not have contention with his brother?"

"Trouble occurred in the cloakroom," said Catricha. "Yes. But this is about something else."

"As long as you promise not to cause more trouble at my party." Nansoela's beaming face told Catricha the hostess wasn't entirely sincere. "I'd tell you Ruar is on the balcony with a fellow gallant by the name of Eram."

“Eram?” said Catricha.

"Yes, the famous gallant lover," said Nansoela. "He's had many of the women in this room asking around for him, and yet you ask for the little Kuldettan brother with the odd stride."

"My matter is personal," said Catricha, "and has little to do with his family heritage or how he walks."

"Did you hear?” Nansoela said. "A new family in the city may be in contention for the throne. They're called the House of Olfrus. Does that seem suspicious to you?"

""Suspicious of what, exactly?" Catricha asked. "There may be a battle for the title of prince, and I'll be here to cover every slimy detail with my poetry."

"So you have no ambitions of ascending to the throne yourself?" Nansoela arched an eyebrow. “Interesting.”

"That's quite forward for a canon poet to say," said Catricha. "But I'd have little chance if I even desired the throne."

"But someone will have it," said Nansoela. "If I'm honest, I'd say the seat has its attractions. Sitting a throne might mean less work perhaps than being a poet, even one famous in canon."

"I'd understand that better if you had more work out recently. I'm still waiting for your next piece." Catricha smirked. "Now please excuse both me and the jab. I must go investigate the balcony."

"Your jab is welcome," said Nansoela. "It's not every evening I get the pleasure of trading barbs, even polite ones, with the steward's wife."

"The steward's widow," said Catricha, halfway to a smile at the thought. "But who knows how much longer I'll be associated with his house."

"No, no. And yet," said Nansoela. "Is that the first thing on your mind?"

"It isn't the last," said Catricha. She gave a proper nod to Nansoela, then turned and made her way across the ballroom toward the balcony on the other side, where the windows overlooked the river.

Nansoela giggled behind Catricha. Catricha smiled as she walked away.

Catricha stepped into the chill night air, feeling the cold close about her, still listening to the party behind.

"Where are you, Ruar?" she asked the darkness.

She looked around the balcony. Despite the walkway' breadth and how it wrapped around the entire outside of the Paroth manor, few people braved the dark of night. None were in sight. With the autumn beginning to turn the leaves around the city colors, Catricha understood the desire to spend the evening inside.

She hunted through the shadows, following the small lamp sconces a few paces in either direction and found no one in sight. Footfalls approached from around the curve of the building. She retreated into the light spilling from the ballroom doors. Two pairs of feet drew nearer. Both seemed as loud and manly as any in the dim light and dull sounds.

One of them, though, she recognized as the distinctive nearly-limping gait of Ruar Kuldettan. Ruar had been born painfully, and his legs never quite worked as others' did. Most men walked with the swagger with little consistent motion to the sides, and became more deliberate when moving faster. Ruar, on the other hand, always rolled his feet back and forth. His steps alternated in an irregular gait, rarely repeating in rhythm. Seemingly, even his legs sought originality above all else. The pattern Catricha detected from years of listening for it around the corner in the family gardens.

Houses Maltos and Kuldettan lost little love between them.

Their's, if it could be called love, was the only one.

"You see," said another man's voice. "Women are more attracted to strength than even appearance. I've experienced that fact many times. They say my hands are skilled, but it's a simple matter of evenly applied pressure."

"You say that," said Ruar. "But if I'm not mistaken, you are not only more experienced but naturally talented with the fairer sex."

"Skill comes through experience," said the other man.

That must be Eram, Catricha thought. *Why is Ruar asking him about these things?*

"That much. We can agree on," said Ruar. "Now, who's that?"

"It's me," said Catricha. "Lady Maltos."

"My lady," said Ruar, stopping in a pool of shimmering lamplight. Eram bowed his head, then raised his eyes and grinned. "Wearing white? Now that is daring, even at a party like this, but especially on a night like tonight."

"I can't see you clearly," said Ruar. "Catricha, what kind of pattern is that on the dress?"

"The markings are of teeth." Catricha glanced through the doors at the party. "I made an entrance just a few minutes ago. A shame you missed it."

"A shame. Indeed," said Eram as he and Ruar entered the doorway's bright glow.

Eram was taller than Ruar and overmatched the swarthy tan of the younger Kuldettan brother's looks with lithe muscles and a broad smile. His jaw was firm, strong enough to make Catricha notice.

"Good to see you in the proper light, gentlemen."

"It's been too long," said Ruar. "How many weeks?"

"Time has passed, indeed," said Eram, bowing his head. "I don't believe we've formally met, Lady Catricha Maltos?"

He reached out a hand, moving his fingers toward her wrist.

She shook her head, drawing her hand out of his reach. "Mine is a dire family's name," she said. "But I'll relent this time. After all, I'm no stodgy canon poet. I'm professionally outrageous, not always outraged in public."

"Professionally outrageous," said Eram. "You certainly looked the part."

"If you say so," said Catricha with a smile at Ruar. "Perhaps we can speak alone."

"Not tonight," said Ruar.

She frowned. "Not tonight?"

"I've heard rumors of what you said at the family funerals," said Ruar. "Your husband was my brother's finest friend."

"I'll take that as your condolences." Catricha folded her arms, frustration growing. "For my husband."

"Yet," said Ruar. "I'm afraid that won't be enough."

"Enough for what?" asked Catricha.

"You understand Vual's rage," said Ruar. "But I don't think you understand his purpose."

"And what purpose is that?" said Catricha. "Besides being heir to your house and probably bidding for the throne as well?"

"Excuse me," said Eram. "It seems you two have things to discuss."

"Stay for a moment, please," said Ruar. "I may need your counsel."

"That's enough to sway me for now," said Eram. "You're lucky we're friends, Ruar." He flashed his teeth at Catricha. "Though I see very little to be afraid of from this lady."

"Then you're not looking hard enough," said Catricha with a smile that betrayed her uneasy nerves at Ruar's request for Eram's continued presence. *Could he think I'm guilty of the murders?* "Unfortunately, it is rather chill out here, perhaps we should head back inside?"

"If that's what you desire," said Ruar.

"Then, in we go," said Eram. The three of them marched into the brilliant light of the ballroom.

CHAPTER 11

MELISSA

The servants announced Bethanelle's name as Melissa followed the Graef heiress into the ballroom. She took in the scene of elegantly-dressed noblemen and women. Many danced. Others conversed in the corners, talking in hushed tones over the sound of fast piano music.

The songs of sprites kept in the lanterns around the room only added to Melissa's uneasy stomach. She was not properly attired for this, lacking even the formality of a gentle servant's garb. Not that she preferred to dress as a servant.

Melissa wore the formal clothes given to her by the governor in Soucot. The dark-colored tunic and trousers brought back sad memories of her fallen friends. Though the waist had a buckle to hold a sword belt, she'd had to leave her spear at the Graef's manor. Her clothes matched, both dark gray and black. The pattern was pleasing to Melissa's eyes but ultimately unremarkable compared to noble garb.

"It's been too long since I've been to a party like this," said Elaine. "I still remember what to do."

"Then what do we do?" Melissa whispered to her friend.

Bethanelle made her way into the center of the ballroom, unaccompanied, straight-backed, and confident. Other guests greeted her with curtsy's or bows.

"Stay on the periphery, if you like," said Elaine. "We're not named figures in Alliance, so neither of us has a much responsibility to mingle."

"Then mingle, we won't," said Melissa. "Though there are some fair people here, I'm sure."

"Let me correct you on that," said Elaine. "You've dealt with nobility before, but none in these circles recognizes a former retainer the same way as a current one. That aside, the nobility is no less a nest of vipers than any other people you'll ever meet."

"I'll keep that in mind." Melissa gazed around the room. Possibly one or more people at the ball could be responsible for the former prince's death, and therefore a threat to her new employer, Heron, or his allies. "So, I won't get comfortable."

"That's for the best." Elaine glanced over her shoulder at the exit of the ballroom. "Shall we explore a little?"

They made their way around the periphery of the party, watching dancers and listening to conversation. Melissa didn't bother picking most sounds out of the crowd. Between the music and the voices, she gave up distinguishing what any individual was saying.

Instead, her eyes remained on Bethanelle. The air of Graef talked and danced with a few different gentlemen that night. After half an hour by the clock moving by the lights of contained essences, Melissa finally decided to move away from the wall where she'd stopped to linger with Elaine.

"I have the idea of what's going on here," she said. "I want to get a little closer."

"Careful," said Elaine. "Remember the nest of vipers."

"Thanks." Melissa stepped away from the wall. "I'm a quick learner, remember?"

"I won't forget." Elaine smiled. "Still, be careful."

Melissa walked a few paces from the wall. She moved past a group of men and women talking animatedly around the party's hostess, Nansoela Paroth, a yellow-haired palavian woman with a delicate gown and slender build.

Many of the other nobility resembled the kind of rich, well-fed people Melissa had grown to resent as a caravan guard. But as a mage, she approached their level of status in society. Her standing in Alliance might not be public like in Soucot or the south, but she had served and earned respect both in battle and out.

A figure detached from a cluster of people nearby, turning toward Melissa. He wore a strange evening mask, not like the heavily patterned ones that Melissa remembered seeing among the nobility in the east of mercy's lands. His mask resembled a burst of feathers around the eyes, barely concealing his features. He had long, palavian-yellow hair and was built tall and broad. His eyes glimmered an unusually dark blue.

She frowned as he approached her. "May I assist you?"

"That's not my worry," said the man. "Quite the contrary, I mean to help you."

"My friends and I have a history of bad luck with men in masks," said Melissa. "Your kind always changes tune quickly, is that true?"

"My kind is not the same as those you've met before. I'm higher born than almost anyone here."

"You'll forgive my caution, as your face is still hidden."

"My name is Galocai, and I'm the twin brother of the hostess."

Melissa laughed freely. "Then, why don't you show your face, Lord Paroth?"

"I'm not supposed to be here," he said in a low voice. "I was sent to study magic in Chos Valley to the east with the clan."

"You're funny," said Melissa. "I suppose you can hear my essences, then? I can't hear yours."

"I heard yours from a distance, but I'm dampening mine. You have quite an unusual song about you. May I hear your name?"

"My name is Melissa," she said. "I'm a wizardess. I've studied magic in Lowenrane."

"Is that so?" said the man. Interesting news from Lowenrane of late, I've heard. Not good, but interesting."

"I only left Soucot weeks ago."

"You were there during the fighting, then. Perhaps we could talk somewhere more private, Melissa from Lowenrane?"

"Forgive me, but no." Melissa shrugged. "I'm here with my friend as guards for Bethanelle Graef."

"You're a bodyguard? That's unusual work for a mage with the kind of power you must possess."

"Perhaps it is," said Melissa. "My friend and I needed coin when we arrived in Alliance. Soon, we'll be free of that position."

"You speak quite articulately," said Galocai. "But, I suppose that follows, given your studies."

"Surely, you can tell I'm not noble, though," said Melissa.

"Easily." Galocai smiled, his lips curving under the feathered edge of his mask. "I was never given to the rough-and-tumble, but I can tell that you are."

"It suits me," said Melissa. "So does magic."

"Obviously." His smile broadened. "Take care, Melissa. The upper crust of Alliance is soft like sinking sand."

"Galocai?" Melissa raised her eyebrows. "You can't simply be here to give advice to strangers. What brought you back to Alliance if you were studying in the Valley?"

"I'm not a remarkable mage," said Galocai. "Here, where the mages are fewer, I'm already a noble gentleman, so I thought I'd return and surprise everyone. You may find that odd, but I'm sure you don't find it is annoying or disturbing as the other houses will."

"Why would they be annoyed for you to return?" Melissa leaned closer to better hear his reply.

"I am well-liked among the common people." Galocai glanced back and forth as if making sure no one was listening in. "In fact, I may well be the next prince of the city, or the steward, perhaps. I'm open to possibilities."

"A mage and a ruler," said Melissa. "You'd be formidable in that role if what you say is true."

"I'm a middling mage." Galocai said. "A sacra form, and with it the title of a wizard, is beyond my grasp."

"Sacra forms are difficult. It took me some time to master mine. I wish I'd done it sooner."

"You achieved control of a sacra form. Impressive to wield the body of a demon as your own, isn't it?"

"Yes. Though, I gained my power too late."

The image of the fallen members of the governor's hand swam into mind, presented by Melissa's inner demon, Fanhedon. The demon remained silent, still resting as much as possible even after weeks following the final battle in Soucot.

"Too late for what?" asked Galocai gently.

"Too late to save a friend." Melissa turned away from the masked man, her heart hammering and lungs feeling inadequate to the task demanded of them. "I need space to breathe."

"If you need air, I'll escort you to the balcony."

"If you wish." Melissa gave an ignoble grunt. "But, I'm sure you'll find a better conversation in here than out there, with me."

"Nonsense." Galocai motioned toward the balcony with one hand. "We'll take a moment. Your fellow mage can stay to guard Bethanelle for now."

Melissa nodded, her head feeling light with the memories of war and death.

She and Galocai moved between two sets of nobles in conversation, making their way toward the balcony doors.

Through the doors came a lone woman with dark skin and a white gown. She was flanked by two well-dressed men, one taller and more handsome, the other tanned and slightly bow-legged.

The smaller man shielded his eyes against the lamps, while the larger one, on the woman's other side, beamed like he was proud of himself. The attention of everyone else seemed focused on the woman between them. Melissa recognized the woman from the poetry market.

Catricha wore a dress patterned with human teeth. Gleaming silver shards, carved into smaller versions of the same shapes, dangled from her skirt's side. Her shoulders arched slightly at the edges, looking like incisors.

Melissa wrinkled her nose. "Lady Maltos certainly dresss differently than the rest."

Galocai stopped at Melissa's side. "That is Catricha for you. She's the steward's widow. I fear she is also provocative, one of the more outrageous members of polite society."

"She's drawing attention, certainly." Melissa continued past the three, walking on the periphery of the room. "I can't even begin to guess what would possess someone to wear a dress like that, especially when her husband just died."

"The rumor is well known among my circle. She never exactly preferred her husband."

"Maybe that big man?" Melissa said. "He seems to be involved."

"I don't know the men well, but Catricha is a special case for many. Her parents weren't both nobles, entered mixed heritage is evident for all to see. The rumor is her husband never wanted her as a result."

"Their parents forced them to marry, anyway?" said Melissa. "Is that how you nobility work?"

Galocai nodded. "Sometimes. My sister is not one of those who fall into such traps. I for one, am a proud bachelor, despite my years."

"As a bachelor then," said Melissa. "Do you suspect foul play?"

"Foul play is its own league. Most everyone here knows all too well what happened that night. I heard about it from my sister. Apparently, the prince and his steward were killed in Catricha's absence."

Melissa glanced at the white-clad young noblewoman across the room. "Then, she couldn't have done it without magic."

An odd song resonated within the girl, flaring and chiming even over the physical sounds filling the room. Melissa kept walking.

Galocai followed Melissa onto the balcony, leaving the party and the intrigue behind.

Melissa gazed into the night. She glimpsed lights moving on the street below. The glow grew as it approached, torches borne aloft by countless hands. *A mob. Could there be an uprising afoot?*

"Who are those people?" Melissa pointed to the crowd with the torches, marching below.

"Don't worry," said Galocai. "They're harmless, just insomniacs who choose not to rest at night. They've been out more since the prince's untimely end. Prince Saviron knew he couldn't suppress all the unsightly things in the city, so he let them march."

Melissa frowned, wondering at Galocai's words. "Unsightly? All they're doing is lighting the street at night."

"A fair point, Melissa. They've never attacked or bothered anyone. They simply don't want to sleep or shut their eyes. I, for one, can somewhat relate. At times, I envy Lord Hadrian."

"Hadrian is in the city. I saw him at the funeral." She put her hands on the railing.

"As did most of us." Galocai put his hand on the railing beside Melissa. "Oh, to be a man who not only lives in eternal youth but bears no weight of fatigue in all his years."

"He does rest, sometimes," said Melissa. "His mind suffers from fatigue. Even if his body does not."

"How do you know that?" asked Galocai. "Your studies?"

She shook her head. "He told me so, himself. I met Lord Hadrian in the south. He is strange, but helped in defending Soucot."

"I imagine he's quite powerful. The battle there still troubles you, though. Doesn't it?"

"It does." Melissa closed her eyes, but the torches still glimmered as afterimages. "I only attained my second form in the fray, and if I hadn't, I might not have survived the fight."

"Danger comes with magic. All my tutors have told me that."

"Your tutors taught you well then," said Melissa. "Most of my breakthroughs came through stress, not peace or introspection."

"There's little time for introspection enough these days." He sighed. "I suppose we should be grateful that magic doesn't require such a rarity as peace, either."

Melissa laughed. "That's one way to think about things." She turned to Galocai's finely-cut silhouette. "I'm glad I met you, Lord Paroth."

"Thank you. May I ask if you have a name besides Melissa?"

"My surname is Dorian. I once belonged to a merchant family that operates in the north, with holdings all over Tancuon."

"Are you looking for someone in Alliance?" asked Galocai. "A family member?"

"Good guess. Though, I haven't seen my parents in years."

"What happened?" he asked.

"I didn't want to see them after I was banned from studying magic, and they did nothing," said Melissa. "I only recently overturned the will of the guild in Soucot. The entire order of magic in Lowenrane has opened up because of my defiance of the magisters."

"Amazing." Galocai's eyes widened as he looked at her. "You're an accomplished woman, Melissa."

She looked away from him to face the torches, cheeks burning like the lights below. "I wasn't alone. We worked together, the governor's hand and I, to achieve what we did. I only had the most to gain."

"Sounds like you gained indeed. And you have my condolences for your friend."

Melissa felt tears in her eyes. "Thank you." She wiped her eyes. "I didn't realize I needed to hear that. It seems so obvious now."

"Are you ready to return to the party?" he asked.

"Not yet," said Melissa, glancing at him. "Would you stay here with me a little longer?"

He smiled. "Gladly."

CHAPTER 12

CATRICHA

Ruar stood on Catricha's right and Eram on the left while she surveyed the party. Other guests all around gawked at her dress.

A single glowing moat of essence floated from Ruar and settled on one of Catricha's silver tear-drop earrings.

The essence spoke, with a tiny sliver of Ruar's voice. "I've dreamt of you."

Catricha gazed at the crowd of agitated nobles before her, fighting the urge to cry at his words.

In the crowd, Nansoela clapped, stepping forward. She turned this way and that, motioning to the poets and nobles staring at Catricha, Eram, and Ruar.

"That's enough," she said. "You all know Catricha Maltos. She satirizes our most important moments, even our moments of sorrow."

"I wouldn't say I exist for that," said Catricha. "But that's my position as a poet."

"So this is visual poetry?" asked one canon poet toward the front of the crowd.

"How uncouth," said a noblewoman nearby.

"Be still," said Nansoela. "You are all welcome to leave if you find my taste in guests deplorable."

"Nansoela, Lady Paroth," said a man stepping forth the crowd, his voice soft but deadly serious. "I would ask you not to defy good sense in this matter. It's natural for us to be infuriated by such displays as this."

"Of course, Lord Benton," said Nansoela. "That changes nothing about Catricha's right, perhaps duty, to perform her role in our society."

"You're a Canon poet," said Benton, "how can you defend her?"

"We've all done things that cross lines, but at the least, all she is doing is wearing hers." Nansoela smiled.

Lord Benton shook his head. "You've departed your senses, Lady Paroth, with all due respect."

"I agree," said a noblewoman.

"Then you're welcome," said Nansoela with a smirk. "To leave."

Benton waved at Nansoela, while he glowered at Catricha. "It's not your party I protest, Lady Paroth, but this wench."

"I'm nobility." Catricha raised the hem of her skirt in a slight curtsy, "and I know when I can perform my role as an outrage poet, and when I must be polite like the rest of you."

"You demean us all." Lord Benton scowled.

Vual's sheathed sword's hilt trembled under his fingertips as he stepped forward. He stared at Catricha, then turned to his brother.

"Don't approach further, Vual. What would our mother say?" Ruar asked.

Vual grunted. "Ruar, stand away from that woman."

"Brother," said Ruar, "you know not what you're saying."

"I know you play at being a poet," said Vual. "But these matters are of life, death, and honor."

"Then let your honor go," said Catricha in a soft voice that only Ruar could hear."

"I understand," said Ruar under his breath.

"What did you say?" asked Vual. "Are you trying to defy me? I'm the elder, I am the air."

"You're not Lord Kuldettan yet," said Ruar.

"I am indeed still your superior." Vual clenched his jaw tight. "Obey your superior, my brother."

"That's enough," said Catricha.

"Indeed, figure this out in your own spaces," said Nansoela. "We have a party to attend to."

"Go on with your party," said Vual. "My brother and I will not attend a murderer's conspiracy ball." He placed shot a glare at Nansoela. "And you of all people should know, you were friends with Adias as well. There is no way that Catricha Maltos is not guilty in some way for his passing."

"That's quite enough unfounded accusations," said Nansoela.

Catricha's face grew hot.

She should be able to defend herself without relying on others. Here she stood, a mere centerpiece with no speaking lines. She hated what Nansoela had gotten her into at that moment. Her dress dragged down the entire evening. If only she could rip it off and throw it on the floor. That would only make things worse.

"Go then," said Nansoela. "This is the last time I'll say it."

"We are gone." Vual shot a scowl at Nansoela. "Ruar, with me."

Ruar glanced at Catricha but said nothing. He left her side to join his brother. The two sons of House Kuldettan left the party and Catricha in silence. Other guests exchanged open-mouthed expressions of shock.

Catricha hesitated only a moment before going after them as fast as her dignity allowed. Anxious tears overwhelmed her. She ignored the rest of the room, frustration consuming her attention. Sion and Porifiria would be fine. She had to talk to Ruar.

* * *

"Wait!" Catricha called as she rushed from the Paroth estate into the street.

But she didn't see Vual and Ruar. The night closed in, filling everything outside the small pools of lamplight by the gates. She retreated a few steps from the gloom. As she neared the doors, a hand snaked out of the shadows and seized her wrist. Long fingers tightened in an intense grip.

Catricha glared at Vual. "You were waiting to trap me?"

"A trick for a trickster," said Vual. "It seemed fitting."

"Where's Ruar?"

"My brother is on his way back to the Kuldettan household with our carriage."

Catricha's breath caught. "Wait! You can't mean—?"

"I can mean whatever I want," said Vual. "Now. I'm in control."

"How dare you threaten me?" said Catricha. "Our families may be rivals, but we have no other quarrel."

"Except for my friends' deaths." Vual grunted and tightened his grip. His other hand moved along her shoulder as he faced into the night. "Don't turn your head."

"What do you mean to do?"

"We're going to talk," said Vual. "For now."

"If you insist," said Catricha. "But promise me you'll do nothing unseemly."

"I'll promise you nothing, not until I hear your answers."

Catricha bit her lip. His hand moved from her shoulder and down her neck, fingers kneading along her spine. She flinched, and he tightened his grip.

"Now," said Vual. "Did you have any part in killing Adias or Saviron?"

"No. You're a lousy interrogator."

"What would you say if I don't believe you?"

"You can choose not to believe me," said Catricha. "But I can't be clearer than I've already been."

"Of course you'd say that."

"Because it's the truth," said Catricha.

"You hated Adias." Vual loosened his fingers, but not by much. "I don't know how you felt about Saviron, but they were both friends to me and my house."

"We all mourn their deaths," said Catricha. "But some mourn more than others."

"You don't," said Vual. "You've been waiting to put that dagger in the tombs to separate you from Adias forever."

Catricha scowled into the night, obeying his command, not turning her head, despite the pain as he tightened his grip around her shoulders and once more.

"You have nothing else to say?" asked Vual.

"Nothing that won't make you hate me more," said Catricha. "But I've answered everything you've asked."

"Everything I asked? I need to know who killed my friends before a new prince is chosen. Whoever is picked, whether it's myself or someone else, could be in danger as long as that killer is loose. I know you did it. Did something."

"I had no reason or desire to kill Saviron." Catricha shivered in the cold of night. "I would never go so far to retaliate against Adias, either."

"Naturally, you'd say that," said Vual.

"I say it—" Vual pinched her chin, and Catricha bit her tongue. She gave a hiss of pain and gritted her teeth. "I speak the truth."

"Your timing couldn't be worse," said a man's voice from above them.

"Who's there?" Vual craned his head, looking into the dark. Thanks to the lantern light behind them, Catricha couldn't see anything from the second floor up.

"Release your peer," said the voice as a figure settled to the ground before Catricha and Vual. "In the name of Mother Mercy."

"Not in your own name, then?" Vual glared at the flowing shape of the shadow.

"And in my name." Deckard Hadrian stepped out of the shadows. His iron robe rustled about him, shifting soundlessly in the light breeze.

The immortal took a step forward, and Vual released Catricha's throat. She stepped toward the man in the iron robe. Deckard backed away, not allowing her to close the distance. Evidently, the immortal wasn't as lascivious as Catricha had heard. Strangely, Vual proved far more eager to touch.

"Deckard Hadrian." Catricha touched her neck with her palm. "Lord of Feathers, this man attacked me."

"I saw," said Deckard. "You'd best be more careful after tonight, Catricha Maltos."

"You know who I am?" said Catricha.

"I spoke with your father," said Deckard. "I'll escort you home. I have some questions of my own."

Vual lunged forward, catching up with Catricha. His fingers wrapped around her wrist. "No, immortal ancestor, you're no part of justice in this city. The Order of Dreams is yours, but they're not the law. Only the prince is the law."

"And the prince's guards?" Deckard shook his head. "They attend his palace and his tomb. They keep their barracks, but they don't protect the streets tonight. The Cult of the Sleepless is out, and I fear they're not mourners for the prince, but celebrating his end."

"Sleepless?" said Vual. "What do you know of them?"

"Little so far." Deckard's pale features furrowed in a grimace. "Now, go your own way. Find a path home, my young descendant."

"Do you even know how many generations it has been?" asked Vual.

"I haven't counted," said Deckard. "It could have been just a blink of an eye."

Vual fumed, turned, and then marched down the street past the gates. His shape faded into the darkness.

"Catricha," said Deckard.

"What?" She turned to face him.

I'm alone with the immortal, Catricha thought. *What an opportunity.*

Deckard Hadrian's face was as chiseled and handsome as the rumors said, but he kept his hands within his robe. His shape beneath the iron garment was almost invisible in the dark.

"Thank you," she said, "my lord."

"No formalities are necessary," said Deckard. "As I said, I have questions for you. You witnessed the scene and were close to both murders."

"Murder." Catricha sighed. "Funny word. When folk kill each other in war, that is glory. The same act in the night, at a party, becomes wicked."

"Incisive," said Deckard. "But I take it what you told him was the case? You didn't kill either of them."

"No," said Catricha. "I mean, what I said was true."

Deckard raised an eyebrow, then took a step toward her. "I see. Though, there is something else unusual about you, Lady Maltos."

"What is it?" asked Catricha, heat rushing to her face. "The dress wasn't my idea."

"That's not it. The dress conceals your form, but within your heart, there's something strange, a song I've not heard before."

"Is this some attempt at seduction?" asked Catricha. "Lord Hadrian?"

Deckard smiled, shaking his head. He looked close to laughter but made no sound of mirth. "I have sensed the same kind of essence song an another only recently. Yours is a different kind, but similar in strength."

"In strength?" Catricha folded her arms, the cold creeping through. "Surely you don't mean my heart is stronger than it feels? Spare me those platitudes, immortal. The cold still hurts me."

"Oh, my words are literal," said Deckard. "I believe you have magical talent, Catricha. It remains untrained, but it is there and powerful."

"You can hear it?" said Catricha. "I have some sensitivity myself, but I've never been able to hear my inner song before."

"It is difficult to hear your own heart song," said Deckard. "But tonight, the more danger you were in, the louder your heart sang."

"Please." Catricha shuddered, shaken, and cold. "Escort me home, and I will tell you everything I know about what happened that night."

"Excellent." Deckard turned his back on her. "Follow me."

Catricha traced after the immortal into the darkness, following him on the path to the Maltos' manor.

CHAPTER 13

MELISSA

The party continued late into the evening hours. Melissa and Elaine talked with Galocai and the handful of nobles he'd introduced to them. None of the other men knew his identity, it seemed, but he knew each of them.

Melissa never once saw his full face without the mask, but what was there treated her. He was a mage, though not as skilled or talented as she'd been initially. Despite his noble rank placing him above her socially, he'd noticed her.

"...And so." Galocai folded his hands as he rounded out his story. "My master sent me back to Alliance. He didn't think I'd be able to focus unless I returned here first."

"Why haven't you told your sister?" asked Elaine. "It seems she should know."

"I wish to remain private for now. Even from her," said Galocai. "This is the closest I've been since I arrived in the city a week ago."

"Where are you staying?" asked Melissa.

"The Inn of the River's Serpent. Have you heard of it?"

Melissa shook her head. "It must be more expensive than the kind where mercenaries stay when they arrive from the road."

"That's one way to put it." Galocai's lips twitched in a smirk. "You see, the River's Serpent is the oldest tavern in Alliance. Some say it even predates the conquest by Jadik."

"How could the building be so old?" Elaine frowned.

Galocai grinned, still looking at Melissa. "It's a handsome structure, but I think it still stands today because the foundation was laid in demon stone."

Elaine rolled her eyes in Galocai's peripheral vision.

"Demon stone," said Melissa. "That material can be useful for many things. It's almost unbreakable."

"Almost?" Galocai's curious smile curled his lips further. "I wonder, Melissa if perhaps you know more than you're letting on about such architecture?"

"I have read a few books. Some of the more recent texts were quite illuminating. Even demon stone not made by the demons themselves hardens into the one material even their most deadly weapons cannot cut."

"More recent books, huh?" Galocai leaned toward Melissa. "Surely, they would touch on that in the older texts as well."

"Of course." Melissa nodded and smiled. "In the oldest volumes, the authors frequently mention how some ancient immortals could alter the shape of demon stone. Those are all long gone. The last one able to shape demon stone is thought to have been the conqueror of Alliance called Zidon."

"Zidon could alter demon stone?" Galocai's eyes widened slightly behind his mask. "So, he was more than an immortal monk."

"It seems so." Melissa shrugged. "Though, I haven't read any detailed accounts of how he controlled the stone."

"Fascinating." Galocai's hangers-on began to drift away, making their way through the party to join other groups.

Bethanelle walked over to the three of them. "Melissa, Elaine, who is this?"

"My name is not important," said Galocai. "I take it you've been employing these two fine mages as guards?"

"I borrowed them for the evening. You could say their true employer is Lord Olfrus, who reached the city only recently."

"Lord Olfrus? The name sounds familiar, but I can't place from where."

"Of course," said Bethanelle. "I only recently heard his name myself. He only lately became a lord and vacated his position in the Chos Valley to travel here."

"So, he might be here for the throne?" said Galocai.

Melissa folded her arms and frowned. She didn't like thinking Galocai could be an enemy of Heron. If they clashed, she could be in an awkward position.

"Many seek the throne," said Bethanelle. "I've heard our hostess might even be angling for it. I doubt that, because of her position as the most famous canon poet in the city."

"What about yourself?" asked Galocai. "You are of House Graef, correct?"

"I am. Bethanelle Fel-Graef at your service."

"I take it you are eager to leave now that the party is diminishing," said Galocai. "I understand, though, I'm going to miss my company in the form of your sterling bodyguards."

"The party is less dangerous than I anticipated, at least now that Lady Maltos and the Kuldettans have left," said Bethanelle. "But leaving the city by night can often be risky, especially given the torch-bearers outside."

Galocai nodded. "You believe the sleepless might cause trouble?"

"I've seen the signs." Bethanelle inclined her head toward Melissa and Elaine. "When I hunt in the ravine, I pay attention to the danger there, and when I dance in the city, I pay attention to the dangers here."

"What dangers?" said Galocai. "I mean, besides the potential of murderers lurking in the shadows?"

"The sleepless formed a large crowd, even in the dead of night. Are they still outside?" Melissa said.

"Yes," said Bethanelle. "I just came from the balcony."

"Interesting," said Galocai. "Alas, I lack a bodyguard to assist my retreat to the tavern."

"Are you suggesting I share?" Bethanelle laughed and flipped the length of her hair across her shoulders. "Lord No-Name, I can't part with either of them tonight. As I said, my way home could be dangerous."

"But you also said that you don't actually pay either of them," said Galocai with a smile. "You know, remuneration can go a long way if applied correctly."

"Speak for yourself," said Elaine. "Lady Graef, we will surely return with you. It's our honor."

Melissa nodded. Thought her instincts urged her to say otherwise, propriety under these circumstances would force her further out of place if she refused Bethanelle's suggestion.

"You seem reluctant, Melissa," said Bethanelle. "Is something on your mind?"

"When isn't there?" Melissa murmured. "Forgive me. I did not need to be snide, but I think one escort will be plenty to return you safely home tonight if you take your carriage."

"The crowd is mostly on the riverside of the house, too." Bethanelle shrugged and then turned to Galocai. "Very well, then."

"What should I tell Heron?" asked Elaine.

"Tell him I'll be returning in the morning." A rush of excitement ran through Melissa. She tried her best to steady her tone and not let it float into the air, as if thrown by Deckard Hadrian. "I'll ensure this man makes it to his place safely, and of course, he will be giving me the proper repayment."

"It's settled then," said Galocai. "Splendid."

Bethanelle laughed. "You bounce between nobles faster than anyone I've ever met, Melissa Dorian."

"I'm curious to see the city," said Melissa. "After all, I'm searching, and your household is outside the walls."

"I understand," said Bethanelle. "We won't wait up for you." She turned to Elaine. "My lady mage, please, escort me to the carriage. It is late enough."

"Elaine," said Melissa. "Be careful on the road."

"You too." Elaine smiled slightly at Melissa. "Stay safe in every way." Elaine followed Bethanelle off toward the carriage house.

Melissa turned to Galocai. "Is there anyone else you plan to talk to tonight?"

"No one not within a yard of me." Galocai grinned. "Thank you for accepting my offer."

"I'll walk you to the tavern. The River's Serpent, was it?"

"Indeed it was," said Galocai. "Shall we go?"

"If you wish." Melissa couldn't help the smile creeping across her face. She escorted Galocai out of the ballroom.

* * *

The two of them made their way along a dark thoroughfare toward the river. Alliance's merchant fleets would ply the dark waters again before day returned.

Melissa and Galocai stuck close together, though she sensed only uncertain attraction from his body language. His words told a different story. Every time they turned a corner, Melissa asked if they were getting close. Galocai reminded her with a laugh that the River's Serpent was a fair distance from House Paroth, and there was no faster way to go. Still, Melissa grew impatient to know what lay behind the mask.

He froze ahead of her, holding up a hand to stop Melissa. "We're nearly there," he said. "But..."

Melissa gazed at the waters, noticing a flicker of flames reflected from behind her. She looked up from the river, nervous, expecting to see fire on the rooftops. Instead, the light came from torches in the hands of a crowd in the street. Could they be from the same sleepless group they'd seen earlier?

"More sleepless," said Galocai. "I wouldn't know them, but they've been patrolling the streets every night since I returned to Alliance."

"They must be people who live in the city," said Melissa. "They must be out for a reason."

"Do you want to get a closer look?" asked Galocai. "Our magic should keep us safe if they turn out to be threatening."

"If you do." Melissa stifled a yawn. "I would think you'd be more tired by now."

"The life of nobility pushes one to odd hours. I have less need of daylight than those with less—"

"Less money?"

"Yes. That is one way to put it. I was going to say, resources, but money is close."

"Even though my parents had money. Nobles have other kinds of power."

"The privileges of my station are greater even than wealth. Shall we get closer?"

"I'll lead." Melissa wished she had her spear if only to help direct her essences. "Stay close. I don't want to get separated when my job is to protect you."

"Sure." He smiled with bright teeth, then shook his head.

They crept through the night toward the higher street overlooking the river. The slope leveled out at an intersection. Two crowds met and formed a ring between the buildings. The faces in the crowd looked haggard by exhaustion. Bloodshot eyes stared into the night. Some appeared nearly dead on their feet.

"What are they doing?" Melissa whispered to Galocai.

"I can't say. Do you hear any odd essences? I don't sense any magic from them."

"Neither do I." Melissa glance along the circle's edge. "Maybe we can get a better idea if we get closer?"

"Let's not risk it," said Galocai. "The sleepless have rituals they observe, and this is one of them."

"Rituals? Why?"

"The sleepless are among the oddest members of our society. In Alliance, they frequently fast from sleep for as many nights as they can. I had no idea there were so many."

"Perhaps there are more since the prince's terrible fate."

"That could be," said Galocai. "We should head the other way, toward the river."

Melissa and Galocai carefully crept through the darkness toward the riverside. They covered the rest of the way to the inn and stopped before the tall, stone structure.

"This is it," said Galocai. "Thank you, Melissa Dorian, for escorting me here."

"Is that all? If so, have a good evening, and I hope you sleep well."

"It's...not quite everything." Galocai smiled in the dim lamps from the inn's doors. "I was hoping perhaps would you step inside with me?"

A thrill of fear and anticipation ran down Melissa's spine. "I'd like that, but that mask of yours will have to go."

"Very well." Galocai brought his hands together, and a slight essence song emanated from him. The feather mask was not constructed. The shape around his eyes broke apart and fell into a cluster of actual feathers that rested in his open palm.

"You kept them there with magic?"

"I like to practice the small details as well as the large forms."

"Attention to detail? That's good to see." Melissa smiled.

"I'm sure you feel the same about other things as well." Galocai stepped toward her and reached for her hand. "The halls are already dark. Let me guide you."

Melissa took his hand. Firm fingers juxtaposed their pressure with the light touch of his palm. She let him lead her inside, then up the steps. With every pace, her breath quickened. They approached his rooms in the suite above the third story. *Is this how other lovers feel before they reach their destinations?*

She frowned, but enough out of her mind. She had only just met this man, and they were nowhere near lovers, not yet. But could they be?

Outside the door, he moved his hand up her wrist, touching her skin and spreading warmth. She waited for him to find the key with the other hand. Melissa pressed her palm against his wrist, stopping the progress of his fingers.

"Lord Paroth, you had another motive, after all."

"You might say so." He inhaled a deep breath. “I don't know why, but something about you has been serious since I first laid eyes upon you, Lady Dorian."

"I'm no lady," said Melissa. "Just a merchant's daughter and a mage."

"A more powerful mage than me. I'm sure."

"What makes you so certain?" asked Melissa." "Is it the sacra form?"

"Yes," said Galocai, “many who study for years can't master one, but you did in months."

"There's something else I should tell you."

"What is it, my dear?"

"I have unique essences. Two of them live in my heart." Melissa touched her chest with her hand. "I possess an iron bane and a shatter sprite, two forms of unknown magic. Both are extremely powerful, and no doubt, gave me the edge in developing my skills."

"So you had your own brand of a lucky birth. Praise Mother Mercy." He found the key and fished it from his pocket.

"You might say so," said Melissa. "Otherwise, you could say misfortune has always followed me."

"You don't consider yourself lucky?" Galocai asked, turning the key in the lock.

"How could I? I was even banned from magic until very recently."

"But that state has ended, and your renown is greater for it."

"My renown doesn't concern me," said Melissa. "Does it concern you?"

"Not at all, Melissa." Galocai put his other hand on her shoulder.

He guided her through the doorway.

They sat opposite each other in small chairs, a lantern glowing on the dark table between them. Melissa frowned, as the shadows danced on Galocai's face.

"I have wine?" said Galocai. "Would you like some?"

"I'm fine without," said Melissa. "I tend to indulge too much when I drink alcohol."

"You're safe. The night is long, but it is nearly over." Galocai yawned.

"Don't rest just yet, Lord Paroth. Melissa climbed from the chair where she'd sat. She walked around the table and eased into the seat beside him, sliding down close to him. The two of them fit well together.

"I say," said Galocai. Then he leaned toward her and gently kissed her lips. They leaned into each other, and their warmth mingled together. Sprite songs danced in Melissa's ears as she pressed against him, hoping the moment would last.

He ran his finger along her cheek, then cupped her ear. She wrapped her arms around his shoulders, feeling his muscles go taut.

The window, overlooking the dark river, shattered with a crash behind her. Melissa's eyes flew open.

CHAPTER 14

MELISSA

Melissa leapt off her seat, rushing from Galocai's side. The shadow before them tracked her with coal-black eyes. Galocai shouted a warning and circled in the opposite direction. She skidded to a stop and glared at the shadowy form crouching on the broken table at the center of the room.

She wished she'd brought her spear, despite how impossible it would have been at the party. The excitement she felt at Galocai's touch combine with her fear and adrenaline into tremors that made focus difficult. She redirected her sprites, keeping the iron bane close to her heart. She jumped forward as the beast bounded on all fours toward Galocai.

The creature possessed catlike moves, jumping and darting before Melissa, in a flicker, as if not fully solid, like smoke or airborne ink. Whatever this thing was composed of, it was no ordinary material. Loud bane songs roared from within the beast. Melissa sensed more than the usual amount of battle-fear in herself. She flexed her hands, drawing on her iron bane for stamina.

"Get out of here." Galocai waved at Melissa, staring, wide-eyed, at the shadow beast. "It's after me."

"How do you know?" asked Melissa.

"No one else knows who you are," said Galocai, his face grim in the shadows.

Melissa grunted. "You were supposed to be disguised."

"I tried." Galocai narrowed his eyes at the shadow beast. "But I have enemies in Alliance, not to mention the Chos Valley."

Melissa rushed toward the shifting form of the beast. The amorphous shape distorted, bulging and shifting, then solidified into a leonine form. A mane of pure darkness radiated from behind feline jaws.

The fangs slashed the air, nipping at Melissa's fist, before she could even strike. She darted backward, skating on the floorboards, cracking a path behind her. She stumbled, then fell on her back.

Galocai was weaving some kind of sprite-spell it with his hands, emitting a sonorous hum, opposing the chaotic sounds that emanated from the beast.

"Is it a demon?" Galocai's voice shook.

"We'll find out." Melissa got to her feet. "Once we kill it."

"If it's the demon, we won't win," said Galocai. "They are immortal."

"Immortal," said Melissa. "It's just a word."

Galocai finished his spell and a wind gust punched the shadow lion off the wreckage of the table.

The lion struck against the chair where they'd been sitting. The padded furniture toppled over backward. Melissa leapt to her feet, reaching inside herself for the source of her sacra form, her inner demon.

"Fanhedon," said Melissa. "I need your help."

"I could tell," said the demon from the back of her mind.

Despite Melissa mastering the demon's scroll over the summer, she'd not called upon Fanhedon for anything after leaving Soucot.

In the next moment, she sensed a pure heaviness from the din of music coming from the lion of shadows. Then, Melissa launched herself at the beast. Her shape shifted into the gleaming form of Fanhedon.

The lion roared and slashed at her with razor-claws. Fanhedon's armor, covered Melissa in an instant, head-to-toe. Her fingers became talons of iron and silver.

She cut at the lion-creature and threw it back across the room. Ribbons of shadow trailed from where she sliced through the beast.

"Melissa," said Galocai, "careful. That thing isn't what it seems."

Melissa nodded.

"What am I seeing?" Fanhedon asked.

“This beast is just a messenger. Look!” Galocai pointed.

Melissa held her fighting stance between the lion in the doorway and Galocai. She stared at where she’d cut the lion.

Blood. Actual human blood ran red from the wounds she’d dealt the beast. The hint of a skinny rib cage was visible beneath layers of shadow magic.

"The beast is human," said Melissa. "Is that it?"

"Don't destroy it completely," said Galocai. "We must know."

"Agreed.”

Melissa hurled herself at the shadow beast. She slammed her shoulder into its side, bashing the lion against the door-frame. Then, she balled her talons into fists and smashed them down on the monster’s back.

The shadow lion hit the floor. It’s back claws raked across her legs, but she feared nothing from the strike thanks to Fanhedon’s armor. Despite her demonic protection, the force of the impact almost took her off her feet.

"You...” The lion’s voice sounded vaguely human.

Melissa couldn’t tell if the raspy voice belonged to a man or a woman.

"Who are you?" asked Melissa.

"I’m as your friend said...a messenger."

"What message did you bring?" asked Melissa.

"Your days are numbered," said the beast. "Galocai."

"Is that all?" Galocai snorted, composure returning. "All humans have limited time."

"Your lifeline runs short," said the beast. "Shorter even than you can believe."

Melissa delivered another blow to the lion's head. The shadowy form began to disintegrate around the body of a young boy, he lay on the floor, unconscious. His wounds matched those of the lion beast that once surrounded him.

"I didn't realize they were going to come after me so quickly. The family of Kuldettan is my bet."

"Kuldettan?" said Melissa. "They’re another noble house in the city, right?"

Galocai scowled. "Yes. They have their own magic. Kuldettan may be the greatest challenge to anyone else becoming prince. I’ll revise my ambitions.

Still, I doubt this is one of their people. More likely he's one of Filavaye's dreaming pawns. Whoever controlled him simply needed a vessel for their shadow summoning."

"Dreaming is a dangerous ability." Melissa folded her arms. "I've encountered it before."

The song of banes dissipated from the shadow lion's fragments and the essences drifted into the air. The dissonant song carried out the window and over the river, the waves lapping dark against the shore.

Melissa listened carefully, still on guard. Galocai walked over to her.

"Are you alright?" he asked.

"Are you?" She raised an eyebrow. "You were right. It was after you."

"Alas, being correct has limited benefits in this case," said Galocai. "Please, let us go inform the innkeeper." Galocai motioned to the broken table and window. "He needs to hear about this."

Melissa nodded, and the two of them left the room together.

* * *

After they notified the innkeeper and gathered guards to the tavern, Melissa and Galocai took seats in the bar below the rooms. The two of them were both drifting toward exhaustion in the long hours of night.

Melissa made a glance in Galocai's direction. He appeared as confident and coolheaded as back at the party. Even so, the attempt on his life clearly put him ill at ease, and with good reason. Even if the lion was just a messenger, the fact that his rivals and enemies knew he was in the city, made for an issue.

"Where will you stay?" asked Melissa.

"I don't know," said Galocai. "I don't feel that my sister's house will be welcoming, given my attempt at secrecy. I'm certain, in fact, that she is merely waiting to reveal the truth and present if the Kuldettans indeed sent this beast after me."

"Perhaps," said Melissa. "You can return with me to House Graef tonight?"

"You have quarters waiting there," said Galocai. "Is that so?"

"Yes," said Melissa. "Though they are ruder than these, by far."

"I'd take anyplace that's safe at this point," said Galocai. "But it's the middle of the night, and the northeast edge of the city is too far to go at this time of night."

"Agreed. We'll need to find somewhere closer to stay for the evening, but I'd ask you to consider allying with Heron Olfrus in the morning. He has a keen ear for magic, as does his sister." Melissa smiled wearily.

"His sister?" Galocai arched an eyebrow. "You made it sound as though you just met those two."

Melissa shrugged. "I did. They met us on the road, Elaine and I, and it was through them that we met Bethanelle of House Graef."

"Graef hasn't been a friend of Paroth in the past, but their weakness politically places them within our power. If I join with Olfrus, I could perhaps have their estate calling in our favors before long."

"That might be worth it," said Melissa. "Though I'll confess I know little of politics."

"I'm not sure of the situation at the moment." Galocai frowned at the mirror behind the bar. "But I do know there is a place nearby in the city. It is said to be haunted, but rarely are such stories true. It stays abandoned, so we can use it."

"You think that's a good idea this late at night?" asked Melissa. "It must be getting cold."

"It's not winter yet," said Galocai. "I spent some time on the streets at night in different cities. Here in Alliance, things are safe until the cold becomes such that it tempts people to kill."

Melissa supported herself against the bar top. "I'll keep an eye out and we can make sure it's safe together."

"A good idea," said Galocai. "Let us go. The place is called the Tower of the Fallen."

"Ominous." Melissa winked.

"Very." He smirked. "Bodyguard."

The two of them walked into the dark night.

* * *

The Tower of the Fallen loomed over them, twice as tall as every building around it's jagged spire.

"Why is this place said to be haunted?" asked Melissa.

"The fallen mages of Fulster were once kept here," said Galocai. "Imprisoned by Deckard Hadrian for their crimes. That's how the tower got it's name."

"How long ago was that?" asked Melissa.

"The last one was said to be lost when the tower was condemned a hundred years ago," said Galocai. "But who knows what's in there now. The lower floors should be clear of danger, I'm certain."

"Have you been here before?" asked Melissa.

"Yes," said Galocai. "I'll lead the way."

"Be ready with your magic in case of an attack. Have your essences ready to fight."

"You take great care." Galocai summoned his sprites to the surface. Electricity crackled at his fingertips. "And yet you came with me the first time we met."

"Yes," said Melissa, but I had my reasons to trust you."

"What were those?"

"Men in masks might be mysterious at first," said Melissa. "But I'm beginning to understand your reason to hide your identity. I saw something in those feathers you are wearing, something that drew me closer. I think I can trust you."

"I'm glad you think that," said Galocai. "Because you can."

The two of them walked up to the doors. Thick, wrought-iron studs glimmered in the starlight. They drew their sprites and lit the scene with their combined magic. The song of Galocai's sprites was gentle, and reminded Melissa of his kiss.

"Can we simply walk in?"

"I think so," said Galocai. "No one should be here."

He gently pulled the door open. Melissa slipped past him, moving fast, and darted into the shadows within the room. She stood beside the door as Galocai entered more slowly.

Melissa gazed into the gloom, taking in the pockmarks of decay everywhere. Chipped fragments of stonework littered the floor. Despite the tower's pristine outside appearance, the interior was strewn with discarded materials from magical wards. The remnant-songs of scattered essences still played within the walls.

"Mages were imprisoned here." Galocai turned to Melissa. "I don't remember most of the histories, but Lord Hadrian was said to have put them here. Maybe because of their fallen nature. Or maybe they couldn't maintain themselves as users of magic or even free humans any longer? They fell too far."

"Is that last part from the book?" asked Melissa.

"Yes," said Galocai. "It's close to a direct quote."

"It sounded like you were quoting." Melissa peered forward, taking in the dingy square room around the spiral staircase at the center. "We shouldn't go any further inside if we can avoid it. Staying right where we stand might be the best choice."

"I agree," said Galocai. "Get some rest, I'll take the first watch."

CHAPTER 15

DECKARD

The Fortress of Sleep loomed over even the tallest nearby buildings, casting a long shadow on the city's northeast side. Deckard Hadrian alighted on the battlements surrounding the central keep. He turned his gaze toward the narrow courtyard that lay behind the outer wall.

Knights were already moving in the early morning hours. Two in partial armor fenced in the yard, while others watched, or marched in formation nearby. The Order of Dreams kept their fortress pristine, and everywhere Deckard looked the servants and order soldiers busied themselves with training or chores.

Deckard took a deep breath, feeling the air swell his lungs. He nearly floated off the battlements thanks to his lightness. He let the wind take him up, then descended by replacing a portion of his weight, then glided into the courtyard.

He landed near the two knights as they clashed blade-to-blade. Neither of them seemed to notice him, both so intent on their opponent.

One was slim while the other was larger in frame. Though they fenced back and forth, the one with the lighter build seemed to have the edge in skill.

The smaller knight wore her long red hair tied back. She drove her opponent toward the far side of the dueling ground. In the yard, there could be only fifty hand-spans between each wall at the widest point. There was virtually no space for retreat.

Deckard folded his arms and watched.

The woman backed her larger opponent to the wall, driving him toward the cold embrace of demon stone. The fortress walls were all built from the black material known across the world as indestructible. Deckard floated slightly off the ground and then let the wind carry him in a wide arc around the battle. He kept his eye on the two, almost certain he had seen the woman before. She fought with stern rigor, and her blade always seemed light in her hands.

Deckard dropped from the air and landed on the grass. This time, the sound of his impact, drew the woman's attention. The next moment, she put her opponent to her mercy. The big man raised his hands and the bout was over. The woman glanced at Deckard, before turning her whole frame to face him.

"Who goes there?" she asked.

"It is I, Deckard Hadrian."

"My Lord Hadrian." The knight's voice went higher and her eyes were wide. Deckard guessed she must be less than twenty years old.

She knelt on one knee. The knight she'd just defeated did the same. "We didn't know if you would come here," she said. "You rarely touched this place in years past."

"Even so." Deckard smiled. "I feel no enmity toward you or your order."

"We serve," said the woman. "Allow me to go and get my father, he's the highest Knight of our Order in Alliance."

"Take me to him," said Deckard. "No matter how early, he's no doubt awake."

"You sound as if you know him," said the girl.

"I once did. Though it has been some years."

"I am," said the red-haired knight. "Rosanna Berline, at your service."

"A pleasure." Deckard fell into place a few yards behind her. He followed Rosanna through the yard to the inner keep's open gate.

They climbed the steps to a chamber with narrow slits in one wall that overlooked the yard, then through ther hall to a chamber of pale stone. Not quite white, but not quite gray, the stone glowed from inside. Someone could achieve that by investing the stone with essences, but Deckard could detect no inner song from inside.

Within the chamber, a knight before a wide altar. Two horns surmounted the ritual surface, one on each side of the flat center. The horns rose and curved in mirrored arcs, nearly meeting in the center over the flat space below.

Shrines to Mother Mercy came in all shapes and sizes. This one was of a kind Deckard knew to from the other knightly orders he commanded. Defeating another immortal centuries ago had resulted in his position over a few such dedicated groups. They had been loyal to their former leader, but that man's ruinous deeds had demanded him overthrown.

In spite of how Deckard gained his status over them, the Order of Dreams made for a strong ally, if not a comfortable friend.

A man kneeling before the altar, wore a blue surcoat and white linen trousers. Whatever his specific purpose, he offered supplication before the altar. Rosanna and Deckard waited for him to finish the ritual by lighting a flame in each of the horns above the stone slab. He rose and turned to face them.

"Daughter," said Giovanni Berline. "And Deckard Hadrian. Lord of Winds, I didn't expect you."

"I was told the same by Rosanna. Nonetheless, here I stand."

"Nonetheless." Giovanni nodded. "It is good to see you, Lord Hadrian."

"You call me lord," said Deckard, "but you shouldn't."

"Whatever you wish, Hadrian," said Giovanni. "You fought by my side before. But I was a different man all those years ago."

"You went to the war," said Deckard. "I saw you in the east. You acquitted yourself well."

"And you." Giovanni smiled. "You did as an immortal man should, and covered yourself in glory. You fought the Kism Avatar known as Jalung hand-to-hand, if I remember."

"We fought him," said Deckard. "If I recall."

"Perhaps, perhaps." Giovanni's smile widened, though a grim steadiness remained in his eyes. He offered Deckard his hand. "You have come to Alliance at a dark time."

"Indeed." Deckard shook Giovanni's hand. "But dawn is breaking."

"I hope so. My friend, Sir Jon Arver, has found little evidence in the prince's case."

"You have a knight looking into the murder already?" said Deckard.

"Indeed." Giovanni's smile faded like the colors if dyed cloth. "Sir Arver, is known for his meticulous nature."

"I've not heard his name," said Deckard. "I've been away too long."

"It is natural to lose track of home when you travel all of Tancuon to hunt demons."

"I appreciate your understanding." Deckard folded his hands. "But there are other reasons I have not sat in Fulster or my hall of glass for over fifty years."

"I know," said Giovanni. "Or at least, I can guess. Do you plan to tell me?"

"You may continue to guess, my friend." Deckard nodded with a small smile. "For now, that is fitting."

"Have you come to safeguard the city?" asked Rosanna, brow furrowed.

"Partially. That's why I attended to the funeral service and spoke to the nobility. My primary mission is to hunt whatever slew Prince Saviron and his steward."

"You're not here to take over the city yourself?" Giovanni snorted. "I suppose not."

"Would you be pleased with me if I was?"

"A good point," said Giovanni. "You must have already begun investigating. Any possible suspects?"

"I interrogated Catricha Maltos for a moment," said Deckard. "And I've spoken with Lord Enrin Maltos as well. I doubt either of them is anywhere near guilty. Their family had just achieved the second most powerful position in the city by marrying Catricha to the steward."

"Adias Halth," said Giovanni. "A lecher if ever there was one, and he never seemed to care the least for his bride."

"Interesting that you know so much," said Deckard. "She told me the same."

"It was known." Rosanna folded her arms. "Even my cousin on the outskirts was familiar with their problems."

"Your cousin?" asked Deckard. "You mean Lady Fel-Graef?"

"Bethanelle," said Rosanna. "Yes."

"She is a potential heir to the prince's throne. The same can be said for members of the other four families, and these newcomers from the east, the Olfrus Household." Deckard folded his arms.

"That makes five potential heirs," said Giovanni. "And five potential motives."

"Or more." Deckard released a long breath. "After all, those families each have multiple members of age. Sadly, I suspect that none of them are as likely to bear the blame as my blood in the House of Kuldettan."

"You suspect the Kuldettans?" Giovanni's lips curled with grim amusement. "This is why I like you, Hadrian. You ignore sentiment so well that you're practically not human."

Deckard frowned, and turned his back on Giovanni. "I am human. And I'm not perfect in any way."

"Forgiveness. I won't deride you again in such a fashion, Lord Hadrian."

"Deckard will do." He looked over his shoulder at Giovanni. "Now, follow me, both of you Sir Berlines. It is time we took clearer stock of the situation."

CATRICHA

Dawn broke over the city, casting long streams of light into Catricha's chambers.

She woke slowly, moving from her bed to her writing desk, and then to the chamber mirror to prepare herself for presentation below. Even eating breakfast with the family, she needed to look presentable.

Catricha shot a glare at the tooth dress where it hung on a rack beside her dresser.

She donned a pale-gray skirt and a finely-tailored green tunic before tying up her hair. She tucked a clean quill into the inner band of her skirt, just in case she needed it.

Finally, she descended the stairs to the dining room. She was early, and felt glad for the quill as she rounded the corner before the long and vacant table. Birds sang in the garden outside.

Catricha froze in her step. The table, though mostly empty, was occupied at the far end by a single figure, her father. Lord Maltos wore a tense expression on his pale features.

"Good morning," said Enrin. "I take it you had a caller during Nansoela's party last night."

"If you mean Deckard Hadrian, than yes. He asked me questions for most of the time I was walking home."

"I'm glad you had a bodyguard, at least." Enrin scowled. "The streets weren't safe last night."

"The sleepless were out," said Catricha. "I wasn't worried about them. I've never heard of them attacking anyone, even a noble in an outrageous gown."

"There's a first time for any event. I'm glad it wasn't last night." Enrin rubbed at one of his eyes. "You know, I also had a visitor yesterday."

"Hadrian." Catricha stared at her father. "He was here? He asked me what happened that night."

"You told me as well," he said. "But Hadrian will be more difficult to convince of your innocence."

"Possibly." Catricha sat down at her place at the table. "But I wasn't exactly trying to convince him I was innocent last night, just not guilty."

"Too much wit will kill you," said Enrin.

"Maybe. But perhaps a little more won't hurt."

"If you're capable of delivering just a little, my dear, I'd be more comfortable with that assessment."

Catricha laughed, a hand to her mouth. "Father, you have some wit, yourself."

"Don't belittle me." Enrin smirked. "I've found ways to impress people that you never have considered."

"Ways to impress mother?" Catricha rolled her eyes. "I'd rather not hear about those."

"Not my meaning. Ways to impress other nobility," said Enrin. "After all, you can't remain a widow forever."

"With respect, father, I've just become a widow. Perhaps I should continue to experiment with it a little longer."

"Then we have turned to the same page." Enrin put his hands on the tabletop. "You're career may return, but I fear for you. If you don't do something to aid your reputation, it will be difficult to attain more power when the time comes."

"When the time comes? Do you wish for me to become the prince of the city?"

"The thought has crossed my mind." Enrin drummed two fingers on the table. "I'm too old, and your mother wouldn't allow me to attempt something so dangerous, given the threat of death looming over the office. If you were to try, a threat by an assassin could prove you innocent of the crime."

"You don't think I could actually become prince?" Catricha frowned. "Should I take that as a challenge or compliment?"

"Take it as a caution," said Enrin. "I don't want you in danger, but it seems to me that if your story is true, you may already be under threat."

"Perils of the body concern me little," said Catricha. "Perils of the heart keep me occupied at the moment."

Enrin put a hand to his forehead. "You've found another."

"Another lover? Father, I would rather not discuss such things with you, at least not bluntly."

"For the best. I would rather not hear of any indiscretions as long as you're safe about them."

"I know how to make a preventative," said Catricha. "It's as if I'm not the only noblewoman in the city who ever had to deny a child entrance into the world."

"As long as prevention is your choice, I'll accept your dalliances."

"I appreciate that, father."

"However." Enrin's brows bent together. "If you are to maintain your reputation, others must not know the truth. They must not know if you're unfaithful to your husband, even after his death."

"I was faithful to him for a week while he was alive and we were married. Wouldn't you say that's time enough?"

"Hardly." Enrin snorted. "Given the situation, perhaps you should let yourself rest, rather than seek out more trouble."

"Trouble? Father, you call me trouble all the time."

"For now," he said. "I'd rather use your given name."

"If that's your will," father. "I will do my best to keep things under wraps."

"As long as no one knows." Enrin tapped the table with one finger. "Now might be a good time for breakfast."

* * *

Later that morning, Catricha and Porfiria took a carriage to the Halth estate, south of the city. A quarter-mile from Alliance's walls the site of the two murders lay in the woods. The black demon stone looming behind them provided a curtain of shade.

A slight gray of high clouds stretched like gravelly fingers across the blue horizon. A glimmer of metal beyond the clouds shone in faint gold beyond the gray curtains.

The Halth Estate was still under investigation, likely by a knight present, based on the guards outside.

"Who goes there?" asked one of the men at arms.

Catricha stuck her head out the carriage door, grateful for the fresh air. "I am the widow of Adias Halth."

"This is your house, my lady," said the man. "What purpose do you have here?"

"My friend and I wish to study the invitations of the final party of summer."

"That would be useful to have," said a man stepping through the iron gates of the estate. "I've not found such records yet."

Catricha recognized the thin, graying beard and harsh voice as belonging to Sion's father.

"Sir Jon Arver?" said Catricha. "What are you doing outside the city?"

The skinny knight put a hand to his heart. "I've been assigned to investigate the steward's house and I intend to find the truth."

"Perhaps you'd like to go with us then?" Porfiria put a foot on the step of the carriage behind Catricha. "My dear friend, Lady Maltos knows where Lord Halth kept the invitation rosters."

"Take me to them," said Sir Arver. "I'm eager to see it as well."

The three of them walked past the guards at the gate and then into the quiet house. They climbed the stairs, and took a corner at the top. Catricha led the way, proceeding into the lord's study. The room was full of books of all kinds.

Histories adorned the tables and chairs. Magical tomes resided on the far wall. Adias had read much, and he'd studied more esoterica than Catricha ever felt understood herself. Even as a poet, she'd not matched his voracious appetite for consuming art and history.

"There!" Catricha pointed to the table at the center of the study. A layer of dust clung to the surface, but underneath that, lay two sheets of parchment and a quill pen between them.

The sheet closer to the door was scribed with a diagram of a wide circle with four smaller circles adjoining it. None of the points were labeled, but the ink had a dull, red tinge to it.

The other parchment appeared was partially wrinkled. Upon that page, in columns, written in Adias's hand, were the names of those he'd invited to his final party. Catricha walked to the table and stared at the names, wondering if the culprit's identity was among the symbols scribed there.

CHAPTER 16

VUAL

Within the corridor of House Kuldettan's manor, every word at normal volume echoed.

"What did you say to her?" Vual's voice came out as a harsh rasp "What did she tell you last night?" He slammed his fist onto the writing desk beside where Ruar sat before the page of poetry he'd been working on. "Tell me, brother!"

Ruar narrowed his eyes at Vual and grunted. "We talked of nothing alone. Eram was with us the entire time."

"I don't care about him," said Vual. "I care about your words with that murderess."

"Murderess? That term does not describe her, brother." Ruar shifted his awkward legs on the stool.

"Fine. If you're going to utter contrivances as your opinion, be silent. Answer only when you have a real information to share."

"If you demand my silence and my answers, perhaps I should request your absence altogether." Ruar glared at Vual.

"Look." Vual took a deep breath. "I know she killed them."

Ruar made an animal sound of annoyance. "No. No, you don't. Nobody knows who was behind what happened that night."

"I'll tell you how I know." Vual released his breath, seething. "She hated Adias. By extension, she probably despised Prince Saviron as well. Saviron enabled her husband, who she clearly hated."

"That's a guess." Ruar clucked with his tongue. "And only a guess."

"Catricha Maltos is guilty." Vual bellowed a sigh. "I'm going now, and I'll leave you to your poem, brother. Know that once I have the truth, I expect you to back me."

"Expect what you will," said Ruar. "It's not my job to please you, brother."

"It's not your job to please her either." Vual grimaced, then stormed from the room.

* * *

Vual rode south, escorted by a pair of bodyguards toward the town of Fulster. The closeness of the town to the city, left Fulster always in Alliance's shadow.

After speaking with Ruar that morning, he'd only grown frustrated thinking of Catricha and the killings.

"This day," muttered Vual as his steed outpaced his guards. "Will stay inauspicious if I don't do something. I require assistance, if I'm going to uncover the truth."

He rode fast, nearly leaving his guards behind by spurring his steed. He approached the village with its palisade walls, he rode straight through the open gate. The guards followed, but far behind.

Dismounting, Vual took his sword from the saddle. He buckled the weapon to his belt.

"The keepers of Fulster," he muttered. "If I owe them anything, it's simply friendship."

"Sir!" called the gaurd who caught up with him first on a racing steed, "what do you wish us to do?"

"Stay with the horses," said Vual. "Make sure no one tampers with the saddles or tries to steal one."

"As you wish, my lord," said the guard. "Will you be long?"

Vual shrugged. "Find some shade, just in case."

"As you wish." The guard bowed his head and took Vual's horse by her dangling reins.

He left them behind and made his way toward the town hall where the keepers of Fulster made their residence. The family, the so-called Nim-Fulsters, had two things of interest to Vual at the moment.

The first, and less important element he'd come to investigate, was their tie with Deckard Hadrian. The family line of Kuldettan had begun with Hadrian's heirs, but they separated from the town of Fulster afterward. Never before had the princely family of Alliance owed the town of Fulster than if Vual became prince. The second, and more important element, was the daughter of the Nim-Fulsters, Osestra.

Osestra Nim-Fulster was a lovely girl. Even Vual, with his focus on magic and swordplay over romance could admit that. The two of them have been friends for years. Still, he'd not made the time to call on her privately of late. The guards no doubt, had their suspicions for his motivation. Let them ponder his intentions toward the keeper's daughter. Vual was done pondering.

He knocked at the side door of the town hall.

An elderly house servant opened the door-slat. "Who is there?"

"Vual Kuldettan," he said. "I've come to call on Osestra."

"Come to call," said the servant behind the door. "Then enter. You may wait inside, where the sun won't bother you as it climbs."

"The sun seems high to me already, but people do things more slowly in the countryside."

"That we do," said the servant as he opened the door. Vual took in the sight of a wrinkled face and shaking hands. "Right this way, my lord."

"Just a moment," said Vual. "What's wrong with your fingers?"

"My fingers? They're nothing special. Age has simply left them infirm."

"I can see." Vual nodded. "I can tell your years...Are you afraid of me?"

"Of course not. I know you, my Lord Kuldettan."

"I've been studying recently. I think I can help with your tremors."

The servant smiled. "Magic is a powerful tool. Even this old man knows that much."

"I'll realign your essences." Vual listened to the man's heartbeat. "With your heart out of order, the effects of aging are worse on every part, including your extremities. Would you say you experience pain in your hands?"

"Frequently, but what can I do about it?" I take the healers herb every day."

"Herbs help," said Vual. "But they only treat the pain, not the cause. Give me your hands. I'll take care."

The servant held out his shaking, weathered hands. Fingers on one were bent almost beyond recognition, like a claw.

Vual took both hands in his, and then separated two of his scalpel sprites. He sent the essences through the man's body. The sting of Vual's swiftly-moving sprites made the old servant flinch.

"The pain is brief," said Vual. "The healing will last."

"I can handle pain." The servant forced a smile.

Vual used his sprites to tug at the heart sprite of the man, pulling the tiny essence into alignment with the bane opposing it from the other side of the heart.

All humans have but two essences to start, Vual thought as he worked quietly. His sprites took hold and adjusted the position of the two shimmering heart-essences until they formed an ideal dichotomy.

The man smiled as Vual withdrew his scalpel sprites.

"Excuse the intrusion," said Vual.

"There's no pain." The servant held his hands completely steady.

"Care to show me directly to Osestra's chambers?" asked Vual.

* * *

Vual climbed the stairs, following the aged servant. A young lord calling on the lady of a lesser house must always show proper etiquette. To be appropriate, he needed company at her chambers.

The servant knocked at the door, a wooden affair carved with the twin symbols of dawn and dusk. Every door had a different pattern in the town hall. Fulster might contain less wealth than even a single noble house in the city of Alliance, but it was still an impressive work of art. Vual didn't understand architecture, but he appreciated art in the form of carvings, paintings, and reliefs.

The door opened. Osestra greeted Vual with a surprised smile. "You didn't send a letter. I didn't expect you."

"There was no time to write," said Vual. "I simply rode."

Osestra's delicate features transformed into an amused smile. "I'm pleased to see you, Lord Kuldettan. I've been worried ever since the last summer party."

"The losses." Vual nodded. "That's part of the reason I'm here." He stepped through the doorway, and took a seat on the cushion of a chair nearby. "I mean to ask for your assistance."

"How can I help?" asked Osestra, slender brows bending with her question. "I don't know much about the situation in the city beyond the obvious that everyone must've heard by now."

The aged servant closed the door behind Vual, while staying in the hall. As alone as he was going to get with Osestra, Vual stood up. He took a step toward her, then hesitated, bowing his head. "My dear Osestra, I fear the threat of the killing shadow has distracted people from the source of it's magic. There must be someone controlling it."

"The shadow?" asked Osestra. "I heard the way the prince fell, but know nothing about the culprit."

"No one knows the actual culprit, yet. I fear if we don't examine the evidence, we may be misled."

"What you propose?" Osestra inclined her head toward him. "You and I need somewhere to start our investigation."

"I have a place." Vual nodded. "I'll need your help to get inside."

"I enjoy the sound of an adventure, and I think that's what you're suggesting."

"An adventure of sorts," said Vual. "But the only thing we're questing for is the knowledge of who killed Prince Saviron and Lord Adias Halth."

"I'm with you." She smiled. "Where should we begin?"

"We'll solve the mystery by asking who could do such a thing, and then why would they? I have ideas..." said Vual. "But first, we should reexamine the place they were killed."

"The Halth Estate is but a short ride from here," said Osestra. "Allow me to dress appropriately, and we will go at once."

"Excellent. I'm glad you're willing to help."

"I'm glad you asked me," said Osestra. "Why didn't you simply enlist the aid of your men?"

"I would," said Vual. "But I don't trust the house's men like I trust you."

"Why, Lord Kuldettan," she said, face reddening. "You're making me flush."

He put a hand on her hand. "Lady Nim-Fulster, that was not my intention."

She leaned against him then took a step back. "Allow me to get dressed. I'll need my riding clothes."

* * *

City guards were waiting outside the gates of Halth as Vual and Osestra's horses carried them toward the estate, Vual's house guards close behind them. The long halls and towering gateways stood vacant after the death of the last member of the steward's family.

Vual despised the idea of nobility as important only due to their bloodlines, but Adias had been his friend.

"Who are they?" Osestra pointed at the sentries.

"City watch," said Vual, "we mustn't let them spot us."

"Should we circle round the back?" asked Osestra. "Is there another way in?"

Vual nodded to her. "Guards, stay here. The lady and I are going around the house. We'll move in from the forest side."

"Take care my lord," said one guard.

"We'll watch the front," said the other.

The guards took all four horses, while Osestra and Vual entered the trees on foot. The two of them crept through the forest, both wearing riding leathers and caps. They reached the low wall topped by a spiked fence at the back of the house.

Osestra looked along the length of the barrier. "There's no gate back here. What's your plan?"

"Take my hand, then hold on tight."

She reached for his hand. Her warm fingers interlocked with his. He tightened his grip and she took his arm in hers. "I'm ready," she said.

"Hang on." Vual put his sprite's strength into his legs. He pushed off with half his strength.

His leap carried easily over the wall, taking Osestra with him. He landed with a thump in the yard on the other side. Trees dotted the yard, providing cover. The house was probably too far away to allow anyone inside to see them clearly through the foliage.

Vual crept toward the back of the house, leading Osestra by the hand. She kept her fingers intertwined with his, but let her arm relax, giving them both distance. The two of them reached the house where the porch extended in a circle around the base of the mansion.

"This is it," said Vual. "Our way in."

"You've learned much magic," said Osestra. "I'm surprised they didn't realize you could do that."

"I've been training as hard as I can," said Vual. "Now, we must be silent. Follow me."

CHAPTER 17

CATRICHA

In the study of the Halth Estate, Sir Jon Arver yawned. Catricha glanced in the knight's direction, raising her eyebrows.

"It may seem exceptionally dull to sit here reading," said Porfiria. "But I assure you, Sir Arver, Lady Maltos and I will be fine on our own."

Jon folded his arms and slouched against one of the bookshelves. "If all I thought imperiled you was boredom I would leave you to it."

"You suspect that the killer might return for us." Catricha's eyes flicked from the page of records to the knight. "If that was his plan, Sir Arver, perhaps he would've done so at the ball?"

"We don't know the killer's motives," said Jon. "I for one would rather prevent than discover murders."

"I assure you—" Porfiria started.

"No, Lady Amburen," said Jon. "I take my role as protector of the city state as seriously as you can imagine."

"Porfiria," said Catricha. "Leave it be."

"Very well." Porfiria smirked. "I'll let Sir Arver be bored with us."

"If my boredom is the price you must pay for your safety, my lady," said Jon, "I will gladly pay it."

"Someone thinks he's a wit." Porfiria turned to Catricha.

Catricha shook her head. "Be kind. He is trying to protect us."

"Yes, yes," said Porfiria, waving a hand aimlessly.

They pored over the text, scanning the lists for unusual names. Catricha recognized most of the people on the list. Many of them she'd darted with poems at some point.

A few names she didn't know, however. The merchant households, she was less familiar with, because of their lower standing and more recent addition to high society.

If the girl was one of them, she could easily have disappeared from the party that night. She would be missed by her family if she vanished altogether. Yet, if she simply returned home without saying anything, how would investigators ever find her?

"Do you know any of the merchants?" asked Catricha.

"A few of them," said Porfiria. "But I could recognize most their families by blood traits."

"They pass down the traits like we do in a regular fashion, thereby making parentage easy to ascertain?"

"Quite so." Porfiria flipped a page. "For example, the Dorians are usually wavy of hair and slim of build."

"Do you know any that are yellow-haired like palavians and tend toward promiscuity?" asked Catricha.

Porfiria laughed. "Don't all humans tend toward promiscuity?"

Catricha smiled. "Fair point, my friend."

"If it's the promiscuous you're after," said Jon, "I could suggest you examine a few names in-particular."

Catricha turned toward the knight. "Have you been hiding something from us, Sir Arver?"

"I extend my honor to those under my protection." He folded his arms. "If I'm to protect the people and the nobility, I must know where they go in the dark of the night."

"So you keep track of the affairs of others?" said Porfiria. "Literally?"

"Sometimes." Jon shrugged. "When it is important to my position."

"As a knight of dreams, you still let infidelities and indiscretion slide?" Porfiria grinned. "I'm beginning to like you."

"At least someone does." Jon snorted a laugh.

"Do you know any women who match the description I just gave?" asked Catricha.

"Straw-haired women of the merchant class who fool with nobles?" Jon nodded. "A few names come to mind. However, I could use a more distinct description, because that hardly narrows it down."

"Right," said Catricha. "Palavians are an extremely common sight in the north. Too many match that description."

"Then we're at a loss." Porfiria frowned. "Unless you can remember the girls face, Cat."

"I can't describe her exactly." Catricha shook her head. "She was pretty, but more was hard to say from a distance."

"What was she wearing?" asked Porfiria. "Perhaps that could help us?"

"I don't remember clearly." Catricha bit her lip. "When we're there, most of the ball-gowns begin to look the same, despite their attempts to appear different."

Porfiria gave a derisive chuckle. "Too true."

"You're going to dismiss the gown because neither of you can remember it? You truly are spoiled, my ladies." Despite his words, Jon smiled, and his tone stayed light.

"Did I say I liked you?" Porfiria rolled her eyes. "It's not that we see too many gowns. It's that all the gowns begin to blend together because of the style of the day."

"I take your meaning," said Jon. "However, I am detecting more than mockery in your laughter."

"What are you detecting, then?" Porfiria raised her eyebrows.

Catricha put a hand on her friend's sleeve.

"Resentment," said Jon.

"Sir Jon—" Porfiria froze in mid-sentence. "What was that?"

"What?" asked Jon.

"There's someone downstairs," said Porfiria. "One of my sense-sprites just shifted out of position."

"You distributed your essences downstairs?" said Catricha. "Were you worried about someone approaching?"

Porfiria nodded. "Whenever I'm nervous, I lay out a few sensory essences to listen for danger. There are two people in the drawing room. They may be looking for the same information as we are. One of them is a mage."

"I'll call for the guards," said Jon.

"Perhaps you should," said Porfiria. "Yet, if that mage is as powerful as he seems, I suspect your people will be better off sheltering where they are. Whoever he is, the guards aren't prepared for him."

"Then what will we do?" Catricha's eyes widened. "There are two of them, but only one is a mage. Perhaps Jon and I can handle the ordinary one, while you deal with the mage, Porfiria?"

"I'd rather not fight," said Porfiria. "But if we must, that is a fine idea."

"Nonsense," said Jon. "We should drive them out, not just observe them."

"We may outnumber them," said Catricha. "But I'm no fighter."

"You fence, if I recall." Porfiria scowled.

Catricha shook her head. "I don't have a blade and I'm no good with my bare hands."

"Then come with me," said Jon. "We will distract these intruders. Porfiria, you can use magic to detain them."

"A better plan." Porfiria nodded. "Perhaps the ruling is out on whether on you being entertainment or actually useful, Sir Arver."

"I'll take that," said Jon. "Let's go, Lady Maltos."

Catricha folded the list of names and tucked the parchment inside her skirt's waist-binding. She followed Jon from the room. Porfiria sneaked down the hall in the opposite direction, quietly as she could.

Meanwhile, Jon and Catricha descended the high staircase at speed, taking loud steps and pounding on the floor. *Porfiria should be circling around,* Catricha thought.

She would take the side stairs and meet them in the entrance hall when the pair of spies appeared.

Jon drew his sword, turning to face the halls leading to the back of the house. Catricha made her way to the front door. She heard an inner din of unpleasantness, that set her teeth on edge. Hadrian had warned her that her heart's song was noticeable.

"Damn it," she said under her breath. "Not now."

"What's wrong?" asked Jon.

"It's," said Catricha. "It's my magic, I have some problems with it."

"You have magic too?" said Jon. "I thought you said otherwise?"

"I can't control it," said Catricha. "It's not an asset to us."

Jon put both hands on the hilt of his blade. "In that case, the two of us make even better bait."

Catricha grunted. The unladylike sound reminded her of Ruar. He occasionally lacked interest in speaking real words. Sometimes, she doubted how he could be a poet and still make such sounds. At that moment she understood, and her annoyance transcended language.

"Who's there?" bellowed Jon. "Show yourselves, intruders."

No one emerged from the back hall. No sounds answered Jon's challenge.

"Are you trying to scare them off?" asked Catricha.

"Yeah." Jon scowled and shook his head. "I don't fancy being attacked by a mage out of nowhere."

"Magic can be very dangerous," said Catricha. "It's a sound plan to take care."

He gritted his teeth. "Thanks for your permission, Lady Maltos."

Catricha shrugged. "Perhaps I'm wrong?"

They faced the hallways together, waiting for sound or movement. For a full five minutes they waited, and then Porfiria appeared at the top of the staircase.

"Whoever they were. They left in a hurry," said Catricha's friend. "We should be safe."

"Good," said Jon. "But if you care to find a merchant's daughter, perhaps the best place to look would be the mercantile docks at in the river district."

"Ask around the offices?" Catricha glanced at Porfiria.

"A good idea." Porfiria descended the stairs.

"Take the list," said Jon. "You'll do more with it than I can."

"He speaks the truth," said Porfiria.

Jon wrinkled his nose. "And you speak of him as if he's not here."

"Never mind that," said Catricha. "You should post more guards at the back of the estate, Sir Arver. "

He nodded. "Go, you two. I'll see to this place's security."

CHAPTER 18

CATRICHA

The carriage took them from the countryside into Alliance, rolling toward the docks.

Porfiria and Catricha took the turn toward the water and descended the slope of the hillside on the western edge of the Duenn. The docks that lay before them were abuzz with activity. Riverboats and larger ships, from as far north as the Lake of Zahon, arrived in Alliance on the waters. Most of the vessels were too small to carry horses or other large beasts, but pack animals were plentiful on the docks, helping the laborers unload.

Catricha peered out the window, gazing at the workers, while the wagon rolled closer to the water. The ships at anchor were mostly empty by that time of day. Dockworkers came and went up and down the gangways. They were not Catricha's concern.

Her main worry came not from locating the girl with the gold hair, but in convincing the family to let Catricha talk with her. Given Adias's long guest list, deception became all too possible. Potentially, the girl was an accomplice in Adias and Saviron's deaths. The idea made Catricha's bones feel cold. She leaned against the carriage seat and shivered.

Porfiria glanced at her. "What's the matter? Besides the obvious, I mean."

"I'm not certain we have the right idea," she said. "Going to look for the killer ourselves could prove dangerous. Think of Sir Arver and those people following us at the country estate."

"I have my magic," said Porfiria. "I'll protect us both."

"I don't want to put that on you," said Catricha. "I really ought to learn how to use the power I've been given."

"What power?" asked Porfiria.

"Last night, after I left the party, I encountered Deckard Hadrian. He told me that I had some kind of unusual essence song in my heart. He didn't tell me much."

Porfiria frowned in thought. "Did he think the song would make you a stronger mage?"

"I don't know." Catricha sighed. "It seemed so."

"Then, given time, I shall tutor you." Porfiria smiled. "After all, I have to practice, and you are my friend."

"Maybe I should be writing instead," said Catricha. "I don't know for sure."

"If you have any doubts I assure you the danger in training is nothing compared to the potential of what we're facing right now."

"I don't feel like we're in danger now." Catricha furrowed her brow. "I know we are."

"Is there any other path to take?" Porfiria shook her head.

"You're right. I just wish this mystery wasn't so heavily shrouded."

The carriage stopped as Porfiria nodded. She arranged her cloak about her shoulders and the two of them dismounted from the carriage.

* * *

Catricha led the way to the office near one of the dock houses, a building owned by a family on the list. They had sent their daughter to the party that night in summer when Saviron and Adias had been killed.

They climbed a flight of wooden chairs to reach the office door. She knocked against the frame. At first there was no answer, then a scramble movement came from inside along with a rattling and shifting of papers.

"Who's there?" asked a voice from inside, one belonging to a man in a hurry.

"I'm Catricha Maltos and I have questions that must be answered."

The doors swung inward. "Look," said the thick-set merchant inside. "My lady, I am afraid I don't know what you're talking about. I'm the head of this house, but we are small. We barely reach your social circles."

"Do you have a daughter who attended the prince's final ball?" asked Catricha.

"What do you mean to imply? I mean—No." The merchant furrowed his brow. "My sister attended. She must have been beneath your notice, Lady Maltos."

Porfiria took a step forward, holding the door open with one hand. Catricha paced a few spans into the room. The man retreated from the doorway, making room for her.

"Does your sister have yellow hair as you do?" asked Catricha, appraised the man's thinning blond scalp from a distance. "It's of interest to both of us." She nodded toward Porfiria.

"We don't—My family has little power, and not a single reason to wish a fate so terrible on anyone, let alone the prince."

"That is your claim." Porfiria sniffed, arms folded. "But how can we trust it before knowing what your sister did that night?"

The merchant clenched his fists, shaking with fury. "Why her?"

Catricha glanced at Porfiria. Her friend nodded. Catricha turned toward the merchant. "We know there was a girl involved that night."

"A young woman with yellow hair," said Porfiria.

"What? You can't accuse my sister of being an accomplice in a prince's murder with so little evidence!"

"We're looking for answers," said Catricha. "And I've said worse without prompting. I'm a professional at rudeness, after all."

"Professionally rude." The merchant scoffed. "Get out of here. Leave now, and I won't hold a grudge."

"That doesn't sound like the truth." Porfiria laughed. "And you can't make us leave. You said yourself that your family is powerless compared to ours."

The merchant snarled. "I'll ask kindly when you go to any effort not to offend me!"

"No one told you to be offended." Catricha tapped her finger against her chin. "I suspect your protestations have a lot to do with the suspicion you feel. Do you know what your sister did that night?"

"That's private!" the merchant snapped. "Don't presume to interrogate me."

"Oh," said Porfiria. "I think we will."

His voice got cold. "How dare you?"

"We dare," said Catricha. "Because my good name is on the line, and by extension so is Lady Amburen's."

"The city would be better off without the both of you." The merchant seethed. "Go."

"How very polite." Catricha paced forward to the man's desk. "I'd say, given we don't even know your name, plump merchant, perhaps you should explain more clearly. After all, we are just a widow and spinster. It could be we are quite simple and we'll never understand your world or work."

"I never—"

"You never what?" said Catricha. "You never saw the point of speaking to your sister?"

"What do you think?" asked Porfiria.

"I doubt he even knows what his sister is doing now, or who."

"By my honor," said the merchant, his hands pinching the corners of his desk. "What are you trying to say?"

Catricha shrugged. "Nothing. Clearly you're ignorant of happenings even in your own household."

"If I was, you'd never know the difference."

"Perhaps. Or perhaps we can read you as easily as a line of poetry." Porfiria winked at Catricha. "You appear nervous, but on the other hand, you act offended. This is covering your offensive nature, if I take your meaning."

"We're not accusing you of anything." Catricha stared at the man across his paper-strewn desk top. "We suspect your sister."

"My sister is the next heir of the house until I find a bride. You cannot attack her!"

"Oh, no bride," said Porfiria. "Not surprising."

The man's face reddened. He clenched his fist and backed away from the desk. "You are both wicked poets."

"Renowned poets," said Catricha with a grin. "Renowned for our wickedness."

"And proud of your evil." The merchant gritted his teeth "My family takes the utmost care. Though we lack your status, we pay homage directly to the throne of Mother Mercy. Your households take everything for granted. You've been given all you have by your histories. My house struggles, strives, and works to create the wealth of Tancuon. The two of you have no right to attack me."

"Or your sister?" asked Catricha. "What do you think, Porfiria? Does he sound innocent to you?"

"I-Innocent?" The merchant wilted. His slack fingers fell like flower petals from the side of his desk.

Porfiria smiled. "He certainly appears nonplussed."

"On the other hand, perhaps he is simply aloof to our banter."

"Aloof, yes that is the word," said Porfiria. "He doesn't appear to have any further words for himself."

The man's face turned a shade of purple. He balled his fists and raised one, preparing to strike. He must have recognized Porfiria's magic because he froze and the color drained from his expression before he could swing at one of them.

"You..." said the man through his teeth. "You two must go."

"No must about that." Catricha looked at the desk. "We must talk to your sister. Where can we find her?"

"And what was her name?" asked Porfiria.

"Sariah is not here," said the merchant. "She doesn't help with business at the river, because she is a lady."

"So are we," said Porfiria. "Yet, here we are."

"Indeed." The man clenched his jaw so tight the teeth looked ready to break. "Now leave my business, before I grind you out of here myself."

"Grind?" Catricha laughed. "Why, sir, I don't think you've ground anything, especially not a lady, in quite some time."

"Not married, after all." Porfiria laughed.

"That's what he said." Catricha turned her back on the man and his desk. "But I think we have what we need, as long as you know the address."

"You're not going to my house," said the man. "I'll stop you here."

"How?" asked Catricha. "With your fist? Or your belly?"

He stared at her. Porfiria unfolded one hand slowly. The song of a bane made the air tremble as if a bell just struck a low note. The merchant said nothing.

"You seem lost for words," said Catricha. "Be ready, because every family who joins the noble ranks must deal with me from now on."

"With us," said Porfiria. "Cat, don't forget about me. You may be better at getting a rise from people but I still serve a purpose in pointing out certain flaws. For example, I noticed a distinct lack of internal decor in this room."

“It seems a little low," said Catricha. "To impugne a man with money for his lack of taste, grotesque as it may be."

"We start with the low hanging fruit. The easy game. The prey that cannot help but wander into your trap."

Catricha put a palm to her forehead and laughed. “Of course. You taught me that, years ago."

"The faster you climb the tree of derision," said Porfiria. "The sooner you mention how a man doesn't know where his sister went on the night of a tremendous event. Of course, such men are found lacking, as he wasn't invited to the party. You can further point out that the man himself, with his palavian yellow hair, definitely fits what you expect a merchant to look like."

Catricha smirked. “Porfiria, you're being overly polite to explain all these things."

"Am I?" Porfiria chuckled. “Perhaps?”

She nodded, arms folded. “Though, you failed to point out how disgraceful his lifestyle appears. This man lacks not only taste in furnishings, but his own palate might be less studied than one would guess." Catricha pointed to the used plates, on the desk. "Too many people in Alliance starve. This man eats brunch at his office while the laborers toil outside."

The merchant lurched toward Catricha. He raised his fist. “You!”

"Yes," said Catricha. "Me."

The fist raced toward Catricha's head. "I'll punish you for your wickedness."

"Of course," said Catricha.

The man's knuckles never reached her.

Two essences pinned the man to the wall behind his desk. Porfiria pulled the banes back with a flick of her wrist.

Porfiria glanced at Catricha. "I think we have what we need."

"The address," Catricha said. "Where did the you say you lived again, merchant?"

The man's face turned puce. "Just north of the tombs."

"Thank you." She smiled. "We'll call upon you again if we need further help."

CHAPTER 19

CATRICHA

They arrived at the merchant's home in western Alliance. With the head of the house at work, the two of them would be uninvited guests at best, and invaders at worst.

Porfiria turned to Catricha. "Let me lead. If needed, I have enough magic to protect our retreat."

Catricha shook her head. "I appreciate the idea. Though, I'm not certain it matters which of us goes first."

"Do you suspect something in-particular?"

Catricha shrugged. "Not exactly. Still, if I'm right behind you, if someone throws a fireball or such I doubt I'd escape unscathed if you won't."

"Magic as we know it is surprisingly low on hurling fire, Cat. So, don't worry. From my understanding, these merchants lack magical training and aptitude. I wouldn't expect pyrotechnics anytime soon."

"I suppose." Catricha laughed. "One wouldn't throw a fireball in one's own house. Quite the mess would result."

"Quite," said Porfiria.

They dismounted the carriage and made their way through and open gate and up the steps. *Shouldn't the gate be closed?* Catricha wondered if the open entrance boded well or poorly for them.

They passed by a stable inside the small compound, and approached a set of tall doors leading into the house. Nothing here held a candle to the decadence of the greater house's estates, but the courtyard was well-appointed with flowing geometries and floral patterns.

The addition of ruby-set and brightly gilded knockers on the door was out of place with the more subdued finery on display. Porfiria's townhouse might be small but it demonstrated greater elegance with it's decor.

Certainly, the merchants that dwelt here possessed far greater income than anyone Catricha knew personally. Gold filigree glittered in subtle shapes that became more obvious on every surface with a pattern before them. The small fountain of fish-mouths carved of stone at the center of the yard gleamed with treated-silver beneath the water.

Catricha followed Porfiria to the doorway and then knocked with the obscene gold clacker. At first there came no answer. Porfiria rapped her knuckles on the door frame.

A wispy middle-aged servant came to the door. "May I ask who is calling?" she asked.

"Porfiria Amburen," said Porfiria. "And her friend."

"Lady Amburen. Who are you calling upon?"

"We're here to see the lady of the house," said Porfiria. "Please asked her downstairs to meet us."

"My lady is resting."

"Then, please let us wait inside." Porfiria motioned to the fountain and the leaves floating in it. "The chill of autumn is growing."

"I don't know if that's a good idea, my ladies."

"Perhaps you don't understand," said Porfiria. "If the most famed cynic poet in the city wishes to speak to your mistress, she will be disappointed if you do not let us in."

"I know little of the ways of poets." The servant's color waned toward a pallid white. "My Lady Amburen, I shall go tell my mistress you're here."

"May we wait inside?" asked Catricha. "It is cold and we are two ladies not accustomed to such icy days."

The servant fidgeted with her empty hands. She bowed twice to Porfiria and once to Catricha, then swung the door open, and curtsied to them.

"Forgiveness, my ladies. Please, come in."

The two of them crossed the threshold with grateful smiles.

Up the stairs, the servant scurried in silence. Once out of sight, Catricha couldn't trace her movements at all.

Unlike the House Maltos manor where her parents and her younger siblings moved here and there at will, the merchant's house was quiet without the servant in attendance. The knowledge that the head of the house was unmarried, might have made Catricha slightly uneasy at being here if she was alone. The tempers she would surely induce simply by appearing about town as a widow thrilled her with excitement.

"Catricha," said Porfiria. "That was a strong play, but let's not snoop about. We don't want to reveal our intentions yet."

"Agreed." Catricha sat in a soft-backed chair. "Porfiria, perhaps you can use your sprites to poke around."

"I don't share their senses fully," said Porfiria. "They are of limited use in exploration."

"If we find the culprit today, what should we do?"

"Most likely? Take flight and then return with guards. I doubt based on what we've seen that this girl was the one who took their lives."

"We will see," said Catricha.

The stairs above them shook with the footsteps of a pair of male servants, descending. Built broad and thickly-muscled, they resembled bodyguards more than household servants. Both men wore house uniforms and carried wooden clubs, each heavily adorned with painful-looking golden bands and ending in a pronounced steel cap.

Catricha arched her eyebrows as the men approached.

"Is there some issue?" she asked. "We were allowed inside by one of your fellow servants."

"The mistress wishes us to escort you to her chambers," said one of the men. "It's not usual for her to have visitors."

"Is she afraid?" asked Catricha. "Of us? Why ever would she be?"

"We don't question her," said the man. He motioned with his club's tip toward the stairs.

The other man nodded. "We're paid plenty to obey."

Catricha and Porfiria exchanged glances, then rose and climbed the stairs in silence. At the top, the guards led them along a short hallway to a circular tower room on the north side of the house. They waited for a moment while one of the guards knocked on the door to an adjoining room.

In the chamber beyond the door they found the female servant from before, and a yellow-haired girl. The lady of the house sat on a tall feather-bed, wearing a dressing gown.

She looked a few years younger than Catricha, seventeen or eighteen. Her palavian-blonde hair was wild and unkempt, but there was no mistaking the shade. Her light frame and generous proportions spoke of Adias's favored type. Her round face matched with the glimpse from Catricha's memory of the party, leaving no further doubt.

"What brings you here, my lady poets?"

"Did your servant give you our names?" asked Porfiria. "If not, you may already have a guess."

"Names?" The girl's eyes widened. "You're Porfiria Amburen and Catricha Maltos of course. What do such esteemed poets want with me?"

"We want to ask some questions," said Catricha. "Be completely honest and we'll share only what we must with others."

The girl's cheeks turned red and she hunched, pulling in her knees with both arms. "You're the steward's widow."

Catricha nodded.

The merchant girl sighed. "You followed us that night."

"Indeed," said Catricha. "But it wasn't personal toward you. I'd always longed for a divorce."

"I didn't know. I thought I was betraying you, though I didn't know you personally." The girl hung her head.

"Betrayals are common. I'd expect as much from any member of our class. You played your part well."

Bright heat glowed on the girl's face. "Forgive me! I didn't mean—I didn't mean for anything to happen."

"What did happen?" asked Catricha, taking a step forward and leaning down. "We must know what happened to Adias that night."

"Before he died," Porfiria said.

The girl nodded, tears beading in her eyes. "I knew you saw us leave the dance floor." She took a deep breath. "I don't know what came over me, but he was so charming, and he invited me to...take up with him."

"A common enough occurrence," said Catricha. "Go on."

"I didn't think the steward wanted anything to do with me," said the girl. "But his charm had an effect on me. As we danced, I saw his desire grow."

Catricha grimaced, biting her lip.

Porfiria nodded. "What is your name, girl?"

"Sariah Ganatz. I'm the younger sister of the head of House Ganatz. Of course we're only merchants, few in number, so we go unnoticed in most scenes of the city."

Catricha unlocked her jaw. "You are no longer beneath our notice."

"I didn't kill him." Sariah's eyes grew thick with tears. She wiped at them hopelessly. "A man by the gate told me to approach the steward when I first arrived. After we left the ball room...I didn't see what happened to him at first. There was a noise like a lion's roar. I knew you were close behind, so I left him and fled. I'm a coward." She put her head in her hands, tears dripping between her fingers.

"You didn't see what happened?" Catricha took a step back from Sariah.

"I heard many footsteps coming down the hallway, like an army was after me. I took a side passage, toward the back of the house, but I never saw anyone, despite the sounds that seemed to follow me. I returned to the ballroom before anyone else noticed what was happening. I didn't see the prince fall. I didn't know what to do, to scream or cry, because I didn't know what happened to Adias."

"You heard footsteps. What did they sound like?"

"There were too many to distinguish," said Sariah. "It was a stampede, the sound of a thousand feet all moving as one."

"A thousand feet." Catricha closed her eyes and pressed a palm to her forehead. The girl's account sounded impossible.

Porfiria put her hand on Catricha's shoulder. "That is a clue, if only an oblique one."

"You're looking for what happened," said Sariah. "There may not be any way of knowing now."

"We need to ask more questions." Catricha took a deep breath. "And that's what we intend to do. Thank you, Lady Ganatz."

"You have my best wishes." Sariah sighed, eyes still tearful. "I didn't mean for anything bad to happen."

"I understand." Catricha glanced at Porfiria. "We believe you. The terrible things that happened that night could occur again, unless we can put a stop to the killer."

"You said you wanted a divorce," said Sariah. "But you're still looking for his killer?"

"My husband and Saviron may not of been good people," said Catricha. "And my husband was among my least favorite, but without knowledge of what happened, the throne may never be safe. The city could devolve into chaos."

"Anything else you can tell us might be helpful," said Porfiria. "So please, tell us everything."

"I'm afraid I already have." Sariah bowed her head. "Best luck, my ladies."

"Thanks," said Catricha. "We'll call again if we think you can help further."

They turned and left the room, walking past the guards. The men stood at attention, making no move to intercept them. Catricha and Porfiria made their way back to the carriage.

CHAPTER 20

MELISSA

She and Galocai made their way through the city and then out toward the northeastern hills.

They arrived at the house of Graef, a few miles from the edge of Alliance. Walking left them both sweaty, after more than an hour under the autumn sun. Galocai removed his mask of feathers to cool off a little. Relief filled Melissa as she approached the great house where her spear rested in the stables. She'd not gone so long without the weapon in some time.

While they walked they exchanged few words. Melissa couldn't figure how to make small talk without a little wine to reduce her nerves.

She barely believed the ease with which they'd talked and kissed after drinking just small amount at the party the previous night. Still, the attack of a shadowy beast was hardly what she wanted to associate with romantic thoughts. Who knew what Galocai thought, though? She couldn't read him like a history or book of magic.

As they climbed the hill to the walled estate, they spotted a guard atop one of the gatehouse tower. Melissa waved her arm and called out.

"We're guests returning from the city."

The guard on the tower squinted at them for a moment, then began to crank the gate open. Melissa and Galocai entered through the gateway, then proceeded into the yard. Elaine was outside, practicing her sprite wards while Niba Olfrus watched from nearby on the grass.

The shimmering, singing barriers made of threaded sprites floated in the air near each of Elaine's hands, barely connected to her fingertips. Melissa smiled at the sight and silvery sounds emanating from her friend.

"Elaine." She and Galocai drew closer. "Enjoying the show, Lady Olfrus?"

"Niba will do," said the noblewoman. "I don't require formality, from someone I consider a potential friend."

"Potential." Melissa laughed, awed by how easily Niba spoke of friendship. "I like that."

"Who is this?" Niba turned her gaze toward Galocai.

He swept his arm low in a dramatic bow. "My name is Galocai Paroth, one of the twin heirs of my family."

"Yet you came here?" Niba raised a brow. "You know you're in contention for the throne with my brother?"

"I'm also a mage." Galocai smiled. "I've come back to the city from training in secret, so I'm not yet officially in contention for the throne."

"But you're keeping your options open?" Niba shook her head. "Melissa, I didn't realize you would be so dutiful in bringing us guests like Lord Paroth."

"It is indeed her doing, in large part." Galocai shot a smile at Melissa that made the back of her neck heat up. "I need protection. My room at the River's Serpent was attacked late last night by a beast."

"A beast in the city? That can't be a common event."

"It's not unless the creature is magical in nature. This was one of those. I'm lucky Melissa was with me."

Melissa folded her arms and nodded. "Indeed. I'll vouch for his story."

Niba glanced at Elaine, who began to reel in her essences. "My brother must hear about this," she said.

Elaine finished withdrawing her wards. The group entered the great hall where Lord Graef sat across the high table from Heron. The long table at the center of the room showed remnants of breakfast, empty dishes half-cleared away by the house servants.

Melissa's stomach complained audibly. She wished she'd stopped for food before returning to House Graef.

"Melissa Dorian," said Lord Graef. "You've returned."

Melissa took a swift bow. "I only felt the need to moonlight for one evening."

Lord Graef nodded. "That is for the best. Bethanelle was impressed with you, you know."

"I'll thank her when I see her next."

"Brother." Niba walked down the long side of the table. "We have interesting news."

Heron rose from his seat, dabbing at his mouth with a napkin. He descended from the high table and approached them. "What is it sister?"

"This man." Niba motioned to Galocai. "This man claims to be an heir to House Paroth."

"That would bring two of the four highest houses together." Heron tapped his chin. "If we could simply make an alliance with the other two...I would suspect, we'd have an excellent claim to the throne. Excellent work, sister."

Niba waved both hands to Melissa. "Melissa found Lord Paroth."

"Found is the wrong word. We ran into each other at the party."

"So you negotiated." Heron smirked. "Good."

"Negotiated." Melissa smiled. "I suppose you could say that."

Elaine glanced at Melissa, raising her eyebrows. "Do you think this means we'll have more access to resources in the city?"

Melissa turned to Galocai and waited for his answer.

"I don't know for sure," he said. "There are possibilities, though."

"Go on," said Heron.

"I have many connections in the city, and I'm willing to put them at your disposal in exchange for your protection. There are mages out to find me. I suspect they're members of House Kuldettan."

"Mages that wish to kill you?" Heron whistled. "Or merely capture you?"

"I cannot say for sure. Someone sent a beast after me last night and if it wasn't for Melissa Dorian I would be either slain or in their clutches by now."

Melissa flushed and shook her head. "You're capable of guarding yourself without me."

"Nonsense. You wield a sacra form and I don't. That makes the difference."

"Sacra forms are not invincible," said Melissa. "I know that all too well."

Elaine nodded, brows pinched together.

"If we give you our protection, can you offer us more than contacts?" Heron asked.

"I'll support you as a member of one of the four families. I can't offer you full support from House Paroth without some doubt, though. I imagine my sister will protest."

"I've heard rumors Nansoela may not be interested in the crown," said Heron. "Is that the same for you?"

"I've had my thoughts. In all honesty, my family is likely too small and insular to claim the throne, despite the reputation of our powers."

"Then we are not rivals," said Heron. "And I daresay we may be friends."

"You dare." Galocai grinned. "Beware. Houses Maltos and Kuldettan will be difficult to contest. They are the strongest of the four families."

"Two is still better than four." Heron motioned toward the side of the dining room. "Better opposed by a few than by all."

"Sadly, Kuldettan has the most mages in the city. I can assist you with that. I suspect if anyone will be our opponent, it would be them."

"They may have already sent an assassin after you," Melissa said. "Can we negotiate with them."

Elaine mouthed the word. "Negotiate." She made quote-marks in the air with her fingers.

Melissa's face grew hot and she turned away from the group to hide her embarrassment.

"We don't know for certain the motives, but the threat was credible, despite its grandiosity in telling me my days were numbered. That could mean they intend to kill me, or it could have been a decoy threat."

"Something just to put you on guard?" Melissa frowned over her shoulder at Galocai.

"Yeah," he said. "I suspect the shadow lion was not completely under their control either. Who can say exactly what it was or why it said those precise words."

Elaine touched Melissa's sleeve. "I remember this from my studies. That monster you describe bore the form of a lion, but used the body of a human, correct?"

"That's it." Melissa raised chuckled. "I should have known you'd have an idea what it was."

"It could have been an essence revenant, shaped into the form of whatever creature it's controller desires. One requires a powerful swell of sprites or banes, and to control such a revenant remotely, would be difficult."

"So whoever sent out that revenant, may have been nearby?" said Melissa.

Galocai scowled. "It's possible we are dealing with a stronger foe than I guessed. Lady Filavaye Kuldettan probably does not have the kind of power to control all that essence at once as a revenant."

"The creature did not seem very tough," said Melissa. "Dangerous, yes, but it didn't hold out for long, once I turned my sacra form against it."

"It wasn't weak." Galocai snorted. "We'd best be on guard in case more of them are about."

Elaine squeezed her eyes shut and nodded. "You're correct. If it was a revenant, then defeating it once won't be enough. As long as there are bodies to be controlled nearby, that revenant could arise at any moment again."

"That's not comforting," said Melissa. "Did you and Bethanelle return without incident last night?"

"We did," said Elaine. "Lady Graef is still resting, but she should be downstairs soon."

"It's nearly noon," said Heron. "It took you some time to return."

"After last night's attack, we sheltered in the city. Forgive me for taking so long," she said.

"No need to apologize, Melissa." Heron smiled. "I'm glad you're safe, given the circumstances."

"Your concern is noted." Melissa smiled and nodded. Elaine stifled a laugh.

"It wouldn't do for any of my mages to be easily embarrassed or defeated." Heron paced back toward the head of the table. "I think you've earned more than a day's wage by bringing us a new ally." He nodded to Galocai. "Allow me to offer you my hand in friendship, sir."

Galocai held out his hand and Heron shook it. Melissa stole a scrap of bread from one of the remaining breakfast plates. She ate it quickly, relieving her hunger a little. Heron, Niba, and Galocai discussed possible approaches to the princely claim. Melissa tuned out, too tired to listen closely. Her eyes closed until Elaine shook her again.

"The meeting's over."

Melissa blinked. "Did things go well?"

"I think so. Care to spar?"

"Always," said Melissa.

Despite training, practicing their resonances and essence muscle enhancements, Melissa always held the edge in strength and speed. Thanks to her shatter sprite and her iron bane's powers, she could diminish pain and enhance her fortitude. She recovered faster than most, and training took less of a toll on her.

She and Elaine trained less intensely back in Soucot. The techniques they used in a magical sparring match took her back to where she first learned magic. Too many people she'd met there had died.

Melissa and Elaine broke off their practice as the sun rolled into afternoon. Hunger returned soon after, but they still returned to practice before long. By the time Niba called to them from the doors of the great hall, Melissa was tired and hungry once again. "It's time. You two train hard."

Melissa and Elaine made their way into the great hall for the night's feast.

CHAPTER 21

DECKARD

Dusk fell as the wind picked up. Deckard descended upon the palace at the center of Alliance. The halls were mostly vacant with only one surviving member of the princely household remaining to serve as regent.

Kizoni Duhikzo had arrived from the desert of Rosado, and her time in Alliance had been brief to this point. She married Prince Saviron just months before his death.

Deckard had questions for her.

He flew through a flock of milling birds that circled over the walls, then descended onto the balcony to enter the palace. Though there were guards, the palace nevertheless seemed more at ease than Deckard expected. The halls inside were vacant, except for a few gentle servants setting out and lighting the lamps for the evening.

Deckard made his way through the halls, approaching the chambers of the ladies who once stood beside the princes of Alliance. The spousal chambers were traditionally reserved not for the prince's brides but for the dowagers of the household. Each regent held power in their own way. Deckard wondered if Kizoni would ever wield that kind of authority.

A cluster of guards waited outside Kizoni's chambers. One of them stepped forward, his hand on the hilt of his sword. Deckard recognized his stern, ruddy features.

"Stay where you are, immortal. I am Terrel Varder, his majesty's sword, servant, and the regent's chosen protector."

"His majesty lies buried," said Deckard. "His spirit is at peace. I'm here to offer condolences to his wife."

"His wife?" Varder frowned. "You speak poorly, my lord. If Saviron still lived, perhaps I'd forgive you."

"My apologies, Sir Varder. But I have little patience to discuss etiquette with guards, no matter how high of station or what sword they carry, even one belonging to a prince." Deckard stepped forward with confidence born of centuries of dealing with noble oafs.

Varder grimaced.

"Be at ease," Deckard said. "No one is going to harm your lady tonight. I have come to ask the nature of her marriage. For this, I require privacy for the two of us, Terrel."

"Guards." Varder's face became a thunderhead. "Stand aside and let this man pass."

"Thank you," said Deckard.

"Indeed," said the man.

"You make a fine sword servant, Terrel." Deckard nodded to him. "Stay close to witness what I ask. That way there can be no doubt that I am doing Mother Mercy's work tonight."

The sword servant bowed his head. "As you wish, Lord Hadrian."

Deckard swept past the other guards and entered Kizoni's chambers. She turned as he crossed the threshold. Her maidens waited on either side of her, both of them Rosadon in heritage, like their lady.

The Rosads were of dusky complexion, but nowhere near as dark as the inhabitants of lands further to the southwest. They belonged to the desert from which they took their name and of a strong heritage all their own.

Kizoni stood in her fine black mourning gown. She'd just removed, the veil a second ago, but raised the black gossamer and set it back into place with her shawl as Deckard entered. Her eyes widened when she saw him.

"Lord Hadrian, what brings you here?"

"I have questions for you, poor lady."

"I suppose that makes sense. Mercy knows that when a prince dies, the world wonders."

"When anyone dies the world mourns." Deckard bowed his head. "And when any soul passes through the gates of remorse, every spirit must pay heed or lose part of themselves."

"You would know more of life and death than any other human yet living," said Kizoni.

"Except for one other," said Deckard.

"Cyrus Bode, yes. But no immortals can say what lies beyond, the same as those who have passed."

"Those who dream have an inkling, perhaps."

"Dreaming is not the same as death," said Kizoni. "Sleep is closer."

"Under those terms." Deckard sighed. "I have little knowledge of death."

"The Sleepless Lord," said Kizoni. "The prince of dreams, and yet you can never experience them."

"That title was given to me under unfortunate circumstances, ones I do not wish to recall."

"Neither do I relish recalling the death of my husband," said Kizoni. "But here we stand."

She put a hand to the side of her neck, touching the edge of the ruby-inlaid choker that emerged from beneath her dark blue scarf. "He gave me these two jewels as a sign of our oneness, more than the crowns we both wore."

"And the veil you now wear." Deckard stepped past Varder and Kizoni's maidens. He paced closer to the dowager regent. "I need to know, what happened and what transpired between you and Prince Saviron before he perished."

"I saw him die and watched my world evaporate." Tears beaded in her eyes. She reached toward one of her servants who offered her handkerchief. The maiden retreated as Kizoni wiped her eyes. "My Lord Hadrian, it is difficult for me to talk of such things."

"I understand."

"Do you?" said Kizoni. "I've lived thirty years and you over three-hundred. What is loss to one who has seen everything he knows disappear before his eyes?"

"The loss of one is always felt. The loss of a lifetime happens in a lifetime. If I dwell in the past, I lose myself there." Deckard looked into Kizoni's eyes.

She gazed up at him, meeting his stare. "You wouldn't go back even if you could?"

"I would not dare," said Deckard. "Living in the world one cannot change is not a fate worthy of any human, either mortal or immortal."

"No mortal nor immortal can change what has passed." Kizoni lowered her eyes, then hung her head. Dark hair fell in trails from around her veil. "My Lord, I think you understand me better than you know."

"Illuminate something for me," said Deckard. "Tell me so that all becomes clear."

"Yes, gladly, but not with ease."

"Take your time."

Kizoni handed her handkerchief back to the maiden beside her. The Rosadon maiden folded the cloth gently, then retreated with reverence.

"I married Prince Saviron at the behest of my brother, the Prince of Ettayeed," said Kizoni. "But when I arrived here in Alliance, Saviron made me feel welcome to the point where I was glad to have come. I left my home, and I left my people. He compensated perfectly for both."

"You loved him," said Deckard.

"Yes."

"Take your time."

"I have," said Kizoni. "Now, I will share what I can." Kizoni brushed away the tears from her face. She straightened her back. "I loved the prince in every way. Yet until a few weeks ago, I did not realize how fruitful my time in Alliance had been."

"How fruitful?"

Kizoni touched her stomach. "What grows within me now is Saviron's heir."

Deckard's eyebrows rose. "This is news to me. Who else have you told?"

"No one but those present," said Kizoni. "I carry the next Prince of Alliance within me. And whether he or she should someday take the throne is dependent on if she is born in the first place."

"Yes," said Deckard. "I understand."

"When Saviron fell," said Kizoni. "I did not know yet that I was with child,"

"No one else knew either, then."

"Almost no one," said Kizoni. "Only the few guards and maidens I trust, and my sword servant."

"Is that why you've closed the palace?" asked Deckard. "Why you refuse to take visitors?"

"I've said I'm still in mourning," said Kizoni. "Which provides good cover to protect my child."

"Protecting you and your child," said Deckard.

He listened carefully, inclining his head and waiting for the sprite songs within Kizoni to tell what kind of child she carried. The process of creation required much energy and labor, even more than the kind of magic wielded by mages both skilled and powerful.

"Your child is still half-formed but the time is coming, when a new soul will be born within you."

"Soul?" asked Kizoni.

"The essences Mother Mercy gives do not arrive until birth," said Deckard. "What happens before that is a mystery. Your essences feed the spirit within you."

Kizoni said, "the spirit I'm carrying is small, still weak, and fragile."

"Yes." Deckard bowed his head. "But trust me, your secret is safe."

"Thank you, immortal."

"Is there anything else you can tell me?" Any other secrets I can help you bear?"

Kizoni bowed her head. "You have my greatest secret already," she said. "But Lord Hadrian, with your protection, I'm confident my child will be safe."

CHAPTER 22

VUAL

He returned to Fulster with Osestra. The road grew dark as they approached the town walls on horseback. Better to keep their honor in clear view, and never in doubt, than to risk anything by returning later than sunset.

The two of them rode through the gates, then gave their horses to the servants for care, before joining Osestra's family for supper.

Vual was once a frequent guest here, but not since he was a boy. He remembered visiting the keepers Ruar and their mother. The three of them and had enjoyed the keepers' company once a week in those days. Despite the ten years gone by, he still recalled playing with Osestra. Her older brothers, heirs to the family, always lurked, waiting for the right moment to shove him over or mock him.

They once chased him up a tree, when he was just days older than eleven. From the branches, he'd used his essences to strike them from above. Despite his inexperience, they eventually fled, rather than climbing to catch him. Ruar and Osestra had helped him down after hours of him being trapped and afraid. He'd been too scared to come down.

Vual hated weakness and no weakness more than his own.

In the present, one of the brothers was talking.

"To Vual Kuldettan," said the older of Osestra's brothers, Tomas, raising his wineglass from the table. "For his honorable bearing, and his refusal to ever put down that damn sword."

"Have you been listening to Catricha Maltos?" asked Vual in a hiss. "You sound as if you're quoting her."

"What if I am?" Osestra's brother sneered. "She has a good sense of humor about her. Beautiful to the eye and ear. and I even read her plates occasionally." He laughed, waving a hand through the air beside the table. "Of course, who wouldn't around the city? We don't dwell in Alliance, but we bear a great weight for you who do."

"Oh?" Vual glared over his plate at Tomas. "What manner of burden do you consider yourselves to carry, keeper's son?"

"Be still," said Osestra's father, nodding to his son. "Our guest does not deserve your ridicule, Tomas. They returned before nightfall." The keeper smiled. "I take it the two of you had a fine day?"

"We found things," said Osestra. "Apparently, the steward of the city, Lord Halth, was a meticulous note keeper. He has countless sets of records at his estate. Looks like he kept track of every party there. Almost all the guest lists are still present."

"Oh?" asked Osestra's brother. "That's interesting, I suppose."

The younger of the two brothers snickered. "Vual probably doesn't know what to do with a woman. He only thinks about investigating old news."

"He didn't investigate anything too deeply," said Tomas. "Right, Osestra?"

"Don't." Osestra flushed, looking down at the table for a moment. Her eyes pinched together as frustrated tears welled in her eyes. She pushed herself from the table, then fled the room, wiping her eyes.

Vual rose, leaving the remains of his plate unfinished. He followed Osestra outside.

"My brothers are awful," said Osestra, as he emerged from the family hall. "I'm sorry for both of us."

"Don't worry," said Vual. "They're only petty because they're weak."

"My brothers have always had it in for you."

"I remember," said Vual. "Again, because they can never have the blood of Hadrian in them."

"They can't," said Osestra. "But I don't feel the same way."

Vual sighed. "Perhaps," he said. "You and I are of an age, and the two of us aren't rivals. We're..."

"Friends?" Osestra's eyes beaded with fresh tears.

"Not precisely."

She flushed deeper, her face turning dark red.

"Don't be embarrassed, please," said Vual. "I've noticed you for some time."

"You never let on that much before," said Osestra. "Not like they do."

"None of us can read minds," said Vual with a sigh. "Your heart is always a mystery to me."

"It shouldn't be," said Osestra. "We have known each other for a long time, Vual."

"That we have. But, I fear the time is coming when we can't be friends or allies any longer."

"Perhaps we can become something else instead," said Osestra softly.

"Perhaps." Vual put his hand on the small of Osestra's back. He felt her breathing and a quick pulse of life beneath the skin. "I must catch my friend's murderer first. I have to know the truth."

"Then, will you tell me how you really feel?"

"I already did," He closed his eyes, focusing on her touch. "Someday I may become Prince of Alliance, as my mother wishes. If so, you'll never inherit the keeping of Fulster. Instead, you'd inherit the city's throne."

"We truly are allies," said Osestra, wiping away lingering tears. "But don't lead me on, Vual. Surely there are more eligible women in the city?"

"Not to my eyes." Vual's face grew hot. "I've never dueled over a woman before, and I've fought duels over less."

"What do you suggest?" Osestra's breath quickened.

"We ought to finish dinner," said Vual. "Then, I'll teach your brothers a lesson."

"Don't hurt them. I don't need that."

Vual rubbed his palm along Osestra's shoulder. "I won't damage anything but their pride. If I chose to duel them, it would only be to first blood."

"A duel?" said Osestra. "With my brothers?"

"Perhaps with one of them," said Vual. "Either of those bullies will surely accept a challenge. Just watch."

"You plan to fight, is that it?" asked Osestra, frowning. “Please, don’t bring greater trouble on yourself."

"Don’t fear. I'm confident I can best either of them."

"As long as you can do so without killing or crippling, they deserve a lesson. I don't want their blood or suffering on my hands. You don't need to defend my honor."

"I do," said Vual. "I won’t let someone I care for be insulted without the pain being returned."

"You mean—"

“Yes.” Vual pressed himself against her side. "I truly mean I care for you, Osestra."

"You have an odd way of showing it.” Osestra leaned against him. "You haven't visited in weeks.”

"I don't want people to talk," said Vual. "But I’ll write more often from now on.”

"I'd like that. We need to keep our flame alive, Vual."

"We can agree that if I don't test your brothers for honor, there can be no correspondence without shame."

"Should there be shame between us? You said it yourself, we've been friends since childhood."

"We are no longer children." Vual gazed into her eyes.

She craned her neck, their gazes meeting. "I just wish time didn’t change so much."

"I know.”

“Shall we go inside?" asked Osestra. Her tears had dried on her cheeks.

"Let us," said Vual.

The two of them walked into the hall. The family was eating, their plates almost cleared of the meal.

"You return?" asked the older brother, Tomas. "Do you plan to take another lashing from us, Vual?"

"That's Lord Kuldettan, to you," said Vual. "Keeper Nim-Fulster.” He turned to the head of the family. “Your sons do you no favors.”

"They're rude," said the keeper. "But I disciplined them often in their younger days, and this is the best I could get."

"Father?" said Tomas. "I merely jest at the expense of this man. He's bitter and worthy of ridicule for his absurd carrying of that cursed blade."

"You carry a bow when you travel," said Osestra. "Don't mock him further, please."

"Why shouldn't I?" said Tomas. "Are you really so head-over for him?"

Osestra turned scarlet but then shook her head. "It isn't that."

"Which is it? You don't care for him, or that's not why you're upset?" asked Tomas.

"As you ridicule him, you ridicule me," said Osestra. "Stop attacking both of us."

"I didn't mean to hurt you, little sister."

"Of course you meant to hurt her." Vual rested his hands on his chair's back. "You're cruel."

"And you're savage," said Tomas. "I may be a hunter, but I don't go around challenging everyone by carrying a damn sword all the time." Vual touched the side of his scabbard, then raised the sheathed weapon. He held it before him, the table between him and Osestra's oldest brother. "You know why I carry the sword, don't you?"

The man scoffed. "You're a nervous man for a high noble. Everyone knows you fear lacking an answer to insults. According to Catricha Maltos, you use it as a replacement for your wits."

"Wit is worthless without anger."

"Without anger," said Osestra's other brother. "Wit is free."

Vual lowered the sword. "We can resolve our differences without violence."

"What do you fancy?" asked Tomas. "A challenge of some kind?"

"A challenge of wits," said Vual. "Have you ever heard or played any table games of strategy?"

"I have tested my skills on tables at times," said Tomas. "But I'm surely no match for someone of your training. You studied for the greatest battles. You're to be a general if there is another war with the Kism. I'd merely be a ranger."

"If," said Vual. "There is no doubt about that war coming someday."

Tomas chuckled. "Table games are for children, regardless."

"Is it fair?" Vual shook his head. "If we look for a fair struggle between the two of us, we'll be searching until your death."

The younger of the brothers laughed. "Is that a threat?"

"No," said Vual. "Merely a statement of your combined incompetence."

The younger brother rolled his eyes.

Tomas grunted. "Now who's throwing insults?"

Osestra pressed her hands together. "Both of you. Resolve this like gentlemen, please."

"Like gentlemen?" said Vual. "You know, I'm not expected back in the city until morning."

"What do you imply?" Tomas asked.

"You fancy yourself a hunter." Vual's lip curled. "Then, you won't be averse to a night hunt?"

"A night hunt in these demon-haunted woods? You're insane."

"Insane?" said Vual. "You baited me to this. If it wasn't your intention to answer my challenge, perhaps your honor and wit should sit down in silence."

Tomas glared at Vual, teeth bared. "Fine. We'll hunt on foot. Bow and arrow."

"As you wish," said Vual. "I won't use battle magic, for courtesy's sake."

"Whoever shall return with the greatest beast," said Tomas, "shall be the winner of this hunt."

"As you wish. You have named your own terms of defeat."

Osestra glanced at Vual. "Do you mean to go into the glades tonight?" she said. "Surely this can wait for another day?"

"No," said Tomas. "We'll take him tonight. I'll teach you through the hunt that you are not my better. I choose my younger brother as my partner."

"I choose your sister as mine," said Vual. "You country folk all know your way around arrows, after all."

"It shall be settled." Tomas ground his teeth together. "Be careful in the dark, Lord Kuldettan."

CHAPTER 23

VUAL

He and Osestra made their way into the glades west of Fulster's walls. They moved lightly, both of them trained in the dark. Still, he could see little without his sprites out. They focused on their feet to avoid snapping any twigs and making sound.

Osestra's brothers must be nearby, but the forest was still quiet except for the song of the night birds, and the occasional buzz of insects. All was covered by the night.

The two of them crept silently through the forest, looking for prey. The deer Vual sensed could be heard only by their magic, but Vual heard their heart songs. Animal songs were not as balanced as those of humans, because Mother Mercy did not see to them at birth.

Where humans were ushered into the world by the grace of her divine majesty, the animals flourished or faded on their own. Only the beasts in the Imperial Gardens of the Chos Valley were known to demonstrate such blessings.

Osestra held a bow in one hand, and carried an extra quiver for Vual, making three quivers between them. He hoped they wouldn't need so many arrows.

Vual watched quietly as moonlight played on the horns of a large buck in a clearing ahead.

The buck moved in a subtle bow, quieter than Vual expected of a deer of such size. He grazed in the center of the small clearing. Thickets surrounded the clearing, bending the path of other animals around them. The deer stood alone, graceful and powerful.

The prey here was different than west of the city. The woods were less full, and the trees sparser, and the animals less influenced by demonic forces.

He signaled to Osestra with one of his sprites. The essence returned to him in an instant, but made no sound or light after blinking once in front of her.

Vual's signal was for her to stay where she stood. He nocked an arrow to his bow. The buck was just twenty spans away. They wouldn't get much closer without startling the animal.

Shadows floated under the moon, birds on the wing. A larger shadow sliced through the night. The sound of banes played from above.

"Never mind." Vual murmured.

He loosed an arrow at the buck. Tracking the heart song with his ears, Vual skewered the beast in a fatal spot. The mighty deer threw back his antlered head and then fell to the ground. The beast made no further sounds as life ebbed away.

A perfect shot.

Vual lowered the bow. He and Osestra crept toward the deer. On the other side of the clearing, came the sound of footsteps. Osestra's brothers entered the clearing, looking at the fallen buck with terrified eyes.

"What did you do?" asked Tomas. "Osestra, you should know better."

"What's wrong?" said Vual. "Your defeat is certain, but besides that, I see no reason for you to fear."

"No," said the brother. "That's not the point. Do you not hear it?"

Vual shrugged. "Hear what? You fools would fear your own shadows in this dark night."

"It's not our shadows." Tomas' teeth chattered. "The demons visit these woods."

"This deer could have been demon spawn?" said Vual. "I've not heard of one ranging so far south."

"We shouldn't have angered a greater spawn. That buck is one of their children."

"That explains the size." Vual grimaced at the fallen deer. "So this is a demon spawn?"

Osestra took a deep breath. "Brothers, get out of here. Go back to the the town."

"I'd agree if I thought my legs could get me there before the mother of that deer catches us."

"How dangerous can a demon spawn be?" said Vual. "I sense no threat nearby."

"She's a doe, the scouts say," said the younger brother. "She lacks antlers but she has other ways of beguiling or destroying us."

"Beguiling?" Vual snorted. "I'd heard you people south of the city tend to view animals differently than we do."

"That's not funny," said Osestra. "Not now."

Tomas nodded. "We need to band together, Kuldettan. You win the challenge. I give up."

"Good. I accept your surrender," said Vual. "Now run along."

"You're the one who brought us out here," said the younger brother. "You have to save us."

"I don't have to do anything, you insulting fool. I have no obligation to protect you, only myself and Osestra."

"Vual," said Osestra. "Please, help my brothers."

He closed his eyes for a second. "Very well." He turned his back on the brothers. "Follow me and keep your eyes open. It's a good mile back to the town. A shadow passed overhead earlier. Have you any idea what it was?"

"It could have been a demon spawn?" said Osestra.

"It sounded like a heart full of banes." Vual nodded. "That means there could be more danger in this place than even a spawn. An actual demon may lurk here."

"An actual demon?" said the brother. "We'd be doomed."

"Not yet." Vual hefted the heavy deer carcass onto his back and started to walk.

They followed the way Vual and Osestra had to the main road. When they arrived the road was lit by a halo of red-glowing sprites that burned, drawing all four of their eyes toward the great form that blocked the path home. She appeared as a deer, even larger than the buck on Vual's back. He lowered the carcass to the dirt of the road.

The demon spawn's face did not resemble a deer's, but instead that of a woman with flowing black hair on either side that moved in the breeze.

"How dare you," said the beast in a sweet, dangerous voice. "How dare you take my children?"

"That thing is not right." Vual shook with fear and fury.

"Thing?" Hissed the beast. "You would kill us like we are not intelligent, like we are not human."

"From your essence I'd bet you're not a demon." Vual clenched his teeth. "But you definitely aren't human."

"You dare—?"

The beast roared as she charged them, abandoning all vestiges of humanity. Her face contorted into a horrible glare. The demon deer raced toward the hunters.

Vual stepped forward, his hand on the hilt of his relic sword, and his bow slung over his shoulder. Osestra glanced at him. He hoped she couldn't see him shake in the dark. The beast before them, half-demon and half-deer, reared up, hooves in the air. Osestra's brothers cried in fear.

"Do you think that pathetic weapon will keep me from avenging my child's death?" hissed the beast.

"It's possible," said Vual.

The monstrous creature kicked the air, then dropped to all-fours and raced toward them. She barreled toward Vual, head forward and teeth gnashing. Those teeth glimmered with a metallic sheen. The fury of her charge gave her a back and forth motion. He swiped out with his blade. The sword sliced through the air over the deer's head, missing the mark.

The deer-beast's fangs sank into his shoulder. With the human-like face close to his, he felt his skin break. Blood flowed hot from his wound.

Osestra yelled and knocked an arrow to shoot. Lashing hooves pounded the ground around them as Vual lost his footing, and the deer carried him forward with it. He shook himself and shuddered in the monster's bloody jaws.

Vual brought his sword up and pierced the demon-deer. He slashed again but the monstrous demon-spawn didn't react. The blade cut and cut but those teeth sank deeper and deeper into his shoulder. Vual's sword-arm weakened as the muscle tore in places.

The deer hurled Vual to the ground, then turned her bloodied face toward Osestra and her brothers. The three of them had all fitted arrows, but none of them would have a chance to shoot before the creature closed with them. Vual lurched to his feet. As he staggered forward, a shadow descended from the trees above.

The robed form of Deckard Hadrian landed directly on the demon deer's back. Bright sprite strings impaled the beast through each leg, pinning her to the forest floor.

Deckard Hadrian slammed the demon spawn to the ground. The monster lurched around to look at him, but in the next second, he had drawn a blade. His sword carved into the beast's neck. The head flew free and the demon spawn's struggles stilled.

Deckard stepped over the fallen monster. He glanced at Osestra and her brothers, then turned to Vual. "You looked as though you were having difficulty," he said. "It's a good thing I heard the screams."

Vual grimaced, pressing his hand to his wound to stop the blood flow. "I'm glad you made it, ancestor."

"So am I," said Deckard. "But I'm afraid this was a detour, I'll see you safely back to Fulster."

"Then what?" asked Vual.

"Then I'll take you back to Alliance," he said. "You have strayed far today, Vual."

"Did my mother put you up to this?" asked Vual through clenched teeth. "If so, I don't need the help."

"No," said Deckard. "I'm here on my own mission."

Vual gritted his teeth. "I'll be fine without your assistance."

Deckard Hadrian shook his head. "I have questions only you can answer."

"I'll answer them all," said Vual. "Right here."

"I won't force you to go back to the city tonight," said Deckard. "But you're just a boy, so be more careful."

Tomas snickered. Deckard glared at him at the same time as Vual.

"All of you should heed my advice."

"Thank you," said Osestra. "Immortal."

"It's nothing. I'm glad I was able to protect you all."

"You saved us," said Osestra. "I won't forget that."

"See that you return safely to the village," said Deckard. "There are probably other demon spawn out in the woods tonight."

"Can you hear them?" asked Vual.

"Some. But I'm sure there are more." Deckard motioned the four young nobles back toward Fulster.

CHAPTER 24

CATRICHA

She waited a day while Porfiria checked through the records of the party for other possible suspects. When the two of them met up again one question joined them. Which guard had directed Sariah to meet Adias?

We might be grasping at straws, Catricha thought, *but at least we're reaching for something.*

The library on the north side of Alliance, east of the river, had fallen far from what it had once been. Stone walls remained overgrown with vines despite the gathering cold. Birds called to each other from their roosts in the abandoned belfry. The books inside, however, were better preserved than the building.

The path of the carriage took Porfiria and Catricha around the circle at the front of the library and to the smaller entrance at the back. Though the library here contained older books than those in the main branch, the indication over the doorway where they stopped the carriage told her of how much older.

The writing above the door was not imperial script, but in pre-imperial. The writing belonged to the ancient rulers of Tancuon. They had been conquered by Jadik and their empires lay fallen. Now, a thousand years or more later, the Empire of Jadiketz was scattered. Yet, Mother Mercy herself held sway over the land.

Catricha said a small blessing to mercy and then climbed from the carriage. Pre-imperial script was not only odd to look at, but tended toward the occult and strange in meaning. Catricha couldn't make light of such things in writing or in front of a crowd. When the time came to test her belief in the world beyond humanity, she found herself more frightened than she preferred to admit.

The door creaked open as they approached. Porfiria nodded to the slender young librarian as he led them in. "Did you find the book?"

"Did you ever doubt me?" The young man produced a thick book with a worn black cover from one side of the short library desks by the door. "It's one of the oldest volumes in this entire place."

"What is it about?" asked Catricha.

"Lady Maltos," said the librarian. "This book details the shadow's reign over the city."

"The shadow's reign?" said Porfiria. "I thought that was just a subtitle."

"It is." The young man grinned. "I like the subtitle better. The main title is of course, *The Prince of Jasguara*."

"Jasguara?" said Catricha. "That's what Alliance used to be called, right?"

"One of its names." Porfiria nodded. "Before Jadik and Zidon arrived."

"Indeed. Before they toppled the former rulers of the land," said the librarian in a hushed voice. "But no one's come looking for that volume in some time."

Catricha narrowed her eyes at the book. "I'm surprised. If anyone else knew what happened to the steward and the prince, I think more would have heir eyes on it."

"What do you mean?" said librarian.

"Never mind," said Porfiria. "Here's your payment." She handed a pouch of silver coins to the librarian.

"Thank you, my lady." He took the silver and handed Porfiria the book.

* * *

A day later, Porfiria sent a letter to Catricha at her parents' house.

The letter read in the flowing script Porfiria used, a simple request, for Catricha to find Sion Arver and meet Porfiria by the tombs.

The way through the city was cold and damp with fresh rain as Catricha walked the path, dressed down from her elegant evening clothes to a pair of trousers and an unassuming white tunic. In daylight, there was no point in her attempting stealth in Alliance.

She was glad not to go anywhere near the Kuldettan-controlled portion of town. Vual could be there. And Ruar, almost as bad, because he refused to even write Catricha in response to her letters.

"I will solve that problem later." Catricha took a deep breath, and then knocked on the door of the small watch-house where Sion was staying. One of the watchmen who lived there let her in.

She made her way past the table of guards gambling for a few bronze coins and bits of produce. Up the stairs and to the right, she found Sion by the window. He was gazing out at the city streets.

The city itself looked bleak from this angle, given the weather. Gray clouds hung thick and low. The towers seem to spear the sky, piercing but not drawing the rain forth, though another torrent looked soon to come.

"I was wondering when I'd see you again, my lady." Sion bowed his head. "After the party."

"Don't feel bad for what happened that night," said Catricha. "I don't blame you."

"Do you blame Lady Paroth?" said Sion. "I heard she was the one who put you up to wearing that dress."

"I put on the dress of my own free will. I don't blame Nansoela for suggesting it."

"Lady Amburen wrote me." Sion nodded. "She told me to wait here until you arrived."

"Here I am," said Catricha with a smile. "Do you want to stand here admiring this grim city for another few hours or do you want to go meet her?"

* * *

Catricha and Sion met Porfiria at a small marketplace near her home. The three of them gathered under an awning where two shops met. The dark clouds gathered overhead, heavy with rain. Catricha glimpsed the first drops in the distance over the city where the sky opened. She frowned at a knot of shadows in the burgeoning sky.

"Why did you call us, Lady Amburen?" asked Sion.

"I found something in that library book," said Porfiria. "I realized it was about the great families of the city."

Catricha arched her eyebrows. "Does that include House Maltos?"

"I don't know," said Porfiria. "But House Kuldettan, definitely."

"Kuldettan?" Sion frowned.

Porfiria nodded. "Their blood owes its origin to a time before the Empire of Jadiketz."

"Before Jadik?" said Catricha. "But I thought they were descended from Deckard Hadrian?"

"One side of them is," said Porfiria. "The other side was descended from Laban Okogael, who once ruled Alliance as the city's immortal king."

Catricha folded her arms. "I've never heard of Laban."

"He ruled the city before it was called Alliance, so back when it was Jasguara. But he disappeared. A shadow reigned over the city when Jadik arrived. The shadow was some kind of beast, a monstrous force of pure darkness that dominated the land around Jasguara from the central palace."

"The palace is the same," said Catricha. "That much is common knowledge."

"While parts of the palace were damaged in the battle with Zidon, and later replaced," said Porfiria, "What you say is true. The palace is perhaps the oldest building left in the city. It is far older than the conquest."

"What does this mean?" Catricha stared at her friend. "A shadow resembles what killed Prince Saviron and Adias."

"I thought the same thing, Cat." Porfiria met Catricha's eyes. "I'm afraid because this monster could be older and more powerful even than Deckard Hadrian."

CHAPTER 25

MELISSA

A week after she and Elaine arrived in Alliance, Melissa joined Heron to go to the palace in the city to put forth his proposal of exchanging power.

Heron planned to pledge his claim for the throne of Alliance. Despite being an outsider, based on the reading, Melissa had done in the interim, his goal could be attainable, given that the prince's family was all-but gone.

With no one but the dowager regent to bear the family name, Prince Saviron Davaltz's line had ended. His household would have to be replaced by another and the four families of Alliance might actually be among the least likely to win the contest, historically speaking. The princely family had never before been replaced in Alliance, but other princedoms set the precedent.

Melissa had grown used to reading coded text in magical tomes. History proved easier on her eyes and mind.

The family of Davaltz had invaded with Jadik, moving north. In the second generation of conquest, the forces of mercy reached and invaded what was now Alliance.

The plains around the city became a fertile breadbasket for the growing empire. The young nations of the lands of mercy had banded together around Alliance and the spread of power from that center had allowed them to take the Chos Valley.

With the addition of Well Country and the Chos Valley to the Empire, Alliance became the second highest seat of power after the city of Empire in the valley.

The most interesting part of Melissa's recent studies had been a note on the Rosado presence in the city. The nations of the desert always sent envoys to Alliance. Still, the marriage of a prince's daughter from the city of Ettayeed to Saviron of Alliance had been a major advancement in their relationship.

Whoever might become the new prince could maintain some kind of additional bond with the cities in the desert if he married the dowager regent.

The party consisted of Melissa, Elaine, Heron, Bethanelle Graef, and Bethanelle's father. The Lord Graef kept to himself, despite his higher status in the party. He rode in the rear, with a handful of his personal guards. The house guards of Graef appeared to be competent warriors, but rumor suggested they were even more skilled at hunting. The ravine near the Graef estate must be dangerous indeed, heavily pocked with world wells, both obvious and hidden.

Melissa shuddered as she recalled the world well from her time in Soucot. Demons could rise from unprotected wells when the wards were down. Such monsters emerged to stalk the surface. Even those that were banished to the depths by Mother Mercy always scrabbled for light. Such beings made for the most dangerous foes imaginable.

She wondered if Deckard Hadrian might have flown off somewhere. The echoes of his presence in Alliance faded by the day. *Besides, it's not like the city is his home.*

Home. Melissa considered the possibility her parents might be close as they neared the palace. If the Dorians were still in Alliance, Melissa needed to find them as soon as possible. Lord Graef certainly didn't seem eager to give her his help, at least, not while she stayed so close. Her position as a bodyguard and mage limited her time.

She and Heron's party approached the palace gates. She wished Galocai had come with them, but he'd gone to visit some other part of Alliance. His need for further study in his magical arts didn't drive him to train with Elaine and Melissa. Instead, he'd been worlds away in some book the Graef's lent him, staying in a manor room they'd offered for his stay.

A fellow nobleman could be offered a suite where a commoner mage would be offered a hay bale in the stable. Melissa emerged from her reverie.

Heron called to the guard at the gate. "I am Heron Olfrus, here to see the dowager regent."

The guard answered with a hand-to-heart salute, and then started to crank open the gate.

The six guests rode through, followed by two of Lord Graef's trailing bodyguards.

They rode through the yard of the palace into the ringed central garden. There, they dismounted. Valets approached to take the horses to the stables.

The party climbed the long stairs to the inner doors, which stood open despite the increasing cold. Guards waited along the arched walls. The palace, which Melissa had expected to see teeming with petitioners, courtiers, and other hangers-on was all but vacant. Evidently, with no prince or steward, the palace served less purpose.

The situation in the city could grow dire if what remained of the law and government failed.

No one to govern, Melissa thought. No one managed the city's watch apart from the four families. The loss of the prince hit the city harder than she'd have thought before her reading.

They approached the throne room. However, despite the table that sat in the middle of the chamber, the same kind of table that lay in the great hall of the cities of the south, with its ring-shape allowing it to accommodate every prince and governor in the lands of mercy. The throne stood empty.

Probably for the best.

If there had been someone presumptuous on the throne at that moment, Heron's challenge for the seat would be even more difficult.

Instead, they found Kizoni Duhikzo sitting at the ring table. She occupied the place of the Prince of Ettayeed. The more than thirty princedom's and governances of mercy made the table wide and circular. There were formal places for three immortals as well. At least one place would always be empty.

Melissa didn't know the last time all the dignitaries of Tancuon had gathered in one place.

The party approached Kizoni and her two nearest bodyguards. More guards stretched out in a loose column behind them. Kizoni held up a hand to stop them.

"Greetings, Lord Olfrus," she said. "What manner of visit is this?"

"I've come to pledge my claim to the throne," said Heron. "I do not wish to be forward, but with the backing of the family of Graef, I have come to offer my assistance in securing the city's safety."

"So you already have the backing of one of the four families?" Kizoni examined her elegantly manicured fingernails. "Impressive, for only arriving days ago."

"It's been nearly six weeks since the prince's passing." Heron bowed his head. "Another pinnacle day approaches."

"It does," said Kizoni. "But Lord Olfrus, are you not aware of the customs of the city?"

"What custom am I forgetting?" asked Heron.

"The laws of stewardship." Kizoni's eyes betrayed no emotion, flat and neither warm nor cold. "You see, my husband's line has not ended yet."

"You have his name." Heron's brows edged together, but then smoothed. "You will stand as regent of Alliance?"

"That's correct," said Kizoni. "Until the name leaves me, and I don't intend to abandon it, I will govern this city."

"Then why not accept petitioners?" asked Heron. "Do you act out of respect for the fallen prince?"

"Yes. My husband and his steward both require the proper mourning before any further business is done in the palace."

"Forgive my inappropriate gesture, then," said Heron. "But it may be easier to manage the city with two seats. Someone must still assume the throne. Order is maintained by tradition."

"By tradition?" said Kizoni. "I hold the throne. Out of respect for my deceased husband, I sit here instead of in his seat, but it would be my right to take that position if I so desired."

Heron swept his arm in and bowed his head low. "I respect the traditions of Alliance."

"Do you?" Kizoni sniffed. "It seems to me you presume the city will bend to you before it bends to me."

Heron's head remained low. "Not at all," he said. "I assure you, I never intended to usurp. I came to help restore order."

"You see disorder?" Kizoni sighed. "Of course, the sleepless march in the streets. There are always demons in the ravine and the forests, but what would you do about those? My husband acted to appease the sleepless, but they remain. I'm at ease, Lord Olfrus. And the demons in the ravine...they won't respond to any prince of mortal lifespan."

"If a prince cannot solve the problems of the city, perhaps the city does indeed not need a Prince," said Heron. "And there are other ways I can be of service."

"I'll consider what to do with you," said Kizoni. "Heron Olfrus, take your allies and leave us."

Heron looked ready to sputter as he raised his head. Melissa frowned as he turned his back to lead the way out of the room. She disliked the challenge Kizoni presented, but enjoyed the manner of the dowager regent. Something about her reminded Melissa of Governor Tandace Lokoth, who'd employed Melissa in Lowenrane. The firm hand on power may have surprised Heron, but it didn't shock Melissa.

She followed Heron and the others from the hall, shooting a small smile over her shoulder at Kizoni.

The dowager regent nodded back, her expression stern, just before Melissa turned away.

CHAPTER 26

MELISSA

After leaving the palace, Melissa went to meet Galocai by the river's edge. As he emerged from the watch house on the riverside, Melissa spotted him from a rise in the street.

She waved to him and he returned the gesture.

He didn't wear the mask of feathers that day. Instead, his handsome pale features remained open and expressive. Melissa felt the flutter in her heart, wondering if indeed it had been just drink that night a week ago, after Nansoela's party.

She walked briskly to meet him.

"How was your visit to the palace?" he asked.

"The dowager regent appears intransigent to Heron's request," said Melissa. "I mean, Lord Olfrus's request."

"You're so familiar with him. I suppose you've had plenty of time to rub shoulders with powerful people."

"I've been blessed." Melissa shrugged. "Did you find anything about your attacker?"

"The boy is here but it's not him. The beast captured him earlier that evening and he remembers nothing of the attack. I suspect the magic that took him drove him to strike at us. The shadow beast couldn't have held the source of it's power in itself. Those essences weren't strong enough to invest with independence."

“Essences can be powerful without being obvious.” Melissa chewed her lip. "Especially when truly powerful they can cloak their songs to hide their true identities."

"Of course," said Galocai. “Deception is a key part of all conflict.”

"We don't know who sent the beast," said Melissa. “Whoever attacked, could be strong enough to cause us trouble at once, even me, with my iron bane."

"You have the special power in your heart.” Galocai breathed a sigh. "I only wish I carried such a gift.”

"You have your gifts.” Melissa smiled at him.

"Oh?" said Galocai with a smirk. "I wasn't aware."

"I detected at least one.”

Galocai laughed, then lowered his voice. “Don’t be alarmed, but I think you were followed."

"Followed?" Melissa frowned.

Galocai nodded. "He's behind you and wearing a palace guard uniform."

“A palace guard?" said Melissa. "Perhaps a messenger?" She turned.

Galocai stifled a dismayed gasp, then shook his head. "You're too honest.”

Melissa laughed at him. “Perhaps. Guard.” She waved to the man who’d followed her. "What is your business with me?"

The guardsman wore royal blue Alliance livery and carried a sword at his side. He stepped out of the crowd and bowed his head to Melissa. "Lady Dorian," he said. "My mistress wishes to speak with you."

"The dowager regent?" she asked.

He nodded. "Please, you and your fellow should follow me."

Melissa glanced at Galocai. "What do you say to that?"

"I’d rather dine out then visit the palace.” Galocai smirked. "But I'll go with you."

"I appreciate it."

They followed the guard toward the palace.

* * *

At the palace for a second time in one day, Melissa was ushered into a side chamber where Kizoni waited, sitting upon a plush red divan. The elegant couches in the room spoke of rest, of a place where princes relaxed with family and close allies.

"Sit." Kizoni's tone was commanding. "Just because I'm now a dowager, doesn't mean I don't have the authority of a prince's seat."

"As you like." Melissa took a place on one of the soft sofas before Kizoni, across a small table. She reclined slightly on the couch, but not so much as to seem overly-familiar. She'd learned a little about etiquette in the south of Lowenraine. Galocai sat beside her.

"You weren't with Lord Ofrus before." Kizoni waved a hand at him. "Who are you?"

"My name is Galocai," he said. "I'm of House Paroth, though I'd rather not spread that around."

Kizoni nodded. "You couldn't conceal the facts if you tried. You look like your sister."

Galocai sighed. "Nansoela is terribly famous in Alliance."

"Yes." Kizoni's nose wrinkled with a small frown. "She threw a party the night of my husband's funeral."

"Forgiveness," said Galocai. "I was there. We both were, though, neither of us meant an affront by it."

"Don't take my words that way but my husband's memory demands I meet you. You both appeared as rogues on return to the city. Yet..." She turned to Melissa. "...you are someone of note in the Dorian family. True?"

"Is that how your man identified me, as Lady Dorian?" asked Melissa. "Wrong on one count. I'm no lady."

"Of course," said Kizoni. "Our mistake."

Melissa nodded, more steadily than she expected.

Kizoni motioned for them to relax. "I don't intend to confront either of you about wrongdoing. I was intrigued by your attention earlier. What are you called?"

"Melissa is my name," said Melissa. "I only belong to the Dorian family by chance. I'm here looking for my parents."

"They may be difficult to find if they are indeed the heads of the Dorian family."

"They've been here?" asked Melissa. "Can you tell me where their offices are? Their home?"

"I'm only a recent arrival here. I know little of the merchants, though they respect the throne. Your father approached the throne with a request a few weeks before the party that ended my husband's life."

"What request?" asked Melissa, heart racing.

"He wanted safe passage for when he left Alliance," said Kizoni. "I don't know if he's gone yet, or where he planned to go."

"I can't thank you enough." Melissa bowed her head. "I was not sure I'd catch them here."

"If you plan to catch someone you care for, I recommend you don't do so by surprise."

"I know my family," said Melissa, unsure of the truth in those words.

Kizoni steepled her fingers and leaned forward. Her black gown and tresses blended into shadows around her bare shoulders. "I have need of your help. You are both mages, are you not?"

"We are." Melissa leaned into the cushions of her seat. "I mastered my sacra form only recently."

"And I have yet to master one at all," said Galocai.

"I need your help. The Cult of the Sleepless is growing restless, more than ever before since the prince's murder."

"The sleepless," said Melissa. "We saw them a few nights ago."

"As pinnacle day approaches they become more bold. Every week that builds toward the center of the month sees more sleepless in the streets." Kizoni tented her fingers, frowning. "Soon they could strike at their enemies."

"Enemies?" said Melissa. "Are they truly opponents of the throne?"

"I do not understand their motives," said Kizoni. "For men and women who seek to never sleep, they encounter the authorities less than you might guess. Their potential prey concerns me. The sleepless were always at odds with my husband and his steward. There must be a way to figure out what they want and not just wait until they move. They sometimes raid the storehouses because they are lacking in funds. As days grow colder that may increase."

"Do they need money to spread the word of their movements?" said Melissa. "If not, they seem more like brigands than a cult."

"A cult of brigands is more how I consider them," said Kizoni.

Melissa couldn't help a smile at the regent's wordplay.

"Yet the guards don't do anything to stop them," said Galocai. "Why?"

"There are too many sleepless and they travel only by night. Without a means to identify them in the morning, we're locked from investigating effectively."

"So they lead ordinary lives by day? Yet they resist sleep by night?" Melissa scowled. "It's like they seek to emulate Deckard Hadrian."

"Not at all." Kizoni sat back. "I see the cult as destructive. They may cause us all great harm."

"What can we mages do to stop them that a normal person can't?" asked Galocai.

"Because of your magic," said Kizoni, "you could uncover their hiding places. I neglected one detail before. Not all of them return home by daylight. Their leaders never seem to rest, and have no residences of their own. Their head is hidden, a mysterious cabal. If you can find these leaders and their hiding places, I'd be much obliged to assist in whatever way I can with your personal goals."

"I'll see what I can do." Melissa glanced at Galocai. "We will, right?"

He smiled. "How can I refuse the regent of my city?"

"Stay safe," said Kizoni. "And find out what you may."

"We will do the best we can." Melissa bowed again.

"You have my thanks. Now go, quickly, before others notice you've been here. The sleepless are watching, and could target you if they think you're working with me."

"Are you worried for your own safety?" asked Melissa. "My fellow mage, Elaine, might be able to assist you with defense if you let Heron Olfrus and his family dwell within the palace for a time."

"You are loyal to Olfrus. Disappointing."

"He's paid Elaine and me."

Kizoni folded her arms. "You are a mercenary. I suppose money still has power over you."

"After fashion," said Melissa. "I was a caravan guard until recently."

"A strange life you've lead," said Kizoni. "A mage from a caravan guard. I think you will benefit from what you find among the sleepless. I think you will benefit as much as I."

“Hopefully.” Melissa stood. "Thank you for your offer. I will do what I can't find out where the sleepless leaders rest by daylight."

CHAPTER 27

CATRICHA

She met her parents in the manor's dining room. Enrin and Hyla had made fine parents, both to Catricha and her young siblings. Recently, the two of them proved less insightful than Catricha hoped they would.

"Where have you been?" asked her mother.

"I went to the Hill of Forges again," said Catricha. "The new plates are still selling."

"I heard you're already printing more." Hyla smiled.

"Yes," said Catricha. "Thank you, for noticing."

"Of course, I noticed." Mother clucked, but her smile remained.

She hoped Hyla didn't notice that Catricha had only told a half-truth. The half that was a lie had been remained unspoken. Catricha went to the hill forges that day to investigated the old part of the city, the part of Alliance still standing once been Jasguara.

You don't know me, she thought. "Mother," she said aloud. "I'm tired, and wish to write before I rest."

"Go on." Hyla's smile broadened. "You work harder than the rest of us put together."

"Not true." Catricha grinned. "You only see when I'm busy."

Enrin laughed. "I see you're busy more often than not."

"We should all be so occupied," said Hyla. "Go to your pages, Catricha."

She climbed the stairs to her chambers, where she rolled out a scroll and began to write down notes for what she remembered from her trip that day into the old part of the city.

The Hill of Forges had been a quiet part of Jasguara, according to Porfiria's text, but even there, in the depths, the shadow lurked before Jadik arrived.

Catricha unfolded her notes, copied from the entrance to the catacombs near the Hill of Forges, and then began to translate the words. The ancient language of pre-imperial Tancuon, was mostly decipherable, though she'd not say it was easily understood.

Her knowledge of poetry told her where some words were leading. The meanings and sounds of many were similar to more current language. Languages drifted over time. Catricha wondered if the symbols and glyphs on the face of the stone at the entrance to the tombs had been carved in a similar way at a similar time.

She translated for an hour as the sun began to set. She rose, yawning, and went to the door, wearing the same clothes as for her earlier outing. Her parents might be annoyed if she arrived at dinner without changing, she went to the dresser and quickly put on a bright blue shawl and changed her skirt.

She descended the staircase, the shawl and scarf combination warm around her neck for comfort as the air grew colder. Within the next week, the first snow might fall.

Catricha reached the bottom of the staircase and peered out into the yard, noting the barren branches on the ancient oaks within the walls, the fallen leaves long ago swept away by household servants.

Catricha noticed the change of seasons more acutely this year, and sighed. The last summer of ordinariness had slipped away. Her life, as it remained, gazed into her.

She walked to the dining room and took her places between her father at the head of the table and her younger brothers on one side. They had guests that night, though, Catricha hardly notice them. Both were foreign dignitaries from the Clan of Geteren. She picked at her food, mulling over the words she'd been working on earlier.

Whatever occupied the city back before Jadik arrived had come from underground.

Spirits from underground, she thought, *and our city is not any wiser.* Could they be demons? The wells that existed in the ravine and beyond led into the pits of the world. From them, the demonic foes of Mother Mercy sometimes escaped into the mortal world.

World wells were common knowledge among the nobility, but Catricha wondered if demons really were loose in Alliance. Most of the worlds wells in the north of Tancuon were known and mapped. Still, the ancient paths of Alliance's underground beckoned to her mind.

"I notice your daughter is distracted," said the voice of a man from across the table.

"I'm not distracted," said Catricha reflexively. "I merely have my own thoughts."

"As if we don't," said the man softly.

"Not at all." Catricha looked from her plate and found herself across the table from a handsome dominion knight from the Chos Valley, Ysaac Frost, one of the group sent by the Geteren Clan to Alliance. His dark tunic set off his pale skin and light eyes.

"Excuse me, Sir Frost. "I forget my manners at times."

"I'm led to believe you've never had them," said the man.

"Nonsense," said Catricha. "I just don't take them out often."

"It seems so," said Ysaac.

Enrin glowered down the table at Catricha, but she glimpsed a hint of a smile behind his grim expression.

"I ask you to forgive my daughter," Hyla said. "She is tired from her day at the Hill of Forges."

"You're a poet," said the older guest in a parson's black who sat beside Ysaac. "Is that true?"

"I consider myself a poet," said Catricha. "Others are not always so generous."

"Because of your discipline," said the man in black. "You see, I heard you encountered Deckard Hadrian recently. He appears to have some appreciation for you and your work."

"Hardly," said Catricha. "Lord Hadrian only acted to protect me. He is kind, but I wouldn't say he noticed me in any way."

That's just another lie I keep telling.

Catricha thought better than to suggest her true conversation with Deckard and the nature of the magic she held within her. The man in black reverberated with the loud inner-song of a mage. Catricha frowned at her plate. "I don't believe I caught your name, parson?"

"My name is Virgil Silas Dane."

"Virgil," said Catricha, "It's good to make your acquaintance. But I'm afraid I don't know much about Deckard Hadrian, or any other immortals for that matter."

"I'd be shocked if you knew as much as I," said Virgil. "I hardly look for insight in a place like this. Especially not along those lines."

"I don't know about that, Parson Dane," said Ysaac. "I'd suspect a house that produces poets and children who speak as well as these, might be of more interest to you, with all due respect."

"I wouldn't rule out a possible change of opinion," said Virgil.

"So you could change your mind?" said Catricha. "Isn't that the case with all men?"

"I don't know what you mean," Virgil said.

"I mean." Catricha stifled a yawn. "All men, no matter how devout have their own changeability. No offense, but you seem irritable for someone who's been enjoying our company."

The parson smirked. "Enjoying?"

"That might be a strong word," said Catricha. "Tolerating?"

"Your family is pleasant enough," said Virgil. "When you are quiet."

"If you can only enjoy company when they're quiet," said Catricha, "perhaps you're better off lecturing than having a conversation."

Virgil shrugged.

Catricha grinned. "After all, I suppose one becomes a parson to hear oneself speak."

"Catricha!" said Hyla. "Manners."

"Forgive me. I merely detected a level of pomposity that disagreed with me."

"I think you'll find more of the world will disagree with you the more you talk like you did just now." Virgil picked up his napkin. "Thank you for dinner, Lord Maltos."

Enrin took a deep breath. "You're more than welcome, Parson Dane."

"My knight and I must be going now," said Virgil. "Come, Sir Frost."

"As you wish, parson." Ysaac put down his table knife with clink on his plate.

The two men rose in the table, and then swept from the dining room.

Catricha's mind immediately went back to her translations.

If the Kuldettan's are under threat, or perpetrating the deeds of evil in the city...If they have any ties to the underground and to the old city of Jasguara, I have to warn Ruar.

"Please excuse me, father." She stood.

Catricha went up the stairs to her room, and wrote a letter.

The next morning, Catricha took the letter from the house, folded in the small envelope, that bore no seal from her household, but was shut with plain wax. She found a messenger who operated without allegiance to any household, and then sent the letter to Ruar.

* * *

Catricha didn't have to wait long. Ruar's letter came that afternoon, carried by the same messenger she'd sent with hers. The gentle servants of House Maltos admitted the woman. She handed Catricha the letter.

Catricha went upstairs immediately, rolled onto her bed, and broke the seal.

Rain began to fall outside the window as Catricha lit a lamp and began to read.

Ruar told her through several lines of poetry that he was grateful for her reaching out. He'd noticed his brother acting strangely, racing all over the the city and its environs, searching for something that Vual would never fully disclose to Ruar.

His mother was constantly upset and spoke frequently of trying to claim the throne for her family. *Filavaye would be the most suspicious member of the household,* Catricha thought, *if it wasn't for Vual.*

Ruar concluded the letter by suggesting they meet as soon as possible. He proposed the old amphitheater, abandoned for putting on actual plays since about five years ago.

Catricha sent a letter back to tell him she agreed to meet. She would go alone.

CHAPTER 28

CATRICHA

Gloom gathered over the city as Catricha made her way through the streets toward the amphitheater.

She took no carriage and wore trousers rather than a skirt, to make her demeanor as natural as possible, aiming to avoid suspicion on the streets. As a member of the high nobility people might notice her if she dressed out or took the carriage.

With her practical gear and clothing, Catricha carried a short blade hidden in a sheath at the small of her back, tucked between her trousers and tunic. The dagger was a shard of the original Maltos bane sword, reinforced by additional magical essences.

The blade's shape had changed a millennia ago when broken in half during battle with a demon. The weapon's essence was reforged into smaller blades.

House Maltos was descended from one of Jadik's knights, so Catricha could wield the blade without any trouble. Such a magical weapon infused with ancient essences wouldn't allow a human of the wrong bloodline to even pick it up without nausea and pain.

She was well aware of the dagger as she crept through the gates of the theater. In case something happened here, she must be ready. Catricha was not a skilled fencer, but she could be ready for a fight. Given her survival training in the noble household.

She had no intention of fighting anyone. Ruar should be the only other person at their meeting. Catricha feared more that the weapon might actually prove useful. The cold and rain made her skin prickle with goose flesh.

The shape of a man stood at the far side of the amphitheater by the base of the stands. He was as slim and awkward-looking as ever. Ruar was the only other living thing in the entire amphitheater. His shoulders hunched, with his back pressed against the stone wall beside the gateway that led into the actor's chambers. Those chambers extended below the stand, and perhaps further below that.

He did not look at Catricha as she approached. The rain began to intensify as the two of them met before the actors archway.

"Ruar," said Catricha. "I'm glad you wanted to meet."

"And I'm glad you sent your letter. I didn't know how to reach out."

"After Nansoela's party." Catricha sighed. "I don't blame you."

"I'm sorry for what my brother did," said Ruar. "He tricked me."

"More like strong-armed you." Catricha scowled. "I shouldn't have followed you when you left. I'm lucky Hadrian was there to protect me."

Ruar hung his head. "Did my brother hurt you?"

"He might have tried." Catricha shuddered. "But his rudeness is in the past and our need to know the truth is more present."

"Past and present meet in memory." Ruar shook his head.

Catricha smiled slightly. "That's a good line for what we must discuss today."

"My family doesn't remember the times before Jadik least, not like they chronicled the last two-and-a-half centuries."

"Your records go back so far?" said Catricha. "My family legends trace to Jadik, but barely include conquest."

"The family histories of Kuldettan are not complete before Deckard Hadrian entered them." Ruar shivered. "My family had chronicled history with enthusiasm, if not accuracy."

"What good is enthusiasm in history without the truth?" said Catricha. "You might tell fine stories, but you would never know what actually happened in the past."

"That's the problem." Ruar sighed. "I fear the way of the world is to conceal what has gone before."

"Don't fear," said Catricha. "You know it."

"The loss of history is tragic," said Ruar. "But we must endure it."

"Yes." Catricha leaned against the wall beside him. "Did you find anything else beyond what I wrote you about?"

"The city beneath the city exists. My family once used it in the legend. Before Jadik arrived, my ancestors went into the catacombs to hide, before we were called House Kuldettan. They hid below the tombs."

"Below the tombs?" she said. "The catacombs go that deep?"

"That's what they wrote of," said Ruar.

"So the under-city still exists. We must learn exactly how to enter it."

"The ruins of the city below are not so difficult to reach, according to legend," said Ruar. "My mother told me Vual found a way to enter years ago."

Catricha hissed in frustration. "No doubt he's heard what I'm trying to do."

"Below the city lies another city." Ruar limped a step toward Catricha. "That city is clad in stone and built of souls, or so the old book says."

"The old family legend?" said Catricha.

"Yes."

Catricha nodded, then glanced across the amphitheater floor through the now pouring rain beyond the archway. "Paths exist in more than one place. Do you know if the underground city has anything to do with world wells?"

"No world wells are linked to the catacombs directly, at least not in the family legends."

"If we can trust the legends," said Catricha. "Then we should be safe."

"Yes." Ruar folded his arms. "That's why want to meet here."

"What was special about this place?" she asked.

Ruar motioned into the hall leading to the actors' chambers.

She frowned. "What's in there?"

"A path to the catacombs," said Ruar.

"The catacombs have an entrance below the amphitheater?" Catricha rubbed her cold hands together. "I suppose the actors aren't the only ones playing parts."

Ruar laughed. "Clever as ever."

"Don't act too comfortable," said Catricha. "What lies below us will be dangerous, regardless of it there are demons or not."

"I know." Ruar touched the hilt of his short sword, sheathed at his waist. "I brought this just in case."

"Is it an infused blade?" asked Catricha.

"It has three banes borne within it. Not a powerful magical weapon, but it is enough to wound by getting close to the target."

"I brought my dagger," she said. "But I'm glad we're both armed if we choose to go below. Is that what you want?"

Ruar shook his head. "I didn't plan to descend today, but with my brother trying to become the prince in his own roundabout way. He may be at odds with you and the newcomers, the Olfrus Family. We would be best to move quickly to end the conflict and protect everyone."

"Do you really care to protect Heron Olfrus?" Catricha frowned. "Your brother, I understand, but you don't even know Olfrus."

"True, but Catricha, we have a responsibility to protect Alliance. We must ensure another prince is found soon, or the city is in danger, despite Kizoni Duhikzo trying to hold things together."

"How much do you know of the regent?" asked Catricha. "She seems capable of managing the palace on her own."

"Then she is also in danger." Ruar sighed. "Anyone who tries to govern the city will face the shadow's peril, according to the killer's threat."

"It's true," said Catricha. "I heard the words."

"Shall we go, then?"

"Go below? I fear this may be risky, Ruar, but I trust you."

"I trust you, too." Ruar smiled at her. "What danger can two people who trust each other find in the dark?"

"As long as we're alone." Catricha smiled at him. "None."

"Then let's hope we stay a step ahead of whatever or whoever else might be down there. I've heard of people moving into the depths. We must be both quiet and careful."

"I can keep my head down and my footsteps light. Now or never." Catricha started into the passage.

The two made their way into the actor's chambers. They searched for a while in the circular room until they found a hidden door marked by a grimy word in the ancient tongue of the city.

The word read aloud said, "Jasguara."

When Ruar touched the point of his infused blade to the word experimentally, the wall around the marking shifted and the floor lurched. The staircase opened, leading down into the gloom of the catacombs.

Catricha stared for a moment before taking the lead.

* * *

Ruar lit the path ahead of them with his sprites and banes. Essences chattered like teeth in the cavern as they continued below the actors' quarters. They were frequently surprised by drips of water or occasional echoes of sound from ahead of them.

Despite herself, Catricha cringed toward Ruar when they rounded a corner and found light ahead of them not projected by him in the vast room ahead.

While the storm raged above, bright lanterns lit the huge cavern below. An amphitheater of sorts, but reversed, so that the large edge opened toward the bottom and the stairs led downward between rows of inverted seats.

They could walk down, because the reversed stairs appeared the same as those in the theater above. Below them, on a tiny circular stage, stood what looked like a washbasin. Around the basin, forms of people gathered in the light.

The people around the washbasin carried lanterns. Others steadied larger standing lamps. The light shed by all these bright glowing flames illuminated a stony shape at the center of the giant washbasin. Whatever it was, it had been carved to barely resemble a human.

Tusks protruded from the edges of the mouth, but every other feature of the head, could have belonged to a stone human. Below the neck, though the creature extended into a long, spidery form, lurking in stone. It only appeared to be sculpture. *But why are these people washing it?*

Catricha glanced at Ruar, silent.

"I don't know what they're doing," he whispered. "But I think we should avoid them."

"Sleepless." Catricha recognized the tune playing over the entire scene from a harpist at the bottom of the room.

"The sleepless?" said Ruar. "You're sure?"

"Absolutely."

Ruar shivered. "Those are sleepless down there."

"Others might be interested to know where they've been going," said Catricha. "But we're looking for the hidden truth about Jasguara."

"The Shadow of Jasguara." Ruar sounded awed. "I'm glad you asked me for help."

"It seemed right."

Ruar said nothing. The two of them crept along the periphery of the scene, looking into the deep chamber.

The sleepless worked, scrubbing at the side of the spidery human-faced thing in the washbasin. The five of them left the washbasin after a few moments. Two others dismantled the wooden basin around the statue. The soapy water flowed off the stage and into a dark abyss. On every side of the circular platform where they stood, the people bowed their heads to the spidery statue.

"They're worshiping it?" said Catricha. "By mercy."

"Mercy!" Ruar breathed in sharply. "Blasphemers."

"Idolaters." Catricha frowned. "But still, what they're doing is not murder."

"Maybe, but it offends me as it offends Mother Mercy."

Catricha didn't feel the same way, but the shock of encountering someone offering respect to any being but Mother Mercy sent a cold chill creeping down her spine. The penalty for blasphemy was always steep, when uncovered.

Catricha motioned Ruar to keep moving forward. They made their way to the top of the steps, and then descended on one of the side staircases. A doorway led deeper into the underground, as on the other side of the theater. They passed through the gap and then followed the side passage deeper into the dark.

She noticed scrawlings on the walls, ancient handwork. Stone reliefs depicted scenes of demons and humans living in a world together. At the center of the room at the end of the passage there stood another statue, one of a different demon. This one, was not spidery, but shaped like a lion with a finely-crafted mane of black spikes. And the face...

Catricha's eyes narrowed. "This lion has a human face. The demon it represents..."

"What?" asked Ruar. "What is it?"

"I'm just—I feel cold," said Catricha. She spoke true. The chill from creeping up her spine to the base of her neck spread toward her extremities.

"We should leave," said Ruar. "We should go, and return with more people."

"Agreed." The two of them turned to leave the small room but footsteps echoed from the passage they just come down. There were no other exits.

"If the sleepless come this way we won't be able to fight them all."

Ruar grimaced. "There's always surrender, or negotiation."

"Let's see who they are, first." Catricha put a hand to her icy forehead. "Then we'll decide what to do."

He nodded. "Our blades might yet be enough to help us escape."

"I don't want to shed blood," said Catricha. "I'm not all that good at fighting to begin with."

"Me neither." Ruar's teeth clenched.

They crept along the passage toward the sound of the footsteps. Catricha's arms folded and she shivered, but the chill continued to spread through her limbs. She felt slower, almost numb.

"Ruar," she said. "I don't feel well. I think I could faint."

"Just hang on," said Ruar. "We have to get out of here."

"Right." Catricha put her hand against the wall to support herself, barely able to feel her fingertips.

They faced two forms shifting in the shadows before them. Behind those, there were others Catricha couldn't see as clearly. One of the two was a man, and the other a woman, with long, wavy hair. The man wore a feathery mask over his eyes. Catricha recognized them from Nansoela's party.

Where did I see that girl before? The tunnel swirled with light and darkness. *The market—Right.*

Catricha's fingers slid down the wall. She sank her knees.

"I told you I would faint," she murmured.

Her head swam with the freezing waters of an icy ocean. She felt Ruar's arms around her and she collapsed into unconsciousness.

CHAPTER 29

CATRICHA

She knew she was dreaming but couldn't force herself awake. She lay frozen as a shadowy shape stalked toward her. The face of a lioness yawned, jaws wide and teeth cold. The chill of night pervaded her very being, spreading from the head downward. She stared into the eyes of the ghostly beast.

The great cat roared and gnashed rotting teeth. Dark eyes met Catricha's gaze and spoke of approaching death. She fought to cry for help, but made no sound in her paralysis. The faces of her friends, of Porfiria, Sion, and Ruar, flickered before her, each taking the place of the lion for an instant.

The monstrous shadow pounced.

* * *

Catricha woke in a warm bed, a chill, wet cloth on her forehead. The sensible clothes she'd worn for the meeting with Ruar were gone and she was naked beneath the fine linen sheets. Carefully, she removed the cold compress from her forehead and set it beside her on the mattress.

She sat up, looked around, but found the room empty except for a chair by the door and a chest of drawers with a mirror behind it. Worse, the place looked as unfamiliar as it did barren.

The people in the passage, she thought, *had they done something to Ruar? To her?*

Perhaps they were from the sleepless and clearly up to no good. Whatever the sleepless did beneath the city, they intended to remain hidden. Catricha frowned and climbed out of bed.

She found a pair of trousers by the high chair by the door. The floorboards creaked as she walked over them. She put on the trousers, realizing they were the pair she'd worn to the meeting. The tunic she'd been wearing also lay nearby on the seat of the chair. She picked up the shirt and began to put it on as quickly as she could. A tap at the door made her turn before she could completely finish with the tie at the back.

A glint of metal from the partially-unsheathed blade of her bane dagger gleamed at her from the chair. The weapon had been hidden beneath her tunic.

Catricha gave up fastening the shirt's tie. She snatched the knife in both hands as the door began to open. The sheath thudded to the floor between her and the woman who stood in the doorway.

Catricha looked at the face of the woman from the underground passage, pale features haloed by waves of dark hair. "Who are you?"

"I'm Melissa Dorian. I'm a mage," said the woman. "Please, put down the knife, Lady Maltos."

"You know who I am. If you think that's clever I won't bother to correct you." Catricha glared at Melissa. "Where is Ruar? What did you do to him?"

"The young Kuldettan is in the next room," said Melissa. "We wouldn't hurt him."

"You didn't—" Catricha's breath caught in her chest. *Thank Mercy,* she thought. "Where are we?"

"An apartment owned by House Paroth." Melissa half-turned, motioning into the adjoining room.

"Paroth? Let me see Ruar."

"Are you sure you want him to see you as you are?"

Catricha looked down at herself, and realized with growing heat she still only wore her trousers. The tunic she'd failed to tie lay fallen on the floor behind her. The blood rose to her face.

"I catch your meaning. I thought mages were supposed to be the more absent-minded, but that shows how little we nobles think."

"No need to insult yourself," Melissa said.

“Dorian, was it? You’re new to the city, but when something here is out of step, I point it out. Thank you very much.”

Melissa’s eyebrows rose as Catricha set the dagger on the chair’s seat. She turned to leave.

“Wait a moment,” said Catricha quickly.

Melissa turned, silent.

Catricha lowered her voice. “Could you help me get the ties at the back?”

Melissa smiled and nodded to Catricha, letting the door close behind her.

* * *

Catricha looked around the room, taking in the people gathered in the Paroth safe house. Ruar rose and took a step toward her as she entered.

He wore a concerned frown, and his face flushed as he looked at her. The man in the feathery mask sat by the window, overlooking a street covered by dark clouds as light faded in the afternoon hours. Catricha’s stomach rumbled, reminding her she’d missed lunch. Too many people in the city went without food all day.

Catricha considered herself spoiled by her life as a noble. Entertaining people by deriding other nobility did not make up for everything she gained from her position.

Melissa, walked to the man in the mask and nodded to him. "It looks like she'll be all right. I heard strange sprite songs from inside the room, but I think it was just hers."

"You heard my heart song?” said Catricha.

"I can still hear it,” said Melissa. "Do you have any magic?"

"None I know how to use.” Catricha sighed. "Maybe that's why had trouble down there. Monsters and demons...their ilk can play hell with magic, can’t they?"

Melissa arching an eyebrow. “How much do you know about magic?”

"Not enough," said Catricha.

Ruar’s brow furrowed. He took an awkward step toward her. "We need to let your parents know you’re alright."

"I'm not a child," said Catricha. "I don't have to return just yet." She looked out the window. "Besides, we may have company to attend to before any of us can go."

Outside the window, swarms of bright torches, sizzled in the rain. The lights glowed over a crowd of sleepless, their eyes hidden by the glare. Catricha guessed every single one would be strained and bloodshot from days without rest.

"What are they doing here?" asked Catricha. "Did they follow us?"

"We didn't get away clean," said the man in the feather mask.

"So they are after me?" said Catricha. "Perfect."

"Don't fear." Melissa smiled. "They've not done anything violent, but if they try anything, you have myself and my friend here."

"Who is your friend?" asked Catricha. "I can nearly guess because we're sitting in a Paroth house."

"It is obvious, isn't it?" The man whisked his hand to the air, tugging the feathers from his face and suspending them on shimmering strings. "You found me out." Galocai smiled. "You've grown a little since I last saw you, Catricha."

"A little?" Catricha gave a loud laugh. "It's been five years."

"Five years since you last attended one of your sister's parties?" Ruar stared at the other man. "Galocai?"

"Indeed." Galocai laughed. I ended my absence only recently."

Melissa folded her arms, lips curving with amusement. "It was for the best."

"I think so." Galocai winked at Melissa.

Melissa laughed, then straightened herself noticeably. "Right. I don't want them to surround us."

"We're mages." Galocai snorted. "They can't defeat us in a fight, especially with your sacra form."

"I don't want to hurt them if we can avoid it," said Melissa. "To rip through a crowd, even if they are cultists to some underground demons would be murder."

Ruar grunted, then snapped his fingers. "The city guard! They'll do something at the least. We may be able to get some of the palace guards if we need them as well."

"The city guard might act if they knew what was going on," said Catricha. "But we have no way of contacting them without leaving the building."

"That may not be true," said Melissa. "Galocai." She turned to the other mage.

"I've already sent some feathers carrying notes across town to the nearest guardhouse," said Galocai. "Hopefully, the guards will be here soon."

"What will we do until then?" Catricha glanced out the window at the crowd. "Waiting here for an hour or two while the guards break up the mess outside feels wrong."

Melissa shrugged. "While you were sleeping you seemed a little less tense."

"Funny," said Catricha. "I guess my dreams didn't show."

"What kind of dreams did you have?" asked Galocai. "They may be important."

"There was a beast made of shadows with awful teeth...It was just a dream." Catricha shook her head. "But it felt very real."

"Your strong essences could be fooling with your mind. I never encountered that kind of thing, but my strong essences are based on physical abilities, not mental ones."

"You have strong essences too?" Catricha narrowed her eyes. "Who are you, really?"

"I was once the heir to the Dorian merchant family." Melissa grimaced. "I was banned from mage-craft in the south, where my family lived at the time. I left to become a caravan guard. But you don't need to know the rest. I've become a mage recently."

"What are your strong essences?" asked Catricha. "Will they be useful if we have to fight the cultists?"

"My strong essences are iron and shatter," said Melissa. "The iron is a bane and the shatter a sprite, but I don't understand the one as well as the bane."

"You have two?" Catricha stared at Melissa. "Have you had them your whole life?"

"I think so," the mage said. "They only awakened at the start of this past summer."

"Regardless." Ruar nodded. "They must enhance your physical abilities, so should be useful in battle."

"They are," said Melissa. "I've used them before, and they can be devastating, but only if I can fight without holding back."

"Do you think that's necessary now?" said Galocai. "They are ordinary people, as far as we've seen. There are no mages among them, just rabble."

"That rabble outnumbers us fifty-to-one." Melissa shook her head. "They gathered even more people from the streets, rather than just pursuing us straight from the underground."

"Whether they are two or two-hundred," said Galocai with a snort. "They are no match for us as a group."

"You mean, no match for you two mages?" Catricha motioned to Melissa and Galocai. "If that's true, you must've learned something since we last saw each other."

"I certainly have," said Galocai. "But I wouldn't put myself up against them alone. Thanks to Melissa, I feel that we will be safe."

"We wait for the guards." Melissa turned to Galocai. "That's final."

"I like it when a woman tells me what to do." Galocai smirked.

Melissa's face flushed. "It's not like that."

"Don't worry," said Galocai. "My nature is to speak plainly, mask or no mask."

"It always has been." Catricha recalled numerous occasions when Galocai had been nearly as blunt as Catricha herself. His reputation once soured as a result.

Ruar glanced to Galocai, frowning. "I don't know you well, but Catricha trusts you, and I think we can rely on Melissa's judgment. You say she's the better mage. Perhaps we shouldn't risk fighting if she feels out of her depth."

"Thank you," said Melissa. "Master Kuldettan."

"It's nothing," said Ruar. "I'm trying to be judicious. The risk to myself and Catricha would be high in the street. Neither of us has powerful magic to wield. I only know a little, and she only has strong essence she doesn't know how to wield."

"What kind of song did you hear from me?" asked Catricha, turning to Melissa with a fluttering stomach. "Was that what drew you in there?"

"I heard a dark tune, low and humming with discord. I've never heard anything quite like it, before, so I investigated."

Galocai nodded. "Honestly, I found it slightly frightening."

"Slightly?" Ruar laughed. "You were noticeably shaken when the song started."

"Noticeably." Galocai sat back, eyes twinkling. "But not greatly."

Melissa shook her head. "You men and your pride. There's no shame in admitting you were afraid."

"There was nothing to fear, though," said Galocai. "So, let's revise that history slightly."

"You Paroth do like your revision." Catricha shook her head and smiled. "I don't mean to be ungrateful but you and your sister have gotten me into enough trouble, lately."

"Nansoela doesn't need any more hangers-on," said Galocai. "If that's what you mean."

"Nonsense. I'd sooner hang on to the top of the tower and dangle over the city then try to ride your sister's path," said Catricha. "We are of different disciplines. I intend things to stay that way."

"You're determined." Galocai grinned. "I enjoy that, Catricha."

Catricha rolled her eyes. "Charming as always. But you say such things to every woman."

Melissa frowned slightly and looked away from Galocai. She returned to the window. "It looks like they're moving."

Catricha approached the window to look out, beside the mages. In the midst of the mob below, a scuffle broke out in the street. Some torches fell, while others scattered, their bearers fleeing into the gathering darkness. A sound like ice cracking ripped through the air.

The noise reached Catricha in the building high above. She must be two stories up, and she could still hear every note of pain in the horrified voice. Their were no words, nothing but a scream of pure agony. In the next moment the shriek cut off. Ruar's eyes went wide.

Catricha nodded. Her face felt cold as the blood fled her cheeks. Melissa and Galocai exchanged glances.

"I'll check the street," said Melissa. "We need to know what's going on down there."

"I'll go with you." Catricha stepped forward. "I want to see it myself."

"Whatever happened," said Ruar. "It could be dangerous."

"Then we'll all go," said Galocai. "Strength in numbers and all that."

The four of them descended the steps in the building, then went into the dark to find what lay on the street. Little remained of the victim. All that Catricha found was a body with a still-attached head. She gagged. All of the large man's limbs had been rent off at the joints.

Blood dripped and flowed, and the smell of it, almost sweet on the evening wind, filled the air. There was no sound of sprites or banes in the darkness and no evidence of the man's attackers. Fallen torches guttered nearby, lighting the horrific scene. Melissa and Catricha stood over the body and looked down into dead eyes. The expression on the man's face was not one of horror. On those slack lips, in those staring eyes, an epiphanic smile graced dead features.

Catricha stood, stunned by the brutality of the killing. In the light of the fallen torches there was no sign of the man's arms or legs. Like Adias' heart and eyes, the man's limbs were simply gone, taken in his final moments.

She put a hand to her mouth and turned away. The kind of tears she'd never managed for her unfaithful husband flowed freely down her face. Ruar put his arm around her, but he was shaking too. Catricha felt his oddly twisted hip against her side and clutched at his arm.

"I'll take you home," said Ruar.

She nodded, unable to force words through her tight throat.

Behind them, Melissa said in a quiet voice. "It wasn't us they were chasing. Whoever this man was...I doubt they could have done worse to him."

"Then why is he smiling?" Catricha murmured. "He shouldn't be smiling."

Ruar pressed her to him closely and they made their way from the scene before the guards could arrive to slow them down.

One way or another, Catricha swore to find the truth behind the murders. The thought terrified her spirit, thrilled her mind and tortured her heart. Yet, she vowed not to abandon the search she'd begun, even if she had to return to it alone.

CHAPTER 30

MELISSA

Heron's chambers at House Graef was lit by a tall lamp.

"Enlighten me on what happened." Heron frowned. "Is there danger beneath the city?"

"We saw a man dismembered on the street." Melissa closed her eyes, trying to shut out the image. "And there could be demons in the catacombs underground."

"Demonic statues maybe. You didn't describe any proof of actual demons, only sculptures made to look like them."

Melissa scowled at her feet. "I know what demons are like. I've encountered more than one in the past."

"Of course, but you don't know exactly what any possible demons below Alliance are doing. You never saw one move. They could just be stone props for the Cult of the Sleepless."

"A stone demon is still a threat to the city if they are related to the sleepless," said Melissa.

"The sleepless are not as harmless as we thought." Bethanelle entered on the other side of the room. "That much I overheard."

"We'll tackle them when the time comes." Heron folded his hands. "I'll see to it myself."

"I'm trying to tell you," said Melissa. "The time is now."

"Perhaps. Or perhaps you're just eager for a fight after so long without one."

"I'm not bloodthirsty." Melissa folded her arms and sighed. "My instinct is to protect people. And you're paying me to protect you, right?"

"A true point." Heron shrugged. "Am I supposed to investigate underground to improve my name with the people?"

"It would help, for certain," said Bethanelle. "Perhaps now is more dangerous than Melissa thinks."

Melissa's gaze flicked to Bethanelle. "The underground is perilous, but I'm willing to face that."

"We all must be willing," said Heron. "As your current employer, with no illusions of how long that will last, I request you use caution when you explore the under-city. I'll need your help to protect myself if the sleepless are as dangerous you presume."

"We don't even know if the sleepless were the ones who killed that man." Bethanelle frowned. "Though his horrible death bears a certain resemblance to what happened to the steward."

"Missing limbs and body parts." Melissa took a deep breath. "What parts was the steward missing?"

"His eyes," said Galocai. "And his heart."

"Not the same parts by any means." Elaine she flipped through her book of spells. "If I had a sacra form I'd be behind you in exploring underground. With demonic threats possible it may be too risky just for the two of us to go alone."

"The three of us," said Galocai.

Melissa glanced at Galocai, taking in his determined expression, set jaw, and fierce eyes.

"Perhaps if we assemble enough people," said Melissa. "We could make an attempt."

"Do you really want to explore under the city so badly?" Heron's mouth shifted, almost like he was mouthing a grumble. "We'll need more than the the city guards, as most won't marshal for a plunge into the depths."

"The house guard." Bethanelle snapped her fingers. "I'll ask my father if we can use them."

“A good idea, my lady.” Melissa nodded. “Your guards should be enough to suppress the crowds of sleepless. They are mostly unarmed people and always lack rest."

"We don't know what kind of magic they wield," Elaine said. "We must take care, Melissa."

Melissa unfolded her arms. "Three mages and a team of house guard, should be enough to at least make an expedition to explore what the sleepless were actually doing under the theater."

"Other than cleaning stone demons?" Heron shrugged. "It seems to me we know very well what they were trying to do. They were trying to spruce up old statuary."

"Witty," said Galocai. "But they're potentially dangerous regardless. We don't know what those statues actually mean or why they're in the catacombs."

"You're the natives," said Heron. "Bethanelle, Galocai. Do you have any idea of what's going on with the cult?"

Bethanelle shook her head. “My family doesn't have much to do with the catacombs or the underground."

"My family on the other hand," said Galocai. "Is native to the darkness of the city. We've had to hide there in the past, or so our legends say."

"Your family hid in the catacombs?" said Melissa. "When and why?"

"Long before my generation, my ancestors were in hiding from a battle between powerful immortals, so they took to the depths of Alliance. Whatever they found there must've disconcerted them, because my family has rarely gone below since."

"Well that doesn't encourage me," said Heron. "The danger might be too great even for mages with guard assistance."

"It's a danger we must confront.” Melissa turned toward Heron, eyes determined. “I'm not going to risk instead letting them go completely unmanaged down there."

"They seem to be tied to the killing," said Heron. "I'll give you that."

"Then let me lead a group into the catacombs," said Melissa. "We'll find what we can and we'll punish the cult for their evil."

"Their evil?" Heron raised an eyebrow. "That's an unusual term for you to use."

"Evil, is a curse," said Melissa. "And that curse must be rooted out by those blessed who defy it."

"A bold statement," said Elaine. "Be careful, Melissa."

"Tomorrow," said Bethanelle. "You three will go below the city, and I'll go with you."

"Are you sure that's wise?" Galocai asked. "After all, my dear, you don't have much magic of your own."

"I have enough," said Bethanelle. "And my arrows will be of use if there's a battle."

"Very well. I'm not one to tell a lady what to do."

"I've heard by reputation you're not a man to push anyone around."

"Guilty." Galocai smiled.

Melissa's heart fluttered with his words. "We should get some rest. Tomorrow we'll go underground again."

* * *

"What is it named...Your sacra form?" Galocai turned to Melissa in the shadows as they crept up the stairs in the Graef estate.

Elaine had gone to sleep below in the stable, where they'd quartered her and Melissa since the first night. Melissa was only supposed to be escorting Galocai up to his chambers.

"She's called Fanhedon," said Melissa.

"Fanhedon? I'm not familiar with the name, but I don't know as much as I should."

"Neither do I." Melissa sighed. "I only know how to access my sacra from, and I can't even imagine more."

"There is a man in the north of Geteren who learned three." They reached Galocai's door.

"Three?" said Melissa. "That's fantastic. Is it just a myth, though?"

"Not a myth." Galocai smiled slightly. "I believe he's still with us, living as a man."

"What is his name?" asked Melissa.

"He's known as Virgil Silas Dane, a parson of the Chos Valley."

"The Valley," said Melissa. "That place is strange. I've been there only in passing."

Galocai fumbled with the lock the door to his chambers. He got the mechanism open and they stepped into the moonlit room beyond. The clouds parted. What remained of the rain still drizzled in the distance over the city, but in the pale light of the silver moon, they sat in the dark, on the couch of animal hide.

Melissa leaned against him, feeling his breathing. "You don't need to know about sacra forms, not yet."

"Why not?" asked Galocai.

"Because as long as I'm in the city, I'll protect you."

"I won't be in the city for much time," said Galocai. "Unless, of course, I somehow become the prince."

"It's possible," said Melissa. "Don't let Heron hear me say this, but I think you'd make a good prince."

"I'm beginning to doubt he would, though," said Galocai. "He seems a little cautious and possibly less trusting then I would hope."

"Less trusting?" Melissa raised her eyebrows. "I don't know if that's a good quality for a prince."

"Not being able to trust your subordinates to do what you ask them of them," said Galocai. "Is not a hallmark of a successful administrator."

"If he can't trust anyone to do anything for him, then he won't be powerful. He'll become a man with a lot of authority and no support."

"Yes," said Galocai. "That's it exactly."

"I have my insights." Melissa wrapped her arm around his shoulders.

"I know you do," said Galocai. "Too many women and men are empty-headed these days."

"Are they the same way in the Chos Valley?" asked Melissa. "I imagine things are different there."

"Well Country is a dangerous place. That ensures the people there are more serious than we in Alliance."

"Not as many poets in the Chos Valley?" said Melissa.

"Very few indeed." Galocai smiled. "Though, I suspect Catricha Maltos would fare all right there. She might be an outrage poet but she has a toughness to her."

"I saw some of that today," said Melissa. "She pulled a knife when I entered the room."

"She's too quick to take up a blade." Galocai frowned. "She's always been that way."

"What aggressive?" said Melissa.

"No," said Galocai. "Uneasy. Part of the reason I think she chose to become a poet that insults the nobility is to use up her anger. She's always been an angry person."

"She has a swift temper, but wit is her tool."

"A good observation," said Galocai. "I suppose the case."

"I've never been funny when I'm angry," said Melissa. "I just get cold inside."

"Cold?" said Galocai. "I've heard warriors compare battle to a raging fire, but you say cold."

"I'm not cold now," said Melissa. "But in battle, I can be icy as a blade's edge."

"I'm glad you're not an ice woman now."

She looked into his smiling eyes, then tugged him closer by the lapels, and they kissed in the moonlight.

CHAPTER 31

DECKARD

Deckard flew to the palace, carrying with him the vision of the bloody street.

The murder of a man by removing all four limbs, struck a bizarre chord within. Ritual killings could hardly be concealed. The theft of all four limbs spoke of a brutal pact with some kind of demon. Deckard didn't know everything about the underground of Alliance, but he knew enough lore to recognize what had happened. Someone was performing sacrifices and the one last night was not the first.

The sleepless might look harmless but their bizarre proclivity for the night and avoidance of sleep may have driven them to darker places than mere self-flagellation through fatigue. Deckard landed on the battlements overlooking the street below. He glided off the wall toward the palace's center, landing on a balcony outside the prince's chambers. There the dowager regent waited for him.

She smiled as his feet touched the stone. "For a man of such skill and power to be remarked upon for his beauty before the rest, is remarkable, don't you think Lord Hadrian?"

Deckard stepped in from the cold, closing the balcony door behind him. The windows rattled with the force of the wind from the north.

Kizoni wore her dressing gown at the late hour, but her eyes were brighter than ever. Perhaps she was simply a night owl by nature.

"What did you find?" she asked.

"Murder," said Deckard. "I suspect whoever did it is the threat to the city we feared."

"Could they be a threat to me?" Kizoni's Rosadon accident made her voice sound gentler in the dark.

"I wouldn't deny they threaten you and your child."

"I'll double the guard on the palace and my chambers."

"Your servant, Varder is a powerful warrior," said Deckard. "I've heard of his exploits in the past."

"Varder can protect me from one attacker." Kizoni sighed softly. "But the dear man can't guard an entire palace himself."

"I only wish I had the same power," Deckard said.

"You've defeated countless demons. I've been hearing of you since I was a girl."

"There are always stories. Only children dream of heroes."

Kizoni sat on the side of her finely upholstered bed. "You know, Lord Hadrian, it isn't often we speak of childish dreams in these chambers."

"The dreams of children may be petty but they are often beautiful."

"I never dreamed of becoming a widow, even with the power of being regent of Alliance."

"You grew up not in this cold city and a dream is not a wish."

"True, but now, I have more power than I would've ever gained as a prince's sister or wife."

"As one's dowager, you are the most powerful woman or man in the city."

"Power does not interest me." Kizoni tugged at the sides of her gown. "It's only a tool to achieve my other dreams."

Deckard, pacing in front of her, paused. "What dreams do you speak of now?"

"Not the dreams of the child," said Kizoni. "I dream as a woman."

Deckard turned toward her. "I must caution you, honorable regent of Alliance. I'm not the man you think you desire."

Kizoni bowed her head, hiding her face from the dim lamplight. "But you are."

"I can protect you or I can love you. Not both."

"Do I not have guards to protect me? None of them can offer me the other service."

"Is that what you call love, now? I've been gone from Alliance, and from Rosado for too long."

"You've tasted a world most humans never dream of," said Kizoni. "But you've grown bored of it, because after decades, centuries, I'm sure the to any taste becomes dull."

"Everything goes stale over time." Deckard put his hand to the clasp of his iron robe. The metallic garment was still light as feathers around him, effortlessly carried by his magic.

"Perhaps. You could give me just a taste of your immortality, just an hour, maybe a little more."

"Why would you want to taste what has driven me to boredom?"

"It will be new to me." Kizoni reached for his hand. He held back for a second, then he let her take his fingers in hers. He felt the coursing of the monster within his heart.

He never mentioned the affliction openly, never shared the nature of the curse with another. His love and lust were always together as one being, both condemned by Mother Mercy. His purpose transcended urges of the flesh. And in that night, as Kizoni drew him close to her, he bowed his head and submitted.

The battle of daylight was over for the moment. At dusk, Deckard Hadrian's most difficult hours began. The night swarmed like a flurry of black insects.

His robe fell to the floor with a clank as it's weight returned upon leaving Deckard's shoulders. He settled onto the bed beside Kizoni.

"Is this what you want?" he asked.

She said nothing, but began to undo the fastenings of his tunic at the front.

He worked on the ties with her. Until his tunic fell away. Moonlight crept through the window, illuminating his many scars.

"Will you," said Kizoni. "Undress me?"

Without a word, Deckard shifted the gown carefully from Kizoni's shoulders. He folded the dress away, and gently laid her against the bed. Their love made the night warm for a time. She cried out when he changed, and he saw fear in her eyes when they were finished.

Weakness overcomes will.

Hours later, he fled the palace in the dark before dawn. Shadows hid his wretched deformity in the hours before the sun rose, concealing the beast that emerged from within him when the curse took hold.

VUAL

Vual met his brother at the foot of the stairs in the morning. The lightened sound of Ruar's irregular gait on the staircase told him the younger man's mood had improved. Vual hated seeing Ruar sneak out to meet with Catricha the previous day. His brother showed a real sign of their intentions together.

He never liked Catricha, but he could've borne her and his brother joining as one before the murders began. The rain after last night's killing threatened to wash all that freshly-spilled blood into the gutters. Vual folded his arms and regarded Ruar as his younger brother reached the bottom of the stairs.

"Where you going?" he asked.

"I'm going to meet with some friends," said Ruar. "Fellow gallant poets."

"I think you mean you're going to meet with one poet in particular."

Ruar inclined his head toward Vual and grunted. "Who do you suspect?"

"Catricha Maltos." Vual added a bite of bitterness to his voice. "Or did my eyes deceive me yesterday?"

"They deceived you not," Ruar said through clenched teeth. "Don't follow me again, brother."

"I was following her. She is the one behind the death of my friends."

"I knew Adias as you did," said Ruar. "I liked Saviron too."

"Then how can you court that harlot, still?" Vual bared his teeth in a snarl. "She had something to do with their deaths', even if she didn't directly attack them."

"No. You're wrong. You won't change my mind."

"Change your mind?" Vual growled. "Brother, I will not take your lecture."

"And I've no reason to endure yours. Stand aside."

"Make me," said Vual.

"You won't allow anything." Ruar's face flushed with anger. "But I will take my freedom from you."

"Is that a challenge?" said Vual. "I'm a far stronger warrior and mage than you, brother."

"I'll give you my best strike."

"Don't," said Filavaye from the corner passage.

Their mother stepped into the front hall of the house. The entryway to the dining room was brightly lit by morning sunlight, but Filavaye's face was a stern storm cloud.

"My sons won't clash in my house. Nor shall you do battle outside. You must measure your words, Vual. As of now, you and Ruar are evenly matched."

"Mother." Vual glared at Ruar. "I know things he refuses to believe about House Maltos."

Filavaye shook her head. "The Maltos have been family rivals for a long time, and though we both know your positions, I suspect one of you is more pragmatic than the other in this regard."

"Neither of us is pragmatic," said Vual. "If I may correct you slightly mother."

"Maybe so." Filavaye smiled like viper. "But an alliance is more valuable than a vendetta, and your blood feud with Catricha Maltos is no longer of any interest to me, son."

"You're not on my side, are you mother?" Vual said.

"Hardly, but one of you will become the Prince of Alliance. When that happens, that one will have the power to do whatever they wish. The other will be unable to prevent you."

"So if I become prince," said Ruar. "I can have my way?"

"In some regards."

Ruar's eyes widened. "I don't believe you'd allow that."

"You'd better," said Vual. "Because now you're my rival too. If you are a potential prince. Now that you have a reason to become ruler of the city, I must beat you as thoroughly as if you were a member of another house."

"Both of you must beware of Hadrian." Filavaye scowled. "He may be our ancestor, but he is not our friend."

"What makes you say so, mother?" said Ruar. "I've not even met him and you're afraid of him?"

"Not afraid," said Filavaye. "Wary."

Vual grunted as the heat rose to his face. "He followed me a week ago when I went riding."

"Where were you?" Ruar glanced at him. "Do you know why he followed you, Vual?"

"He followed me into the forest when I was hunting south of the city in the night. He protected my rivals and me by slaying a demon spawn."

"A demon spawn?" said Filavaye. "Were you planning to tell me about this at any point, son?"

"I just told you now." Vual's teeth clenched. "I don't feel the need to share every detail of my life with you, mother. I'm a man now."

"You're better off sharing what you know," said Filavaye. "Because we are on the same side, you and I."

"Not if you'll help Ruar supplant me as prince." Vual's essences hummed in his ears, though he might not be a match for Filavaye's magic. "If either of us become prince and that shadow is still out there, we will not have long to live."

"The shadow threatened all potential princes," said Filavaye. "But that shadow is not what you should be afraid of. Neither should you fear Deckard Hadrian. Fear me, because I'm the one who can release you from this family. Your life or death no longer matter if you aren't a Kuldettan."

Ruar stared at Filavaye, eyes wide. "You may miss me less than Vual."

"I mean it for both of you," said their mother. "Don't consider yourselves unique."

"So." Vual folded his arms. "It's begun."

"What is?" Ruar clucked. "What has begun?"

"Our rivalry. I won't crush you outright." Vual felt his face grow wide with a savage grin. "Not without a small hint of regret, brother. For now, you're not going anywhere."

Ruar hissed, then retreated up the steps, his feet pounding at an odd tempo on the stone.

CHAPTER 32

MELISSA

The party met at the gate to the amphitheater, then went inside. Melissa led the way, with Galocai behind her. The rest of the hunters from House Graef followed them, Bethanelle among as their leader.

The eight hunters with Bethanelle, Elaine, Galocai, and Melissa descended into the catacombs.

Bows and swords hung upon their shoulders. They held lighter weapons in their hands. Melissa carried her spear forward, pointing the tip along the passage. Elaine and Galocai carried short swords, though Elaine seemed unsure what to do with hers. She kept the weapon buckled to her belt in a scabbard.

I hope you won't need that, my friend.

The twelve of them made their way through the passages toward the inverted theater below the great amphitheater of Alliance. They gazed upon the same sights Catricha and Ruar had witnessed the previous day. In grim silence, they moved. Through shadows lit only by sprites with their songs almost entirely quieted, they crept into the depths.

Melissa and Galocai exchanged glances as they stepped into the stands of the inverted amphitheater. On the stage below them, no sign remained of the statue the sleepless had been cleaning. *No people either*, Melissa thought. she knew there were sleepless around from the faint songs of essences resonating from the pits between the seats surrounding the stage.

"How deep does this go?" asked Elaine.

"I don't know." Melissa raised an eyebrow. "Galocai?"

"We'll find out," he said.

"Yes." Melissa continued to lead with her spear as they descended the steps. She kept her thoughts close to Fanhedon, ready to summon the spirit of the demon at any moment.

"Demons live within these statues." Elaine pointed at the ceiling and the faces that leered at them from the angles of the amphitheater walls.

"Are you certain?" asked Galocai.

"They must be demons because their hearts resonate with only banes, and they are definitely resonating."

"But they're not moving," said Melissa. "They're just waiting. I can scarcely even hear anything from them."

"They're sleeping," said Elaine. "Their heart-songs are quieter as a result."

"Demons sleep?" Galocai frowned at Elaine. "Are they sleeping here for some particular reason?"

Elaine shrugged without a word.

"Hunters." Bethanelle motioned for her people to fan out. "Protect the passages to the surface. Let the mages proceed forward if true demons are afoot."

Melissa nodded and stiffened her resolve with her spine. "You can stay with your hunters, Bethanelle. We'll find the people below."

"If you have any trouble, rush back and we'll assist you." said Bethanelle.

Melissa shook her head. "No, my lady. If you hear us in too much trouble, you should head for the surface to tell the city what is happening. We can escape on our own, as we have magic on our side."

"We'll take any warning you give as a chance to escape ourselves?" said Bethanelle. "That seems cowardly."

"Do what you have to do," said Melissa. "If it looks like we can't win, though, plan to flee."

"Life as a coward is better than death." Galocai gave Bethanelle a grin. "That's always been my philosophy."

Elaine folded her hands and then spread them, sending her sprites flying through the amphitheater to illuminate the deep pits on either side of the tiny stage.

Long ladders carved into the stonework on both sides of the pits were barely wide enough for a human to traverse vertically.

Melissa frowned. "Do we think that's where they went?" She pointed toward the ladders.

"We'll have to check," said Galocai.

Elaine directed her sprites to gather on the stage. They formed a brilliant, circular beacon. "We have to make sure that they're not plotting more murders down here."

"Murders." Melissa nodded. "People can be as monstrous as demons."

Galocai took the first step forward. "I agree. Let's go."

The three of them descended the stairs to reach the stage. There, they gazed into one of the shafts, standing side-by-side. Below them lay a vast chamber. The stone ladders remained intact and led directly into an abyss of darkness lit by small torches.

"How big is this room?" asked Elaine.

"Enormous," said Galocai. "Far more extensive than the catacombs under any other city as far as I know."

"We in the east aren't known for our underground territories." Elaine whistled. "This is new to me."

"And to me," said Melissa. "But this place is stranger. It must predate what stands above us."

"A city beneath a city?" said Galocai.

"Possibly," said Melissa. "Catricha Maltos and Ruar Kuldettan seemed to think such a thing was possible."

"Terrifying." Galocai's face looked like a grim mask, though he didn't wear his feathers, but let them float in the grip of the essences by his side.

"Who wants to go first?" asked Elaine.

"I'll go," said Melissa. "If anything happens, I can assume Fanhedon's form."

"It's a long way down." Elaine turned to Melissa. "Be careful, my friend."

"I will be."

Melissa climbed onto a ladder and descended into the depths of the pit. The shaft widened into a huge atrium below. Using Elaine's sprites for light, she was able to see through the darkness. Torches and small fires flickered like sparks on the sprawling cavern floor below her. Columns rose from the floor to support an arching ceiling, the center of which Melissa hung on the ladder's stone grips.

The amphitheater in the cavern above isn't an theater at all, but the highest chamber of a vast dome. What is this place? Who built it?

Melissa didn't have time to think much further as she descended.

A bolt of screaming sprite-flame shot from below. The fire streaked toward her and the ladder where she climbed, still more than a hundred spans above the floor.

Assuming Fanhedon's form, Melissa hurled herself from the ladder. She yelled a warning to her friends above as she fell, and reinforced her spear with her iron bane, holding the weapon above her until the last second before impact.

Melissa struck outward with as much force as she could against the floor, tossing a vast cloud of dust upward. Flames guttered or went out completely throughout the chamber.

The blast of her windy impact shattered the silence and sent rocks and debris flying from her landing. Her legs shuddered but held thanks to Fanhedon's armored might.

She raised her shimmering metallic mask and straighted her back, her sacra form under her will.

"You called upon me quickly," Fanhedon said through Melissa's mind. "I'm glad for your trust, Melissa."

"I need more than I can do on my own," Melissa answered silently. "I must defeat these foes if we're going to get back the surface with the others."

She looked this way and that, eyes piercing the darkness with the help of Fanhedon's demonic senses. She spotted people scurrying from the ruins of their fires. The ragged sleepless disappeared into passages on either side of the chamber. Only a single form stood before her, the shape of a demonic statue with spidery legs. It moved slightly, turning glistening eyes on her.

Melissa took her spear in both hands. She rushed at the demon.

The demon's face was slender and toothy. A bulbous back sat behind the face. Eight legs protruded from the body to carry the monster's weight. Two additional forearms of human proportion and shape hung in front of the body, and the demon held glowing sprite strings between those human hands.

“A spider would spread silk.” Melissa rushed at the demon.

"Why do you intrude?" the demon asked in an archaic imperial dialect. "This hall is not for you."

Melissa spoke only to Fanhedon. "This hall is for no one, just a pit beneath the earth." She said nothing out loud, but thrust her spear at the demon’s face.

"No, no, no," said the demon. "That won't do." He brought both hands together to deflect her spearhead.

She twisted her grip to change the angle. Melissa's weapon glanced from the demon's forearm, but cut a gash across the grotesque mockery of a human limb. The flesh immediately repaired in a rush of tiny motions. The wound healed over in an instant.

"As you can see, sleep has give me much power."

"Sleep?" said Melissa in Fanhedon's voice. "You’ve been at rest?"

"We promortals sleep beneath the earth, waiting to awaken." The demon hissed with a long tongue. "Not like you, Fanhedon, who fell centuries before your appointed time. I know you. I know."

Fanhedon responded on her own. "I fell before my time?” she roared. “You cowards dwelt here, while I fought to defend the world from what came upon us."

"Demons are not heroes," said the spider demon. "We all know that.”

The demon leapt toward Melissa and his tongue shifted backward, revealing an even longer second tongue with a stinger at it’s tip. The tongue’s point stabbed at Fanhedon shoulder.

She and Melissa lurched one side, the pain, intense as venom pumped through a break in the armor plate and into the demonic flesh beneath. If Melissa had not been in her sacra from, she’d not survive that wound for long.

She held the demon at arms length, Fanhedon’s gauntlet wrapped around the monster's throat. She hurled the beast backward through the air, tugging the stinger from her wounded shoulder.

"Are we all right?" she asked Fanhedon.

"It's nothing,” answered her demon.

“Can we beat him?" Melissa asked out loud, voice echoing.

"I can best any number of these spider monks. Most promortals are not well-versed in battle."

"That sting hurts," said Melissa. "Do you feel it too?"

"I do." Fanhedon's words echoed internally. "But don't fear, Melissa. We will be triumphant."

Melissa and Fanhedon raced as one being toward the spider demon. They darted out of the path of a net of sprite-silk, then stabbed the foe's side with the iron bane-reinforced spear.

The spider demon squealed in pain and spun, swatting at the spearhead with his human forelimbs. Melissa gritted her mind within Fanhedon's steely mask.

Another essence song approached, and Melissa recognized the tune of the leading sprite, dark and low, rippling with chaos, like a cloudy night sky. Catricha Maltos was near the fray. *Why did she come back?*

Melissa searched the darkness. The spider demon released a giggling sound, then retreated a few paces. The foe bounded away, racing toward a side passage in the great cavern. There, Catricha stood squinting in the flickering gloom.

Melissa shouted a warning as she gave chase.

CHAPTER 33

CATRICHA

In the darkness beneath the city, Catricha emerged from a descending labyrinth of narrow tunnels and stairways into a vast cavern. A din of essences at war assailed her ears across the stony plain. Catricha had never considered how loud a battle between magic-wielders could become.

She stood, transfixed, looking into the darkness, only making out flickers of movement and flashes of light. Essences' battle songs filled the cavern, vibrating the stone with their echoes. A piercing cry cut through the chaos.

"Catricha, get back!" shouted a metallic voice.

At the same moment, a gaunt face emerged from the clouds of debris and shifting darkness. Catricha recoiled, cold sweat trickling down her spine as spidery limbs followed the howling visage toward her. Before the grasping hands could reach Catricha, a thunderous roar and a flurry of dust cut into the spider demon's path. The two forms collided in a booming clash of flesh and steel.

Catricha retreated into the passage, up the path the way she had just come. Her hair flew in front of her face, adding to the confusion and chaos of the near-total darkness around her.

She fled along the tunnel, darting past a side passage where drifting lights glimmered in the dark. She didn't turn toward them, remembering the way back to the surface. Catricha could tell she was still far from the world of light. She scrambled up more than one flight of stairs, breathing hard.

The demon beast raced behind her. The spider and the steel demon clashed and tore at each other through the passages, ripping chunks from the walls and shattering columns as they fought to pursue her. *They must not be allies,* Catricha thought, but in their pursuit of her, they were singular.

"Damn it." Catricha gasped for breath. "I have to get out of here."

How foolish she'd been to go below the streets alone. She'd written to Ruar again, but he'd not replied or joined her at the meeting place, despite her hopes.

His brother must've got in his way. *Or his honor.* She hated her second thought, but the first was almost as bad. Ruar and Vual might be enemies now, not that it mattered much to Catricha if the demons caught her.

She climbed more stairs toward the surface, taking another flight upward. She panted out breaths as she raced up, up, and up. The two demons battling behind her, smashed through another side passage, but then quickly barreled back after Catricha. They fought in a flurry of limbs and spear strikes. Catricha saw the gray light of day ahead of her. The sun peeked through a cloudy sky.

She ran for the light. As she approached the exit, the sound of distant bells echoed in her head. She stumbled, and then came face-to-face with a new monster.

The demon outside the underground passage was tall and built strong, with heavily muscled arms. He bore a triangular scar on his face, but the mark appeared etched into the flesh on purpose rather than suffered in some battle. Catricha stumbled to a halt as the creature ducked his tall head and stepped into the passage in front of her.

"Who are you?" she asked. "What are you?"

"I'm your protector," said the demon. "I'm also your judge."

"That sounds familiar," she said. "Vual?"

"I'm wielding my sacra form," said Vual. "I was told keep it secret, but now I'm here to punish the monsters that lie below as well as you, for your complicity with them."

"Complicity? You know nothing, and your lack of knowledge will cost us our lives if you don't stand aside."

"Do you think those demons behind you are going to defeat me?"

"They're getting closer," said Catricha.

"I don't care," said Vual. "I'm here to punish you."

MELISSA

Fanhedon growled, a low sound that only Melissa could hear through her link with the demon in body and spirit. They faced the spider demon across the street from the surface amphitheater's open gate. The clouds opened just as they emerged from the building.

Rain pattered down only lightly at first.

The spider demon prowled toward Melissa. Fanhedon's power held her upright, and her iron bane kept her unfeeling and strong despite the battering. Melissa's resolve grew as she held the spear in demonic metal hands.

"How much more stamina can you give me?"

"As much as you need," said Fanhedon. "I'm not seriously hurt, and pain won't be enough to stop me if this is the best he can fight."

Melissa nodded. She desperately wanted to breathe despite the metallic mask that replaced her face. She couldn't breathe, because Fanhedon didn't breathe, but the sensation was unnerving at best and terrifying at worst.

What kind of demon is this? Fanhedon seemed to think he was a weak spider monk, but Melissa had yet to land a telling blow despite multiple attempts with her spear. The weapon reinforced by her iron bane had done serious damage to foes in the past. She'd felled demons more powerful than the spider, for certain.

"Do you know why he's so tough?" she asked in silence.

"No," Fanhedon answered in the same quiet. "I've never faced a spider demon as enduring as this one."

As enduring, Melissa thought, *that's one word for it.* She twirled the spear before her and set the butt of the weapon on the cobblestones of the street.

They faced each other along the thoroughfare. The handful of people who'd been out in the rain kept their distance from the fray.

The spider threw back his head and laughed "You humans and your attempts to be like us...You can take the form of another, but none who has not fallen before."

"To be reborn is an honor," said Fanhedon. "One afforded only to those who fell in glory."

"Continue to lie," said the spider. "If you must."

"Who are you?" asked Melissa. "What is your name, spider demon?"

"I joined myself to the conclave that rests beneath the streets. We serve a lower power now." The demon giggled. "Beware Jasguara's name."

"Jasguara? Whom do you serve?" hissed Melissa.

Despite her low voice, the sound reached the spider demon over the falling rain.

He inclined his head and smiled. "We all need our secrets, and I will keep mine."

Fanhedon tensed her muscles. "Then it's time you're destroyed, as in any battle against a superior being."

"Fanhedon is it? I suspect being you're less than truly immortal yourself, my form is the stronger. I will match you blood for blood."

The spider demon rose up on two pairs of his middle legs and spun a blade of silk that hung whip-like from his human fingers. The edge of the silk glittered with essence-disrupting banes.

"We are in the light," said the spider. "It is time to end this."

Melissa spoke in her mind. "Time to show your power, Fanhedon."

"We are in agreement," said her demon. "Time to strike." Melissa hurled herself forward, thrusting her spear toward the spider demon.

The foe recoiled, swinging his new blade of essence-silk to connect with the end of Melissa's spear. The iron bane reinforcement kept the weapon in one piece, but the point deflected from the dissonant essences on the edge of the spider demon's whip blade.

Melissa kicked out, pivoting on the spear butt planted on the ground. She drove both of Fanhedon's taloned feet into the demon's face. The spider demon caught the blow along the jaw and the cuts opened in the flesh there, though the wounds began to seal immediately.

The spider demon leapt backward and flew toward the tunnel opening. Catricha and the other mage in his sacra form retreated to either side as the spider demon flew between them. The thickly-muscled sacra form jumped over the spider demon and returned to the ground beside Catricha.

"You won't escape that easily," he said.

"Catricha," said Melissa. "Keep still. I'll be there in a moment."

"This man is out more odious than you know," Catricha called in reply. "His form matches him well."

Before the unknown sacra form wielder could respond, the spider demon hopped back on all fours toward Melissa. Melissa didn't hear the other mage's retort.

She and the spider demon clashed back and forth.

Melissa retreated a few paces, battering back blows from the long and ever-growing whip. The silk and attached essences left gouges in the street where it struck. The disruptive banes made stone burst with a mere touch.

"A formidable weapon," said Fanhedon inside Melissa's mind. "But, I have means to defeat it."

"Tell me," said Melissa in silence.

"His essence is feeding the blade," said Fanhedon, "We must strike his spirit. Sever his link to the whip and you will be able to damage his connection to his weapon and disrupt its power."

"Separate his essences from the weapon." Melissa parried another strike with a crack of the whip. "A good plan."

Fanhedon and Melissa dodged to one side, skating along the stone street. They darted toward the spider demon's flank. The spider demon lashed in their direction, but Melissa hurdled it. She flew through the air, then landed on the other side of the demon.

Her spear blocked the next whip strike. Fanhedon's taloned hand jabbed toward the spider's wrist. The human hand of the demon contained a resident bane connecting all the power in the demon's body to the whip, just as Fanhedon suggested. Melissa understood the din of loud musical notes better as she stepped closer. Amid the chaotic sounds, she sliced at the bane on the spider demon's wrist.

Her teasing fingertips sliced through demon-skin, but the bane eluded her touch. Her essences couldn't grip the monster's inner power as the bane flew into the spider's hand, narrowly avoiding her severing attack.

Melissa lurched backward, then leapt upward and blocked another strike with the spear's haft. The whip coiled around her spear and the spider demon tried to yank the weapon from Melissa's hands. She reinforced her strength, using all Fanhedon's might and held the spear fast.

She dived toward the ground and landed, bouncing on both feet. She kept her grip on the spear while trying to twist it to break the demon's grasp on the weapon. Her eyes narrowed within the mask.

She shoved out with all her strength, and forced the spider demon back another pace. The creature dug in his hind claws and pointed feet dove into stones of the street, pinning the monster in place.

Melissa lashed the spider with Fanhedon's feet, cutting at the demon's belly again. The spider recoiled, and released her spear from the coiling whip. In an instant, the demon redoubled his attack, but Fanhedon's armor proved enough to defend against every ensuing blow. In spite of the flurry of strikes, Fanhedon flinched mentally as the silk whip cracked across the street and propelled fragments of stone into her knees and shins.

"The pain is tolerable," said Fanhedon. "I will endure it for your sake, awakener."

"What's wrong?" asked the spider demon. "Are you two conferring?"

Melissa said nothing, but pressed the attack. She drove the spider to retreat toward the passage as the demon retaliated with a flurry of strikes and whips snaps.

Street stones cracked and flew out of place. After thirty minutes, as the bells tolled one o'clock, in the distant towers, Melissa began to tire. The spider appeared no worse for wear.

Fanhedon spoke to Melissa, "the pain is growing, but I will assist you as long as I can."

"As long as you can," said Melissa. "How much more can you take?"

"At this rate, it could be another hour, but we may be able to fight longer if we are careful."

"Once we take him down we can rest."

"I don't see a weakness in him," said Fanhedon. "I can't sever any of his essences."

"He must be protecting them somehow." Melissa said.

"There is a presence about him. I can't be certain why, but he's to be resilient to essence manipulation."

"Are you figuring me out?" The spider demon grinned. "When we awaken, we do not require rest for some time, and while we wake, we are resilient without limit."

How much time?

"So you there is a limit to what you can do?" Melissa said.

"There are limits to everything any being can do," said the spider demon. "Fanhedon should know this best, among all of us, as a fallen form."

"This fallen form is more than enough to end your prattle. " said Fanhedon. "Let me show you."

Melissa let the demon speak through her, but Fanhedon's temper appear to be rising even more than at the battle of Soucot. The boiling heat of rage coursed through Melissa. Her mind charged with the demon's fury. *Can I control Fanhedon for much longer?*

The spider demon raised his whip blade, then slashed outward, but failed to wrap the weapon around the spear as Fanhedon accelerated faster than before. The rage driving Fanhedon forced the spider backward. Her spear broke through the monster's defenses and sliced through the demon's torso.

Still, not a single essence changed tune because of the blade. All their songs continued in discordant chaos. The spider demon's lash cracked across Fanhedon's shoulder. White-hot pain burned more intense than the fury of Melissa's inner demon. Fanhedon's armor plate cracked and buckled with the force of the impact and the destructive power of the banes.

Nevertheless, Fanhedon did not release the spear or retreat from the demon. Her talons shot out from below, and tore at the other demon's flesh. The spider demon's skin hung in shreds, inner organs exposed. Black blood splattered the street. The spider still grinned manically as if he could feel no pain.

"Why won't you fall?" Fanhedon growled.

"The magic I wield is of the oldest kind."

"Division! You've made a cluster of external essences to protect yourself."

"All demons must find some way to live," said the spider demon in a husky voice. "I have found a way to live eternally alongside my brothers."

"You monks will never achieve what you want."

"On the contrary," the spider demon. "The conclave is close to an end."

Melissa grimaced. She twisted the spear in the demon's chest. Fanhedon's talons continued to rake and tear at the demon's lower body. The creature appeared no weaker mentally, and his stamina remained despite the damage done to his body.

The whip-blade struck Fanhedon's head. Her mask cracked from the impact, and Melissa stumbled backward. She released her grip on the spear. The spider demon pulled the weapon from its chest with fluid motion.

"Now it is my turn to hurt you." A grin etched itself on the spider's bloodstained features.

Shouts came from either side of them. She retreated a pace and found Galocai and Elaine along with Bethanelle and her hunters approaching along the street, opposite the direction where Catricha and Vual watched the fray.

"I have assistance," said Melissa. "And we will beat you now that they've arrived."

She took a defensive stance, both bloody claws raised. Despite Fanhedon's mental daze, Melissa remained clear of thought and in mind. The pain in the demonic form she wore did not extend to her human mind.

The spider demon laughed. "Then, I will have to punish you as well as them." He reeled his arm back and hurled Melissa spear straight at Catricha.

Melissa dove for the weapon, closing to intercepting it by grabbing the handle but she moved too slow to get a firm grip. She twisted, tackling the spear out of the air with every bit of Fanhedon's speed. The weapon skittered and bounced across the ravaged street and then rolled to a stop at Catricha's feet.

The spider jumped onto Fanhedon's back and pummeled her from behind. Blow after blow rained on her back, neck, and head. Melissa's view rattled and she rolled onto the stones.

The demon's spidery legs dug into Fanhedon's armor. The sharp points couldn't break it like they could the street, but the weight of the monster pinned her. She got her arms beneath the monster and then hurled the demon off. Melissa regained her feet.

"Should I finish them before or after you?" The spider demon cackled. "I have plenty of time for both."

"Your fight is with me." Melissa raised her sharp hands.

"I will teach you what I please, Fanhedon, and your awakener, too." The spider demon tugged on his silk strings and flew to land on Fanhedon's back once more. The monster clung to demonic armor as easily as any wall or floor.

"Melissa!" called Elaine. "Are you alright?"

The pain and haze of the demon's slashes on her back raced through Melissa. "Elaine, stay back."

Galocai put his hands together, completing a woven spell, and shot a bolt of hardened air. He knocked the spider demon from Fanhedon's back. Melissa whirled to face the monster, gaze flickering with pain as she looked from Fanhedon's cracked mask.

She retrieved her spear with a quick kick and catch, then grimaced with pain. A shadow flitted passed overhead. She heard the same song as the first day she'd met Deckard Hadrian. The sound of divine trumpets blasted through Alliance.

Deckard Hadrian slammed onto the spider demon's back, crashing down with more force than a man of six-and-a-half spans in height could ever wield without magic. His impact smashed the spider into the cracked earth, cratering the street beneath them. Deckard stooped. He picked up the spider demon, as if the stunned monster was light as a feather. He hurled the promortal demon into the air.

"No," the demon screamed. "Hadrian?"

Deckard did not wait, but flew into the air after the spider. The airborne demon caught the harsh breeze on a band of silk, narrowly avoiding Deckard's next strike.

The spider demon cut his silk tethers and fell back to the street. He scuttled through the tunnel in the amphitheater, and into the darkness of the catacombs. The sound of his heart song receded.

Deckard land beside Melissa. The sun above was obscured by clouds. Rain began to fall heavily.

"Fanhedon," said Melissa. "Rest."

"Thank you, awakener." Fanhedon's form faded from Melissa and she regained her own shape.

She stared at Deckard. "I didn't expect you," she said.

"Surely you knew I was present in the city," said Deckard. "I'm not exactly surreptitious. I'm surprised that spider demon could handle you in your sacra form for so long."

"You ought to know." Melissa gulped a breath. "No demon or Sacra form is invincible."

"Wait." Deckard's eyes narrowed. "There's something wrong."

He turned in the direction of the palace, where rain struck the dome and a heavy shadow descended from the clouds over the city center.

The clouds parted for moment, and the ring around the world, where the city of the maladrites stood, appeared in the heavens. For a moment, even the weak sunlight illuminating the ring brightened the sky to brilliance. The clouds rejoined as suddenly as they'd parted. Deckard's attention snapped back to Melissa.

"I must go," he said. "Don't return underground today."

"What's happening?" Melissa glared at him. "Tell me."

"There's been an attack at the palace."

He took to the air and raced toward the city center. Melissa charged after him, reinforcing her limbs with her already-weary essences to accelerate herself faster.

CHAPTER 34

DECKARD

He raced through the corridors of the prince's palace, bounding toward Kizoni's chambers. The smell of blood and the sound of disrupted essence-songs filled the dim passageways. Deckard hated to be tricked, and the growing pit of dread in his stomach told him the spider demon had gotten the better of all of them.

In the hall outside Kizoni's chamber, beneath a derelict lantern with the lights of the sprites, Deckard hesitated. He stared at the open doorway. The glimmering of orange, fading sunlight out the window told him the day was growing late. Through the doorway and the window lay the shapes of the two guards who usually stood in attendance of the dowager regent's chambers.

Deckard clenched his fists and marched to the doorway.

The sunlight cast a bitter glare on the bodies in the room. The fallen form of Terrel Varder slumped beside one of the handmaidens, strewn upon the elegant couch near the window. Two more guards, lay collapsed in the wings of the entryway. Whatever had struck them had struck fast and hard.

There was no sign of Kizoni.

Deckard's teeth ground together. He forced his jaws to still, unwilling to increased the suffering he endured at that moment. Kizoni would have sent him away, but he ought to have known they were planning an attack against her.

Whoever they are.

The strike had come from above, from the city in the sky. The maladrites of the highest city interfered with the mortal world for as long as Deckard could recall. Destroying the leader of a major city in Jadiketz was once an impossible move, Most in the maladrite city respected Mother Mercy's power.

No one in the city could lie behind this attack. It must be someone in Alliance.

Deckard picked up the darkened infused sword Terrell Varder had wielded from where it lay near the man's mangled right hand.

"This," said Deckard softly. "Was not enough to stop whatever attacked."

Behind him came footsteps, fast, powerful and thunderous. Melissa's heart-song pounded through the hallway, reverberating toward Deckard. He turned to face her as she stumbled to a stop in the doorway.

"What happened?" she asked.

"Something powerful attacked from above," said Deckard, "while we were distracted."

"We? You haven't spoken to me since you arrived in the city. There is no 'we' here."

"Forgive me," said Deckard. "I doubt either of us could've protected her in that moment."

"What happened? Where is Kizoni?"

"Whoever struck the palace has taken Kizoni with them." He felt tears bead unbidden in his eyes, but they wouldn't flow.

Melissa's expression hardened. "We'll find her."

"I appreciate the sentiment," said Deckard. "We must find the regent before time runs out."

"She hired me to look into the sleepless cult. Could they have anything to do with this?"

"They may," said Deckard. "But they lack the power to deliver an attack of this strength."

"Demons did this?" Melissa gazed in horror around the chamber. "Or was it beings from on high?"

"I should've known." Deckard put his face in his hands, but his tears still didn't flow. His shoulders shook and he turned from Melissa and sank to his knees before the sunlight flowing through the open window. Wind made the curtains flap against the frame. "I should have known, because this is what demons do. They strike when you least suspect."

"That spider monk couldn't have done this alone." said Melissa. "There must be more of them."

"Likely, there are many more."

"How many more?"

"I can't say for certain, but I'd guess the city below is home to many."

"What should we do?" said Melissa. "We can't let the city go without a leader."

"It is neither of our place to determine the next prince. I only want the city to be stable again."

She nodded, somehow still calm despite the carnage before her. "Do you have a plan?"

"Not yet." Deckard pushed himself to his feet with his hands. "I will, once we get to the throne room. I must prepare to address the people."

"We should go. We can't do anything for the dead right now." Melissa gestured at the fallen forms of the slain defenders in the room.

"They are beyond help." Deckard heaved as sigh. "Their essences have departed."

Melissa gritted her teeth, then turned and marched into the corridor outside. *It must not be easy to see such death so soon after the battles in Soucot that claimed the lives of some she considered friends.*

To be immortal meant to see the death of all mortal humans that one knew. Immortality brought pain that mortals never understood, but it was merely amplified grief from what each soul endured in an ordinary lifetime.

Deckard went between the bodies and closed their eyes. The expression of shock on Varder's face and the horror in the sightless eyes of the handmaidens made him shiver. The guards appeared as loyal and taciturn as ever, but their silence was cold and vacant now, opposite the sense of security they provided in life.

With what little he could do complete, he went into the hall and joined Melissa.

* * *

The two of them marched into the throne room, making their way through the halls as quickly as they could. Melissa carried her spear. Deckard didn't know what good it would do to have the young mage at his side if he told the people he'd assumed the position of regent.

Nobility and common people from the street flowed in through the broken gates of the palace. Deckard glimpsed Catricha Maltos and Vual Kuldettan in the crowd. Evidently they'd followed him, along with Elaine Tanlos and Galocai Paroth with the hunters from House Graef.

Those present must be innocent of the crime. Deckard heard their surprise in the essence songs rising from them. Deckard approached the throne, through the crowd. He drew close to the seat of Alliance, then he saw he'd been beaten to the ornate chair.

Standing before the throne was Virgil Silas Dane. The old man, his face weathered by a wind and storm, and lined by age, waited in silence. His black parson's vestments helped him cast an imposing shadow upon the crowd below the raised dais where the throne stood.

Virgil served only one master, and it wasn't Mother Mercy directly. He served Cyrus Bode, Deckard's brother in blood and cause. He served Deckard's enemy, and Cyrus had been a foe for too long for Deckard not to know what Virgil's presence here meant.

Over the decades of Virgil's life, he'd hunted Deckard more than once at the will of his true master. Deckard gazed upon the throne and Virgil before it. The aged parson's white hair hung around his head, having grown out some since Deckard last saw him almost a full year ago.

He held a walking stick, but didn't need it to support his weight. He held the stick in both hands at his back. "Alliance," said Virgil. "I don't know how to tell you what happened to your honored dowager regent."

Deckard listen for any disturbance inside in Virgil's essence song but found no dissonance from lies or deceit. The cloak of calm remained as his veneer. He appeared as innocent of the horror that occurred in Kizoni's chambers as any of the others.

"I have been chosen to become regent of the city for as long as you need my help. Though it is unusual for a parson to hold such a position, it is not without precedent in other lands of mercy. Alliance has never had an interregnum before. I will assure an orderly transition to your next princely household."

He motioned to the waiting pair of armored figures who detached from the shadows and approached on either side of the throne.

"These are holy knights of the Geteren Clan. They're here to help me keep the peace for the moment."

Catricha stepped forward within the crowd, and the people parted around her. "With respect, Parson Dane, what kind of foreigner dares name himself regent of the city?"

"I carry a letter from Cyrus Bode," said Virgil. "The immortal foresaw the extent of this chaos. I will protect Alliance with all my resources and abilities. I do this, because I've been commanded to do so, not because I seek power for myself."

The two knights advanced. Deckard grimaced within the crowd. Of all his rivalries, and all his enemies, Virgil always brought the worst of both with him.

Melissa glanced at Deckard. "The clan sent knights?"

"Have you heard that they hate me?" Deckard said under his breath.

"Cyrus Bode hates you?"

"Yes," he said.

Virgil spoke. "I have taken this seat in the name of order and in the name of Mother Mercy."

"I see no mercy here," said Catricha. "Only ruthlessness. You would take the city for the Chos Valley, for Well Country and your master there. We here are not pawns of Cyrus Bode."

"Hardly would I call you pawns, Lady Maltos." Virgil bowed to the people before him. "I have come to officiate a means to determine which noble house shall inherit the throne. You will have your chance, and you'll have your words to speak, Lady Maltos, but not today."

Galocai Paroth stepped out of the crowd and put a hand on Catricha's arm. "Excuse us, Parson Dane." He turned and said something to Catricha that Deckard missed in the hubbub of the crowd that followed. The two nobles retreated from the front of the crowd.

Melissa glanced in their direction. Time had ways to disillusion everyone from their attractions.

Deckard slipped away to the crowd. He had no time to deal with Virgil's words or the clan's knights. He had to find Kizoni as quickly as possible. *If that remains possible.* He had to get to the maladrite city. Deckard left the palace, passed through the crowd, and then took to the sky.

CHAPTER 35

CATRICHA

Snow fell lightly on the last day of the tenth month as Catricha made her way back to the palace, remembering her footsteps on the second day she'd gone underground. Fear assailed her more than ever as the memory arose.

Sion Arver walked with her in the present, and Porfiria at her other side.

Parson Dane's conditions for passing the throne were still unknown. And after four weeks of uncertainty, the city needed to know what happened next. Enrin and Hyla Maltos walked behind Catricha, Porfiria, and Sion on the way to the palace.

A carriage would be more convenient normally, but in the crowded street, foot travel was easier.

Catricha led the way toward the palace. She clenched her hand as she thought of what had happened that led to today. Virgil Silas Dane and the knights from the clan had indeed kept order, but with cruel hands toward the people.

Catricha had written many lines about them in the past few weeks, but spoke few of them aloud. She must play her cards closer to her chest than usual.

Keeping the suits clean and the hand fair was a card-players ideal, but Virgil held one more card than anyone else at the table. Whatever game they were playing, he was the only one aware of all the rules because he made them.

Catricha glanced at Porfiria. Her friend head been quiet on the walk from the Maltos manor. Ever since Deckard Hadrian had left the city, following Kizoni's disappearance, Porfiria head been disconnected from events. She'd published a poetry plate, but that made the only recent exposure of her cynicism to the public. Even Catricha had not seen much of her friend recently. Porfiria had emerged from her house a week after the attack sent a portion of the nobility into hiding.

They made their way up the path up into the palace. The ice in the river grew thicker day after day, and the current began to slow. Snow fell lightly as the lords and ladies of Alliance made their way under the palace domes of stone and crystal. White flakes spiraled along the rooftops in drifting patterns.

The nobility gathered in the throne room, where Virgil and the empty seat of the prince stood at the front.

The parson looked as much like an aged snake as any man Catricha could imagine. His pallor looked gray, and his hair white. Virgil's very essence song sounded colder than the air outside.

Despite his reputation as a powerful wizard, Catricha saw no sign of the new regent's hidden magic in the past few weeks. Unlike Hadrian, who flew everywhere on the power of his sprites, the parson appeared more at ease in the political situation than controlling essences.

She spotted Ruar and Vual with their mother, Filavaye, at the front of the Kuldettan group, but Ruar wouldn't look at her.

Nansoela and Galocai Paroth stood opposite each other, one with the retainers of her house, and the other with House Greaf and Melissa Dorian. Heron Olfrus stood between the two. He and his sister had made themselves a presence in the city over the past month, but not as oppressively as the other new arrivals from the Chos Valley who stood before them.

These five families made up the most aggressive elements vying for the throne. Few others could even dream of challenging them. Even the merchant families couldn't declare one of their number the next prince.

Only old blood can afford such risks.

Catricha's family might be more mixed than the others, with Hyla hailing from a common background. Still, every household here but one was known for honor. The Olfrus family might be powerful in wealth, but they lacked in standing in the city.

Porfiria spoke softly. "I wonder what Dane will suggest?"

"We'll see soon enough," said Catricha. "I'm sure he'll want to bloviate."

"More like oh-bloviate." Porfiria sighed. "He's going to talk until we're all destroyed."

"Why did you come with us, then?" asked Catricha with a slight smirk. "Was the suspense too great for you?"

"The tension is high," Porfiria said. "But no, I am curious to see what he says even if he buries us in a sea of platitudes."

"More like a blizzard of platitudes." Catricha nodded.

"That's better," Porfiria said. "Well done."

"But you didn't laugh."

"This is no laughing matter."

"I'm still disappointed," said Catricha. "Once I could make you laugh."

"You haven't been practicing enough." Porfiria shrugged. "If I'm going to crack a smile or release a giggle, I need more stimulation than that, my dear friend."

"More stimulation? Do you miss the immortal so badly?"

"Don't speak nonsense." Porfiria wrinkled her nose. "I'd never."

"He was staying at your house," said Catricha. "Surely, people will talk?"

"I suppose we are people."

"We certainly are," said Catricha. "Oh, the parson seems to be ready to say his piece."

Catricha and Porfiria looked toward the dais where Virgil stood near the throne. Virgil folded his hands on the round cap of his cane, and leaned on the length of wood. "It has been some time. I have assessed the situation in the city along with my advisers."

"Here we go." Porfiria whispered. "Bloviating."

"I have seen what you nobility are capable of," said Virgil. "We have no opinion on which of you is more worthy to lead the city, yet."

He paced back and forth on the stage of that before the throne. "You each have your desired outcome, but it is up to me to choose the next

Prince of the city. Ever since Deckard Hadrian took his leave, I am the only authority present to adjudicate the situation. Given my general lack of knowledge of what goes on among your households, I declare a challenge to see which of you will put forth the best heir to the throne. Each family may select one candidate to challenge for the name of prince. The challengers shall then compete to become the next Prince of Alliance. In the end, I and a few others will judge the outcome, but it is not my place to determine, alone, who the next prince shall be."

Virgil nodded. "Be patient, and I will determine what I can from the challenge, which will be of the classical variety, as determined by the poetry of Jadik. We will test who the greatest ruler will be, just as Jadik suggested in his short trials of succession."

"Does that please you?" Virgil asked. "The great houses will not be the only ones capable of competing. Any noble or knight of age can become the heir to the throne as long as they prove themselves."

"So," muttered Porfiria. "A free-for-all."

"Certainly seems that way," said Catricha. "Seems frightening."

"Don't be afraid." Porfiria shook her head as people began to mutter all around. "I won't challenge you or your claim."

"My claim?" Catricha asked. "I suppose I'm the only member of my household of age, who is eligible."

"Indeed, but your training with your strong essences is going well, from what I understand. We can move to teach you actual techniques soon."

Between Porfiria's help, attempts to arrange lessons with the master mage Baltas Truncheon, and Catricha's occasional encounters with Melissa and Elaine, her control of her strong essences might be in reach. Still, she could hardly qualify how powerful her magic might be. Melissa had been generous in offering her assistance, though Catricha wished she'd had Ruar's help as well during training.

"That is all that needs be divulged now," said Virgil. "The first part of the challenge is one of wit and honor. The rules will be put forth soon enough, and challengers will have time to train."

Good, thought Catricha. "I don't think he knows how ruthless the households can be," she said to Porfiria. "We'll all bleed before the end of this ordeal."

"Cat, you can do this. You can win."

Catricha still only wanted to find the truth behind who killed Adias and Saviron. *No doubt, the destroyer of the Prince also stole away his widow.*

"Did you hear?" Catricha asked. "There have been rumors that Kizoni was pregnant before she disappeared."

"It's possible," Porfiria said. "If so, Prince Saviron may have a true heir, yet here we stand."

"I certainly pray Mother Mercy shields Kizoni, wherever she is," said Catricha.

"Are you more pious than before?" said Porfiria. "At times even I regret lacking my ability to pray."

"It's not difficult for those of us without a cynical attitude."

"My cynicism is all I have, my dear."

"Perhaps." Catricha smiled. "Being outrageous is my primary ability. I could offend everyone in this room, but then I would have even less chance of becoming the princess of the city. The princess is always going to be the most outrageous person in the city."

"I'm a bit too old to fight for accolades and titles," said Porfiria. "You have at it."

"Will you keep helping with my magic?" asked Catricha. "There's no way I'll be able to compete in the challenge of a warrior without your help."

"You've had some help already," said Porfiria. "Or is that sacra form-wielding Melissa Dorian, no one to you?"

"I miss your friendship," said Catricha. "Admittedly, more than your skill as a mage."

"Regardless, I can help you."

"Thank you," said Catricha. "Shall we?"

The crowd began to break up. People began to stream from the throne room, muttering and talking among themselves. Catricha, and Porfiria, and the others returned to the snowy world outside.

CHAPTER 36

VUAL

In the weeks since the arrival of Virgil Silas Dane and his knights in Alliance, Vual head seen his mother go from eager, to annoyed with the state of the city. She wanted to see power transition to House Kuldettan as soon as possible. The presence of the Chos Valley delegation in control of the throne began to rankle her before long.

Soon the presence of Virgil in place of Deckard Hadrian began to set her as ill at ease as it did Vual. Cyrus Bode was Hadrian's rival, and Virgil worked directly for the immortal of the Chos Valley.

As descendants of Deckard Hadrian, the Kuldettans might not be direct foes of Cyrus Bone and the Geteren Clan he ruled. Still, there was always the possibility they'd become enemies at any moment.

Cyrus, though Vual, *always rests like a shadow over the northern lands.* Bode's military forces were capable of projecting the strength of the immortal master wherever he desired within the lands of mercy, but the closer to the Chos Valley, the more easily they achieved such things.

Vual and not seen nor heard of the immortal carrying out such brutal action in his lifetime, only remembering a little from his youth. Cyrus had been the one to command the gathering of so many nobles and knights from the cities to go to war with the Kism in the east. The radical opponents of

Mother Mercy had demanded more assistance than the clan could provide alone, to do battle with them.

Though that time seemed long ago, Vual only felt more uneasy at the presence of the elder mage, Virgil. Most wizards knew his name. Virgil Silas Dane was one of most powerful and skilled wielders of sacra forms in the entirety of the land of mercy, not just the north.

Normally, if Virgil had not been Cyrus Bode's servant, Vual might have been eager to prove himself as Filavaye had assured him he should earlier in the month. However, as the pinnacle of the final month, Tigalas, approached and snow began to fall again, the challenge that lay before them became clear. If the contest Virgil suggested went forward, and anyone with enough support could join the fray, Vual might have more competition in the approaching contest.

Would I be afraid if someone from the southern lands had arrived with a similar position? No, he thought. No, he would not be afraid. And thus, he decided, he would not fear Virgil Silas Dane.

Vual met with his mother in the parlor of the Kuldettan mansion. She was pale, sick, suffering from the same cold-borne illness that came each winter in recent years.

She sat, bundled in a great chair near the embers of a fire. The blankets covered her form almost completely up to the neck. She looked toward him as he entered.

"Son," she said. "Are you prepared to begin your training for the challenges?"

"Training?" Vual laughed. "Mother, the challenges won't begin until the new year."

“If you don't train now, you will not be prepared. I've asked your uncle to prepare lessons for you."

"You gave me a sacra scroll, and he told me my sacra form was ready." Vual scowled at his mother. "I fail to see what any others could do against me with such power now at my command. I control a demon now."

"I'm not worried about your physical combat abilities, but you must realize the challenges will demand more than your honor, courage, and magic."

"I realize that." Vual turned away from his mother. "My sword and my sacra form should be enough to tackle every challenge before me. Before I took the form of Nalneth, I couldn't tell his intelligence, his glorious overflowing power in both mind and body. But when I took his shape, all of that suffused me."

"Not all take to their sacra form as easily as you, my son."

"Is it true that Virgil has more than one inner demon?" asked Vual.

"My spies tell me the stories are true," said Filavaye. "He's mastered three."

"How can one man master three sacra forms?" Vual said. "Even I ache in the mind to think of such a crowded spirit, and Nalneth rarely speaks to me."

"Dane found a way." Filavaye shook her head. "But you will need to impress more than him if you are to become prince."

"Of course, mother. What do you know of the other judges?"

"All will be drawn from nobility, except for Virgil himself."

"The fact that Dane is positioning himself to be the ultimate judge of the city's ruler makes me suspicious, mother," said Vual. "Doesn't it bother you?"

"If I thought it mattered, I would confront him myself."

"Mother." Vual nodded. "I would advise you remain indoors for the time being, at least until the sickness passes."

"Thank you for the respectful suggestion. I'll do what I must, however." Filavaye motioned Vual closer with her chin. "Of the three classical challenges. One of them is wit, one of them is war, and one of them is ruling. I don't know exactly what each one of consist of, but the training for war is the one we have the greatest advantage in. But that is the second challenge of Jadik. The first challenge is wit. Son, you must think faster."

"Is this some sort of joke?" Vual laughed. "I've looked into the skill of writing, but I'll never be like Ruar or Catricha Maltos. I don't have that kind of cunning."

"And Nalneth won't supply it for you?" said Filavaye. "He is an incredibly intelligent demon, as was said of him when he walked the land as a free being."

"When Nalneth walked the land of his own accord, I had yet to be born. If I'm not mistaken, so had you."

"You're not mistaken. But Nalneth has more to tell you then just how to calculate the strength needed to shatter a boulder or how activate his wings of fire or his flaming blades. No, Nalneth is a more powerful sacra form than even you know."

"Should I rely on Nalneth for every test as well?" said Vual.

"Don't lean on him like a crutch," said Filavaye. "Your sacra form cannot hold the throne. Still, listen to him. I assure you, if you fail to perform in one challenge it will be your wit that brings you down."

"I'll go practice making remarks, then, mother."

"I suggest, you find someone to spar with verbally."

"Spar verbally," said Vual. "I think I know the person."

"Are you planning to go to Fulster again?" Filavaye smiled slyly, chin buried in her blankets

"Mother, you wound me with your accuracy."

"Accuracy." Filavaye laughed. "You just want to meet with Osestra Nim-Fulster again."

"Why not?" Vual said. "She and I have always gotten along since we were young."

"You are still young," said Filavaye. "Go, then. Ride to Fulster, if you wish. The snow is falling, but it should still be light on the road."

"I'll take my personal guards," said Vual.

"See that you all are well-dressed for the journey." Filavaye waved him away with an open hand.

* * *

Vual and his guards rode to Fulster in the biting wind. Even as they moved south, the gale turned against them. They approached the stockade around Fulster and the howling of the wind intensified. The snow began to fall more heavily on the road and the forests west of them. The fields on the eastern side turned whiter with every passing moment.

He dismounted at the gates of Fulster, and then led his horse inside. The gate closed behind him and his bodyguards. They approached the town hall where Osestra stepped onto the top step to greet him. She looked stunning in her snow-colored scarf, her hair pulled back then left to fall over her shoulders. Her eyes sparkled like fresh ice crystals. Her gown and winter mantle shimmered different shades of almost-blue, hinting at sea-green.

"You came in spite of the storm. I didn't think even you would brave weather like this, when the sentries told me you might be on your way."

"If the sentinels spotted us a mile away, even in this." Vual took off his riding gloves and blew on his chilly fingers. "I need to thank them, because they had the gate open when we arrived."

"I'll send them your regards." Osestra beamed. "Vual, you and your men should come inside. The guards can get out of the cold in the kitchen."

"Thank you." Vual and his men bowed their heads.

They entered through the patterned doors. Separating from the guards, Vual and Osestra took their seats beside the hearth at the center of the keeper's hall. She poured a cup of tea for each of them. The rest of her family was occupied elsewhere, so Vual and Osestra sat in easy chairs near the fire.

"Are you worried, Vual? The arrival of those men from the Chos Valley can't be good news, can it? They must be up to something."

"I don't know." Vual stared into the flames crackling in the fireplace. "To be honest, my mother agrees with your thought. She may be glad for Parson Dane's presence, but his knights make her uneasy. His attitude toward the city only adds to the trouble."

"Attitude?" Osestra reached for his hand. "What is his attitude?"

"He's dismissive." Vual took her hand in his, palm to palm. "He treats Alliance like we're some colony, not very nearly the center of old Jadiketz, second only to the city called Empire."

"I suppose when one comes from the Chos Valley." Osestra intertwined her fingers with his. "Anywhere else seems provincial."

"Perhaps." Vual sighed. "Regardless, I don't like his dismissal of our culture in the land of mercy. After all, Chos Valley, despite being the heart of the old Empire, is practically a wasteland compared to Alliance."

"Will you participate in his challenge?" asked Osestra. "You could become prince if you do."

"I intend to try." Vual frowned. "But I don't have to appreciate the man who gives me the opportunity."

"I suppose not." Osestra smiled slightly. "Once you become prince, perhaps then, as you said before..."

"Perhaps we can marry?" whispered Vual. "I suppose you're right."

"You suppose?" Osestra blinked in surprise, looked indignant for a moment, then turned to look into the fire.

"I know it. I know it and I'm glad."

"Have you spoken to your mother?"

"Not about that, yet," said Vual. "She is occupied by other matters at the moment, but the time is drawing near when I will do as we planned."

"I'm glad." Osestra smiled at him. "Vual."

She wrapped her slender hands around the cup of hot tea she held and then raised the porcelain to her lips.

Vual looked at the tea she'd poured for him. His reflection looked warped and brown in the surface of the liquid. "Do you really want that?" he asked. "Not many in the city appreciate me. Despite your brothers, and all, how you can remain so enthusiastic?"

"I can remain however I wish," said Osestra. "I'm free, as are you. That is the power afforded to us by our position in the hierarchy of mercy."

"The hierarchy of mercy," murmured Vual, "is not enough to put me at ease. Osestra, I will find a way even if I cannot become prince. But I don't know if that will be the true issue or not. After all, I have skills with the blade and with essences. My wit is the only thing I find lacking."

"You don't lack wit," said Osestra. "You just need to use it more often." She laughed.

Her tea shook slightly with the motion of her body.

Vual chuckled. He set his cup on the small table between them.

"Perhaps you could help me?"

"Of course." Osestra gazed into his eyes. "I'm happy to assist you, my friend and my lord."

CHAPTER 37

DECKARD

Ilrona's chambers in the House of Mercy lacked the concept of orientation. In the cool air of the dark room, objects and beings floated adrift, weightless. The disruption of ordinary material laws put even Deckard Hadrian ill at ease.

He disliked the place, but his questions demanded answers. Why had Mother Mercy sent him to Alliance? Did she, did either of them, know the nature of the shadow being Zidon vanquished all those ages past during the conquest?

The lack of a pull in any direction left Deckard floating without sense of up or down while he waited for Ilrona to appear. After a few hours, she emerged from one of the fluid gates that occupied the edges of perception in the room. Those portals led countless places, but Deckard could not tell where each one ended, knowledge only Ilrona held.

She liked her secrets.

Ilrona drifted toward him, as effortless and forceless as everything else in her chambers. The dark banes singing on one side terminated their dissonance where they met the glowing brightness of her other half.

She always seemed larger here, as she bent to address the few petitioners who accessed her rooms.

"How long have you been here, immortal?" asked the demon lady from the bright side of her mouth. "I didn't expect your presence."

She brought her bright side close to him, no eyes but clearly able to perceive him as surely as if she'd been covered in them.

Deckard closed his eyes, shutting out the glare of her brightness. "I'm sure you'd be lonely without me."

The chittering staccato of her light essences served as laughter. Ilrona's glow diminished, telling Deckard she'd drawn back, even behind his eyelids. He opened one eye to look.

She folded her arms, light and darkness interlocking. "Why are you here, demon hunter?"

He bowed his head best as he could in a place where the very concept of up and down was an absent memory. "Lady of light and dark, I request your advice on my mission."

"Questions? Ask them." Ilrona's voice echoed in the chamber.

"Why did Cyrus send Virgil to take Alliance? Does Mother Mercy accept his actions as legitimate?"

"You human sons of mercy ought to seek better terms, demon hunter. After all, only you two remain upon the world, after what you did to—"

"After Tetzirat's fall, yes." Deckard scowled. "That is beside my aim. Cyrus is shaking the order of all the land by trying to claim Alliance through a proxy."

"Take it up with him yourself, as I cannot." Ilrona's voice was cold, deadened and without affect. "Do you have anything else to say?"

"Do you know anything about the Shadow of Jasguara?"

"You speak the old name of Alliance. Zidon bested the shadow for me there, almost a thousand years ago. Have you a reason for asking?"

"I suspect the shadow has returned to the city."

"How could he?" Ilrona with a smirk in her voice. "When you look upon him now?" She held out her dark arm, fluidly stretching the limb what would be an unnatural length for a human. "I took the essences Zidon claimed from him for my own."

Deckard's brow furrowed. "You've been collecting dark essences, of course."

"Perhaps I should be more curious about events in Alliance, demon hunter. Your unease tells me more. Have you encountered any of these dark essences?"

Deckard thought of Catricha, recalling the sound of her strong essences. She possessed a shadow sprite, and a cursed bane by his estimation. Wherever those essences had come from Deckard had no plans to turn them over to Mother Mercy's handmaiden. Separating strong essences permanently could kill a mortal owner.

"No," said Deckard. "But the reports of Prince Saviron's murder spoke of a shadow appearing as the culprit. Could it be a demon or a mage?"

"Either is possible, but I have no more answers for you now, demon hunter. Leave my chambers."

"As you will, Ilrona."

"I will be watching, demon hunter."

Deckard nodded. "I'm certain of that." He closed his eyes as the sensation of directions began to return. When he felt solid ground beneath him, he looked around.

Deckcard stood in one of the central plazas of Alliance, a few streets south of the tombs, within a worn-down shrine to Mother Mercy. The sun climbed high and cold overhead, and the clouds were few in the pale sky.

Ilrona's quiet insistence remained implied. She'd sent him back to the city where he'd prefer not to be for the moment. Virgil sat as steward now. The time for courage was here again, ever it be cursed.

He flexed his fingers, sickening nausea afflicting him momentarily as he readjusted to the reality of vertical movement and positioning. Deckard left the shrine and marched toward the palace. As he moved he regained control of his stomach. He chose to walk, remembering times past he'd attempted to take to the air while disoriented. Deckard went to confront Virgil Silas Dane, the greatest mage in the service of the immortal Cyrus Bode.

Deckard stepped into the throne room of the palace and gazed at the tapestry Virgil had set up behind the princely seat.

Thunder clouds and blue-tinged lightning warred over a scene of battle. Deckard knew the story well. Jadik, depicted in the center of the tapestry in his silver armor, fought the forces of Aush as he advanced north, out of the desert of Rosado.

The conquest must have been bloody, and the tapestry's art did little to diminish the horror. Deckard turned his gaze from the tapestry to the man pacing before the throne.

Virgil wore black, the uniform of his priestly station. Strands of Virgil's white hair drifted in the breeze from the open door behind Deckard. Age took its toll on all mortals, no matter how magically powerful. Nevertheless, a firmness remained around the priest's eyes.

"How long has it been since you and I spoke?" Virgil asked, turning his piercing blue Palavian eyes on Deckard.

"Last winter, though there wasn't much to say."

"It's been nearly a whole year, Hadrian. Thanks for the sacra scroll you brought to Empire. My master continues to keep it safe."

"Cyrus is the only one with the power to hold that scroll securely for as long as required." Deckard paced closer to the throne.

"You feign my end in praising him." Virgil shook his head. "But I'm not dead yet."

"How long since you first chased me across the valley, Dane?"

"Fifty years, Hadrian. I was just a child then, with only one sacra form to my heart. Have you any clues as to the whereabouts of the dowager regent?"

"No," Deckard muttered. "Her fate remains mysterious."

"Someone knows." Virgil shrugged. "Though little hope remains."

"More hope exists than if we'd found her slain in her chambers." Deckard clenched a fist, sprite strings at his fingertips.

"Why have you returned to Alliance?"

"I was sent back by Ilrona. She has concerns in this city."

"You speak the name of Mother Mercy's handmaiden with such familiarity, yet still, you've bent no resources to your will. Hadrian, you're quite the disappointment of late. Do you know anything I haven't already learned?"

"Kizoni was pregnant before she disappeared." Deckard climbed the steps to the raised portion of the room by the throne.

Virgil inclined his head to hold Deckard's gaze now that they stood on the same level. Of the two of them, Virgil had always been built smaller and lighter. He stood perhaps half a span shorter than Deckard, and this close together the difference was noticeable.

The priest glared at Deckard. "Your doing?"

The implied jab would once have made Deckard's face go red. After three centuries, the old chill creeping along his spine was the same as the weakness left to him in the wake of lust.

"Not mine," said Deckard. "Her husband left her a parting gift."

"A potential heir?" said Virgil. "I appreciate you unburdening yourself, but with the regent missing, I will carry forward the tournament. This city needs a prince."

"I agree," said Deckard. "But that man you brought with you will not take the throne."

Virgil smirked. "Ysaac Frost is a master of the blade, a skilled speaker, and a valiant retainer. Why shouldn't he have his chance to sit a throne? All men deserve at least a fleeting glimpse of glory."

"I know not what he deserves," said Deckard. "But Cyrus may reign in Empire, and content himself with the powers he already holds. A puppet prince here is in no other human's interest."

"You act as if Lord Bode holds every leash so tightly."

Deckard scoffed. "You'd not have come to this place without his orders."

"I'm my own man, Hadrian."

"Indeed." Deckard glanced at the throne. "But your days of glory are fading."

"I've more power in me now than you'll ever wield in your entire immortal life. Do not tempt me to demonstrate my skills."

"Mastering three sacra forms is an impressive feat," said Deckard. "But calm yourself, parson. A battle between us could see this ancient palace in ruins. I'd rather hand it to the next prince as it is than as a pile of rubble."

"Fair point." Virgil grinned, showing mostly-well-preserved teeth, slightly yellow from age. "If there's no other business at the moment, Hadrian, I have a tournament to organize."

"How do you plan to choose victors?" Deckard asked.

"The head of each of the four houses will cast a vote for each of the three events, and I will cast one as well."

"Three events? Are you looking to draw matters out?"

"Hadrian, you guessed one point correctly earlier. I wouldn't be here by choice. You may leave your family to fly in the wind, but my second grandson was just born before I departed Geteren. I'd rather play the doting elder than preside over the chaos in this city. I speak truthfully."

"Another grandchild," said Deckard. "Congratulations."

"Don't pretend you care. My line is but a petty abrasion on the surface of time to one like you."

"If your talent carries down the generations, I'd say that's far from the case."

"Sadly, my daughter never showed the least interest in magic, let alone sacra forms." Virgil shook his head. "But at least she's brought this old man little ones to care for again."

"Keep yourself well, Parson Dane." Deckard turned his back on Virgil. "And I will be watching."

"I hope to see you at the tournament. We stand on neutral ground, immortal. I'd be sad to miss the chance to see your descendants fail before your eyes, so don't fear me, for now."

"I've never feared you," said Deckard. "Powerful or weak, you're a mage like any other."

"Don't lie," said Virgil. "I'm the most formidable hunter ever to quest to take your life. And perhaps I'll yet claim the instrument that breathes within your chest."

"If you ever do, I'll use the last air it gives me to take back what I said about your glory fading." Deckard chuckled, hoping the sound didn't seem forced. "I'll see you at the tournament, parson."

He marched from the palace, then took to the air.

CHAPTER 38

CATRICHA

The sky rippled with moving clouds as darkness fell over Alliance outside her chamber window. Father had invited every challenger for the throne to dinner. She should go downstairs to greet people as they arrived, like a good hostess.

Ruar, Vual, and Heron...all these men are in the way. She hated to think of Ruar like that, in particular, but either Kuldettan brother could contest the princely seat. She didn't want the throne for herself. What use did a poet have for power? Nevertheless...the family's interests demanded she or one of their allies win the contest.

Catricha sighed and turned from the window.

She had to get ready for dinner. Time to look the best she could without donning a gown resembling human remains. She smiled at the memory. *I must be bold tonight as well.*

Under streams of water flowing from the mouths of the gargoyles in the bathroom, she washed away her body's tension. By the time the bath's fire began to cool she was already out and dressing. Catricha covered herself in a black, white, and green gown. The skirt's patterns were of tree-roots, and the blouse's of branches by night with highlights hinting at star-dappled greenery. She added her family's ring, bearing their shield. For her brow she chose a silver circlet set with tiny rose-colored gems.

Garbed like a work of art, she descended the staircase to meet the evening's guests. They began to arrive just as the sun set, by carriages insulated against the winter cold. The entrance hall was drafty and the weather outside was always noticeable in the larger rooms.

Catricha smiled at the first guests to climb the steps to the door. Heron Olfrus arrived like a brooding raven with his pale and slender sister on one side, and his tall mage, Melissa Dorian on the other. Melissa earned that party some respect, for Catricha didn't seek to find fault with someone who might help her wield her newfound magical abilities.

Olfrus and both women were clad in fine clothing. The dress was cut to fit Melissa well, but she looked uncomfortable in it, regardless. She was still not accustomed to attending functions of the noble families, no doubt.

The gentle servant by the door announced the arrival of the second set of guests the moment.

Bethanelle Graef and another young mage, announced simply as Elaine, entered close behind Olfrus. They were followed by Galocai and Nansoela Paroth. Nansoela nodded to Catricha as they passed, following the others to the dining room.

"A good night to be well-dressed." Catricha's mother arrived at the base of the grand staircase beside her. "Thank you for not insisting on taking the opportunity to be outrageous, daughter."

"If I'm to be taken seriously as a competitor for the throne, I must show a new side," said Catricha.

"And you're showing it beautifully, my love."

"Thank you, mother."

Hyla Maltos smiled slightly. "I say what I see. Honesty is an honorable path if not always an easy one."

Catricha glanced at Hyla. "Honor is valuable to others, but I fear I'll never earn enough to make up for my career."

"On the contrary," Hyla said. "Your words and your lines bring distinction to the family. We can be more than the shield of Alliance. We can be the wit as well. Now is too cold by the door for that dress to wait here. Perhaps you should got to the dining room to greet our guests there."

“As you say, mother.” Catricha set off toward the dining room, fighting the urge to look over her shoulder to see if Ruar had arrived. If he came at all tonight, he’d be here soon enough.

* * *

In the dining room, Catricha found the guests already mingling with each other. Melissa, Heron, and Heron’s sister, kept to themselves on one side of the room. Bethanelle and Galocai seemed intent on remaining within earshot of them. Those two members of the lesser great families appeared to have little to say to each other.

On the other side of the table, the guests Catricha had missed while entering, were already engaged in conversation. These consisted of Eram, The gallant poet, and Sion Arver. She paused for a moment to consider him, but his presence shouldn’t have surprised her so much.

Sion glanced at Catricha as she frowned in his direction. Footsteps approached behind her. She looked over her shoulder and saw Ruar and Vual Kuldettan emerge from the entryway. *Perfect timing.*

Of course, they would wait until she had just left the entry hall to arrive. Nansoela waved to Catricha. "Lady Maltos, I'm glad to see you're safe after your troubles underground and everything that’s happened since."

"That was the least of my worries.” As Catricha approached the table, she frowned. "After all, that day the dowager regent disappeared."

"I pray she’ll be found safe," said Nansoela. "We've had too much tragedy in the city as it is."

"Indeed," said Eram. “Though, I fear there will be more danger between now and times of peace."

"Do you fear it?" said Catricha. "Or do you long for it? You gallant poets certainly prefer action over peace much of the time."

"My lady," said Eram. "I'm insulted. After all, what kind of man would wish for war and conflict during the time a new house takes power?”

Catricha arched an eyebrow. “The kind who enters a challenge among nobles, despite having little power himself. That is why you are here, isn't it?"

Eram smiled broadly. “Though only a fool would assume that whoever wins will become the next prince, it would be good for my reputation to compete with such notables as yourself and the others present."

"I'm not sure I will compete," Catricha said. "If I'm honest, and I must be honest, I would rather see the city safely in new hands and the dowager regent returned to power then take the throne myself."

"You speak plainly," said Nansoela. "Have events shaken you?"

"As much as they shook the foundations of the city.” Catricha sighed. “I fear there is much danger still afloat."

"Wise," said Melissa Dorian from across the table. She stood up. "You may consider yourself a comic poet, but you speak more truth than I've heard in a while.”

“Heron?” Melissa turned to Lord Olfrus.

"Of course," he said. "Feel free to speak frankly."

Melissa nodded. "It's not a matter of who becomes the next prince as I understand. It's a matter of how we can protect whoever wins the challenge."

"Protect the next Prince," said Vual, marching in the room. "The only way to protect the next prince would be to place Catricha behind bars."

"Noted.” Catricha grinned at him. “And dismissed."

"Aren't your parents meant to officiate here?" said Vual. “Hosting this gathering doesn't seem fitting for someone with such suspicion on her."

"You're the only one who's suspicious,” Catricha said.

"Am I?" Vual’s nose wrinkled like he’d smelled something foul. "The people know who you really are, Catricha."

"That's quite enough.” Catricha's mother stepped into the room behind Vual and Ruar. "I will hear no more of such talk until after we've entertained you guests. Catricha, you’re hardly doing what I suggested you attempt."

Catricha turned to her mother and shrugged. "Sometimes even an entertainer needs her rest."

Vual snorted. Ruar grunted and glanced toward Catricha, over his brother’s shoulder. He half-nodded to her.

"Very well," said Hyla. "Dinner will be served shortly. The cooks are working as we speak."

"Is that why you called us here?” Heron asked. “You wish to extend your hospitality to all of us challengers?"

"Yes," said Hyla. "But not everyone is here yet."

"Who are we missing?" Eram glanced around the table.

"Only Sir Ysaac Frost," said Hyla.

"Ysaac?" said Catricha. "You invited the knight from the Chos Valley as well?"

"Not everyone here is from Alliance," said Heron. "I came from the Chos Valley recently, myself."

"Don't remind us." Vual gritted his teeth. "Opportunist."

"For once I agree with Vual." Nansoela fixed Heron with an editor's gaze. "You insinuated yourself into our affairs. I don't necessarily see the difference between you and Sir Frost."

"One of us serves the Geteren clan," said Heron without moving an inch. "He does. I am here to seek my fortune."

"You seek your fortune with mercenaries and mages," said Nansoela. "However, if the judges and adjudicators of the challenges consider your wit worthy, I'd understand better why you are here."

"How generous but I won't require your understanding to govern Alliance."

"I will not require your submission to govern, either." Nansoela smiled at Catricha. "But I require loyalty from the other families."

"Now, now," said Hyla. "This dinner's purpose is hospitality. Please keep the claws in, Lady Paroth."

"Hiding your claws is not going to make them go away." Catricha drummed her fingers on the table in front of her. "I say if we all speak openly and perhaps we will have a more productive evening."

"How very mature of you," said Bethanelle Graef.

"Appreciated." Nansoela nodded to Catricha.

Galocai leaned back, tipping his chair on two legs. Catricha guessed he wanted to rest his feet on the table.

Melissa sat back down, putting her hands on the table one on top of the other.

"Shall we begin?" said Catricha. "Unlike my mother, I don't see the need to wait for Ysaac. He may not come at all."

Hyla crossed her arms. "He will attend if he cares anything of the customs of Alliance."

"That assumes much," said Galocai.

"Quite so." Vual glared around the room. "From his arrogance for being a mere knight assigned to this city, he must be the clan's favored choice. He must think himself safe."

"No one here is completely free of danger," said Catricha. "Anyone who's knows what happened to the Prince Saviron should understand the threat the shadow poses."

"Agreed," said Heron. "Lady Maltos, I mean Catricha, may I speak?"

"We don't need adjudicator here," said Catricha. "And you're already speaking."

"I promise I'll be more reasonable than the Kuldettan thug who stands at your side."

"He stands behind me," said Catricha. "Take from that what you will." She glanced at Ruar, who then shook his head. Vual grunted.

"Please take your seats." Hyla extended her arms on either side. "I won't have you springing at each other over the table at dinner."

"Very well." Vual took the seat near the head of the table, opposite Heron and his party. Heron's sister glanced at Melissa. She looked ready to speak, but said nothing, and then lowered her gaze.

The Olfrus girl looked out of place, even among the youth of the city's nobility. Despite her age, Catricha suspected Heron's sister might be more involved with the lord's ambitions than the two of them let on. A noble ingénue would be a difficult woman to arrange courtship without money or a high title. Catricha understood as much first-hand

"Catricha?" said Heron's sister in a small voice. "Would you speak first?"

Catricha shook her head. "I think we ought to start with the way the situation arose. The prince of this city and his steward were slain by a shadow, an evil monster from of some kind. It is my suspicion that this shadow originated before the city's name was changed to Alliance."

"The shadow is that old?" Heron leaned forward, forearms on the table, brows bending inward.

"Is it a demon?" asked his sister.

"We don't know," said Catricha. "But this shadow ruler may have existed in the city for some time. I don't know exactly what happened to bring it back, but having been silent for perhaps a millennia, it chose our time to arise again."

"Where did you learn this?" asked Melissa.

"Wait a moment," said Catricha. "I'll get to that."

She told them as much as she could remember about the shadow of Jasguara as quickly as she could, but as she spoke, a darkness at one corner of the room began to solidify into a humanoid form behind Heron's seat.

Catricha's eyes widened. The same shadowy form that appeared after Saviron's murder materialized behind Lord Olfrus in the dining room.

CHAPTER 39

CATRICHA

"Look out!" she cried just as the shadow slipped away from her perception.

"What?" Heron stood up fast, looking over his shoulder. "What is this?"

"The shadow," said Catricha. "It was here."

"What shadow?" Heron scanned the space behind his seat. "I see nothing but a wall and the tapestries upon it."

"It's not—No, it was there!"

"The killer is here?" Vual's chair shook and his hands trembled on the table. He got to his feet, shoving back the seat so it nearly tottered and fell over. He caught the chair with his other hand before it could crash to the floor.

"I saw it," said Catricha. "The shadow."

"Is it in the room now?" Melissa scowled. "If we catch it, we can put an end to this whole affair."

"It went away. It seems the shadow can appear and vanish at will." Catricha looked this way and that. "How can we stop that?"

"You're the best one to fight it," said Melissa. "I can tell by your essence's mastery of darkness."

"Mastery?" said Catricha. "How can my essence do anything? I know almost no magic."

"You're not very studied," said Melissa. "But your magic is there. Your essences are like mine, that way."

Galocai stood, looking around, essences singing their soothing tunes even in the dire situation. "Sister," he said, "You and Ruar should go."

Melissa said to the Olfrus girl, "Niba, you should go too."

"I'm staying as long as my brother." Niba Olfrus folded her arms. "If this beast is in the darkness, the household is too dangerous for us to go elsewhere without lights of our own."

"A good point." Ruar's teeth set on edge. He glanced at Catricha, hands trembling, but not with the rage that Vual exhibited. Instead, he shook with fear.

"You." Vual turned to Catricha. "You will assist me."

"I'll be the lady of this household someday," said Catricha. "I refuse to accept orders from someone like you."

"Enough of this," said Galocai." Sprites and essences flew, singing from him, carrying glowing feathes to illuminate the entire dining room as bright as day. They chased away every shadow.

"The only ones left are the shadow we cast ourselves," said Melissa.

"Everyone be careful of your back," said Galocai.

Nansoela pushed out her chair and stood up, arms crossed. "I may not be equipped to handle some kind of magical demon, but I'm not leaving this place until we catch that shadow."

"An honorable statement," said Heron. "I can see why you're renowned."

"This is no time for pandering compliments, Lord Olfrus," said Nansoela.

Heron shrugged. "It never will be if we don't get out of here."

"We need to find the shadow." Catricha swept her gaze around the bright room, looking for signs of the living shadow. *Has the killer already fled?*

The table was set, but no food had been placed on the plates. The servers would still be in the kitchen, preparing the meal while the nobles waited. The guests were alone for the moment, but one invited guest wasn't here. Ysaac Frost never arrived. *Could he be the cause of this whole mess?*

Catricha had never heard of the young knight before his arrival in Alliance in late autumn. The day the dowager regent disappeared, Virgil and Ysaac had been present to take advantage. *It can't be a coincidence.*

The lights began to flicker, and then, in the center of the table, billowing cloud of smoke emerged in the dissonant song of sprites. The din engulfed two of Galocai's sprite-feathers, dousing their illumination in the center of the room.

Galocai winced and try to draw his essences and feathers back to him. The magic entities rushed into his arm, but the feathers fell to the wooden tabletop, drained of what little color they'd had left. Galocai clutched his wrist in pain. Blood spotted the floor at his feet.

Melissa ran to Galocai's side, quick as a flash, despite the gown she wore and the skirt keeping her legs from top speed.

"We need help," said Melissa. "That thing." She pointed at the smoke cloud rising over the table. "That thing attacked him."

"Galocai," said Nansoela. "Are you all right?"

"Obviously not." He said through his teeth. "I'm bleeding somewhere inside. My wound is deep."

"We can get you to a healer." Ruar put a hand on Galocai's shoulder. "Just remain calm and conscious."

"Retreat?" said Vual. "I will hold the line for you."

"Everyone wielding strong magic," said Melissa. "You best be out of this room in seconds."

"Right," said Heron. "Everyone follow me." He waved toward the door to the entry hall.

The guests rose as a group and rushed toward the door. Only Vual, Galocai, and Melissa stayed with Catricha. Ruar hesitated at the threshold as the others passed ahead of him. He glanced at Catricha who stood directly behind him, near the doorway. "Come with us," he said. "Get out of the danger."

"I can do something to catch the shadow now, and I'm going to do everything possible."

"That shadow is dangerous," said Ruar. "You can't control your magic yet."

"I'll find a way." said Catricha. "It will not. If no one else can stop it, I'll have to."

Ruar leaned close to her and squeezed her hand. Then he turned and limped after the other guests into the hallway, where they shouted for the servants and other family members to follow them out of the building. Heron led the way.

Catricha turned toward the center of the room. She and the three mages fanned around the table, facing the growing cloud. The warmth of Ruar's touch cooled on her palm.

"Here it comes." Melissa stared at the cloud. "We must prepare as much as possible. Careful with your essences. It can uses them to attack us like it did Galocai."

Galocai nodded. His face was pale, and sweat leaked down his collar.

Vual drew his relic sword. He held the weapon in both hands, then sent sprites playing along its length to enhance the blade. The lethal edge would be difficult to break. He held the weapon between himself and the monster rising from the middle of the table.

Melissa began to weave a spell in the air, though Catricha couldn't tell what she was trying to accomplish.

The three of them left the table's head to Catricha. She would have to fight alone if the shadow turned in her direction. The plume of smoke began to take shape, body forming first a pair of glowing blue-gray eyes that shimmered a familiar color.

Catricha could place the shade of those yes, but didn't dare imagine how they'd come to be there. Then the limbs came, flowing from the smoke, hugely muscled and thick with power. The arms could have belonged to the man who'd been dismembered in front of the aparmtent that night before winter began.

"This," said Catricha. "Those are stolen parts of the dead."

Galocai shuddered. "It's monstrous."

"Humanoid though." Melissa gritted her teeth. "Those eyes..."

"The eyes belonged to Adias Halth," said Catricha. "That monster must have taken them from him."

"Your husband," said Vual. "And my friend."

Vual advanced, sword in both hands, glaring at the shadow. He aimed the point of his sword toward the heart of the the dark.

One other thing was stolen from Adias that night, Catricha thought with a grimace. She may have hated him, but he hadn't deserved to have his heart taken and used by this abomination.

"Stand back," said Melissa. "Lord Kuldettan, you and I will charge together."

"A fine plan," Vual said.

Laughter, deep and echoing, emerged from the shadow. What had been silent became the source of a voice as low as the pits of the earth and his dark as depths of any world well.

Catricha's eyes widened as she stared at the warped being of darkness.

Melissa shot a glance at her. "Catricha, your essences are strong. Focus on what comes naturally. What is the thing you see when you close your eyes? What is the shape that moves your heart?"

"What I see when I close my eyes." *Nothing.* Catricha widened her eyes in realization. "Darkness."

"That's it," said Melissa. "That's why you resonate with the shadow."

The laughter continued. The shadow turned those blue-gray eyes on Catricha.

"You finally realize it," said the unnaturally deep voice. "The truth."

Catricha's blood ran cold and her hands clenched together at her sides. "Realize what?"

"You're realizing how cold death can be when you oppose the true prince."

"Catricha," Galocai said in her ear, seemingly without anyone else hearing.

Catricha realized he spoke through one of the glowing sprites carrying a feather by her shoulder. The sprite spoke soft as a whisper in her ear. "Catricha, you're no mage. If you don't get out of here that thing may kill you."

Catricha grimaced. "I know," she muttered.

Melissa and Vual hurled themselves at the shadow. Catricha took a step toward the table, and then braced her arms against it's short side. As Vual and Melissa raced toward the smoke, the shadow killer turned his blue eyes on Catricha.

CHAPTER 40

MELISSA

Melissa focused on the form within the smoke cloud. She leapt onto the tabletop with a clatter of dinnerware but the thick oak easily held her weight. The shadow turned almost imperceptibly and leered at her from the corner of an obscured face.

"You shouldn't have let the immortal turn away from the city, Catricha..." rumbled the low voice from inside the smoke. "...If he was here perhaps he could protect you."

"To the pit, monster!" Vual cut at the smoky darkness with the beam of light shooting from his sword. The shining blade passed through the shadow's form without harm or trace.

Melissa scowled, recalling her previous bout with an insubstantial foe. "Part of him might be solid," she said, as Vual retreated along the long side of the table.

Melissa kept weaving her lightning spell between her fingers. Electricity made a strong choice for magical attacks and could be more controllable than fire, especially in-doors.

Galocai grimaced, sweat clinging to his brow. He held his illuminating feathers in position, but it was evident he could do little more. She couldn't let him fade further.

Melissa completed the weave of her spell. Electricity crackled between her extended fingers, energy produced and controlled by her essences.

Melissa's electricity flickered and jumped onto the shadow, leaping through the boiling clouds that concealed his limbs and eyes. The shadow prince turned, sweeping with one arm as Vual's blade passed through his other. Despite those limbs having been stolen from a real man, they were as gaseous as the rest of him.

Vual leapt backward, and his sword glimmered in the light of Galocai's sprites.

Melissa glanced at Catricha. "Get out of here. We'll handle the monster."

"No," said Catricha softly. "You can't fight him."

"We can't?" said Melissa. "Why not?"

"That thing isn't just anyone," said Catricha in the same subdued tone.

Galocai brought a pair of lighted feathers in with wave of his hand, striking the shadow from one side. The night the quills of passed through the shadow, missing the solid shape hidden inside the dark cloud.

"You know what it is?" Melissa asked.

"Yes." Catricha's voice was softer, even than before. Her eyes closed. "Last time I saw you, I thought you were gone for good."

The shadow's gaseous face twisted, forming a sneer.

"Little Catricha," he said. "You have guessed well."

"You guessed?" said Melissa.

"You stand in the presence of Adias Halth," said the shadow.

"Halth is dead," Galocai said through trembling lips.

Vual's mouth twitched. "You don't mean? You can't mean that—"

"I do. I am Adias Halth, and I will have my eternal reward for all the patient years my family waited to become the princes of this city."

"Is that all you want?" Vual glanced at Catricha, his eyes narrowed. "This could be a trick. We know Catricha has power over darkness."

"She could never compel me," said Adias. "Just as your blades cannot touch me, nothing her words can do will harm me now."

"Catricha," said Melissa. "You have to leave. Go to safety."

"This is my family's house," said Catricha. "And he was my husband."

"In name only," said the shadow. "And soon, we will be together and you will join me forever."

Melissa made a hissing sound and shook her head. "Not unless you go through everyone in this room."

"Oh?" said Adias. "You believe you can defeat me, little mage. Dorian is it?"

"Get back!" Vual shouted.

Melissa darted forward, her electricity spell flashing toward the shadow.

Adias brought his shadowy hands together in a clap like thunder. The ashen clouds dissipated around him while the table rumbled and then split in half.

Shards of broken dinnerware from House Maltos collapsed to the floor. Melissa spilled into the center of the room, between the two broken halves of wood, now propped on slanting legs. She tried to get up as the shadow loomed over her.

"It's too easy," said Adias. "You mages believe you have all the power. But in reality, you know almost nothing of what lies beyond or below this world."

"Adias, stop this! It's me you want to hurt."

"I'll have you, Catricha," said Adias. "At the time I choose."

Melissa got to her feet, teeth clenched. "You'll never take another life."

"You can't stop me." Adias' voice faded, as if coming from far away. He lunged toward Melissa.

"Fanhedon!" cried Melissa.

The demon's body surrounded her, metal armor, powerful limbs, steel helm and mask. She struck out with taloned gauntlets, ripping at the shadow.

Whatever substance Adias possessed now, he evaded the touch of even Fanhedon's claws.

The blow Melissa received in reply sent her hurtling against the table's broken side and pinned her for an instant against the black wood. Her demonic form slumped into a sitting position on the floor.

Adias turned from her, one foot stepping on her ankle but failing to break through Fanhedon's leg armor. Despite the light touch of the foot, pain exploded through Melissa's entire leg. She lost her senses for an instant, and Fanhedon's form faded from her. Melissa returned to her human shape.

"The sacra form left you?" said Adias. "You still have much to learn, and you are young. Perhaps when things are different I'll return and take you as well." He laughed and vanished into a billowing pall of smoke that spilled forth from his shadowy figure.

Melissa grimaced, struggling to stand as the sounds of the others coughing filled the room. She covered her mouth and nose with a napkin she found on the floor beneath her palm.

The smoke began to resolve, pulled into the place where the shadow had stood, rather than spreading to fill the room. A horrifying scream of bane songs burst from the dense cloud, then faded as quickly as it first arose.

Melissa looked this way and that, trying to see the others. Her eyes fell upon Galocai. He was fighting to remain upright, features twisted in determination, and hand clutching his wounded arm. She struggled to her feet, fell to one knee, then tried once more to stand.

For a long moment she looked at her hands, spotted with dust and tense with nerves. The only sounds came from her and Catricha and Galocai breathing. *Vual. What happened to Vual?*

CATRICHA

She watched the smoke dissipate along with the evidence of Adias's presence apart from the damage he'd done. She shook, her knees knocking together beneath her skirt.

"Are you all right?" Galocai asked, limping toward Melissa at the broken side of the table.

"I'll survive," said Melissa. "What happened the with Vual?"

Catricha looked around, finding the Kuldettan heir nowhere in sight.

"I don't know." Galocai's eyes narrowed. "He disappeared after the shadow called back the clouds."

Catricha took a deep breath. "Adias must have taken him."

"Like Kizoni," Melissa said. "No."

"The dowager regent was attacked as if from nowhere." Catricha stared at the broken dining table

"Whatever happened to Vual." Galocai sagged. "I'm feeling weak."

"It's the loss of blood," said Melissa.

"That I have." Galocai leaned against the broken table.

“We need to get help," said Melissa. "I don’t know any healers in the city yet."

"I know some," said Catricha. "I'll take you."

"It's late at night.” Galocai wheezed out a breath. “How far is the nearest one?"

"First, we get to the carriage house," said Catricha. "We'll be faster from there.”

"Thank you,” Galocai breathed.

Melissa nodded.

"I suppose your friends now.” Catricha turned to the mage. "Thank you, Melissa, for defending me."

"It was the right thing to do.”

"This way.” Catricha started toward the door to the entry hall. Ruar and a number of other guests remained outside. Nansoela put a hand over her mouth when she saw them emerge.

“Catricha, are you all right?" said Ruar. "Where is my brother?"

"We don't know what happened to Vual," said Catricha. "He disappeared when the shadow vanished."

"The shadow—We need to go after them."

"Yes," said Nansoela. "We must put an end to that fiend once and for all."

Bethanelle nodded.

Galocai’s wounded arm was losing blood fast. His dripping hand left a trail of red on the floor tiles as Catricha pushed her way past the others and led the way to the carriage house.

"We need a healer," Catricha said. "Someone has to help Galocai, and quickly."

"Then we’ll hurry," said Nansoela. "I'll ride with you."

Catricha nodded.

The four of them rushed to the carriage house, Galocai supported on Melissa's shoulder. They climbed into the lighter of the carriages, while a yard servant hooked up the horses. Catricha glanced behind her, and saw Galocai’s head lolling against the seat where he sat. Melissa supported him and he leaned against her.

Nansoela took the seat across from the two mages. Catricha sat on the driving board and drove the horses out of the stable with the crack of the whip.

The carriage bumped along the road. They made their way north, along the riverside.

"Where is this healer?" said Melissa. "He may not have much longer."

"We need to hurry," said Catricha.

Nansoela shook her head. "I've heard of a place."

"How far is it?" Melissa asked.

"Near here," said Nansoela, "There is a shrine. It can take any mage to the city above."

"Any mage?" said Melissa. "Both Galocai and I are, but how will the city help?"

"Is there a healer there?" Catricha frowned.

"In a way," said Nansoela. "I've read there is a maladrite fountain in the city above, with waters that heal any wound they touch."

"It's his essence that's wounded," said Melissa. "The shadow did it somehow."

Nansoela frowned. "If anything can heal a wounded essence, this maladrite fountain can."

"Then let's go." Nansoela turned and told Catricha the directions to reach the fountain shrine.

Catricha brought the carriage to a halt in front of a tiny temple with steps leading to the walled shrine outside. The temples and shrines of Mother Mercy were grand, but this was no shrine to her. *No,* Catricha thought, *this place belongs to the night, and the evils that roam the world above and below.* She stared at the jagged, irregular shapes behind the altar.

"What do we do to use the shrine?" asked Melissa.

Nansoela frowned. "Have you ever been to the city on high?"

"I know I can get there with my second form," said Melissa. "But I've never done it."

"This is your first time attempting it." Nansoela opened the carriage door. She and Melissa supported Galocai, carrying him from the steps of the carriage to the shrine. Catricha climbed down from the driving board, awkwardly thanks to her skirt. She patted the horse's nose.

"What do we do?" She turned to Nansoela.

"We're poets," said Nansoela. "Not wizards. We'll wait and see if they return swiftly. I don't remember much about how the shrine works, and I lack training in sorcery."

"I've studied only a little, myself."

"There are many things about us that are the same," said Nansoela, gazing at Catricha.

"What is it?" asked Catricha.

"I mean," Nansoela said in a whisper. "We share blood, the two of us."

"Impossible," said Catricha.

Nansoela looked along the snowy street, but her gaze shifted steadily toward Catricha's face.

"It's as I said. Galocai and I are your half-siblings, Catricha. We needed to hide from each other, but your father before he married your mother, could not stop his lusts."

"Why are you telling me this now?" Catricha said with a wrinkled lip.

Nansoela's eyes sank, tears beading at their edges. "You should know, that I've always thought of you as a sister."

"Is that why you gave me that dress?"

"I've always envied what you do with your outrage, where my canon poetry can never go."

"It's not time to learn something like this." Catricha shivered, on the verge of tears. "Who else knew?"

"No one left alive, except your father and Galocai," said Nansoela.

They watched as Melissa laid Galocai down at the top of the shrine's steps. She shifted into her steely sacra form, the glittering Fanhedon.

"Mages are amazing," said Catricha. "But even she couldn't stop the man who attacked us."

"She'll have to try again," said Nansoela.

"We will try again." Catrich bowed her head. "Though, there is something I need to tell you, Nansoela."

"What is it?"

"That shadow in the dining room," said Catricha. "The shadow is my former husband."

"Adias? How?" Nansoela stifled Catricha's repyly with a finger to the lips. She then pointed as Fanhedon lifted Galocai. The two forms on the steps vanished, into nothingness as if they'd never been.

"Incredible," said Nansoela. "I've never seen a shrine work before."

"Have they reached the city?"

"I hope so," said Nansoela. "My brother is stubborn and hoping to live as long as he can."

Catricha wrapped her arms about herself. "I hope you're right. I want them both back safe."

"Of course you do," said Nansoela. "Because despite all the rudeness, and all the jabs and jokes at the expense of our nobility, you are a good person, Catricha. You didn't flee with the rest of us. You didn't run from battle, though you knew you could do little to help. That's who you are."

"How can you say that?" asked Catricha. "I've never thought myself brave."

"We'll talk later," said Nansoela. "But your house isn't safe tonight. Come and stay at my place for now. We'll get out of the cold and work things out in the morning.

"I'll have to let my parents know in the morning. Until dawn, we need to be wary of every shadow."

"I'll send a messenger tonight," said Nansoela. "We can't have them assuming you were taken as well."

Catricha nodded "A good idea. I only hope the streets aren't too dangerous after dark."

"Don't fear for my servants. They are able, as always, to carry words safely."

CHAPTER 41

MELISSA

Melissa arrived in the maladrite city, shaking and sweating within Fanhedon's shell. She held Galocai in her arms and made her way toward the luminous bath near the shrine. They'd appeared in the city directly before the great building of enormous columns, huge galleries, and vaulted ceilings. Shimmering steam wafted from inside, drifting over the cold street.

Galocai looked weakly around, his eyes seemingly unable to focus on anything in the chaotic metal-sculpted structures around them.

"It's all right," said Melissa. "I won't let anything get close to you."

"We're close enough," said Galocai.

Melissa carried Galocai up the stone steps of the bath. They entered under an archway that towered hundreds of spans above their heads.

The enormous structure was wreathed in dense clouds of steam and mist rising from the baths themselves. The sound of running water reached Melissa's ears from all around as she stepped through the archway.

The ceiling glowed with airborne candles dodging above the steam clouds on what looked like large bubbles of soap.

Essence songs came from everywhere, describing a menagerie of higher creatures. Melissa looked inward and asked Fanhedon a question she'd conssidered the moment they'd decided to enter the city. "When did you last come here?"

"Several human generations passed before I was defeated in battle those many centuries ago. I've only been here once before."

"When?"

"It's a time I prefer not to recall," said Fanhedon. "But I can lead you to the healing fountain."

"A fountain," said Melissa out loud. "We'll find the way there."

"Did you just talk to your inner demon?" asked Galocai.

Melissa nodded. "She told me to look for a fountain somewhere in this building."

"At the center," said Fanhedon in Melissa's mind. "Go to the center of the great bath."

"Melissa, there!" Galocai pointed through the steam to a bloom of motion. Boiling water hot, and white with foam, rushed up from the floor. Illuminated in the central pool of the bath before Melissa and Galocai, the fountain bubbled, rushing with power and essences Melissa had never heard on earth below. Even world wells were quiet by comparison.

"That's it," said Galocai. "It has to be."

"Definitely." Melissa bent her armored knees, and sprang into the center of the fountain. They flew over the shapes of maladrites and demons wading in the water all around. There were many kinds, not all of them humanoid. As Melissa descended, she realized the area around the fountain was even more densely populated by forms both bizarre and unnatural, too many to take in quickly.

She hit the water feet-first, then leapt onto the steps encircling the fountain's center. The tiles held against the impact of Fanhedon's talons. The floor must be made of some material akin to demon stone.

Everything on high gleamed as if made new every moment.

Melissa lowered Galocai gently into the water before her. His wounded arm touched the surface and sprites began to flow up his wrist and enter the wound.

"I can feel it working." He flexed his fingers.

"I feared an essence wound might be too much for the water to heal. It could have killed you. I don't know much about such attacks."

"It almost did." Galocai gazed at her face. "You saved my life, Melissa."

She felt hot, and her metal-clad arms trembled. "It's nothing. I mean—"

"No," said Galocai. "It's not nothing because my life is not nothing—"

"On that we can agree."

"—And neither are you." Galocai finished his sentence. "You are not nothing, either, Melissa Dorian."

Despite the impersonal phrasing, his tone and the peace on his features thrilled Melissa with intense desire.

"We shouldn't stay long."

Galocai climbed onto the stones of the fountain steps. "The water has already done its work."

Splashing came from behind her.

Melissa turned and found the two of them surrounded by curious maladrites. A hulking brute with massive forearms and a snakelike tail slithered through the shallow water toward them. The creature's limbs were each a span longer than Melissa was tall. The maladrite pulled itself along like a great ape from the bloom, but with a snake tail instead of legs.

"I am the keeper of the fountain," said the serpentine ape. "Who would bring a mortal to my waters?"

"It is I," said Fanhedon before Melissa could reply. "Fanhedon of the demonic nations. I've come to the city at the behest of my awakener."

"You've become a sacra form Fanhedon," said the keeper of the fountain. "You have my sympathies."

Fanhedon bowed her silver head. "Not all demons die in such a lucky way, but most will never cross into grand remorse."

"Grand Remorse?" Melissa asked internally.

Fanhedon did not reply.

"We bear no ill will to you or the fountain. Your have our gratitude."

"We will have your lives should you ever return," said the maladrite. "The keeping of this fountain and the precious essences within is my honor."

"Your honor means little to the those who dwell below," said Fanhedon.

Melissa nodded. "Keeper of the fountain I speak as the human who awakened this demon to live once more. If you resent us standing, we will take no more of the water than we need."

"You should have taken none of it," said the keeper of the fountain.

"We need to survive," said Melissa. "I'd gladly take a sprite from your fountain if it saved this man's life again."

"You dishonor this place mortal. I should've known you'd be as greedy as any mortal, a lawbreaker as all who dwell below."

"Greed isn't saving a life," said Melissa. "Greed is letting die those you can save."

"Mortal lives do not matter under maladrite law," said the keeper of the fountain. "Now be gone and do not return. If you do, I will have no mercy for you, humans."

Melissa took a deep breath. "Climb on," she told Galocai. He gripped Fanhedon's shoulders.

She jumped out of the fountain, soaring past the floating candles and landing by the entrance, on one knee.

"Melissa," said Galocai. "We need to get back to Alliance."

"I know," she said.

* * *

Melissa and Galocai returned to Alliance the same way they'd gone above. Once more in the dark city, they made their way straight through the midnight streets to Nansoela's house.

They climbed the steps to Galocai's chambers. He'd not stayed there since returning to the city, but the two of them lacked other options.

Melissa glanced at the man she'd saved.

His eyes met hers and his lip curved into a small smile. "If you want to go, I'll be all right."

"I know you will be," said Melissa. "I should return to the Olfrus family."

"They are the ones employing you."

"Yes, but I they don't need me right now."

"Who knows what happened with that shadow," said Galocai. "And Vual..."

"We'll find them all. We will find Vual and we'll find Kizoni."

"I hope you're right. Mother Mercy, have mercy."

"I never heard one said that way."

"It said all the time by some folk in the north," said Galocai. "But mostly just by me."

"But I've never heard you say it before."

"I try to save it for truly serious moments these days." He smiled and opened the door. She followed him into his chambers.

Starlight played on the covers of his bed. It was large enough to easily accommodate three ordinary people side-by-side.

"You don't have to go," he said.

"Then I won't."

"I wouldn't want you to have to go walk in the night. It's not fit for a lady."

"I'm not a lady," said Melissa. "I'm a mage, and a merchant's daughter, but it seems my family are nowhere to be found in Alliance."

"Do you have clues to find your parents?" said Galocai. "The Dorian family was once prominent here. But I suppose their blood-members aren't always present."

"They're all gone," said Melissa. "Maybe they heard I was coming and fled."

"I don't think that's it." Galocai smiled and touched her side gently. "Truly."

His touch sent pleasant shivers creeping through her.

"You don't have to be so kind," said Melissa. "I can take harsh words, and even harsher truth."

"I'm not much for harshness," said Galocai. "That's probably why I don't have sacra form."

"I thought you simply didn't study enough." Melissa walked to the side of the bed.

Galocai followed her. He put his hand on the covers. The mattress was firm under Melissa as she sat. Their fingers brushed, then touched, then locked together.

"What is it you want to do?" he said.

She put her lips to his ear. "I think you know."

"I do. I do."

He lay on the bed before her, his tunic buttons undone and his hair flowing about his head, haloing him with yellow-white locks. She gazed at him for a long moment, admiring his warm features and toned muscles.

"Are you all right?" he asked.

"I think so." Melissa leaned over him.

"We don't have to do anything you don't want."

"That's not very noble of you," said Melissa.

"Have you been taking lessons from Catricha?" said Galocai. "She's too much, too stubborn and too witty."

"I suppose she is."

"Wit isn't everything," said Galocai. "I'm glad you have a voice and you're willing to use it."

"I'm not exactly quiet." Melissa smiled and brushed his cheek.

"But you can be reserved," said Galocai.

"I often prefer myself that way."

"I'm not like most. And being a noble is more than taking what you want. Being noble, at least in the north here means sacrificing what you have. My parents died fighting in the east against the Kism. They fought alongside others of every nation in the lands of mercy, but when they returned, many of our lords and ladies and knights and mages came home straight into their tombs."

"That's a sad tale. That's war." Tears ran freely down Melissa's cheeks, "Everyone loses in war."

"I've never gone to one, and I hope I never must."

"Then we better hope the prince is chosen quickly," said Melissa "Those men from Geteren all look like they would try anything to take Alliance's throne."

"I pray they won't."

"I'll pray for the same," said Melissa. "And hopefully a blessing will follow."

"A blessing from on high is nothing like the present blessing from below."

"A blessing from below?" Melissa arched an eyebrow. "What does that mean?"

"Perhaps I'm too subtle." He put a hand on her hip.

Her face grew hot and her breath came faster. "Is that what you want, Lord Paroth?"

"You know as you did before. You are singularly beautiful, Melissa Dorian."

"Nonsense." Melissa gradually eased onto the bed with him.

"Have you loved others before?" he asked.

"I'd be honored if you were my first." She leaned toward him and their lips met. They kissed in the dim room under wintry stars. The light from the windows began to fade as clouds rolled overhead. And what they did together, they did in the dark without interruption.

CHAPTER 42

MELISSA

She woke in darkness, Galocai sleeping at her side. The light of dawn was hinting at the edge of the windowpane overhead. The room remained mostly as dark as when they made love. Melissa shifted, restless, unable to fall back to sleep, so she rose and dressed. Only having the gown from the previous night, she descended the stairs in fine regalia.

At least for me, it's fine. Normally her attire had to be at home on a battlefield or guarding a caravan more than bedding a nobleman and walking through halls as finely furnished as these. House Paroth was wealthy, no doubt. Indeed, as she approached the kitchen below the bed chambers, she heard the sound of servants at work preparing food and boiling water. No doubt the kettles would be steaming and screaming soon enough.

Melissa sat at the dining room table. She wondered at how far she'd come without finding her parents again. There was no sign of them in the city, beyond their businesses. Nobody seemed to know where they might be except for the secretive Lord Graef. Alliance was another dead end, though a beautiful one.

"So," said a soft voice Melissa almost didn't recognize as Catricha's. "You and Galocai?"

"Yes," she whispered in reply.

"Take care," said Catricha. "He is used to using people."

"Perhaps this time, I'm using him."

"How do you mean?" Catricha stepped in from the hall by the dining room, wearing a slightly ill-fitting white dressing gown. Her hair drifted in loose strands.

"Galocai is known to run around," said Catricha. "I like him, but he isn't the kind of man who would marry anyone, probably not even a noblewoman."

"That's what I've been thinking," said Melissa. "But he is striking."

"Renowned for his looks and respected for his magic. Remind you of anyone?"

"Deckard Hadrian." Melissa scowled. "But that's not why I slept with him."

"Why then, even when you knew he was not serious?"

"I've never done this before. Love? Romance? I don't know about these things. I thought he might be keeping a secret until after...but now I see I might be wrong."

"You saved his life," said Catricha. "That wasn't enough?"

"It would have been." Melissa sighed. "Yet, I still wanted him. Funny, how that goes."

"Many women feel the same way."

"Some men must, as well." Melissa thought of her time traveling, before magic, before war. "I spent a long time hiding from what they wanted."

Catricha nodded. "Did you take any precautions?" asked Catricha.

"Precautions?" Melissa said. "Of what kind?"

"The kind that prevent child-bearing," Catricha said. "If you don't mean to carry a bastard, you must be certain of these things."

"Oh." Melissa's face heated with a flush. "I hadn't thought of that."

"You are clever and well-read, but some things can't be found in history books or mage's tomes."

Melissa nodded. "Is there anything I can do for a precaution now?"

"Follow me," said Catricha. "There is water boiling." In the next moment a faint whistle of steam came from a pot in the kitchen. "I'll fix you some tea that should take care of the matter. We noblewomen know how to use such tools. Some of us use them all too much."

Melissa stifled a laugh. "And people say that Mother Mercy is the only one who determines when children arrive."

"If mother sought to instigate things, she might still have her way, but I don't think she attends to little ones so early, even those of noble blood."

"I wonder what Hadrian would say about that," said Melissa.

"Hadrian's been absent from Alliance for a long time. He is a strange man."

"Have you talked with him?"

"Briefly. He told me you and I were alike, Melissa."

"We both have strong essences. I've read they most often appear in pairs. Not always the same combinations, but there are at least two each time."

"Fascinating." Catricha put the kettle of water onto an insulated pad. "What are yours?"

"I have one called an iron bane," said Melissa. "The other is more mysterious to me, but I call it the shatter Sprite."

"Those names, have a touch of poetry to them."

"They're mostly literal," said Melissa. "The iron bane makes me tougher, stronger, and it can be thrown like a spear that returns to me."

"It returns to you, so you can't just throw it away."

"Yes." Melissa smiled slightly. "All essences return to their bearers. Given the chances. When a sprite or bane is separated from a living thing they try to find a way back. There are ways to delay them, and other ways to make them seek others, but mostly, they're attracted to their one master."

"One master?" said Catricha. "Or one mistress."

"I've separated my iron bane many times. It always returns, frequently with bloody results."

"Have you been in many battles?"

"Some," said Melissa. "Considering the short time I've been a mage, a fair few."

"I need to learn more," said Catricha. "Just as you must learn about noble society. I need to learn about magic."

"I can help teach you some of what I know."

Catricha poured the hot water into a cup with tea leaves at the bottom that carried a bitter scent.

When the water filled the cup, Catricha stirred. Then she reached for a shaker on one side of the stove and put a few dashes into the tea.

"What's that?" said Melissa. "The contraceptive?"

“You have quite a vocabulary. You might be a good poet. But no, the sugar just makes the taste less terrible."

"I shouldn't expect something that assists transgressions to taste good."

"Sometimes a transgression is good enough on its own." Catricha winked. "Hopefully yours was worthwhile."

"It may have been." Melissa took the cup Catricha offered, and held it by the small handle. Catricha also gave her a spoon. "Stir well. It gets easier to take as it cools and you can't drink a cup like that straight off the fire."

"Right. Catricha." She looked at the noblewoman. “Are you used to this kind of thing?"

"What kind of thing?" Catricha asked.

"Nobles sleeping around," said Melissa. "I never assumed people higher up so lacked for morality."

"Morality has little to do with us. We have power and most never know our true transgressions. When we cross the lines we set for ourselves, we hide those moments or tell people the line was never there at all. That's the nature of power."

"From what I've seen, that's very true."

“I need to study magic, thoroughly, If you're willing to be my mentor."

"I don't know as much as my friend Elaine." Melissa sighed. "I'll bring her into the city. She's out at the Graef estate."

"We'll send a messenger at daylight. I'm sure Nansoela will help us with one."

“Why is she treating you so well?" Melissa stirred the tea. "Aren't your families rivals?"

“We've become quite amicable, but I found out something tonight that makes me think we're closer than allies."

"It's a secret, though, isn't it?"

“Yes, but I'll find a messenger to send for Elaine, then we just need a place to train without damaging the city like your bout with that spider."

"I know a place," said Melissa. "The Tower of the Fallen."

"The Fallen? Are you sure that's a good idea?"

"From what I can tell of the place it's protected by powerful wards that will keep us from being sensed by outside listeners. It might be the safest place in the city for a mage right now."

“I'll defer to you, on that." Catricha smiled.

"Thank you," said Melissa. "I won't let you down."

"I'm curious," Catricha said. “What happened between you and Deckard Hadrian?"

"Deckard and I?" Melissa frowned at her cup. "Nothing."

"You know him," said Catricha. "Yet you don't seem to get along."

"I don't think any human can really know an immortal very well."

"He fought alongside you in the south, though."

"That doesn't mean we'll be comrades for life, or even that I trust him now. Immortals have ulterior motives, human or not."

“Interesting," said Catricha. "What happened last night, when you saved me...I don't think Adias is human anymore. Perhaps he is striving for immortality."

"A man with his position must have had some great ambition in mind. Being a steward to a prince should be enough for any human."

"Any mortal, for certain."

"Perhaps." Melissa nodded.

She set the cup on the table. After it cooled a little longer she began to sip the bitter tea.

CHAPTER 43

CATRICHA

She and Melissa joined Elaine by the gates to the Tower of the Fallen. When she arrived, Elaine brought a change of clothes for Melissa, trousers and a tunic more practical than the gallantry worn to Catricha's house the night before.

Galocai had elected to stay behind, perhaps because Nansoela had told him what she'd said to Catricha the night before. If the Paroth twins were her siblings too, that only raised more questions for Catricha.

She waited as Elaine and Melissa drew a warded path between them on the floor in the center of the tower's entryway. The rooms seemed well preserved, all seemed cleaner than they should be, despite the fact that no caretaker was known to attend the place. *Only Deckard Hadrian could explain that,* Catricha thought.

Unlike the demons from Jasguara that had arisen again and joined with Adias, Catricha doubted Deckard would misuse his power, based on his heroic nature.

Elaine drew a larger warding circle on the floor with chalk. "When you practice magic within a city like Alliance, you must take care. I've neglected warding symbols in the past, but I won't do so again."

"In the past? You can't be any older than I am, Elaine."

"It was over the summer." Elaine took a deep breath. "I helped train Melissa and other members of the Governor's mage guard in Soucot."

"So you have experience, teaching. That is excellent."

"Thank you, Lady Maltos," said Elaine. "I have most of a witch's skills, but for now, these wards and the arts of controlling essences will be most useful to you."

"Can you draw either of your strong essences out?" Melissa turned to Catricha.

She shook her head.

"Even so, we can help them emerge, by inciting events that awaken them."

"Such as?" said Catricha.

"We could suggest danger by threatening you somehow. That often prompts powerful essences within someone to defend."

"I know darkness has come out of me before," said Catricha. "I think a dark essence might be one of mine."

Elaine nodded. "That is possible."

"Shall we experiment, then?" Melissa asked.

"I'm ready." Catricha tensed, glad for her bane dagger at her side if anything went too far. Her hand brushed the weapon's hilt.

"That's fine." Melissa set her spear by the doorway. "We won't use weapons."

"No weapons. Right." Catricha unbuckled her bane dagger's sheath from her belt, then set the bloodline weapon on the floor.

"Melissa." Elaine backed away from the two of them. "People may overhear us if we get rambunctious."

"Who are you worried about?" said Catricha. "This tower is fairly far from other buildings."

"If I should engage my sacra form, we could make some noise even if this tower's built as tough as demon stone."

Melissa drew out a mote of darkness surrounded by a kind of pallid halo. Catricha stared at the tiny essence but already sensing a terrible song from it. The bane bent existing light around itself.

"That's the iron bane," she said. "What are you going to do with it?"

"I won't throw it at you unless I know you can stop it."

"Appreciated," said Catricha. "I need to learn quickly, not get killed trying."

"I'm going to toss the iron bane to you underhanded. Try to catch it before it returns to me, alright?"

"Catch? Is that how real mages train?"

"Sometimes," said Elaine. "Only one of your strong essences should really catch the iron bane. Hopefully a simple game will help you draw out one or both of your strong essences."

"I'll try my best."

"Good." Melissa gave Catricha a smile. Elaine nodded.

Melissa tossed the iron bane lightly upward. The essence floated through the air, then descended toward the floor in front of Catricha. She stepped forward, focusing with all her intensity, and drawing her mind together like the point of a needle dragging thread.

Pushing out with her arms, hands pressed together at the wrists, Catricha caught the iron bane on one up-turned palm. The halo of light around it began to fade, and Catricha gradually made out the shape of another essence beside the iron bane holding to Melissa's essence. The essence that emerged was made of pure darkness, and larger than the iron bane thanks to a halo, not of faint light, but a ring of additional darkness.

"I think that's a night bane," said Elaine.

Melissa laughed. "It worked. You're a genius, Elaine! Now, pass my iron bane back, Catricha."

"Right," Catricha carefully tossed the iron bane underhand toward Melissa.

Melissa caught her bane in her palm and the strong essence disappeared back into her body. She stood straighter with the iron bane in her, Catricha noticed.

"So, one of your strong essences is a night bane. We should still look for another one, a sprite probably."

"Sprites and banes usually work in tandem," said Elaine. "One of them is a push and the other a pull, depending and the relationship of the essences to each other, the arrangement can vary."

"My night bane felt like it was pulling your essence to itself." Catricha smiled. "Intriguing."

Melissa nodded. "We should try a different technique to draw out your strong sprite."

"What kind of technique?"

Catricha glanced at Elaine and Melissa. The two mages exchanged looks of their own. Elaine nodded. Melissa folded her arms. "I want you to try to separate one of my strong essences."

"Separate? As in, remove? Don't they always go back, though?"

"They try," said Melissa. "And you can help it out by pushing it back to me."

"A little like how I tossed you the iron bane?"

Melissa nodded. "I'm going to toss you a more common bane. It should float in front of your hand. Then you can sent it back to me with your strong pushing sprite."

"I wonder," Catricha said. "Are the strong ones my only essences? Or are there others?"

"I can hear that you have at least four," said Elaine. "That's an unusually high amount for an untrained individual in Tancuon, though I've met simple travelers from abroad with far more. I was born with two, like most people in the lands of mercy."

"And Melissa?" said Catricha. "How many sprites were you born with?"

"My essences were a mystery to me until this year," said Melissa. "By the time another year rolls around I'd bet you'll know more about yours than I ever knew about mine before last summer."

Catricha nodded. "Let's try another toss."

The glimmering light of a bane separated from Melissa. She stepped forward, holding her hands crossed one behind the other. She shoved the tiny light toward Catricha.

Catricha focused like a ray of sunlight feeding a blade of grass, and pushed with her mind. The tugging sensation she'd experienced from the night bane reversed completely into a pull on her heart. A glimmer of violet light left her palm, moving between her and Melissa. The purple hue enveloped Melissa's ordinary bane and then pushed the lesser essence into Melissa's palm. Melissa caught it, then gently pushed Catricha's violet essence back to her.

"That was a strong sprite," said Melissa. "What do you think?"

"The song was almost as dissonant as a bane's." Elaine frowned. "It could have been almost anything."

"Good or bad?" Catricha scowled. "Lately I feel cursed."

"It could be a cursed essence," said Elaine. "One of the sprite forms I've been studying is a curse or hex sprite."

"A curse sprite?" Melissa turned to Elaine. "You never told me such a thing was possible. I suppose my bane is more solid but the sprite has always been less material."

Elaine snapped her fingers. "Melissa, you're onto something there. Catricha, If you're going to fight for yourself, you'll need to know how to resonate with your essences."

"Resonate?" said Catricha. "Another kind of magic?"

Melissa nodded. "The most basic form of the matching technique. You try to access something you already know and infuse it into your essence. The essences already have some of your nature infused into them, so it should be easy enough to accomplish."

"All I'm really good at is taunting people with poetry," said Catricha. "Are you saying that if I need to make someone mad, I might be able to use magic for it?"

"I'd bet your curse sprite would be good at that," said Melissa. "Try it now."

"Focus on what you know," said Elaine.

"Right. Focus."

Melissa nodded. "Close your eyes."

Catricha squeezed her eyes shut. "Now I should focus on what makes people angry?"

"Yeah," said Melissa. "Focus on what would enrage someone you know. Any of them will do."

Catricha pressed her eyelids tighter. She focused on the words she would use, her tone, and the very exciting moment of fury sparking in the eyes. She let the concepts flow into her essence. The cursed sprite jumped into her mind, filling her head with more ideas, parting the veils of confusion that always surrounded her. Before she attempted to begin a difficult piece.

The curse sprite made everything fit together with ease. She could see the holes in the morality and logic of her theoretical targets, one she'd previously found unassailable. *Even Nansoela could be no match for my wit with this kind of magic at her disposal. And she's my sister.*

"This is easier than I thought it'd be," she said.

"Strong essences add to your powers," said Elaine. "I suppose the other word for curse would be an epithet."

"Epithet has more than one meaning. High-brow name-calling is just the beginning."

"If you can say something that would drive someone mad with rage," said Melissa. "You may be able to figure out how to calm them, as well."

"Reversing fury is different than causing it," said Catricha. "I'll try my best."

"Good," said Elaine. "Keep focusing."

"It's getting chilly," said Melissa. "That should help Catricha stay alert."

"You lived too long in the south, Melissa," said Elaine. "It's winter here."

"I should have brought something heavier," said Melissa. "These are my summer clothes."

"You can afford warmer clothes, you know. Stop distracting Catricha."

Catricha opened her eyes, and the two mages turned toward her. "What's wrong, you two?" she asked.

"Do you want the long list, my lady?" Melissa arched her brows.

"Right," said Catricha. "I should go see Ruar. I want to see how he's doing."

"Why is that?" asked Elaine.

"I..." Catricha hesitated. "His brother was taken, and I...I care for him."

Melissa folded her arms.

Catricha sighed. "Look, I'll go by myself. I promise I won't take more than an hour."

"We should go with you," said Melissa. "We can keep you safe."

"It's broad daylight," said Catricha. "I'll be fine."

"If you will," Melissa said.

Elaine frowned. "Alright."

"Thank you both," said Catricha. "I won't be long."

* * *

Catricha made her way to the house of Kuldettan. She was stopped by the guards at the gate outside, but Ruar came out to meet her.

"What are you doing here?" he asked.

"I was looking for you. Have you heard anything from Vual?"

"Nothing from, and nothing of him. I fear he may be lost." Ruar brushed at his eyes with his hand.

"Don't cry, please."

“He deserves it," Ruar said through tears.

"He doesn't deserve death."

"For what he tried to do to you?" Ruar’s fists clenched. "Vual is awful."

"Vual fought with us against the shadow," said Catricha.

"Unless you know where to find him, go, but thanks for coming to check on me." He turned his back on her and the guards stepped forward to close the gate.

Catricha took a step forward, but the guards lowered their the bars before her.

"I'm sorry," said Catricha, blinking back tears of her own. "I didn't mean for any of this to happen."

"But it has happened. I need to go. Hadrian is talking with my mother." Ruar marched back toward the house.

Catricha turned, wiping her eyes, and made her way through the mounting blizzard toward the Tower of the Fallen.

She didn’t make it back.

CHAPTER 44

MELISSA

Melissa and Elaine watched for Catricha until snow-bearing clouds began to cover the horizon and the day began to fade into night. Darkness fell, bringing mounting concern and chattering teeth that something happened out in the city.

Catricha should have been back.

“She was going to the Kuldettan’s," said Melissa. "Do you know how to get there?"

"I think you know someone who does," said Elaine.

Melissa nodded. "Let’s find Galocai.”

They set out for House Paroth. Galocai met them there, and the group hurried onward.

With Galocai leading the way, they reached the house of Kuldettan. Snowdrifts formed in the streets, and the people making their way outside were wrapped heavily in the cloth. Winter of the eleventh month crushed in cold. Ice began to form on the rims of decorative fountains. The sky was gray and white.

Melissa led them once Galocai brought them within sight of the Kuldettan house. He fell behind a few paces while she used her essences and spear to cut path through the gathering blanket of snow.

She cast aside drifts of snow to form a path for the others. They reached the gate and the guards stood huddled in the falling snow.

"Have either of you seen Catricha Maltos?" asked Melissa.

"She was here," said one of the guards. "We kept her from entering at our lord's request."

"Which lord?" asked Galocai.

"Young Ruar commanded it. We don't often take orders from him directly, but Lady Filavaye was talking to Deckard Hadrian. They're still inside."

"Deckard is here?" Melissa glanced at Elaine. "Why would he be here except to begin a search for Vual?"

"Can you let us in?" Galocai said. "There is a gold piece in it for each of you."

One of the guards smiled. "If nothing else, we'll get to go inside, and be out of the cold more quickly."

The other guard nodded.

The two men opened the gates and let Melissa and the others inside. One of the men gave a half-nod to Galocai.

"Thank you." Galocai pressed a pair of gold pieces into the guard's hand. Share this with your companion. We have to be on our way quickly."

"We understand." The guard grinned. "You and the young ladies enjoy your visit."

"Enjoyment isn't our objective," said Melissa. "Catricha Maltos disappeared after she came here. She didn't return to meet us."

"That worries me." Galocai nodded. "And if she's out of this, things can be very serious indeed."

"She couldn't have just gotten lost, right?" said Melissa. The three of them made their way into the House of Kuldettan.

* * *

Within the dark sanctuary of House Kuldettan's manor, Melissa, Elaine, and Galocai met with a gentle servant who ushered them into the study. There, Deckard and Filavaye sat across from each other in high-backed chairs. Deckard's robe was the largest light in the room, reflecting the candles glowing from the corners. The high window on the far side was already etched with the tracery of feathery ice spreading across the glass.

Melissa and Elaine froze as Deckard raised his head and looked at them.

"What are you doing here?"

"What are you doing here?" Melissa repeated. "Vual disappeared last night. Catricha's been taken as well."

"Maltos?" said Filavaye.

"Catricha was taken," said Deckard softly, closing his eyes with furrowed brow.

Filavaye looked out from her mountain of blankets. "The shadow is eliminating potential threats to his throne."

"He has taken three already. And if you need more, we don't know but he could come here next."

"Or the Graef estate." Melissa smashed a fist into her palm. "Damn it."

"Bethanelle would be a natural target." Filavaye nodded. "If he's eliminating heirs or challengers."

"That would leave only Nansoela and Galocai," said Melissa.

"Get them here, then," said Galocai. "My sister isn't safe."

"We'll get back to her in time," said Melissa. "We have to find Catricha, Kizoni, and Vual."

"The city." Deckard pressed his hands against his knees. "The city on high if my suspicion."

"The city?" said Filavaye "You can't mean—"

"They must have been taken to the maladrite city."

"The city above?" Filavaye stared at Deckard in shock. "How? And why?"

"I don't know for certain," Deckard said. "My research with Porfiria Amburen suggests they were taken not by the shadow alone, but another being called a meridian, one of the most powerful recorded kinds of demon. Only one dwells above. His name is Anloth."

"You can stop one of these demons, can't you, ancestor?"

"I don't know." Deckard rose from the chair. "I will do what I can."

"You need to go to the city?" said Melissa. "To face this meridian?"

"I intend to rescue Catricha, Vual, and Kizoni, and you can be of help, as well."

"I'll try." Melissa nodded.

"You've just gone to the city for the first time as I understand it. You'll do fine."

Melissa turned to Elaine. "You should protect Bethanelle as best as you can, Heron too."

"Of course." Elaine nodded. "Heron might also be a potential victim."

"I will send as many guards as possible to find Nansoela," said Filavaye.

"Hopefully that will be enough," Melissa said.

Filavaye bowed her head toward Deckard and Melissa. "I'm sure you two have your plans on saving my son and the others. Deckard, you must let me go with you."

"No," said Deckard. "I love you, but I don't trust you, my child."

Filavaye seethed as Deckard turned and led the way out of the study. Melissa, Elaine, and Galocai followed him.

* * *

CATRICHA

Catricha woke in a cold place, but nowhere near as freezing as the streets of Alliance in winter. Metal cruved beneath her as if she sat within a giant spoon. The floor curved slightly, cupping her body against it. She planted her hands and tried to stand up, but the room was dark, and she slipped on the smooth surface. A sound clanged above her, and she turned, noticing her intake of breath. A light glimmered from a doorway above her.

"Who's there?" she called.

"Just me, my bride," said Adias. "But only by proxy."

She squinted against the light and made out a man in the doorway in the wall of the metallic room. The more she saw, the more the room resembled the inside of an eggshell than a spoon. The ceiling followed a similar but inverted curve, compared to the floor.

"You mean you're not really here?" she said.

"I sent my sword servant to look after you," said Adias. "You know Sion."

"Sion?" Catricha remembered a hand clamped over her mouth just before she lost consciousness in Alliance. "He was there."

"Yes," said Adias, as the figure at the top of the stairs descended from the doorway into the bowl where Catricha sat.

"Sion has proven very pliable to my will."

"You're controlling him?" Catricha scowled. "With magic?"

"With dreaming," said Adias. "A dream is all it takes to make life transform into something altogether different."

"Something different?" said Catricha. "You're not creating a dream, but a nightmare."

"Nightmare?" Adias sighed, turning up the palms of both Sion's hands in a shrug. "Obviously, you would say such a thing."

"Sometimes, the obvious is the best response," said Catricha. "You murdered Saviron."

"He had to die," said Adias. "As will you, soon enough, my dear widow."

"Why not just kill me and be done with it?" asked Catricha.

"Is that what you want?" asked Adias. "Because I can think of some things you'd rather live for."

"You don't know anything about me," said Catricha through a grimace of pure hatred. "You never have."

"On the contrary. I know all too much about you, my unfaithful bride." The shape of Sion Arver resolved fully from the shadows as he entered the pool of light falling from the doorway above. He stood over Catricha. "I will punish you," said Adias with a smile curling those lips. "I will take what I wish from you with whatever hands I control at the moment."

Catricha softened her glare, thinking of loyal Sion. "You don't hate me, Sion," she said. "Adias hated me."

"I still do," said Adias using Sion's lips.

"You don't have to do this," said Catricha. "Sion, you can fight him!"

"I'm afraid that's quite impossible for a sleepwalker like him," said Adias. He crouched before Catricha. His hand stroked her cheek, and she pulled back. His other arm swiped out, and he slapped her with all his strength.

Catricha recoiled stunned. She touched her smarting face and glared at him. "Is that all you want?" To beat me?"

"A member of a noble house needs to know how to do battle," said Adias. "But I see you don't have your bane dagger with you."

Catricha realized she'd left the weapon with Melissa and Elaine at the Tower of the Fallen. She gritted her teeth.

"That will do," said Adias. "Your lips and your mouth were meant for nothing but pain. Your defiance will do you no good." He brought Sion's face close to Catricha's. "Or perhaps you'd rather have a taste of what's between his legs with what meets yours."

"No," said Catricha. "Even you wouldn't–"

"Even I wouldn't dare?" said Adias. "Soon, I will rule the entire Princedom of Alliance," he said. "I'll do whatever I please with whoever I want there."

"There?" said Catricha. "Where are we?"

"Above." Adias leered at her. "We are in the city of the maladrites, so even if you escape this chamber, there is no way you will return to Alliance. Any human who the maladrites capture becomes a slave, and that is if they're lucky, as far as I understand."

"The maladrites," said Catricha. "They're ruthless as they are wicked."

"Indeed they are," said Adias. "I've learned much from them. Their lore is what led me to discover the ancient Shadow of Jasguara."

"You always read too much," said Catricha. "You explored too deeply, where you should never have gone at all."

"I can't agree," said Adias. "I am nearly immortal now. I will last forever. Whereas you will perish within days."

"Days?" said Catricha. "You plan to simply let me starve in here?"

"I've always despised you, Catricha," said Adias. "You didn't belong among us. You and your mother's blood combined with your father's ill will meant your family must be purged. I will do this, because my dear, you have been in my way for far too long. I only married you because I thought I would get the chance to destroy you on my terms."

"And my family?" said Catricha. "You hate us because we're not like you."

"Of course," said Adias. "Don't we all hate what we don't understand?"

"We are like you," said Catricha. "Or, we were. Before you became a monster."

"My dear," said Adias. "By your standards, I was always a monster."

Catricha said nothing but glared at him. Her eyes were already welling with tears, uncontrollable, inevitable.

"You," said Adias. "You were considered a great beauty by many of my friends, Catricha. But I always despised you from your appearance, to your manners, to your wit. Everything about you is bleak and lifeless, and soon your life will be mine to take."

"But it isn't yet," said Catricha. "What are you waiting for?"

"I want to hold the blade myself," said Adias. "And a ghost can't hold a dagger."

"What do you mean?" asked Catricha. "You wounded Galocai."

"I can sever essences and disrupt bonds."

"You killed those guards to kidnap the dowager regent."

"No," said Adias. "I had help."

"Who?" said Catricha. "Not Sion?"

"Not him," said Adias. "My dream had yet to take control at the time. No, I had the help of a demon in taking Kizoni. You must know, she is with child."

"What?" said Catricha. "I merely suspected, but I didn't know."

“I'm going to leave you with that thought. I have plans for that child. To live again, this time forever, I'd sacrifice anything. Anything.”

"But it's not time." Catricha smirked. "The child won't be born for months, and you want to have your new body in days."

"Of course," said Adias. "But I have secrets to keep myself, little Catricha."

She spat on the floor of the eggshell. The metal reflected in glimmered with the saliva. Sion's back straightened, and his eyes glazed over. Catricha got to her feet, slowly. Adias said nothing more.

She glanced at Sion. His eyes remained vacant, but she knew he was in there somewhere.

"Can I help you?" she asked his empty features.

Sion still wore the sword of House Halth at his side.

"I need to get out of here," Catricha whispered.

She stared into Sion's face. He blinked twice. He could regain his senses soon, or Adias might return.

Catricha delivered the fiercest blow she could manage, pumping the power and solidity of her night bane into her fist. Her shadow-clad knuckles connected with Sion's jaw. He staggered, moving more like a broken carriage axle rather than a human. Darkness flowed from Catricha's impact point, surrounding his eyes, covering his features, and blocking his senses.

Catricha ran as fast as her legs would carry her up the eggshell, toward the door. Light greeted her, and Catricha stormed onto the ring above the world. Maladrite architecture loomed all around her, alternating sleek and sharp. A nearby tower of black sand cast the longest shadow over the street where she stood, chilled in the evening wind.

Strange forms turned toward her from along the metallic street. The sun glinted on faces and bodies more bizarre than she'd ever read about. The nearest one was a pallid maladrite with the body of a giant crab from which sprouted the upper half of a man. The monster scuttled in her direction.

Catricha's eyes widened. *I can't freeze now, or I'm doomed.*

Left with nowhere to hide, she fled up the black tower's slope. Her breath came in harsh gasps as she fought the sand threatening to trap her feet by sinking away with every step. Looking up, she stopped in her tracks. A cave mouth loomed before her leading into the tower of sand. Rivulets of black dust cast into the air by her passage scattered behind her. The crab-maladrite retreated along the street at the tower's base.

Whatever dwelt within this tower scared even other monsters.

Sion emerged from the tunnel where she had stunned him, at the base of the tower where she'd been taken by Adias. His head turned in her direction.

Adias called after her. "You fled? I expected more from you, Catricha!"

Catricha answered him with a glare.

Sion struggled to climb the tower's wall, steep as ever. His greater weight slowed him in the sand. She scrambled the rest of the way to the mouth of a cave in the sandy wall.

Glancing behind her, she saw Sion was still twenty yards away. She took a deep breath and forced herself to run into the darkness, past caring about what horrors awaited within. Her feet sank into the floor, slow and unsteady.

What could this place be? She asked herself. *What kind of maladrite lives in a tower of sand?*

The black tower surrounded her, walls dark and cold. A skittering sound echoed from deeper within the tower, the only sign of any other creature, maladrite, human, or otherwise. She plunged into the dark. Then came a din like a thousand feet all working as one to carry a single massive weight.

She screamed and ran deeper into the tunnel. Another voice answered her in the darkness, fearful and all too human.

"Who's there?" Catricha asked.

"I am Kizoni Duhikzo," whispered a low voice from ahead of her.

Catricha squinted forward. By the little lights of pale, glowing plants, she saw the face of the dowager regent.She was bound by the plants. Loops connected her to the wall. Then, the demonic monster arose in the tunnel beyond them.

"Welcome," said the deep voice from an unseen body. "Are you here to play a game with the last meridian to dwell on high?"

CHAPTER 45

DECKARD

They entered the city using a shrine near the Kuldettan estate. Standing on high on the street outside the House of Mercy, Fanhedon's emotionless mask turned toward Deckard.

"Where should we look?" Melissa asked in the demons voice.

"I have ideas," said Deckard. "But the place drawing me now is dangerous, the black sand tower."

"The black sand tower."

Deckard pointed at the horizon behind Melissa and across the ring over the bend of the earth. There stood a towering shadow. In the twilight, the shape eclipsed the moon, and cut off all light from above, blackening the stars in that direction.

"A tower outlines the night."

"Poetry, is it?" Melissa grunted. "We'll find Catricha soon enough. Vual, Catricha, and Kizoni."

"Those are the three we know are missing," said Deckard. "But there could be others."

Melissa nodded.

"To work," said Deckard.

They set off through the streets, leaping and bounding across the metal and stone of the city of the maladrites. Deckard glided ahead, catching the wind. The cold of the night closed in around them. The city on high grew extremely cold in the dark. What light was captured by the cities metallic domes and gleaming streets was mostly absorbed or reflected during daylight hours. The city became hot when the sun emerged, and cold when the light failed.

The two of them climbed through the night, making their way far from Mother Mercy's house. Only Deckard caught sight of a winking shape, like half a person standing in the darkness between them and the tower.

"Ilrona," he murmured.

Melissa glanced in his direction. "Who is that?" She skidded to a stop, taking a fighting stance.

"That is Mother Mercy's handmaiden," said Deckard. "Ilrona, the lady of light and dark."

"She's a demon?" asked Melissa.

"Yes. Almost all the denizens above are demons or maladrites."

"So she's here to stop us?" asked Melissa.

"More likely to interrogate me." Deckard shook his head. "You go ahead. I'll deal with her."

"I'll do what I can to search the tower, but it's so large. I don't know if I can a get all the way through it."

"You'll be fine, Melissa. Go."

She took off through the streets running with Fanhedon's long stride.

Deckard flew forward, aiming for Ilrona. She held up her right hand and stopped him in his tracks with two words. "Catricha Maltos."

"What did you say?" Deckard slowed his flight and then landed in front of Ilrona. "What do you want with her?"

"You lied to me, demon hunter."

"I told you I didn't know what her strong essences were. That's all I knew at the time."

"But you didn't report to me as you said you would." The bright side of Ilrona's mouth curved in a scowl.

"I had other things to attend to. Now she's been taken."

"Taken?" Ilrona's nostrils flared. The shadow side of her expanded, seeming to swallow the bright side except for the tiniest sliver of light. "I need to find those essences."

"Ilrona," said Deckard. "I didn't lie to you."

"That remains to be seen, and your failures suggest other facts. Mother will want words with you."

"She can be disappointed when all is said and done tonight."

"Your mission. You and the young mage will find it difficult to intervene at the black tower without my help."

"We seek to rescue a group of nobles kidnapped from Alliance. Mother Mercy should support that."

"Should?" said Ilrona. "Do not show your arrogance any further, Hadrian."

"I refuse to let you stand in our way. I won't be intimidated, Ilrona."

"In that case, perhaps you should simply bow to my will and tell me where you found the night bane."

"I never found any night bane."

"I doubt the shadow prince of Alliance will be as merciful as I toward Catricha Maltos when he finds out what she can do."

Deckard gritted his teeth and drew out the sprite strings between his fingertips. "Don't make me clash with you Ilrona. We'll both be harmed."

"Again, arrogance," Ilrona. "I'm standing in your path, Hadrian, because you are a betrayer at heart, and I suspect you would betray Mother Mercy."

"I've never betrayed anyone who didn't deserve it," said Deckard.

"Continue with that line of speaking. You're idea of the future will be regarded as foolish soon enough."

"I'm not the kind of man to make a plan.

"Mother has noticed," said Ilrona.

"Let her reprimand me later. I have no reason to speak further to you while lives are in danger."

"Yes, you do, unless you want me to pursue that little mage you have running ahead of you."

"You collect those night banes, I know," said Deckard. "You've wanted them for a long time."

"I only want to complete my collection."

Deckard waved toward the tower. "Complete it with the night banes that live in the shadow prince's heart."

"He is like a living death," said Ilrona. "And I will take on what could threaten Mother Mercy's order before serving myself."

"Catricha Maltos is no threat to Mother Mercy," said Deckard. "She doesn't study magic, and she lacks the will to become a real mage."

"Are you certain?" asked Ilrona. "I'll watch her carefully, regardless."

"We must rescue her, first," said Deckard. "Let me past and I will forget this."

"Very well," said Ilrona. "But I go with you."

"Fine," said Deckard. "Follow me."

MELISSA

Melissa glanced over her shoulder as they approached the black tower, Ilrona and Hadrian followed her.

A man was walking up the tower's side, struggling against the sand. *He has to be human*, Melissa thought, or he *wouldn't be having such trouble*. A maladrite wouldn't be struggling to climb a tower of sand in their own city.

"That's Sir Sion Arver," said Deckard, squinting ahead.

"one of the missing nobles?" asked Ilrona.

"Not one we were looking for," said Melissa.

"A human without a second form in the city," said Ilrona. "Any maladrite can claim a human as a servant of their own, here. The three of us should catch him quickly."

Melissa nodded. "I'll grab him first." She sprang toward Sion, propelled by Fanhedon's steel muscles and reinforced by her iron bane.

She landed on the sand tower's side in front of Sion. He stared at her with vacant eyes. A kind of recognition entered his gaze. "Mage," he said in the heavy voice from the shadow. "A pleasure to see you again, my dear."

"That's the voice of the shadow," said Melissa. "You're Adias Halth."

"Correct, my dear. I can control anyone who dreams through me."

"I've had trouble with dream-crafters before," said Melissa. "I won't let you take this man's life."

"On the contrary," said Adias. "I already possess him."

"For now."

"If you could stop me, woman," said Adias. "I'd be terribly surprised."

Melissa tensed Fanhedon's talons. She prepared a leaping strike at Sion as he drew his sword. The Halth family blade gleamed with the light of a magically-infused weapon. Essences bound within reinforced the blade and the sword might have other abilities as well.

Melissa eyed the weapon, wondering if it could cut through Fanhedon's armor.

"You don't have long. Hadrian will be here soon, along with one of Mother Mercy's most powerful demons."

"In that case," said Adias through Sion's mouth. "I shall have to complete my quest sooner than planned."

"Sooner than planned." Melissa grimaced.

"I'll leave you in suspense with little Sion and his blade." The knight raised the infused sword to swing.

Melissa caught his wrists and forced both hands upward. She didn't close the talons, not wanting to cut through his wrists like butter.

"He is weak," said Adias. "Sion is low even in his dreams."

The sand beneath Melissa's feet began to shift. "I have other ways of defeating you."

With a grunt, Sion staggered to one side.

Melissa shoved forward, pushing Sion down the slope of the tower. The sand where she'd been standing parted. Smaller, human-sized spider demons began to emerge, all with the same hideous mockeries of human faces as the one she'd battled in the streets of Alliance.

"Damn it," said Melissa under her breath. "Deckard, take care! There's more than just him."

Deckard landed behind Melissa. Sprite strings leapt from his fingers and entangled one of the spider demons by all eight legs at once. He hurled the creature away through the air. "I can see that, but at least they're here and not in Alliance for now."

"Awakened promortals." Melissa grimaced. "They can recover from anything."

"They can try." Deckard winked. "But they're no match for us. How many did you bring, Adias? I only hear six heart songs."

"That will be more than enough to defeat you. Half a dozen demons against two demon hunters? Please, Hadrian."

Melissa snarled. Fanhedon's claws tore through the lesser spider demons. She ripped one down and hurled another deep into the black sand at her feet. Others that Deckard tossed upward came down hard, smashing deep into the tower. Yet, no spider seemed completely beaten. They all scrambled away, scuttling on all their limbs.

Adias laughed. "You see," he said. "The battle you have chosen is not one you can win."

Melissa said nothing. She focused on her iron bane and then loosed it at a spider demon she'd eviscerated. The strong bane punched through the spiders back and pinned it to the tower's soft wall. The sand sank away and then spider fell into a the abyss of darkness below the tower. Sand trailed behind the howling spider demon as it plummeted into oblivion.

Shock passed across Sion's face.

"Did you not expect that? Even if we can't break them, we can beat your spider demons." The iron bane returned to Melissa's hand. She held the strong essence between her fingertips, ready to throw again at any moment.

"Formidable," said Adias. "But how will you fare when you face more to save good Sion?"

"We already have more," said Deckard. "Where is Kizoni?"

"Kizoni and Vual are safe, for now. Catricha on the other hand." Adias grinned. "She just rushed into a certain death—"

Melissa jumped at Sion, swinging a punch Fanhedon's strength but talons closed to avoid a lethal strike. The knight went sprawling onto the sand, a fresh bruise forming on his cheek. Melissa landed before him, and took a defensive stance. *No need.* The dreaming man was unconscious.

DECKARD

Deckard glanced at Melissa as Ilrona caught up with them by the tower of sands. Black spirals of dust scattered into the air before them. Deckard glanced around. "Who lives in the tower?" he asked Ilrona.

"Anloth," said the demoness. "I can approach no further than we are now."

"Anloth the Meridian of Law," said Deckard. "I don't want to confront him if I can avoid it."

"That demon is more powerful than any of us," said Ilrona. "Despite his lower status."

"I have to follow Catricha inside. I must try to save them."

"You really think Kizoni is in there too?" Melissa asked.

"I believe it." Deckard bowed to the lady of light and darkness. "Please, Ilrona, make us a path to the city of Alliance for when we return." He grimaced. "If we return."

He glanced at Melissa. She lifted Sion onto her shoulders.

"We're going to find Vual," said Deckard. "I have a sense of where the boy is being held. Then, we'll search for Catricha and Kizoni."

Melissa nodded with Fanhedon's smooth mask. "I see your logic. Lead the way."

CHAPTER 46

CATRICHA

"What is your name?" Catricha asked, peering into the gloom.

A flicker of silvery luminescence showed an unnaturally wide face set at the front of a chitinous body. Grasping human arms surrounded the demon's visage. His voice boomed when he spoke.

"I am called Anloth."

The darkness surrounding Catricha and Kizoni was absolute, except for the face of the meridian demon, lit by his dimly pulsating silver banes. The demon hissed, a forked tongue flicking out of his mouth. His wide, round face shifted into a sardonic smile, dark eyes glistening in the gloom. He gazed at the two women before him.

"What will you offer as a wager for our game?" he asked.

"I don't know what I have that you'd value."

"An astute observation," said Anloth. "No one ever does."

Catricha glanced at Kizoni. Her gaze lingered on the trembling woman. The dowager regent's skin looked sallow in the weak light. The demon reached out with one of the arms that haloed his head. Thick, human-like fingers extended toward Kizoni. He touched her cheek gently.

She looked at Anloth, then shuddered. Her eyes squeezed shut and she shuddered.

Catricha stood before the demon as more arms extended toward her. They threatened to an trap her in clusters of grasping fingers.

"If I win," said Catricha, "will you let us go?"

"It depends on your wagers," said the demon. "Win well and I'll let you go free."

Catricha took a deep breath. "What's your game?"

"I bend space to serve," he said.

The meridian glittered and shifted his eyes slightly, then lazily flicked a long insect Catricha hadn't notice from her shoulder. The finger of the demon appeared as nimble and dexterous as any human extremity. Catricha a took a deep breath, trying to hold in her fear.

The demon smiled slightly.

"My game is dice," he said. "Are you familiar with the chance-game called life and death?"

"I think I'd remember if I were," said Catricha.

"Let me explain the rules, little human." One of the meridian's other hands produced a pair of stone dice that clicked together. One die was a shiny black and the other bone white.

"Here." The demon dropped the black die into Catricha's hand. "That die represents life. The die that represents death is pale as the dread snow that falls upon Alliance as we speak."

"How do you know it's snowing in Alliance?"

"I can see many things from within this tunnel," said the demon. "Time and space open their secrets before me."

Catricha gritted her teeth. She clasped her hand around the die in her palm. The cube was cool to the touch, with a strange sense of slipperiness. It was like a cube of ice in her hand.

"Kizoni," Anloth said.

The regent looked at him fearfully. "Haven't you done enough to me?"

"Precisely. That is why you will be my first wager."

Catricha a put a hand to her heart. "In that case, I must wager my freedom in return."

"You are perceptive. I would not accept less."

The meridian rolled the white die around in one large palm. "The game is one of pure chance. I can tell you don't know the rules. First, when we roll the dice we each get points."

Catricha of frowned. "Points?"

"The most points at the end of a round wins," said Anloth. "Every round has rolls of each die."

Catricha folded her arms. She still held the black die, feeling as if it was melting in her grip. She relaxed her stance slightly, then looked at the demon's face through the mass of arms that nearly surrounded her.

"Whoever rolls high wins, then?" she said.

"Not exactly." The meridian smiled. "Before you roll the die, pick a number and write it on your palm. You and I won't be able to see each others' in the dark, so that is your secret and I'll write down one for myself as well."

Catricha nodded. "Go on."

"If your number is rolled you get two points. If both our numbers are rolled we each get a single point. If neither of us has the number rolled, we both get no points."

"Sounds simple," said Catricha.

"The one who has the most points at the end of three tosses of the dice shall be the winner. However, there are other wrinkles. First, you may not pick the same number twice in one round. Second, if you roll a higher number thaan your opponent but do not hit your number, you will win with one point. If neither of us rolls our number, but yours is higher, you win a point as well."

"I understand." Catricha sighed. "If I wager my life how do I know I'll get my winnings?"

"You wager not your life," said the demon. "But your freedom. I have no desire to take your life, except in terms of this game."

"I expect we may get to know each other a little. If I win this wager it may not be the last."

The demon laughed from deep within his throat. "I had a feeling you'd say that. You are an odd human."

He withdrew most of his arms from around Catricha, leaving just the one holding the white die before her. He threw down a box with two of his other arms. The box was wooden and open on the top, lit within by a gleaming set of softly singing sprites at the sharp corners.

"Roll in the box when you're ready," said Anloth.

Catricha scribbled a number in her hand, then cast the die. In each round she could take each number only once, and she suspected the demon would aim high first so she picked six. She cast the die and prayed.

The demon cast his white die to rattle in the box along with her black cube. She kept the maladrite quill pen resting on her open palm. The two dice spiraled into the box, bouncing between the sprites at the corners.

At last, the dice both came to a stop. Catricha his heart sank. Her die was a four, not a six.

The demon whistled low, and then said in a low voice. "What are the chances?" He indicated his own die with a wave. The pips showed just one dot.

"What was your guess?" asked Catricha.

"Six," said the demon.

Catricha nodded. "It's my point."

"Indeed," said the demon. "If your die is higher and neither guess is correct, the point is yours."

"I think I understand the game."

"Then write another number on your arm," said the demon. "I will do the same again."

Catricha nodded. She set to guessing the next number, with six being unavailable.

She chose the number four, not five, because she did not want to score even with the demon if the dice matched. If she guessed five, but as she suspected he would, they would more likely end up with equal points.

Catricha a cast her die.

Her teeth chattered in the cold of the tunnel. The demon leered at Kizni, then cast his die almost casually into the box.

The two dice banged off each other in the air and then bounced into the bottom of the box. Catricha rolled a two and the demon a five.

"What do you know." Anloth smirked with fanged teeth. "Two points for me."

Catricha grimaced "So I'm losing by one, now."

"And if you should lose another point to me, I shall keep both of you as my playthings."

"Who brought Kizoni here for you to keep?" Catricha asked.

"I brought her here. Wager for more information later if you win this round," said the meridian.

Catricha scribbled a number on her hand, the number five. That meant that she could not lose to the demon by him picking a higher number.

"If we roll equal numbers, the one of us picked a higher score will get the point."

"That is so," Anloth said.

Catricha nodded. "I understand. If only I could learn this game with a friend instead of a monster."

"Do you think of me as a monster?" said the demon. "I am a meridian, flying keeper of time and space, and I remain the most honorable of my kind. All the rest were expelled from this city on high."

"A thousand legs isn't my idea of a human," said Catricha. "And gambling isn't part of my concept of honor."

"My limbs weren't my idea," said Anloth.

Catricha almost smiled at that. *This demon isn't a lack wit.*

"Cast your die," he said. They rolled as one. Catricha's die, bounded on it's side. She watched the movement carefully. If you roll the four, five, or six she would win at least one point.

The demon scored a five. Catricha's die settled.

She'd scored a six.

The demon clapped his hands together in a cacophony of many pairs of human arms creating applause. As if an audience besides the terrified Kizoni was watching the game.

"Well done," he said. "After two casts you've scored as many points as I. I'm not feeling generous, though. We must break this tie."

"That wasn't part of our deal," said Catricha. "Given all your skill, Kizoni and I should go free in a tie."

"Given my skill at this game of chance you mean?" Anloth roared throaty laugh. "I think not."

"If I'm to roll the die again for my freedom, I think you should raise the stakes on your end."

"Why is that?" said the demon.

"If you don't raise the stakes, I may not honor my side should I lose. Do you want to chase me through this narrow passage. You're practically cheating me by changing the game's terms once by making me cast a fourth roll."

"We must decide the game. I'd not considered that things be resolved in a single round."

Catricha shrugged, trying not to shake in the demon's horrid presence. "Alright. For the next round, I'll barter the freedom of my friend Porfiria in

Alliance. She's a mage and poet of some skill, so should be worth double what you've offered me up to now."

"What would you have me add to compensate?" asked the meridian.

"If I win, you must tell me how the spider demons slept so long beneath Alliance without being known."

"Very well. I will accept your terms in exchange for your wager of Porfiria below."

Catricha went to write the next number. "In each round, can we use the old numbers?"

"You may choose any number once again," said the demon.

Catricha a went back to her hand.

She chose five, going higher seemed to be strong, though choosing low could be a way to mitigate a poor die roll. Still, she feared she picked poorly.

She cast her die. The demon dropped his with a perfunctory clank at the other end of the box. She'd scored a three as did the demon. He revealed his number, shining a light on one palm. The number read as a three.

"I now have four points."

Catricha grunted. "Roll again. Perhaps we should make things more interesting."

"Is it not interesting enough?" asked the demon. "You could soon be my slave, as it is."

"I've asked for freedom and for information," said Catricha, shivering. "But perhaps we can raise the stakes higher."

"You raise the stakes for the pot while the challenge increased?" The demon barked a laugh. "Very well. Name your terms."

"I will wager you the freedom of Deckard Hadrian and his services in exchange for your service to me."

"If you should win, you demand my service? Have you any idea what that would mean, human?"

"I do," said Catricha. "At least as much as what Deckard Hadrian is worth to the world below."

"An immortal man of Mother Mercy..." Anloth whistled. "I accept your wager for it pleases me." Anloth scuttled further forward in the tunnel on his countless legs, bring his face close to Catricha's.

"Scribe the number, then cast the die."

Catricha picked six this time.

They rolled. His die came up a three, once again. Catricha scored a five. She received another point.

"Four to three," said Anloth.

Catricha nodded, silent, calm despite the cold.

She picked four this time. Hoping, she would be able to roll the number exactly. She cast the die. He laughed as he dropped his die into the container. Then, his arms reached out, Catricha a sensed them move the box through the warbling of the sprites inside.

"Wait!" said Catricha as the dice rattled in the box, shifted ever so slightly by the demon's arms. "You're cheating."

"How dare you accuse me of such a crime. Cheating among demons in the city is punished by banishment!"

Catricha's curse sprite flew from her arm and illuminated the hands of the demon clasped around the edges of the box. "I can see it now. By your own rules, you've lost this game."

"No. How could you?" Anloth's face fell and his smug smile vanished.

Kizoni fell to her knees, gasping for breath as the ties binding her to wall released her. Anloth howled and his arms withdrew from the box, Catricha scooped up both his dice, the black and the white. She slipped them into a pocket in her trousers.

"Now, take us from here. I can get my other answers from you later, Anloth."

The demon grimaced, face contorting into a sharp mass of shapes as muscles bunched together.

"By your will. I serve you for one day."

"One day?" Kizoni whispered. "I feel as though I've been here forever."

"You lost your rolls." Anloth's gaze turned toward Catricha.

"Are these terms acceptable to you?"

"I accept," Catricha set her jaw. "Now, take us from this tower."

"As you command." The meridian turned his back on them, and a cluster of arms waved them to climb onto his carapace. "I will take you on my back."

Catricha put an arm around Kizoni. She held the regent to her side, and they rode toward the faint starlight shining at the top of the tower.

"What about the information I've won?" Catricha called as wind began to howl in her ears.

"Simple," answered the demon as they emerged from the cylindrical tunnel at the top of the tower.

He arced to swarm down the side of the tower and raced toward the street, carried by a thousand legs.

"Your spidery foes are promortal demons, cursed to dream but never die. They've slumbered beneath Alliance since before the fall of the Primes."

"Can you return us to Alliance?"

"At your command, Catricha."

Her eyes widened as the demon took off. The rush of cold air made her cringe against the demon's back, holding tight to Kizoni.

CHAPTER 47

DECKARD

Melissa and Deckard raced through the tower, through caverns of black sand. There was no sign of Catricha within their tunnel but in a side passage, set within the walls was a set of cells in the sand, it's base sheet with darker sheets of stony material, like burnt glass.

Vual sat hunched in one cell, his sacra form assumed and essence song angry with chords. Flames billowing from the blazing wings on his back. Deckard pulled the bars apart, with his sprites allowing him to break the metal easily from its hinges.

He hurled the doors to the side. "Vual, are you all right?"

"I live." Vual grunted. "What of the others?"

"We found Sion before we knew he was missing. As for Catricha and Kizoni, we have to keep looking."

"I'll help," said Vual. "Now that I know the truth, I owe them both much to atone for my misdeeds."

The group set off, prowling through the darkened tunnels of the black tower, calling out for Catricha and Kizoni.

MELISSA

Melissa emerged from the side passage she'd been searching, wearing Fanhedon's shape and carrying Sion. She'd found nothing alive in the sandy cells behind her.

Deckard glided out of a vertical tunnel nearby to join her. "We can't search everywhere before the tower shakes to pieces."

"It won't fall," said Ilrona from off further ahead in the passage.

Melissa lifted Sion onto her back and then glanced at Vual. "Can you fly?"

"My sacra form can, but not for long."

"We need to leave," said Melissa.

"If I abandon Catricha now." Vual glowered at her. "I'll prove myself a coward."

Deckard said, "You're no coward, Vual, but if we're going to survive, we need to go now."

Vual beat his flaming wings and took to the air. Fanhedon leapt after him. Deckard darted into the air, gliding on the light wind in the city's night sky. The three of them descended with Ilrona toward the base of the tower. The demoness glanced at Melissa. "The shrine is too far away for our purposes. Alliance is in peril."

"How do you propose we return?" asked Deckard.

"The dream way," said Ilrona. "Brace yourselves, all three of you humans."

"And remove your sacra forms," she said. "A demon cannot cross the dream way."

Deckard nodded. "Open the path."

"It is done," said Ilrona.

Melissa's eyes widened as stairs appeared in the sand, forming a spiral staircase leading toward the world below. She grimaced. "This can't be real. I never even read of such a place as the dream way."

"It is hidden magic," said Deckard. "Once it could be wielded by one of my fellow immortals."

"Vual," said Melissa. "You can go first. I'll bring up the rear to protect our backs."

"No," said Deckard. "I'll go last. I'm not losing either of you in this place."

"Thank you, ancestor." Vual assumed his human form, looking tired and fragile compared to his usual self. He started down the steps into the dream way. Melissa followed with trepidation.

She didn't like to place trust in anything she didn't understand, which made unknown magic frustrating to use. The dream way possessed an ethereal nature she glimpsed images of the past as she put one foot in front of the other. Deckard followed them them inside and the path behind them sealed completely.

They descended the stairs at a rapid pace. The black sand from the tower Ilrona had used to form the dream steps began to disintegrate behind them. "Quicker," said Deckard. "We must hurry."

"How far is it?" asked Vual.

"Not far," said Deckard. "Only as far as we believe, so abandon thoughts of real space and time."

"I see it!" Vual shouted with excitement and charged ahead.

Slipping and sliding along the sandy steps, he reached his a gate of the same color as the stairway. Melissa followed him to the door leading inside Alliance's walls. Melissa stepped through onto the cold street paving stones outside the tombs of the princes of Alliance.

DECKARD

Deckard's experience in the dream way flickered and faded away. His mind raced and his heartbeat echoed in his ears. He stormed through the final gateway and emerged from the dream way into the snowy plaza outside the tombs in Alliance.

The river rushed by on one side of the plaza, ice floating on the surface. Snow and ice lay thick on the ground. No one had yet noticed his presence. As night fell, the way of the world turned from mortals to the immortals that still dwelt below.

No one else noticed the shadow standing before the gateway of the city's necropolis. He cradled a bundle in his arms, and his eyes were blue-gray. The same color as Adias Halth's eyes ever were, even when he was a child. The shadow prince of Alliance waited before the tombs.

"You made it here." Adias' voice boomed unnaturally loud. "But it's too late, immortal."

Deckard squinted at the shadowy man. "What are you holding?"

"I think you know, Deckard Hadrian."

"The heir of the city, Kizoni's child. But how? She shouldn't be born yet."

"Time was of the essence," said Adias. "I had Anloth use his essences to accelerate the growth of this child."

"Anloth..." said Melissa. "What happened to him when we wrecked his tower?"

"The tower will stand as long as the meridian wills it," said Adias.

"So you aren't going to try to destroy us, are you?" Deckard stretched his fingers, ready to release bane darts if Adias moved toward him.

"In good time. You know the mystery of becoming immortal requires taking as well as giving, in my case, mostly taking."

"Your method is not like the one I was subjected to."

"Correct. What I have chosen to become that you cannot?"

"I was never given a choice," said Deckard.

"No wonder you're so angry, Hadrian."

Melissa clenched her teeth.

"Now, now, my dear," said Adias. "Don't hide that temper. It makes you quite beautiful."

She made her hands into fists.

"I will take the created essence of this child to complete myself. Then I will rise as an immortal prince."

"Those who aspire to such power are never worthy of it," Deckard said.

"How would you know? You've not confronted mortality as I have. You've not spoken to demons and destroyed allies and friends. You've never done a thing–"

"Don't be presumptuous," said Deckard. "You know nothing of my deeds and misdeeds."

"I know one thing, Hadrian. You cannot stop me."

"As long as you hold that child." Deckard's mind raced for a bluff. "I won't have to."

"Why not? You know I plan to steal her life for my rebirth."

"Yes, but you left a trail. You're draining the child's essence taking and I may be powerless to stop you. But there are others who aren't."

"Who else would dare?" His shadowy features melted into a toothy smile. "I control this city now. I am the rightful prince and I will simply have the guards remove you the moment I'm human again."

"You will never be human again." Deckard laughed. "You cannot be."

"I'll be more than human."

"No," said Deckard. "You will always be less."

Adias shook his head. From the snow there came the sound of spider demons crawling up from the tunnels below ground. They emerged from the catacombs, a dozen promortal spider monks, and began to creep toward Melissa, Deckard, and Vual.

"Have fun with these three," said Adias. "And as for you, my foes, the promortal monks can endure the most deadly pains inflicted upon them. Now the elders are awake."

Melissa said to Deckard. "I'm going to take on my sacra form."

"Do it," said Deckard. "There is still a battle left to fight."

The spiders rushed at them. Vual and Melissa assumed their sacra forms and they clashed in brilliant light and glinting steel in the cold of night.

MELISSA

Melissa came face-to-face with the spider demon. Her spear clashed with the monster's second tongue. The creature's stinger extended from a wild human-like mouth.

The spear flashed, illuminated by the glow from Melissa's sprites. Her iron bane shimmered around the metal point, reinforcing the weapon. Fanhedon's form shone in the light around her. She darted forward, driving the spider to the ground. The promortal demon looked up at her, eyes furious.

"You cannot destroy me, nor defeat my kind," it rasped.

Melissa said nothing. She impaled the creature through the abdomen. The spider's legs kicked at her, cutting toward Fanhedon, but not able to pierce her armor.

Melissa delivered a thrust to the spiders neck. The creature's wounds healed almost as fast as she cut them, but the spearhead remained stuck in the wound this time as the damage repaired itself, trapping the point of the spear and Melissa's iron bane within the beast.

Melissa retreated a few paces, then pulled the bane to her, tearing the spiders body to shreds as it emerged from the monster's torso.

The pieces of the spider struggled, crawling toward each other. In a flash of flames, a blazing inferno from Vual's Sacra form engulfed the remains. He returned to clashing with another, already flaming, demon on his other side. Melissa retrieved her spear, then hurled it at the spider battling Vual.

The weapon caught the demon in the side and the spider clutched at the haft with his human arms. The spear went all the way through and the point emerged from the spiders opposite flank, breaking open the carapace from within.

"We need to clear the way for Hadrian to go after Adias," Melissa said.

"Right," growled the heir of Kuldettan.

The two of them drove the spiders back pace by pace from the mouth of the tombs. Gates of iron shone in the moonlight.

Snow flickered around their sacra forms as they battered and slashed through their enemies. Foes fell backward, wounds, gaping and burning. The flaming spider parts never returned to each other. Instead, fragments of language began to float in the air, the faint sound of failed incantations.

Other spider monks chanted from their severed heads or torn mouths. One by one the promortal elders of Alliance fell to sleep once more.

Deckard Hadrian sliced between the remaining spiders, charging toward the gates where the shadow stood, waiting.

CHAPTER 48

CATRICHA

Anloth carried Kizoni and Catricha down through the clouds, racing in the night through billowing layers of the snowstorm into Alliance. The great demon moved with ease, though the wind rushed by at a roaring pace. Catricha pointed toward the river as they came into view of the great city. A great light outlined by darkness bloomed within the tombs.

Catricha's heart seized and she pointed toward the light. "There," she said. "That is where we need to go."

"Very well," said Anloth in a rumble. He arrowed to the sky, descending on the river. His great centipede bulk crashed into the water, sending ice flying and showers of freezing wet everywhere. Catricha and Kizoni climbed down, Catricha helping the dowager regent.

The two of them stared at the battle before them. The demons with their spidery limbs clashed with Vual and Melissa in their sacra forms. Deckard Hadrian hurled the spiders this way and that, crushing limbs with each blow of his fists. He hurled spiders in the air. He smashed them into the dust in the snow in the ice. The shadowy form before them simply stood cradling Kizoni's daughter.

"We need to get there." Kizoni stared at Adias.

"I'll go," said Catricha. "I'll protect your child."

"Why?" asked Kizoni. "You've done enough."

"That child is my princess," said Catricha. "I'm going to protect the city as shield should."

"This city's shield is the nobility," said Kizoni. "And the prince's line."

"I'm going," said Catricha. "Stay here. You'll be safe."

"I will protect Kizoni," said Anloth. "As long as I serve you."

"Kizoni glanced nervously at the centipede demon's face. "I understand," she said. "Thank you, Catricha Maltos."

Catricha nodded. For once, lacking words, she ran through the fray, darting past spiders past fighting demonic bodies. She sprinted in the snow as fast as she could toward Adias, abandoning any cover of darkness. She charged straight at the shadow prince. He grinned at her, his bluish eyes, bold and bright.

"There you are, Catricha," he said. "You're in time to witness what I will become." A void of joy and light emanated from him, drawing in all energy from those he touched.

Catricha's essences tugged in her heart, as if pulled toward him, as well. She got to her feet, holding on tightly with her mind.

"You won't have that child," she said. "I'm going to save her."

"Do your best," said Adias. "Because now is the time when I'll kill you."

"You didn't think you'd have to, did you?" said Catricha. "As usual you didn't think about me."

"As always," said Adias. "You are as arrogant as ever."

"That's odd coming from a man who would try to be immortal," said Catricha. "Now," she said. "I will do what I must. Put down the child."

"Do what you will," said Adias. "I have only one need left."

He turned and marched through the open gateway of the tombs. Catricha charged after him.

His footsteps were like ash on the ground, leaving traces of shadowy dust behind. She pounded after him, rushing up stairs and along walkways, past the gaping maws of mausoleums and the towering spires of monuments. She raced in the dark, seeing only by the power of dark bane. The halo of energy around Adias guided her after him. He must be gathering in the the essences of Kizoni's child.

"Adias!" she called. "Stop!"

The shadow prince of Alliance did not wait. The evil being who took his name from the legacy of Jasguara continued toward his own tomb. *What does he need there? Could he need his old body?*

Catricha screamed as she charged after him and ran as fast as she could. Yet he effortlessly evaded her every move and shortcut. She skidded to a halt in front of the tomb. She found the doorway open. The mausoleum of House Halth stood unsealed in the cold night, opened by the horde that now surrounded her. The Cult of the Sleepless occupied the tombs, lurking around every corner, bloodshot eyes now gleamed, reflecting the dim light from Adias's energy drain.

Catricha dodged to continue the chase, but the cultists were everywhere. Her path was blocked just before the yawning doors of the tomb. Dozens of sleepless with their eyes peeled back in starting gazes fixed on her, interposed themselves before Adias health.

"Out of my way," she yelled. "I must stop him."

"None. Must interfere," said a leader among the sleepless, a priest with the eyes more red with blood than any other. "Now is the time we all will awake from this mortal dream."

"Fools," said Catricha. "This can't be the end."

She pushed as hard as possible with her curse sprite and dark bane, joining them together, so the curse and the darkness wove between her and the foes keeping her from her quarry. She darted after the dark bane while her cursed essence followed after her. The dark bane shot ahead, scattering the sleepless in chaos. Catricha came to a stop within the mausoleum.

The sleepless reformed behind her and began to pursue, trapping Catricha between the crowd and the shadow prince. Adias Halth stood over his own corpse in a coffin, holding the infant daughter of one who'd called him a friend.

Catricha gritted her teeth. "Stop." She froze with the glint of steel. Her ritual dagger lay on coffin's lid. That could be her chance, even as an ordinary weapon.

"No." Adias turned to her with a grimace. "You've stopped me long enough, little Catricha."

Catricha barreled toward the deadly shadow. The sleepless behind her surged to enter the mausoleum. But Adias held up a hand and the cultists all froze in their tracks. Catricha ran through his insubstantial body, racing through his smoky body. When she emerged on the other side, her hand found the hilt of the dagger. The symbolic weapon she'd placed on the tomb the day Adias' mortal remains were interred.

The coffin's lid began to shift and then branches emerged from the coffins top. The plant limbs hurled Catricha against the wall, with a painful crunch.

She arched her spine with a grimace, holding onto the dagger. Adias rounded on her. He still held the baby, but now his corpse rose from the box where it had rested. From the eyes of the corpses, removed for his ritual of rebirither, and from the heart issued living branches.

The tree limbs grew before Catricha's eyes, advancing on her, pushing back toward the sleepless cultists on two sides while the one sprouting from his empty ribcage prepared to stab her with a sharp point.

"Your friends cannot protect you," said Adias. "Meet your end, Catricha."

"I'm not out of friends yet."

"What can that mean?" Adias laughed. "You are all alone. You are nothing."

"False," said a soft voice from behind Catricha. A glimmer of light suddenly became a glaring blaze as Ilrona stepped through the wall of the mausoleum, leaving behind no trace of her passage. She stood, half dark and half light, the glowing demoness' dark side screamed with strong banes, an overwhelming dissonance nearly deafening to Catricha.

The cultists retreated in terror, bowing their heads and crying for forgiveness. Ilrona waved her hand and a spray of darkness flew at them, scattering across the sleepless as night banes raced among them. The darkness burrowed deep. Cultists screamed and fell.

"You haven't exhausted your options, Catricha Maltos." said Ilrona. "But you are out of time. Halth."

"No," said Adias with a snarl. He clutched the baby to his shadowy chest and roar.

His corpse body shot more freshly-grown limbs from his eyes and chest, and they raced toward Catricha, threatening to stab into her. One cut across her thigh. Another fine branch encircled her wrist.

Her hand with the dagger stayed free, and she cut the plant from her wrist. Catricha lunged forward. The branch from the corpse's chest cavity lashed toward her, but she darted along the side, turning at the right moment. She brought the dagger to bear in a stab into the corpses neck. The strike accomplished little.

Catricha retrieved the ritual blade with a dusty rattle. There was no blood, but simply a kind of pinkish, chalky texture on the dagger.

"You've traded your old life for another," said Ilrona. "Adias Halth, your essences belong to me."

"You will not take me, demoness," said Adias. "I rule Alliance now, and I will be more than a new shadow of the city. I will govern it as Jasguara was ruled long ago!"

"No, you've already failed."

"I will destroy this child," said Adias, knife to the infant princess. "Stand back, Catricha."

"I can't," said Catricha. "You've destroyed too much already. People are dead because of you. The city is in ruins because of you, my friends are hurt because of you."

"What's one more life for an eternity?" Adias pulled the child to him and his essence halo glowed brighter. "I'm almost there."

Catricha lunged forward, pushing past the bulky form of Adias's corpse body. She closed with his shadow form. The shadow prince twisted himself, so the baby was between her blade and his chest. She raised the weapon and could not bring it down and strike through the child and heir to the throne. The princess, who was to rule Alliance, wriggled and started to cry from the cold and pain of her energy being siphoned away.

"You hesitate," said Adias. "But this child will die regardless."

"No." Catricha sagged, her hesitation too much to bear. She could have killed him.

"Yes, this is the end for all of you. By the time you can reach me now, Ilrona, I'll be stronger than any demon of your kind. Then attempt what you must."

"I will do as Mother Mercy commands."

"What?" said the man. "Will she show up in the sky, descend like you did and confront me here? Time is up. I will soon be a demon stronger than any other."

"You will not be a great one." The lady of light and dark shook her head. "Only the eighty-eight and Mother Mercy will ever have that honor."

"I will be like them in power," said Adias. "But unique. Different."

"Your followers are scattered," Ilrona said. "None will survive this battle unless you relent. If you wish to rule the city, govern your people. Tell them to stand down."

"In the night," said Adias. "I need show no mercy. Catricha, put down the dagger, I will take this child and make her life my own."

Tears welled in Catricha's eyes. "You can't."

"You seem all but lost for words," said Adias. "I didn't expect that."

"I have no words left for you," said Catricha. "Because I didn't dream you were this terrible."

"I'd take a life to save my own," said Adias. "And I would sacrifice my own life to gain eternal power."

"That you've done," said Catricha. "I'm sure the stories will live on when you're gone."

"But I will not die," said Adias. "My time of death is past. I alone will emerge from this tomb. I will be the new prince of the city."

"Your boasts mean nothing," Ilrona said.

"No." Catricha turned to Ilrona. "You're wrong. He knows what it means to be the hero he thinks he is, the hero who holds a baby's life in his hands and threatens to take it without mercy, without love, without forgiveness."

"What you saying?" said Adias. "You mean to mock me, do you, my wife?"

"No." Catricha's lips curved in a cursed grin. "I wouldn't dream of mocking the Prince of Alliance."

"I'll be greater than a prince," said Adias. "I will be a king!"

"If you're a king," said Catricha. "then take my life and spare the child. You've already drained a lot from her. Surely, the power of a young woman will be enough to replenish the life energy you need."

"I will take the life from both of you, but because you've chosen, you will go first Catricha." He appeared before her, and Catricha brought the dagger down low. She dropped it near her foot.

She kicked out with the other leg. Her shoe struck into Adias's knee. He was not fully solid yet, but he was more so than before. His frail leg caved beneath the blow. He shouted in rage as his leg began reforming from the shadows. She held the dagger in hand with a single sprite flying free, her cursed sprite. Catricha plunged the dagger into Adias' neck.

There was no blood, just as with the corpse body, and there was no sound as Adias fell. He lost all substance in his final descent. His ethereal form broke apart in motes of shadow and the princess fell toward the floor of the mausoleum.

A man appeared with a sound like trumpets, flying over the sleepless and into the mausoleum. Deckard Hadrian caught the sleeping princess in the crook of his arm. He landed between Ilrona and Catricha.

"He is gone?" said Catricha. "I truly killed Adias Halth as they all suspected I had."

"No." Deckard shook his head, black hair glittering with ice crystals. "You killed him as he had to be killed."

"The demon is banished." Ilrona flowed to stand before Catricha. "The shadow of Alliance has fallen. You may walk the world for another day, Catricha Maltos. Live now, before I claim the dark bane you've kept hidden within for so long."

"Why would you want my dark bane?" asked Catricha. "Are you greedy for shadows?"

"I require as many as I can find," said Ilrona. "But these will do for now." She drew in the motes of darkness that remained of Adias Halth. When she finished, the lady of light and darkness retreated through the wall leaving as little trace as when she first arrived.

"Deckard." Catricha turned, shivering, to the immortal man. "Thank you."

"I'll talk to her," he said. "Ilrona has no right to take your life or your bane, even if she's willing to wait days or years."

Catricha took a deep breath. "Is it over? He's really gone?"

"We stand within the tomb of a dead man," said Deckard. "Let us all leave this place and not look back."

EPILOGUE

VUAL

Wedding bells rang in the chilly belfries of Alliance. He and his bride, Osestra, made their way up the walkway to say their marriage vows. The two of them had met again in the dead of winter. She'd thrown her arms around his neck and kissed him on the lips when he returned.

No need remained for tension.

He couldn't become the prince, but there was no need left for him to succeed Saviron. *Saviron's daughter will do that herself, someday.*

Some things can't be accidents.

Vual smiled at the thought. Adias's evil seemed unfathomable in the next moment as Vual spoke the words that bound him to Osestra, and she replied with the reverse of the marriage couplet.

They talked and laughed as the night wore on. The festivities drew to a close long after the winter night fell. At last, they joined together.

That night as they lay side-by-side, intertwined Vual gazed at Osestra while their breathing slowed. His eyes overflowed with tears.

He needed to make friends of better folk in the future. From tonight onward, he had someone he could trust, someone he could love. The shadows in their chambers only served to outline rather than conceal what lay between the two of them.

Could it be, that they had achieved something more than a princely throne?

Vual smiled. He could wait to gain power. But couldn't wait for the woman beside him and for that, there no further need.

CATRICHA

She watched the wedding from the tower of the fallen. The care of the procession moved to the city, weaving through the buildings, and waiting only at the places where the bride and groom stopped to kiss. Catricha watched and wondered if Vual really had forgiven her. Would he ever? Would anyone?

She could hardly forgive herself, but killing Adias was the right thing to do. Destroying the evil that dwelt within the city left her with no shame. Leaving her family was a different matter. Leaving Ruar was worse, even as things stood between their families.

Snow began to fall outside her window. She wondered if Vual would've invited her to the wedding if he'd thought she'd attend. Had he truly forgiven her? None of that mattered much.

Catricha frowned, wondering if the houses of Kuldettan and Maltos could ever come to peace. She had to go east simply to get away from all the tension. Porfiria didn't seem willing or eager, though. She insisted on staying to make more poetry plates. *Not as if either of us need the money,* Catricha thought.

Porfiria approached the window and stood beside her.

"You know," she said. "For a heroine, you hardly seem satisfied."

"I don't know if there's such a thing as heroes or heroines of any kind," said Catricha.

"Well," said Porfiria. "I am."

"Where's the cynic, now?"

"The cynic has gone walking for a while."

"I can believe that," said Catricha. "But I still must leave as well. I don't see any way to avoid that demon, Ilrona, if I don't separate this strange essence from me."

"So you're going to go look for a way to free yourself of it?" said Porfiria. "You've made up your mind?"

"I'm never really seen the world outside Alliance. Travel will be quite a different adventure."

"It must be exciting and frightening," said Porfiria. "To wander the world all alone."

"Oh." Catricha shrugged. "I don't know if I'll be alone."

"What do you mean?" asked Porfiria.

"I know you don't intend to travel with me, but there is someone who does."

"You attempt to be mysterious with me?" Porfiria smirked.

"I wouldn't dream of it, Lady Amburen. You can guess."

"After all that's happened," said Porfiria. "I felt we haven't grown closer together, but farther apart."

"You're my teacher," said Catricha. "Perhaps it's time I went to learn on my own for a while."

"I understand." Porfiria smiled. "The age we live in is not one for those who wait to make a move."

"Is that the case?" Catricha laughed. "I'd better go speak with Filavaye and Ruar."

"I thought you planned to leave the city soon?" Porfiria said.

"Yes." Catricha smiled at her friend. "I still intend to leave Alliance to search for a means to free my dark bane."

"How long might you be gone?" Porfiria arched her eyebrows.

Catricha laughed louder this time. She turned from the window. "Perhaps long enough for a betrothal or an elopement."

MELISSA

The snow was deep as Melissa trudged through the ravine with Bethanelle. Elaine was packing their things for travel at the Graef estate. They would leave the moment Melissa had what she needed. She'd not bothered speaking with Galocai about any of it. He'd been absent more often than not, since the shadow prince's defeat.

"Lord Olfrus is quite upset." Bethanelle glanced at Melissa. "I understand why."

"He has his reasons," said Melissa. "But he has no further hold on me or Elaine, with Halth defeated."

"I agree."

Bethanelle and Melissa's boots crunched in the snow.

"And?" asked Melissa.

Bethanelle shrugged. "My father promised to tell you where your parents went when you left the city. I remember the same as you do."

They descended a few paces toward a lean-to a few hundred yards away. The smoke of a cooking fire rose outside the pile of logs and the slanted roof.

"He's been hunting this late in the winter?" said Melissa. "He's brave to go outside so late in Tigalas."

"When you reach my father's age." Bethanelle smiled. "You fear little."

"I understand the concept."

"We're both young," said Bethanelle. "And I'm growing tired of being sheltered."

"You've been hunting in this ravine, yourself." Melissa stared ahead into the gnarled forest. "I wish I'd had the chance."

"Our doors will open for you. Should you wish to return to Alliance some other day."

"We will see," said Melissa.

The approach to lean-to. Lord Graef emerged from the makeshift structure, wiping gore from his hands with a damp cloth.

"A good kill today," he said. "Demon-spawned deer make the best venison, and it is fine to see you, daughter."

"Father." Bethanelle dipped her head in a slight bow. "I came to help Melissa find the way here."

"Well, here I am," said her father.

"Lord Graef," Melissa said. "I am leaving alliance."

"I'm glad to hear that. The Dorian merchants and the Graef family are not always on good terms. I like to think that at least you two have established something of value by now."

"Perhaps that is so." Bethanelle turned to Melissa. "But whatever we established, Melissa has the same request for you as before."

"Then," said Lord Graef. "I shall answer your question, Melissa Dorian."

Melissa bowed her head. "I need to know," she said. "Where are my parents, Lord Graef?"

"Politeness is beside the grace of mercy." He nodded, his weathered face grim. "They went east." Lord Graef set the bloodied cloth on a wooden table within the lean-to. "It wasn't that I didn't warn them of the demons that dwell in the valley. But they'd gone to the live in Empire, the very center of what was once great Jadiketz."

"Their business is there?" Melissa said. "They have not moved on since?"

"They left Alliance only recently." Graef looked down at his still-bloody. "Just earlier this year."

"Perhaps just before I arrived?" Melissa frowned.

That fits with what Kizoni told me.

"Take care." Lord Graef sighed. "When they left, they took their young daughter with them."

"Their daughter?" Melissa furrowed her brow. "But I'm their daughter."

"I should say," said Lord Graef. "Their other, younger daughter."

"Do you know anything else about her?"

"No." Lord Graef brushed his red hands against the cleaning cloth, while he looked at Melissa appraisingly. "Whatever you decide, you must remember that time does not heal every wound."

* * *

Melissa watched the city of Alliance recede as she took a river boat up the Duenn toward the Chos Valley. Well Country was in her future. Heron would stay in Alliance, and join the feuds of the intermediate families. Melissa wished the Olfrus family the best, but she couldn't remain.

Elaine sat with Melissa in the cabin their mercenary coin had bought. They watched as the icy waters grew between the ship and the dock. Another storm was blowing, a harsh squall out of the northwest.

The options had been to leave now or stay until another thaw came.

Freezing spray, cold and damp, filled the air. The boat's oars carried them east as they followed the Duenn toward the Chos Valley and the heart of ancient Jadiketz.

She'd miss the people she'd met within the walls of Alliance. Who could say what lay ahead beyond the city of Empire where the prow angled toward now?

Time moved on.

DECKARD

The storm over the northern land of mercy broke into rain and snow. Lightning flickered and thunder rumbled far below the maladrite city. Deckard Hadrian watched from a gallery of Mother Mercy's house on high, gazing at the world below. He wondered if Ilrona would keep him waiting long this time.

Waters from the fountain in the nearby baths left his cuts and wounds clean after the battle. The pain remained as another day went to die in the west.

At times like this, even an immortal feather mage needed a moment to unburden himself.

Mother Mercy would not allow such rest until after they spoke of the events in Alliance. As an immortal, those who stood over him were few in number. He recalled old words first spoken by a soul long gone.

"A demon hunter ought never bow to demons," he murmured in repetition of his mentor's last instruction. The moment he finished the verse, Ilrona drifted into the silver and gold antechamber. Deckard raised his eyes to meet her divided face.

"Mother Mercy greets you, demon hunter," said the down-turned light side of the demon's mouth. Her dark side gave a mischievous smile.

"Ilrona," said Deckard. "You must give up your quest this time. What is one shadow sprite to you?"

"One shadow sprite," said the demoness, "is as all the rest, vital."

"That can't be the truth."

"I've given Catricha Maltos her life," Ilrona said. "The young lady won't have to meet me again until her dying day. I can be patient."

"You will give me your word?"

"I give you my word, demon hunter." Ilrona's light side reversed her frown into a grin.

Deckard bowed his head. "I will see what Mother Mercy has in store for me."

They stepped through the golden doors into the passages of the house where only Mother Mercy and her greatest servants dared to tread. They followed the gilded hallway, ornate patterns glimmering from every angle with unnaturally bright essence light.

Deckard said nothing until they entered the chamber beyond the hall. There, flowers burst from the rich, black soil at their feet as they stepped through the gateway.

The flowers bloomed in every color, roses both white and red, as well as carnations, lilies, and countless other kinds for which Deckard did not know the names. Many of them could have been found on the earth below, but still others belonged to kinds that never greeted human eyes below. Deckard gazed at the flower garden in the warmth of some abstract sun. "Why does she wish to meet here?" he asked.

"I do not know."

"Well," said Deckard. "At least we didn't have to traverse the grand walkway. The House of Immortals is far from my favorite place."

"Do not let mother here you say so," said Ilrona. "She dotes over her children within the House."

"I'm no child."

Ilrona didn't let her smile go. "Of course, Hadrian. You are a great and powerful demon hunter."

Deckard ignored her condescension. *Certain indignities one learns to bear.*

"When should we expect her?" he asked.

"Mother Mercy has been attending to matters afar," said Ilrona. "But she will be home soon."

"I suppose I'll have to wait a while." Deckard sat down on the path among the flowers, folding his legs under him. "Do you know any card or table games?"

"Just dice. But dice aren't a game without stakes, and you don't want to gamble with me."

"You're right. I'd rather not."

In the field of flowers, somewhere on high, Deckard and the demoness awaited the return of the greatest benefactor of humanity.

THE END

The demon hunters will return.

If you enjoy this novel, please leave a review on the amazon store. Every review helps the author get an idea of what readers want to see more of in the future.

More support means more books in the series.

Look for the next novel in the Demon Hunter series, Well Country, available soon.

Find more books by Tim Niederriter at mentalcellarpublications.com

Thanks for reading.

GLOSSARY

Ancient beings - Beings of any kind that predate the dominance of demons and maladrites.

Bane - An aggressive form of magical essence.

Bowami - Mire dragons, cousins of the vakari.

Charinien Fisher - Shapeshifting magical creatures from the Bay of Charin.

The Conquest - The wars fought to conquer Tancuon many centuries ago.

Demon - An immortal being with heart-essence made of banes, mostly disorderly in nature. Many are imprisoned beneath the Earth.

Dire Families - The descendants of the conquest army that took over Tancuon for Mother Mercy.

The eighty-eight greater beings - The eighty-eight greater demons and maladrites, each one powerful enough to rule countless followers. Most of them are preoccupied with mystic battles with one another. These include Mother Mercy, Voratome Drake, Ordoth, and Gorsheva.

Essence - A general term for the tiny spirit beings that dwell within the hearts of all beings and around world wells.

Hervs - Ancient nature-beings who dominated the world before the demons and maladrites.

Iron bane - A rare form of magical essence that holds the properties of strength and endurance inherent in its nature.

Maladrite - An immortal being with heart-essence of sprites, mostly orderly in nature. Many dwell in the city on the ring.

Palliam - A type of massive demon with a thousand legs.

Promortality - A form of immortality which requires the subject to slumber as if dead before awakening and gaining phenomenal power until sleep claims them again.

Sprite - A peaceful form of magical essence.

Vakari - A race of intelligent lizard people native to Linien.

LOCATIONS

Alliance - A large city in its own princedom in north-central Tancuon, known for poets and knights.

The Bay of Charin - The stretch of sea between Lowenrane and Kanor.

Besany - The city in Lowenrane up the river from Soucot.

The Bloom - Thick forests and swamplands east of Kanor.

The Chos Valley - A valley in north-central Tancuon on the edge of Geteren.

Crinri - A far-eastern nation, home to many artificers.

The River Duenn - A mighty river that runs through Alliance, Geteren, and the Chos Valley from the northeast to the southwest.

Edede - Matriarchal nation east of the Kismlands.

Empire - A city in the Chos Valley, home of the immortal Cyrus Bode and former seat of the emperor of Jadiketz.

Fulster - A small town south of Alliance under the protection of Deckard Hadrian.

Geteren - A governance in north-central Tancuon where many world wells reach the surface. Also called Well Country.

The Inner Ring - The ring closest to the planet's surface. The Maladrite City stands upon this ring.

Jadiketz - Name given to the now-divided empire formed in the Land of Mercy.

Kanor - A peninsula and nation of the same name on the east side of The Bay of Charin.

The Kismlands - Allied nations ruled by greater maladrites, located east of Linien from the lands of mercy.

Lands of mercy - A term encompassing all the princedoms and governances ruled by Mother Mercy, mostly in Tancuon.

Linien - A strip of marshes and lowlands between Tancuon and the eastern continents.

Lowenrane - A southern land with many rivers and governance of the land of mercy.

The Maladrite City - The city build in the ring around the planet where Mother Mercy dwells among the maladrites.

Naje - Far-eastern nation, home of the Palace of Shadows and the Palace of Blades.

Nassio - A nation of vakari lizard men in the southernmost swamps of Linien.

Obnilen - A distant world ruled by exiled demons.

Rei - The Broken Land. A continent destroyed by the fall of the greater demon Gorsheva.

Soucot - Capitol city of Lowenrane, seat of the Governor of Lowenrane. Built at the mouth of the Lowenrane River. Originally Soucot was a fort built of demon stone ages ago to help Prince Geldingstar defeat the rampaging greater demon, Gorsheva.

Tancuon - The north-western continent mostly ruled by Mother Mercy and her governors and princes.

Tenok - An eastern nation on the sea.

Toare - North-eastern nation and rival of Edede.

Wagewood - A governance of the land of mercy near the Chos Valley.

Author's Note

I am pleased beyond all possible belief to present Shadow Prince to you readers. This book took a relatively long time to get right.

I'll have more Demon Hunter stories for you soon. Deckard and Melissa will be back, like a certain indomitable film character.

Catch them soon in Well Country.

Tim Niederriter, September 2020

Also by Tim Niederriter

The Demon Hunter Series

Demon Scroll

Other Series

The Rain Protocol

Shifter Empire

Bondmage

Forces of Empire

Stand Alone Books

Rem's Dream

About the Author

Tim Niederriter, as you've no doubt gathered, writes fantasy stories.

Tim is the son of two physicists from Pennsylvania, transplanted to Minnesota. His parents read him The Hobbit (repeatedly) at a young age. The math adds up. Tim fell in love with fantasy of all kinds. Diagnosed with an autism spectrum disorder at a young age, he immersed himself in fictional worlds his whole life. He studied fiction and literature at Gustavus Adolphus College and also has a strong interest in history and politics.

Tim co-hosts the roleplaying game podcast "Of Mooks and Monsters" and talks with other authors each week on his other podcast, "Alive After Reading."

Milton Keynes UK
Ingram Content Group UK Ltd.
UKHW012209150124
436080UK00006B/751